# LORI FOSTER

# The Little Flower Shop

CANARY STREET PRESS

CANARY
STREET
PRESS™

Recycling programs
for this product may
not exist in your area.

ISBN-13: 978-1-335-00930-2

The Little Flower Shop

First published in 2023. This edition published in 2024.

Copyright © 2023 by Lori Foster

For questions and comments about the quality of this book,
please contact us at CustomerService@Harlequin.com.

TM is a trademark of Harlequin Enterprises ULC.

Canary Street Press
22 Adelaide St. West, 41st Floor
Toronto, Ontario M5H 4E3, Canada
CanaryStPress.com

Printed in U.S.A.

Dear Amazing Readers,

Thank you so much for coming on another adventure with me to the quirky little town in Indiana. It's a special place where a mannequin gets into shenanigans, the people are pushy but caring and love fills the kitschy little shops around the lake. Saul and Emily are happy to welcome you back. Oh, and extra thanks to everyone who wrote a fun review for *The Honeymoon Cottage*, where you first met these characters.

I hope you enjoy *The Little Flower Shop* just as much. Please let me know!

I love connecting with readers. Though I'm most active on Facebook, you'll find me on other social media sites as well. Remember that you can always find out the latest about my books on my website, lorifoster.com.

Here's wishing you lots of happy reading!

*Lori Foster*

# CHAPTER ONE

A BAREFOOT WEDDING on the beach. A novel idea that the tiny town of Cemetery, Indiana, had fully embraced. As Emily Lucretia looked around at all the naked feet on women, men and kids, as well as the bride and groom, she couldn't help but smile. After such a long day, it'd be so nice to do the same, to kick off her dress sandals and wiggle her toes in the summer-warm sand.

Of course, she didn't. For whatever reason, that type of carefree enjoyment wasn't in her DNA. Long ago she'd accepted being the proverbial stick-in-the-mud, as her ex-husband had labeled her.

But, she told herself, she was also a perfectionist, and even after a day in the late-August heat, her flower arrangements still looked incredible. Yardley, the stunning bride, had been thrilled with them all.

Above the sound of music, conversation, and laughter, Emily heard a group splash into the lake. Swimming at a wedding. How fun was that?

The day of celebration had, for many, turned into a real party once the ceremony had concluded. The air was humid but fresh, the mood mellow and festive. Scents from the flowers mingled with sunscreen, roasted pork over an open spit, and breezes across the water.

Nearly everyone from Cemetery had turned out for the wedding until the beach had been filled. It was an unfortunate name for the friendly town, yet the people were wonderful, and Emily loved the quaint area with all her heart.

Carefully maneuvering from one decorative stepping stone to another, Emily fluffed and straightened the various arrangements. From pink peonies and blue hydrangeas to freesia and gardenias, anemones and daisies to rosebuds and baby's breath, it was a beautifully colorful wedding, ideal for the setting and exactly what the bride had requested.

Emily heard laughter and looked up to see a group of women toasting Yardley as she and her new husband prepared to leave. Yardley made such a beautiful bride, and as the town's wedding planner, she was in her element. She'd known exactly what she wanted, and how she wanted it, yet she'd never expected the area businesses to make the wedding a gift.

The entire town loved Yardley—with good reason. Thanks to her, the matriarch and great-granddaughter of the town founder had loosened up enough to remove the town's name of "Cemetery" from every local business.

Before Yardley had won that particular argument through persistence laced with kindness, Emily had suffered the misfortune of running "Cemetery Florals," which made it seem that she only supplied flowers for burials. Actually, the small town didn't even have a cemetery. Those who passed away were buried in Allbee, the next town over.

"You're still wearing shoes."

Jumping at the sound of that deep, rich voice coming from right behind her, Emily turned too fast and almost stumbled off the stepping stone. Saul Culver reached out and caught her arm, his hand big and warm against her bare elbow as he steadied her.

She looked up, way up, into incredibly nice green eyes, then down to those broad shoulders and the open front of Saul's shirt.

"Careful," he said, releasing her and then pressing a wine cooler into her hand. "I didn't mean to startle you."

Emily took the frosty bottle automatically, realized what it was, and tried to hand it back. "I can't have this," she protested. At forty-one, she was well past the age of drinking on the beach, especially during a job. "I'm working."

"Em, *no one* is working."

Saul was the only one who shortened her name… and from him, she liked it. "Says the man who only just stepped away from the firepit." She breathed in the scent of smoked wood laced with his sun-warmed hair and skin—such a pleasant mix.

The wedding, followed immediately by a reception, had gone on for hours now and everyone was a little wilted, pleasantly so.

Somehow, for Saul, it only made him more appealing.

"That wasn't work," he protested. "Not really, since I had plenty of helpers."

Yes, she'd noticed that. A lot of men had enjoyed chatting with Saul as he'd roasted meat over the fire, but then, all the women, married and single, too young and too old, had at one point or another visited with him, also.

Repeatedly, Emily had found her gaze on him.

A few times, he'd gazed back.

*It means nothing.* Over the past few months, she'd

started to wonder if she and Saul might...but no. For one thing, she was older than him. Okay, not by much, but still. At her age, every year counted.

For another thing, Saul was fun—everyone in Cemetery would say so. Within minutes of meeting him, vacationers would smile and relax. The townspeople went to him whenever they had a joke to tell, or if they needed cheering up. His brand of comfort was good food, a drink or two, and plenty of humor.

She, however, was merely pleasant. No one laughed it up with her. No one told her dirty jokes or made sexy suggestions.

She was merely Emily Lucretia, the "flower lady."

Most of her friends treated her like a grandma. Granted, forty-one wasn't young, but she didn't really consider it old, either.

"The food is all but gone," Saul said. "Everyone brought their appetite. Of course, fresh air and sunshine could make anyone hungry."

"Don't be modest," she chided. "It's the excellent food that really mattered."

Being the owner of a local barbecue restaurant, Saul had generously supplied a big portion of the scrumptious meat for the wedding. Sallie had donated a gorgeous wedding cake from her bakery shop, Sallie's By The Shore, and Daniel had gifted the newlyweds a honeymoon at the bride's favorite feature in the town, the Honeymoon Cottage. Emily had, naturally, decorated with flowers, and everyone else had brought side dishes and drinks.

The wedding was the town's gift to Yardley, because she was a gift to all of them.

"Em?" Dipping down to better meet her gaze, Saul asked, "You okay?"

Blinking fast, Emily realized that for a second there she'd been lost in thought. "I'm fine." She tried a quick smile. "Wasn't it a beautiful wedding?"

He nodded. "Casual but somehow classy, too."

"Like Yardley." As the day had progressed and night approached, the sun seemed to rest on the lake, coloring the sky in pastel hues that reflected on the surface of the water. Several men had asked her to dance, but she'd declined. To keep herself busy, she made sure the flowers stayed fresh. "The weather couldn't be more perfect."

Leaning back on the edge of a sturdy picnic table, Saul lifted his drink. "Your flowers were a hit."

"Yardley seemed pleased." She wished she was better at small talk, but everything she said ended up sounding professional instead of friendly.

"I heard different women talking about them." He smiled. "It was nice of Yardley to tell everyone to take some flowers home."

"Oh, she did?" Somehow Emily had missed that, not that she minded. "I'm glad. Flowers are meant to be enjoyed. It would have been a shame to toss them all away." She didn't think she was overly prideful, but she knew without false modesty that she did an incredible job with flower arrangements. It was one of her very few gifts.

Saul leaned closer. "I snagged a few for Kathleen."

Emily couldn't help but grin as she glanced toward the town mannequin. It was a favorite pastime for the locals to dress and arrange Kathleen for different scenarios. No one ever knew where she might show up, but it was all in fun.

Now, dressed up in her wedding finery with a few wilting peonies in her stiff hand, Kathleen sat in the sand, her legs arrowing out in a V before her. Someone had fixed her hair into a fancier style.

"Even Kathleen is barefoot," Saul said.

"But," Emily teased back, "Kathleen is not drinking."

"Are you serious?" After pushing away from the table, Saul looped his arm around her so that his broad hand opened on the side of her waist.

It nearly put her heart into a tailspin. *Be cool*, she warned herself. *He's only a friend.*

Saul steered her three steps to the left so she had a better view. "Look again."

"Oh, my gosh." All around the mannequin, empty bottles and cans had collected. "That lush," she said around a laugh.

Saul smiled down at her. "My gosh?"

Even knowing he was teasing, Emily felt her face go hot. "I don't curse." At least not often, and rarely out loud.

"Of course you don't," said Mimi, the matron of honor and Yardley's best friend. She had Sheena, the groom's sister, with her. Both women had been crying and now had mascara tracks down their flushed cheeks.

Mimi grinned at her. "How is it that I'm falling apart and you look as put together as when you arrived?"

Emily liked both women a lot. Knowing Mimi'd been drinking, she ignored the silly question and smiled. "How are you holding up, Mimi?"

"I'm a little drunk, a lot thrilled, and I'm so…" her voice cracked "…*happy for Yardley.*"

Sheena hugged her close. "Me, too!" she sobbed.

"Not drunk, I mean. I'm pregnant. I can't get drunk, but I'm so thrilled for Travis. He loves her so much, and he deserves someone like her."

Fighting off a grin at the overblown response, Emily asked, "Did you want to take some flowers?"

From somewhere, Saul produced a handful of napkins that he handed to the weepy women.

"I do." Mimi realized what she'd said, then dissolved into laughter. "Or at least, Yardley did."

Also laughing, Sheena said, "Travis, too!"

After she mopped her face, Mimi eyed Emily. "Honest to God, you never get rumpled." Mimi shoved her wildly curling blond hair out of her face. She'd started with it up in an elegant twist, but dancing had taken care of that.

"She's perfect," Sheena said. And then to Emily, she added, "You really are. Your flowers are perfect, and you're perfectly nice, and even now, you look perfectly beautiful."

Emily choked a little. They couldn't know it, of course, but she was touchy about that particular compliment. "I'll agree the flowers are perfect. Thank you."

Saul gave her a glance, then said in a silly formal voice, "All women are perfect in their own unique ways."

Mimi fell against him laughing. "Such a diplomat."

"It's true, Mimi. You were a superior server at my restaurant. There'll never be another you."

"Ahhh…" She gave him a big hug, then turned and did the same to Emily. "Thank you for helping to make Yardley's wedding so special."

"I think that honor goes to you and Yardley." From the time they were kids, Yardley and Mimi had been inseparable best friends dreaming of incomparable beach weddings. It explained why Yardley made an ideal wedding planner. She'd been working on it most of her life.

Mimi's husband, Kevin, along with Sheena's husband, Todd, came to collect their wives. Saul helped Emily to divide up a cluster of flowers for the women.

Once they were gone, he boldly tipped up Emily's chin, making her heart a little topsy-turvy again.

His astute gaze probed hers. "That made you uncomfortable?"

"What? No. I adore both women." It was all the "perfect" nonsense that always made her uneasy. "I think it's amazing that Mimi and Yardley are so dedicated to each other. And now Sheena has them both, too."

In no way did he look convinced—and his fingers lingered. "Do you have a best friend?"

Until this very moment, until he asked, she hadn't thought about the lack of a best friend. Now that she did consider it, it seemed…sad. "Not really." To cover up the sudden feeling of loss, she tried for another smile, but it definitely felt off. "I like everyone."

"I know. It's cute."

Cute? That was hardly a description for a woman her age, but she certainly preferred it to "perfect." And starting right now, she would stop thinking about her age. Forty-one was not old. *It wasn't.*

Dropping his hand, but putting his arm around her again, Saul gave her a squeeze, as if he'd understood things she hadn't said. The gesture brought her closer to his big body in an affectionate way that she couldn't begin to decipher.

He pointed at the mannequin. "Let's get back to

Kathleen, okay? Obviously, she's been drinking. Maybe not as much as Mimi…"

Sharing his amusement, she agreed, "She was a wee bit tipsy."

"Mimi was completely smashed, which is okay. She celebrated hard for Yardley. Hell, everyone here has had a few, so it's definitely okay for you to have a single drink. It's not even a real drink. It's a *wine cooler*."

Hating to admit it, Emily explained, "The thing is… I don't drink."

His brows went up. "Ever?"

See, *that*. His surprise. She'd known Saul for a few years now, but he didn't really know her. Not all the little things. The dumb things.

The things that made her different.

Sighing, she lifted the bottle. "I have no idea what this might do to me."

With a slow grin, he suggested, "Might be interesting to find out."

Was that flirting? She thought it might be and was about to ask him when a few more people joined them.

"Hey, Saul. Now that the rest of the meat's taken, we're going to load all the equipment into the back of your truck. That okay?"

Taking a few steps away from her, Saul answered the guys who were helping out. "That'd be great, thanks. You just have to make sure the tarp is there so nothing gets damaged."

"Tarp? Is it in the back of the truck?"

He hesitated, then said, "Hang on a sec and I'll help." Turning back to Emily, he looked at her eyes, then her mouth, before glancing away. "Sorry, I need to take care of…"

"I understand. I have things to get done now, too, since the party is winding down."

"Emily…" Saul looked as if he wanted to say more. Then, with a quick smile, he gently pried the wine cooler from her hand. "How about we hold off on this until I'm with you? I wouldn't want to be the cause of you tripping, or—"

"Doing anything embarrassing? I agree." Realizing what she said, she added quickly, "Not that I plan to try drinking, so don't feel obligated or anything. At my age, it'd be—"

"Past due, if you're interested." Still he hesitated, standing in front her, his gaze moving warmly over her face again. "I was joking before. You know that, right? You can trust me."

"Of course." Trusting Saul was definitely not the problem. It was everything else, too many things to name.

"You and me, Em. We're past due, don't you think?"

Her jaw loosened. "We…yes?" She didn't even know what he meant, but "yes" seemed to be the polite reply.

Satisfaction filled his expression. "Great. Then I'll see you soon."

He waited for her agreement, so she nodded.

Then, with the other men calling to him, he jogged away.

Emily was still lost in thought when a group of women approached her, each hoping for a flower or two to take home. With care, she separated the different sprays and offered small bundles to each of them. Others pitched in, bringing the arrangements to her as they helped to clear the beach and claimed the remaining flowers. Heavy vases were toted to her florist van, and within an hour, the majority of the guests were gone, with only a few stragglers still packing up. There were general farewells and the quiet closing of car doors and then…the peacefulness of the evening settled around her.

It seemed even vacationers had turned in early tonight.

After securing everything in her white van, Emily consulted the supply list to ensure she wasn't forgetting anything. It was a good idea, because she realized she hadn't yet collected the shepherd's hooks and frame for the flower-draped backdrop used during the vows.

Being alone, she gave up on formality and removed her sandals, putting them on the driver's seat before heading back to the beach. The scene was very different now, the only sounds those of the waves lapping gently at the shore and the melody of frogs in long grasses. The sun had completely set, but a fat moon sent a rippling ribbon of white dancing over the lake. The deep violet sky sparkled with stars.

Stopping, Emily closed her eyes and inhaled slowly, her thoughts dwelling in uncomfortable places.

She'd enjoyed the wedding so much, yet she couldn't deny the touch of envy. She'd been alone for so many years now. Not *alone*-alone, she reminded herself. She had Aunt Mabel and Uncle Sullivan, who she loved dearly. She had her many friends here in Cemetery— not a single best friend, but a lot of people she enjoyed. She had her work, her independence…

Opening her eyes and staring out at the lake, she added that she had a silent house to go home to.

A lonely bed to sleep in.

A tiny coffee maker that only served one person.

"Stop it," she muttered aloud. Standing around moping was ridiculous. She took a determined step forward—and gasped as she spotted a body on the beach. Her heart shot into her throat...until she realized it was Kathleen.

Oh no, the mannequin had been forgotten.

Laughing at herself, she approached the abandoned dummy with sympathy. "Most of the discarded bottles and cans are gone, but they left you? Poor Kathleen." It appeared someone had quit midway in the cleanup. "No worries. I'll finish the job, and I'll take care of you, too."

It dawned on her she was talking to a dummy, and she glanced around guiltily, but still, there was no one. Just her and Kathleen.

Ugh, they had that in common.

Never before had she played with the mannequin, even though every other local resident had at one time or another taken a turn dressing her and placing her somewhere in town. Kathleen had attended town council meetings and church, held pompoms in the bleachers at sporting events, rode on parade floats, perched on the bar at Saul's restaurant...and she'd even been a guest at local weddings.

Yet Emily had never dared to take part.

It seemed too silly, and she'd have been embarrassed to be caught...

She curled her toes into the warm sand. Why had she always resisted? Was it because everyone considered her too prissy for it, or because she really was a killjoy?

She thought of Mimi and Sheena calling her perfect. God, how she hated that word. Too many times her ex had used it to describe her. The problem with perfection, of course, was that no one could be perfect all the time, no matter how hard they might try.

With sudden insight, Emily realized what she needed to do.

She needed to shake up her life.

She needed to change her good-girl image.

She needed excitement and fun—and by God, she'd start right now.

With Kathleen.

EARLY THE NEXT MORNING, Emily stirred in her bed, wondering what had awakened her. After a long night, it took her a moment to realize her phone was buzzing. Bleary-eyed, she lifted her head from her pillow and glanced at the clock. Only 6:15 a.m. On a Sunday. Her *only* day off.

Groaning, she fumbled for the phone and then flopped to her back on the mattress as she looked at the screen.

Aunt Mabel.

Instantly more alert, she jerked upright and answered with a worried, "What's wrong?"

"I'm so sorry to wake you, honey, but Sullivan fell and hurt his hip. He's fine, so don't you dare panic, but they'll probably keep him overnight."

"Wait—what?" She swung her legs over the side of the bed. "They who? Where are you?"

"We're at the hospital. The ambulance brought us here."

"The *ambulance*." Hurrying to her dresser, Emily asked, "How bad is he hurt? Why are they keeping him?" She found a pair of trim white capris and fumbled in a drawer for a bra. "How did he fall?"

"I'll tell you everything when you get here." Lower, Mabel said, "I'm in my housecoat. I wouldn't let them take Sullivan without me, and we hadn't yet gotten dressed, so—"

Oh, God. "I have to pee." Making that blurted admission to someone else would have horrified Emily, but her Aunt Mabel knew her better than anyone, everything about her, all her worries and fears and disappointments. When Emily's parents had died together in a car wreck, it was Aunt Mabel and Uncle Sullivan who'd taken her in. She'd been seventeen and a know-it-all and they'd loved her unconditionally anyway. "I'm sorry," Emily said. "Give me two minutes, okay?"

"Take your time, honey. I'm not going anywhere."

Emily raced through the bathroom, taking care of her most pressing need, then cleaning her face and teeth in record time. She tossed her head forward, caught her hair, and put it in a not-so-smooth ponytail. Immediately she was back to the phone. "Tell me everything you need while I get dressed."

"Well," Mabel said, "first I need you to take a breath."

"Aunt Mabel—"

"Breathe in, hold it, breathe out."

Knowing her aunt would insist, Emily followed along while also pulling on her clothes and stepping into her shoes. "I'm good," she promised as she snatched up her purse and keys. "I'll head to your house now. Want to text me a list of what you need?"

"That would be wonderful. Promise me you'll drive safely."

"Cross my heart."

"I mean it, Emily. Sullivan is off having X-rays and

I'm in a comfy chair with my feet up. It'll be fine, so slow down."

Her dear, darling aunt. The woman was seventy-one years old and hell-bent on denying the effects of age. Her one concession was propping up her feet so her ankles wouldn't swell. Uncle Sullivan was ten years older, legally blind, but still hilarious and determined to do things his own way. And oh, how he adored Mabel.

And how Mabel relished all his affection.

Emily loved them both so much.

As she headed out the door, she promised her aunt that she'd be there soon, she'd drive carefully, she wouldn't rush, and yes, she'd keep breathing. She disconnected the phone and headed for her new Chevy Spark. Though most people paid no attention to the little hatchback, for Emily, the Nitro Yellow color was pure rebellion. All her life she'd owned silver, black, or white cars. Even the shop van was a sensible white.

But her personal car? She considered it very sporty.

No one else did, but that didn't matter.

On the twenty-minute drive to her aunt's house in Allbee, she worried. Twice she heard a text come in on her phone. She assumed it was her aunt telling her what to pick up, and even though there wasn't much traffic between Cemetery and Allbee, she never allowed herself to check texts while driving. If anything critical had come up, her aunt would have called.

The second she pulled into the driveway, she snatched up the phone to be sure—and good heavens. The list was long in the first text, and even longer in the second.

Clothes, meds, snacks, glasses…on and on it went.

Were they moving into the hospital? Was her uncle's injury more serious than Mabel had admitted?

With her fear ratcheting up, Emily used her key to get inside the house, and immediately she saw the overturned step stool in front of the big dining room window. The table was askew and one chair knocked over.

Hand to her mouth, she suddenly knew exactly what had happened.

Sullivan had fallen off the stool.

NOT THE TYPE to sleep in, Saul was already up and driving to the beach for a morning run when he got the call that Kathleen the dummy was outside his restaurant, looking a little hungover from what appeared to be a night of revelry.

Luckily the restaurant didn't open until two on Sundays, so customers wouldn't have seen her—but plenty of beachgoers would. His restaurant was located on the same road that half-circled the beach, with only a short distance between them.

Grinning, he thanked the caller and turned off Main Street onto Lakeshore Drive, all the while suspecting— even hoping—that Emily had put the mannequin there. Deliberately, he'd ensured Kathleen was left behind as a way to coax Emily into loosening up a little. *With him.*

Anyone could have taken the dummy, though.

Kathleen got around.

Emily, however, did not. In so many ways, she was guarded. Always proper and polite, her laughter restrained, her manner professional. Yet every so often, he got a glimpse of more.

It made him hot.

He thought of Emily's cinnamon-colored eyes and

how pretty they'd looked last night in the light of the setting sun, especially when she'd laughed at the bottles and cans deposited around Kathleen.

Whenever she loosened up, which wasn't often, she took his breath away. He wanted her, when she was prim and controlled, when she cut loose a little, when she was in full-on professional mode. He'd wanted her for a long while.

Initially, he'd thought to make his feelings obvious until Emily reciprocated a little. He figured they'd date, ease from friends to—hopefully—lovers, and then go from there. It'd be natural. A building relationship.

So far that hadn't worked out. Emily was aware of him, and attracted to him, he felt that much. Yet she never seemed ready to take the first step with him, and now... Well, now, he wanted a whole lot more. With Emily.

He had his work cut out for him.

Never had he known a woman to possess so many different personas. She was Emily the flower lady, 100 percent. Skilled and talented and great with her clientele. She was also Emily the circumspect friend, easily trusted, always there when someone needed her, but often unsure of how close to get. At times she seemed painfully uncertain, and other times she had a confidence that few could claim.

Always, she was reserved. Kind and polite. Polished in an effortless way where she could make any outfit look like a designer had put it together.

Just once, he'd love to see her all messy.

No, that was a lie. He wanted to see it often—in his bed, when she first woke; stepping from the shower; in the evening after work, when she'd kick off her shoes, release her hair from her usual ponytail, and strip off her bra…

He didn't want to change her. Never that. He enjoyed her buttoned-up manner a lot. But he wanted to be the guy who got her unbuttoned.

He wanted things she wouldn't give to anyone else.

Pulling up to the restaurant and seeing Kathleen, he had to laugh out loud.

The poor mannequin was propped against the side of the building near his front door, her wig crooked, the skirt of her dress riding a little too high, the neck of a wine cooler wedged between her perpetually posed fingers, with the other hand holding her sandals. There were only two other bottles and a can on the ground near her, meaning whoever had put her there had probably cleaned up the rest.

He glanced at the clock on the dash of his truck, saw it was early, but decided why not? After pulling his cell from his pocket, he called Emily.

She answered on the first ring with a harried, panting, "Hello?"

Interesting. "Hey, it's Saul."

The hurried breaths fell silent, and she replied with a tentative, surprised, "Saul?"

"Yeah, see, I just got to the restaurant, and guess who's passed out against my front door."

A lengthy pause preceded a muffled snicker. "I have no idea."

Oh, she knew all right. "It's Kathleen," he murmured, intrigued by Emily's mood this morning. "It appears she stayed out all night drinking." Emily said nothing, but he could hear her moving. "Wine coolers, by the look of it."

Another snicker. "Maybe those things are more po-
tent than you realized."

God, he loved that she was teasing with him, which
allowed him to tease right back. "So it *was* you."

This time she outright laughed—and he loved the
rich, husky sound of it. He had it bad, and he knew it.

"Imagine my shock," he said, "getting a call from
a passerby, telling me I had a drunk lady at my restaurant."

All of her humor fled. "Oh no. Did you really? Saul,
I'm sorry. I thought no one would be at the restaurant
until much later, after you arrived and saw her. It was
just a joke. I didn't mean to embarrass you."

Well, hell. That just derailed all the fun. "Emily,"
he chided softly. "You know me better than that." Or
at least she should. "I'm not embarrassed. It's hilarious
and I love it and I'm glad you did it."

"You are?" He heard what sounded like a drawer
opening and closing. "It seemed funny last night when
I realized Kathleen and I were the last ones there."

Damn. So she'd been alone on the beach? If only he'd
gone back, he could have—

A door closed, and it sounded like Emily was rushing. He asked, "Did I catch you at a bad time, hon?"

"Normally, you'd have woken me," she said. Then
quickly followed with, "Not that I'd mind. I don't mean
that." And then, in a bigger rush, "Not that you *need* to
call. I'm not suggesting—"

"Good to know," he said, cutting off her awkward ex-
planations. If things went the way he wanted, he would
be calling, often. "So if you weren't sleeping, what's
going on?"

"Oh, sorry. It's my Uncle Sullivan. He fell and hurt

his hip. He's at the hospital with my aunt, so I'm grabbing some things for them, only the list is ridiculously long, so now I'm doubly worried even though Aunt Mabel said it wasn't serious."

"He's older, right?"

"Eighty-one and legally blind." She paused, then said on a huff, "I think I know what happened. See, Aunt Mabel is afraid of bugs, so Uncle Sullivan tries to get them for her."

"You said he has trouble with his vision?" Saul left his truck and headed for Kathleen while they spoke.

"He does! But he'd do anything for my aunt, including fumble around and try to catch disgusting bugs that he can't even see. Most of the time it's harmless. Almost like a game."

"I can picture it," Saul said with a smile. He pried the wine cooler from Kathleen's hand, then picked up the other empties and tossed them into a recycle bin. "Pretty funny, actually."

"Usually, I'd agree. But Saul, I think he was on a stool."

Obviously agitated, she detailed the scene she'd found, making Saul whistle. He didn't say it aloud, but it was a good thing her uncle had fallen backward toward the table, rather than forward out the window. "I'm sorry, hon. I can tell you're worried. Will you do me a favor?"

As if dumbfounded, Emily said nothing for several seconds.

Saul glanced at the screen. "You still there?"

"Oh, yes, I am. Sorry. You mentioned a favor?"

He grinned, knowing it was the endearment that had flustered her. Maybe she'd missed it the first time, or thought she'd misheard. Going forward, he'd make certain she knew how he felt.

For too long now, he'd been waiting for Emily to figure out if she was interested or not. It was time to be a little more obvious. "Will you call me after you find out what's going on? And if you need anything, let me know. I'm here, and I'd be glad to help."

"Okay, but…you work more hours than I do."

"True enough." He hefted Kathleen under one arm and walked around to the passenger side of the truck. "I just hired another server, though, so I can reposition a few things easily enough. Seriously, Em, let me know if you need me."

In a more breathless voice, she whispered, "Thank you."

"Anytime."

"I should go now that I've packed up half the house."

Saul laughed. "I hope he's okay. Keep me posted."

"I will. Saul? Really, thank you." And with that, she disconnected.

Progress, Saul thought, as he positioned Kathleen in the seat. He straightened her wig, smoothed down the synthetic hair, then dug out some sunglasses and put them over her eyes. Now that Emily had opened the door to a little teasing, he planned to take full advantage…and with any luck, it'd help to hurry things along.

With recent events, he was juggling a lot. Too much. He'd been forced to really consider his priorities, those that were necessary, and those that were personal desires.

When it came to what he wanted, Emily was right there at the top.

## CHAPTER TWO

EMILY FOUND HER aunt in a padded lounge chair beside an empty spot where a hospital bed should be. She had a pillow behind her back as she used a TV remote to scroll through channels on a TV hung high on the wall. Gently, Emily tapped at the open door.

"Emily! Oh, thank goodness you're here." Struggling to hold her housecoat closed, Aunt Mabel lumbered her way awkwardly out of the deep plastic chair, losing a slipper in the process.

Emily rushed to assist her. "I'm sorry it took me so long to find everything on your list." She set aside what she'd brought: two massive tote bags, her uncle's cane, and the rolling suitcase. With her hands now free, she bent to help Mabel replace her slipper, then rose to embrace her in a tight hug. "Tell me everything. How are you?"

"Everyone here has seen me in my nightclothes, that's how I am! You should have heard Sullivan carrying on. He had a fit, saying I'd entice everyone. The man can't see anything ten feet from his face, and he still tried to put a blanket over my head." Mabel laughed, but it was strained, without her usual humor. Softly, she added, "You know that man thinks I'm irresistible. It's proof that he really is blind."

Unable to smile, Emily held her aunt back, looking

down into her rounded face with concern. Her aunt was a short woman, barely five feet tall, which put her five inches shorter than Emily. Her silver hair, white-streaked in places, was mussed, her blue eyes filled with determination, her downy cheeks flushed with embarrassment. "To Sullivan, you *are* irresistible. Never argue with a man who's madly in love."

Mabel let out a long breath. "I hope his hip isn't broken. Sullivan doesn't like to show pain, so it's difficult to tell." Glancing at the bags, she asked, "Did you bring the change of clothes I wanted?"

For the next few minutes, Emily helped her aunt to find what she needed. Mabel was still in the restroom dressing when they brought Sullivan back. The poor man wore darkened glasses and was busy grumbling. Emily tapped at the bathroom door. "Aunt, they're here with Uncle Sullivan."

The door snapped open as Mabel finished buttoning her blouse. Leaving her shoes behind, she raced over to Sullivan, getting in the way as his bed was repositioned, a mobile pole rolled to one side, and an IV bag rehung. Luckily, the kind nurses were very understanding.

Seeing her uncle in such shape, with tubes coming and going, his face pale, caused Emily's nose to burn and her throat to tighten. She fought back the tears. No matter what, she'd be strong for her aunt.

The nurse explained, "He needs to rest, and we've given him meds for pain."

"He's so bruised," Mabel said, trying to lift the blanket so she could see his hip again.

Sullivan grumped at her, slapping down his gown and saying, "Don't shock the ladies, damn it. I'm naked under here."

Emily thought it might be time to intercede. "I'm here, Uncle Sullivan." She moved close and smoothed her uncle's blanket back into place. After thanking the nurses, she asked, "How long will it be before we hear the results of the X-ray?"

"A doctor will be in shortly to answer all your questions. In the meantime, I think Mr. Thatcher might like to nap."

"Mr. Thatcher," Sullivan said, "wants to eat."

"Uncle," Emily chided. "Let's find out what we're dealing with, and then we'll worry about food."

"You can say that because you're not starving." He reached out for Mabel's hand, which she quickly provided. "You promised me pancakes after I got that bug."

"Dear, I didn't know you'd jump right off the stool, did I?"

"Mabel," he whispered, his tone heavy with anxiety. "Did I hurt you?"

"No, I'm fine. It's not like I caught you."

"You tried," he said, not yet convinced. "If I'd hurt you—"

Mabel lifted his hand to her lips and pressed a lingering kiss to his knuckles. "You're the only one hurt, Sullivan."

Giving them privacy for the tender moment, Emily followed the nurses to the door, thanking them once more. They each smiled, and then quietly left the room. Now with her aunt and uncle alone, Emily turned to face them.

Mabel said in a stage whisper, "Emily's in a huff. She's giving us both the stink-eye."

"No, I'm not." Was she? She cleared her expression

and even smiled. "I love you both so much, and I'm... concerned."

"He'll be fine," Mabel said, settling on the chair beside him, still holding his hand.

"Of course he will. Uncle Sullivan is far from frail." That was just a small lie. She gentled her voice. "But Aunt, he shouldn't have been climbing on anything."

"There was a bug," Mabel said in her defense.

"A nasty stink bug," Sullivan concurred. "Mabel hates those things."

Her aunt shuddered. "It was crawling across my dining room window."

Sullivan squeezed her hand. "She can't stand bugs. I had to get it for her."

"He wanted to do it," Mabel stated.

"Course I do," Sullivan agreed. "I'll always get the bugs for you, honey. You know that."

His devotion to Mabel was touching, making it difficult for Emily to persist. The last thing she wanted to do was make her aunt feel guilty, or cause her uncle more worry. Still, they needed to understand the gravity of the situation. "You fell, Uncle. Thankfully, you didn't go through the window, but what if—"

"That was my own damn fault. Mabel said *left* but I went right."

"The bug flew," Mabel admitted miserably. "I screamed. I think that's what startled him."

"I wasn't startled," he denied. "I just lost my balance, that's all."

Unsure how to continue, or if she even should, Emily settled on saying, "Well, I guess we just need to be more careful."

"We?" Mabel laughed. "Sweetheart, you aren't queen, and Sullivan and I are always careful."

Good grief. How could she reason through that? Clearly it wasn't the time. For now, in a hospital bed, Sullivan was safe from overdoing it. Until he was released, she'd use the time to come up with a plan.

Over the next two hours, Sullivan dozed off and on, Mabel drew out her knitting, and Emily fretted.

Twice, Mabel told her, "Why don't you sit down?" and instead, she'd moved from the window, which overlooked a parking lot, to the bathroom, where she tidied up from Mabel's hasty change of clothes, to the hallway, where she'd walked from one end to the other. She understood that things took time, but unfortunately, she wasn't the patient sort.

All her life, she'd been a doer. When she knew something needed to be done, she came up with a plan. Once she had that plan, she acted on it.

This, waiting to hear from a doctor, was excruciating.

She strongly disliked having things out of her control.

Finally giving up, she went into the room and took a seat by the uninspiring window view. A yawn caught her by surprise, and then her stomach growled.

With Sullivan now snoring, Mabel loudly whispered, "We need food."

Food would be *amazing*. That morning she'd jumped from the bed and started running without coffee or a single bite to eat. If she was this hungry, how must Mabel feel?

Emily whispered, "Why don't you go down to the

cafeteria, get some lunch, and relax? I'll sit with Uncle Sullivan."

"I'm not leaving him, and the cafeteria won't open until lunch." She dipped her chin, giving Emily a familiar cajoling look. "You could go out and get us something. It'd do you good to expend some energy. You were never one to suffer idle time."

Emily suspected that her aunt just wanted her out of the room so she could relax without distractions. She and Sullivan enjoyed a sedate routine, and even though Mabel was ten years younger than Sullivan, she was still aging and likely tired.

"I'm sorry, Aunt. My pacing is probably driving you batty."

"Nothing about you makes me batty. I adore every inch of you. You know that."

Over the years, she'd heard that sentiment many, many times. "I adore you, too. Both of you."

Mabel intensified "the look," adding a softness to her voice that never failed to sway Emily. "I'll pay for the food."

"No, you absolutely will not. But… I don't want to leave you."

"The fresh air would do you good, and just think how wonderful food would be. I bet you missed breakfast, too."

"Me? You were planning pancakes and didn't get them." Emily didn't want to chance leaving the room because she was afraid she'd miss the doctor when he came in. She preferred to hear the particulars directly from the professional, not secondhand. While her aunt had an enormous heart, she did have a way of losing the details.

Just then her cell phone buzzed. She pulled it from her purse, saw with surprise that it was Saul, and although she immediately felt rejuvenated, she hesitated to answer.

"Who is it?" Mabel asked with new alertness. "I can tell by your expression that you're excited. Take a breath, then say hello."

Dutifully, Emily drew a breath, smiled at her aunt, then answered with, "Hello, Saul."

*Saul?* Mabel silently mouthed, her brows up in interest.

"Hey, you," Saul said. "Any news yet?"

"Not a lot. My uncle is napping, my aunt is hungry, but we're waiting on test results."

Wide-eyed, Mabel said, "Tell him you're hungry, too."

Emily didn't get the chance.

Voice lowered, Saul asked, "Are you hungry, Emily?"

She blinked at that unfamiliar, husky tone, and the way it made her breath catch. "You heard my aunt?"

"Was I not supposed to?"

"She probably didn't realize..." With Mabel grinning at her, Emily could barely think. "Yes, I'm also hungry, but the cafeteria won't open for another hour yet."

"Trust me, you don't want the cafeteria food. How about I run something over to you?"

Honest to God, her jaw dropped. Stunned at the offer, she looked at her aunt.

Mabel promptly asked, "What? *What?*"

"Um... Saul offered to bring us some food."

"Yes! Tell him *yes* right now." Under her breath, Mabel murmured, "This is exciting."

"No, it's not," Emily whispered back while tucking the phone close to muffle her voice. "He's a friend."

With another of her patented looks, Mabel grinned. "Of course he is. Friends like that should be cherished— and they should visit with your loving aunt."

Oh Lord.

"Emily?" Saul said with a laugh, proving he'd heard all of that, too.

"Yes, sorry, I'm still here." What should she do? She hated to put him out... "It's a twenty-minute drive from Cemetery."

"I know. It's not a problem. What should I pick up?"

Emily tried to think of the restaurants he'd pass along the way, but mostly her thoughts were caught on the fact that Saul was willing to go out of his way for her. "What should you pick up?" She knew she sounded silly, but her brain was on the fritz. "I don't know..."

Mabel quickly said, "Get us something good. Oh, I know. Chicken wings and french fries. Maybe with ranch dip."

"I don't think there's a restaurant like that along the way," Emily said.

Having overheard them again, Saul said, "I'll take care of it. Give me about thirty-five minutes, okay?"

Because she couldn't bear sitting a moment longer, Emily shot to her feet to gaze blindly out the window. "This is so nice of you. Thank you."

"It's my pleasure, hon. I'm glad to do it. So what's the room number?"

*Hon*, again. What did that mean? Anything, nothing? With her aunt staring at her, taking in her every blink, Emily couldn't sort it out right now.

Since there was only the one hospital to service Cemetery and Allbee, he didn't need that info. She gave him the floor and room number and, avoiding Mabel's gaze, disconnected.

"Quick, come here." After scooching to the side of the big chair and then patting the empty space on the cushion beside her, Mabel began to dig in one of the bags.

"What are you doing?" Emily asked, easing onto the seat next to her.

"This." She withdrew a brush and hastily pulled the band from Emily's hair.

"Aunt." Emily laughed as the messy locks fell free. "I'm not seventeen anymore. I can brush my own hair."

"But I've always enjoyed doing it, and I could tell you pulled it back in a rush today, probably worrying about us."

"I love you both." They were the only family she had. "Of course I was worried."

A nurse came in to check Sullivan's blood pressure just as Mabel finished fussing with her hair. Emily's ponytail was now smoother, and much higher. It brought back memories of when her mother and father had suddenly been taken from her. Many nights, Mabel would sit with her and fuss with her hair, just touching and talking quietly, supplying the human contact Emily badly needed. Those were quiet, careful times—that meant so much to her.

In contrast, Sullivan would take her out to the garden with him when his eyesight was still good. They'd spend hours in the sun, sweating and joking as they weeded around flowers and vegetables alike. Without being obvious about it, he helped her to burn up nervous energy so she could finally sleep at night instead of crying with the suffocating hurt of losing both parents.

In their gentle, insistent, quirky ways, they'd saved her from her overwhelming grief. Emily knew she owed them more than she could ever repay.

And now they were older, and the thought of anything happening to either of them...

Mabel's arms closed around her shoulders from behind, hugging her warmly as if she sensed Emily's mood. Her hands, weathered but still strong, crossed loosely over her collarbone. "He's okay," Mabel whispered.

Emily put her hands over her aunt's. "Yes, I'm sure he is." She reassured herself that no one at the hospital had seemed desperate or anxious. So far they'd treated Sullivan in a kind but routine way.

"Tell me about your caller."

Grinning, Emily turned her head to press a kiss to her aunt's cheek. "He's not *my* caller, so don't make more of it than it is. He's just..." The hottest guy in Cemetery. The most eligible bachelor. A certifiable hunk.

Also the friendliest, the easiest to be around, tall and sexy and... "He's younger than me."

"So?" Mabel gave her one more squeeze, then released her. "I'm younger than Sullivan."

"That's different."

"Only to a sexist. And Emily, I refuse to believe that of you. In fact, I was reading an article the other day about the advantages of women dating younger men. All the celebrities do it. God knows men have been doing it for years."

"I'm not a celebrity, Aunt." She was *the flower lady*.

"You'll like Saul, though. He has a family-owned restaurant with amazing food."

From the bed, Sullivan asked, "How old is he?"

Ha! Emily should have known her uncle would wake
for any gossip. "Thirty-nine."

With a snort, Sullivan said, "That's not younger."

"It is by two years."

"Mabel, explain to her that two years is nothing."

"It's nothing," Mabel dutifully agreed. "You're being
ridiculous and you know it."

"It's not just age." *It's everything.* Hearing the exhaustion in Sullivan's voice, Emily went to him and
smoothed his blankets.

Feeling her touch, he removed his glasses, and his
faded blue eyes focused on her face. When she was
close enough, and directly in front of him, he could still
see her, at least enough to recognize her.

"Do you want a drink, Uncle?"

"God, yes. Got a beer?"

Her mouth quirked. "Sorry, only water for now."

"It'll have to do." He opened his mouth, making her
grin as she put the straw to his lips. When he finished,
he said, "I could use some food, too."

"I'll ask about your tray." After pressing a kiss to
Sullivan's mostly bald head, she headed out of the
room, grateful to escape the questions she knew would
come. Unfortunately, the interrogation waited only long
enough for her to say that the doctor would be in shortly
and a tray was ordered. Then her aunt and uncle both
gave in to their curiosity.

Used to them and the over-the-top ways they tried to
encourage her, Emily wasn't at all surprised that they
were geared up and ready to go.

"Tell me what he looks like," Mabel demanded.

"Tall, fit." Hoping to sound indifferent, Emily gave them the basics. "Brown hair steaked by the sun, green eyes. A little tanned, because he enjoys running on the beach." Oh, how she loved watching him run on the beach, not that she was overt about it. She couldn't be. But Saul definitely drew attention. He usually ran shirtless, his strong, wide shoulders flexing as his arms moved and his muscled thighs—

Breathless, Mabel stared at her face, touched her arm and purred, "Tell me more."

Oh, no. Mabel always knew when she started day-dreaming. "I—"

Before she could come up with something plausible, Sullivan asked, "His restaurant serves good food?"

"Delicious food." Whew. A safe topic. "It's called Saul's Pit Stop, and he advertises as 'the most remarkable ribs from the town of Cemetery.' You'd love them."

Sullivan snorted. "*Just* from Cemetery? I could throw a rock from one end of that town to the other. I doubt there are any other rib joints."

Emily laughed. "I'm sure he's being modest. I'd say the ribs are easily the best in Indiana. Maybe even this side of the country."

"Damn it, I need food."

As Mabel patted his hand, she stated, "He's nice, I'm sure. You wouldn't like anyone who wasn't nice."

"Of course he's nice. Everyone likes Saul, *but*…we're only friends, so get that gleam out of your eye."

"You're the one who got all dreamy when you said he likes to jog on the beach."

Yes, she probably had. "Fine." Emily had never been able to fool her aunt, so there was no point in trying now. "I may be a stick-in-the-mud, but I can enjoy..." how to put it? "...*eye candy*, the same as any other healthy person."

Immediate protests ensued, not at her description of Saul, but at the perceived putdown of her character.

"You are not a stick-in-the-mud!"

"Thank you, Aunt."

"I should have gotten Rob alone," Sullivan growled, "and beat some manners into him."

He looked angry enough to do it, as if the age difference wouldn't have factored in. Never mind that Rob had been an extremely good athlete, strong and energetic.

Right up until he wasn't anymore.

She hated remembering Rob and how drastically he had changed after the accident. "We're not a violent family, Uncle Sullivan. You know that, so please don't get all flustered."

"Flustered!" Now he really looked put out. "I don't get flustered—not unless your aunt is teasing me, and then it's because—"

"Sullivan!" Mabel snapped. "Don't embarrass the girl."

Which immediately told Emily that the type of teasing and flustering Sullivan meant was not something she wanted to hear. Not in detail anyway. Her aunt and uncle had always been open about their love—sometimes a little too open, especially considering that her parents had been affectionate but private, and they'd never used innuendoes to tease each other.

Two different types of love, and Emily admired both. In fact, she'd been noticing the different manners of love for a while now. For her parents, her aunt and uncle, friends, soon-to-be-wed couples who bought flowers from her—it seemed every love was different. For some it was quiet and reserved, others playful, or downright sexy, and a few that were more formal. With each couple, there'd been something special to admire, as if they'd created their own language.

Someday she'd like to discover *her* type of love, but at her age, the chance of that grew slimmer every day.

"Emily?"

She looked up to see the doctor in the doorway, and surprise, surprise, she knew the woman. "Angela? Angela Bower!"

Grinning, she came forward to embrace Emily. "Yes, though it's Dr. Angela Randall now." After setting her back, she said, "It's so good to see you. How have you been?"

"I'm wonderful." Realizing what she said, Emily turned to her uncle. "Or at least I will be once we find out how Uncle Sullivan is doing."

Striding forward, Angela explained to Sullivan and Mabel, "Emily and I attended college together. I was so envious of her. She was always so perfect."

Emily choked at hearing that dreaded word yet again. "No, I wasn't."

"You were," Aunt Mabel insisted. "And she still is."

"She was always so nice to everyone, even those of us who were awkward." Angela shook her head. "I considered her a saint."

"What?" Emily gave an uncomfortable laugh. "Everyone liked you."

"Not true." To her aunt and uncle, Angela said, "I was such a social misfit back then. That studious girl who didn't know how to fit in—except with Emily."

"Because I was also a studious girl!"

Mabel beamed at Angela. "Emily befriends everyone. She's never given us a moment of trouble. She always knows the right thing to do."

No, damn it, she didn't. With her serene expression in place, Emily said, "Thank you both, but you're being silly. I'm horribly flawed."

And to that, they all chuckled, including Sullivan.

Emily would have said more—really, the expectations were too much—but Angela went into doctor mode, and Emily forgot everything but her uncle's health.

"I hear you've been climbing on stools, Mr. Thatcher."

Mabel flushed. "That was my fault..."

Very matter-of-fact about it, Sullivan said, "Mabel's afraid of bugs. I had to get it for her."

"I understand, but let's avoid that in the future, agreed?" Without waiting for an answer, Angela said, "The good news is, your hip is not broken, but that doesn't mean it isn't traumatized, and it definitely doesn't mean you can go home."

Sullivan grumbled.

"I'm a little concerned by the dizziness you felt, so—"

Mabel and Emily said, "*Dizziness*?" at the same time.

Angela gave him a look. "You didn't tell either of them?"

"Wasn't a big deal."

Emily knew it was more about not wanting her aunt to suffer guilt, since she was the one who sent Sullivan on the bug hunt. In fact, Emily felt far more guilt than her aunt. For some time now, she'd suspected that they needed more assistance from her.

So far, she hadn't pressed the issue. Not because she didn't care, but because they valued their independence so much, they resisted all her efforts to help.

"Your labs came back normal," Angela continued. "Overall, you're in great health."

"Mabel takes real good care of me."

"I can tell that she does. You're a fit man for eighty-one."

"I do my best," Mabel said. "I can promise you, he'll never get near another stool unless it's to sit on it."

"Excellent." Angela gave them each a glance. "He should also avoid climbing of any kind."

With a firm nod, Mabel said, "I'll see to it."

"I assume you have a cane."

"I do." Sullivan gestured toward the room. "Should be here somewhere."

Emily came forward. "I brought it. After he fell, my aunt was focused on getting him to the hospital." She put her hand on Mabel's shoulder in a show of support. "I did some light packing for her and brought what she'd need."

"Good." To Sullivan, Angela said, "I'd like to keep you for now."

"All the women feel that way," Mabel teased.

Emily couldn't help but smile, especially when she saw Angela's amusement.

"A dietician will be in," Angela explained, "as well as a physical therapist who can evaluate you. I've ordered a CT scan to rule out a TIA, or a small stroke."

That caused Emily and Mabel both to suck in air.

"It's a precaution," Angela explained. "I'd also like to have an ophthalmologist check your vision, just in case it's worsened, and an otologist to rule out any hearing issues."

"Good Lord," Sullivan grumbled. "You going to send in a mechanic, too?"

Shaken, Mabel spoke over him, stating, "He doesn't mind any of that, but I'll be staying here with him."

Though her aunt said it like a challenge, Angela only nodded. "You have a private room, so that's not a problem, though we probably don't have any cots available."

"The chair is fine."

Emily could see that even the floor would be fine, as long as Mabel could stay by Sullivan's side. They were so dedicated to each other that her worry amplified. They relied on each other so much. At Sullivan's age... No, she couldn't even think of her aunt going through a loss like that.

"I'll be back to see you in the morning, Mr. Thatcher. In the meantime, I've ordered a tray for you. Please don't attempt leaving the bed unless you call a nurse first. If you need anything, don't hesitate to ask."

"I need to go home."

"We'll do our best to get you out of here as soon as we can." Angela was about to speak to Mabel, but the older woman was already hovering over the bed, kissing Sullivan's cheek and whispering to him while petting his shoulder through the thin gown.

Emily walked Angela to the hallway instead. "Thank you for explaining everything."

"It's really good to see you, Emily, though I wish it was under better circumstances. It's never easy to see one of our elders hurt."

"He'll be okay?" Emily asked, voicing her top concern.

"From everything I've seen, he'll be fine. He really is fit for a man his age. No cholesterol or diabetes problems." Angela smiled. "You help care for them?"

"As much as they'll let me. Until now, it hasn't really been an issue, but I've been concerned. They're all I have—and I'm all they have."

Angela hesitated, as if confused.

"You probably remember that I married my second year of college." Emily had no issue sharing her status. "We divorced a long time ago."

"Rob Masters. Of course I remember. You two were such a popular couple. He was a big athlete, easy on the eyes, and he seemed so madly in love with you."

Rob had been in love with an illusion. He'd put her on a pedestal, thinking she could always solve every problem. Unfortunately, she hadn't been able to solve him. "Shortly after we married, Rob was in a car wreck. It was bad enough that it ended his athletic career."

"Oh no." With no sign of judgment, Angela said, "That had to be hard for both of you."

Harder for Rob. She'd loved him anyway and had been happy to make any adjustments necessary. Nothing she did helped, and Rob became so distant. Drinking, drugs… Thinking he'd get better, she'd given up her education to help pay for his bills. So, so dumb. "We lasted five years before it ended." Only because she'd kept trying. And trying… Emily didn't resent those lost years, yet she hoped she had learned from them.

"I'm sorry," Angela said.

Emily wanted to reply, *See, I'm not so perfect.* Instead, she shook her head. "I'm happy with my life." Overall.

"I can tell. Plus you're still beautiful and as friendly

as ever." Angela touched her forearm. "I was just the opposite, you know. I was so focused on my education and then establishing myself that it took me a long time to get interested in anyone. I'll admit, I didn't have much faith in marriage, not after the ugly way my parents divorced, but now I've been married five years." With a smile, she added, "So far, so good."

"Is he a doctor as well?"

"Ha! No. One of us is enough, believe me. He's a schoolteacher, very down to earth, and…he's my rock. I don't know what I'd do without him."

Wow, to hear that from such an accomplished person surprised Emily. "I'm sure he feels the same."

"He says he does. Honestly, we both have some horror stories. They're just very different." After checking her watch, Angela asked, "What do you do now?"

"I'm a florist in Cemetery."

"Not just any florist," came a deep, amused voice. "She's *the* flower lady."

Emily turned to see Saul stepping up behind her, a large bag of food held in one hand.

Before she could even say hi, he leaned in and put a kiss to her forehead. "Sorry it took me so long. How's your uncle?"

The imprint of his warm lips against her skin left Emily flustered. "Oh, he, ah…" Never before had Saul kissed her, and she didn't know how to react. "This is Dr. Randall. We knew each other in college. Angela, this is…" *How should she describe Saul?* "…my friend, Saul Culver." Moving past that awkwardness, she explained, "Dr. Randall says overall he's fine, but they'll keep him for now to do more tests."

Angela looked from Saul to Emily and back again

before giving them both a knowing grin. "Obviously, Emily, we need to catch up. Hopefully I'll see you again soon."

Was there anything to tell? Saul stood close enough to her to give the doctor that impression. "I'll be checking in on my uncle as often as I can."

"Excellent. For now, try not to worry too much, okay? We'll take good care of him." She patted Emily's shoulder. "It's nice to meet you, Saul."

"You as well," he said easily, paying the beautiful doctor very little attention.

Once she'd walked on down the hall, Saul focused solely on Emily. And wow, that green-eyed gaze had the power to push her off balance, especially when he said, "Sorry if I overstepped."

A little lost, she shook her head.

"This," he said, brushing another kiss to her temple, then asking, "You're okay?"

"With the…" She gestured at her head. "Yes." *Absolutely yes*.

His mouth quirked. "I meant with your family. Your uncle. Having to rush up to the hospital."

Emily stared at his mouth, wondering if she could get another kiss, this time lips to lips. Maybe when they weren't in a hospital hallway… She took a breath. "Yes, I'm fine. Relieved now that I know Uncle Sullivan will be okay."

"So you and Dr. Randall were already acquainted?"

"Small world, right? Last I'd heard, Angela was in Ohio." Trying to get back on track, she nodded at the bag he carried. "That smells good."

"Can your uncle eat any?"

"I don't think so, not until they finish with all their tests. Angela said his tray should be here soon."

"Better not let him smell it, then." He propped a shoulder on the wall, his gaze drifting over her face as if tracking each feature before meeting her eyes. "I asked an aide, and he told me there's a visitor's lounge just down the hall. Why don't you and your aunt go eat, and I'll sit with your uncle."

Incredible. Why would he offer such a thing? Emily was trying to think of an answer when Mabel peeked out the door, spotted Saul, and joined them with her eyes wide and her lips parted. She didn't even blink.

Saul said, "Hi," in a way that would make any woman's toes curl.

Never one to falter, Mabel shook off her stupor and smiled hugely. "And hello to you, too."

Oh for the love of… Emily cleared her throat. "Aunt Mabel, this is Saul Culver. He's brought the food."

Mabel gaped at Emily. "This is your *friend*?" She dropped back against the door frame, her hand on her chest. "He's…"

"Yes, I know." Emily tried clearing her throat again, but it didn't faze her aunt. Saul had that effect on people, a sort of punch of awareness comprised of his good looks, his fit bod, engaging smile, and those compelling eyes.

Without missing a beat, Saul smiled and held out his hand. "Aunt Mabel. How nice it is to meet you."

## CHAPTER THREE

EMILY WAS STILL in a daze when she arrived at the floral shop the next day and parked her yellow Chevy at the side of the building, leaving the street parking for customers. By rote, she exited the car and headed to the entrance.

Her stalwart aunt had all but melted for Saul. *Melted*.

Emily had heard her giggle. Repeatedly, Mabel had given Emily encouraging looks, as if she wanted her to…what? Pounce on Saul? Proposition him?

Mabel knew her better than that.

Although, since Emily wanted to change up her image, maybe a little pouncing…but no. She was not the pouncing type. She'd need to think of another way to shake things up.

She'd gone to the hospital first thing that morning to check on her aunt and uncle, and they'd barely said hello before they started talking about Saul.

The funny part was, Mabel said very little about how incredible he looked. Most of her praise was for the easy way he'd entertained Sullivan, how gallant he'd been in bringing them food…and how he'd looked at Emily.

According to her aunt, there was a lot going on in Saul's gaze.

*What*, though? That's what Emily would like to know.

Sure, there was friendliness. Saul was that way with everyone. She'd often seen him kiss Mimi on the cheek, or hug Yardley, so she really couldn't put too much stock in the small pecks he'd given her, either.

Her aunt was of a different opinion. According to Mabel, it was all in the eyes.

It pleased Emily that within minutes of meeting them, Saul had them both treating him like part of the family. He and Sullivan found a dozen topics to share, and Mabel did everything she could to play matchmaker.

It had shocked Emily when, after introducing the men, Sullivan had insisted that the women go off to eat so he and Saul could "get to know each other." Even more alarming, Mabel had agreed. In fact, she'd practically dragged Emily out of the room and down the hall to the visitor's lounge, where, around eating, she'd grilled Emily to learn everything she could about Saul. If Emily hadn't resisted, Mabel might have asked for his shoe size. It seemed no detail was too small or insignificant.

It had struck Emily that she actually *did* know a lot about him…and that made her wonder how much Saul knew about her. Okay, so he hadn't known she didn't drink. That was a small detail that anyone might miss.

But what else? She had serious doubts that he'd ever been as aware of her as she was of him.

That thought had irked her. She was a mature woman, not an insecure girl with an unrequited infatuation for the local hottie. She was no longer the same person she'd been in college.

Yet that's what she felt like.

All because Saul had suddenly—what? Been wonderful?

The man was always wonderful.

Too many things had played on her mind when she'd tried to sleep last night, and so here she was, in a fog of exhaustion. She yawned as she took in the sparkling clean front window of her shop, dragging a little even as the morning slipped away and noon approached.

Sallie Sheldrake waved from the front walk of her bakery. "It's a scorcher today."

"Not unexpected for late August in Indiana," Emily called back with a smile.

Two laughing kids ducked around her on the sidewalk, each carrying a float and beach towel, while a harried father rushed to catch up, and the mother pushed a stroller in a more leisurely way.

She murmured, "Sorry," as she went past Emily.

"No apology necessary. Have fun." The scent of the lake, carried on the barely stirring air, mingled with the acrid smell of hot pavement.

Someone tooted the horn of a golf cart.

A dog barked happily at the end of a long leash.

Visitors to the tourist town were busy browsing the shops along Lakeshore Drive, while others were on their way to or from the beach.

Thankfully, Gentry McAdams, her one and only fulltime employee, had opened for her today. In the four months that he'd been working for her, he'd repeatedly impressed Emily with his work ethic.

She strode in through the front door, already saying, "Thank you so much, Gentry. I owe you."

"Not a problem." He rang up a customer and thanked her. As she left, he asked Emily, "How's your uncle?"

"Sore," she admitted. Poor Sullivan had grimaced anytime he'd moved. "Fortunately, the CT scan didn't show any sign of stroke, but his vision has worsened."

Amazingly, PT would start working with him today. If he had enough mobility, he might be able to go home on Wednesday.

"At eighty-one, I bet he already has aches and pains, and then to fall…" Gentry shook his head while he misted a display of flowers. Just shy of six feet tall, with black hair and gray eyes, he was a handsome young man, solid, patient, and always respectful to customers. Emily liked him a lot, and valued him as an employee.

"He has some horrible bruises. He's a sturdy guy, but right now, he looks so fragile."

"Don't share that with him," Gentry advised with a slight grin. "No dude, regardless of age, wants to be called fragile."

Emily agreed. Sullivan would have a fit if he heard her use that word. "I'm glad I was able to see them both this morning. My poor aunt." She put her purse behind the counter and hastily pulled on her apron. "I don't think she slept very well in that chair."

"I'm sure she's right where she wants to be."

Amazing that Gentry understood that. "That's exactly what she said." Rushing around, hoping to catch up after her very late start, she removed a little loamy dirt from a potted hyacinth. Then she rearranged the cut flowers that Gentry had set out, ensuring they were in the vases just right. Gentry was absolutely amazing, but he didn't quite have her eye for design.

When she'd first hired him, he'd only done the outside work on the wildflowers Emily grew in the field behind her home. She and Sullivan had started the massive garden years ago, and as it expanded and thrived, she got the idea to incorporate it into her business. New brides would take photos in rows of flowers, or they'd make it an outing for the bridesmaids to choose their own bouquets. It was a beautiful backdrop, but often more work than she could handle alone.

Gentry loved it. He had endless stores of energy, and according to him, he preferred to be outdoors whenever possible. That hadn't stopped him from taking on additional duties at the shop, though, when one of her two part-time employees moved away. Whenever it was necessary, Emily could count on him.

"We got a delivery a few hours ago," Gentry said.

Pivoting on her heel, Emily started for the back of the store, but Gentry caught her, gently turning her to face him.

Holding her shoulders, he smiled down at her and said, "Slow down, Boss. I already took care of it."

Huffing a laugh, Emily said, "I swear, I feel like I fell out of bed behind schedule."

Just then the door chimed as someone entered.

She and Gentry both turned to look—and there stood Saul, poised half in, half out, his gaze locked on them. The hazy sunshine haloed his brown hair, making it look more golden and leaving his expression in shadow.

All but his eyes.

They seemed to express a lot of…something. Emily wasn't sure what.

His gaze moved from her face, to Gentry, and the way he held her shoulders.

"Saul." Feeling more harried than ever, Emily moved toward him. "I didn't expect you."

It took him a second to get his attention off Gentry, then he took another step in and let the door close behind him. "Should I have called?"

"Of course not. It's always good to see you." It was

*great* to see him. Inspiring. Rejuvenating. Seriously, her heart was already pumping faster, making her feel somewhat…nervous? Ha. Women her age did not get nervous over an early afternoon visit from a friend. "I thought you'd be at the restaurant."

"I'm heading back there shortly." He held up a bag. "What do you bring a woman who already has flowers?"

Oh my goodness, he'd come bearing gifts? An appalling, silly schoolgirl giggle escaped her, and she almost slapped a hand over her mouth. Instead, she cleared her throat and smiled gently. "You didn't need to bring me anything."

Gentry sniffed the air. "I smell food, and I think it might be lunch."

"From the restaurant," Saul said. "I know Emily likes the potato soup and hot rolls, but I figured you'd be working too, Gentry, so I brought enough for two."

"Thanks, man. Appreciate it." He nodded at Emily. "She's been in fast-forward mode all morning. I doubt she even had breakfast."

Emily looked back and forth between the men. "Guys, I swear, I do eat. It's not like I'm wasting away." She opened the bag Saul handed her, breathed in the delicious aromas of yeasty bread, melted cheese and green onions, and closed her eyes. "This smells *amazing*. Way better than the protein bar I devoured on the way to the hospital."

Saul spent a minute asking after her uncle and aunt, then he surprised her by stepping closer. Something in his manner seemed different, leaving Emily flustered.

"I'll be in back," Gentry said with a grin, drawing her attention. "If anyone needs me."

"Thank you." She turned back to Saul. "He's such a great kid."

A curious half smile curled Saul's mouth. "He's not a kid, Em."

"Well, no, but he's only twenty-five, so close enough."

"Twenty-five is a grown man and you know it."

"I guess." She didn't understand why he stressed the point.

"You two have something going on?"

Lifting her brows, Emily asked, "Who two?"

"You and Gentry."

It took her a second for the gist of the question to sink in. Then she laughed at the absurdity of it.

Saul crowded closer in the sexy way guys did when interested. His voice lowered. "Is that funny, hon?"

The closeness threw her off a little. "Me and Gentry?" Emily tried not to stare at Saul's mouth. "Very funny. Seriously. You do know I'm forty-one, right?"

"Yeah, so?"

There was no way he didn't recognize the age disparity.

One rough-tipped finger touched her cheek. "I'm thirty-nine."

"Also younger." Something she already knew. She gave him a playful push—that didn't budge him an inch. "Thanks for reminding me."

Eyes narrowing, Saul lifted that teasing finger to the bridge of her nose. "Would it be okay if I put one right here?"

A surge of awareness swept through Emily. She hoped he meant what her surging hormones thought he meant, but to be sure, she asked, "One what?"

In answer, he leaned down and pressed his mouth

to the spot, lingering for one, two, three seconds. With him that close, Emily was acutely aware of the musky heat of his body, the size of him, and his strength.

She'd thought about his random kisses all night long, and she also thought about how she despised being such a proper person all the time. Always doing the right thing. Always doing the expected. It was what caused people to call her perfect.

What would have happened if she'd taken the wine cooler at the wedding?

Or if she'd randomly kissed him back when he'd pecked her cheek at the hospital?

At some point during her drive back from the hospital, after stewing on too many things for too long, she'd made up her mind on how she'd do a few things differently. Angela was wrong. Her aunt and uncle were wrong. She was far from perfect.

Now she'd be imperfect on purpose.

Looking into Saul's eyes, she said, "I'd rather you put one right here," and she touched her lips. Yup, her heart stampeded as if trying to escape her chest, but she didn't falter.

Without a word, Saul's gaze dropped to her mouth... and the front door opened right behind them.

Betty Cemetery, great-granddaughter to the town founder and older than Emily's uncle by a few years, gave them both an arrested look, then muttered, "Right in the front of the flower shop. Shame on you, Emily Lucretia."

Laughing, Saul put an arm around Betty's low, plump shoulders and gave her a gentle squeeze. "You shouldn't be jealous, Betty." Bending, he pressed a kiss to her cheek. "Better?"

"Oh, stop." A bloom of color filled her papery cheeks, and she smiled. "The younger generation knows no shame."

From behind them, Gentry said, "Feel free to move that to the back room. I'll take care of the customer."

Good Lord, Emily realized that she'd forgotten all about Gentry. Actually, she'd forgotten she was in the shop, too. In front of the big display window.

And now both Gentry and Betty had seen her flirting. "I can't ask you to… You've already been here alone all morning and—"

Saul said, "Thanks, Gentry," and took Emily's elbow. Fortunately, he didn't lead her to the back room, which would have felt too obvious, but to a quieter corner of the shop, where colorful vases caught the sunlight and created a rainbow across the floor. "So."

She leaned in to whisper, "I rescind the request." Then in embarrassed honesty, she added, "I forgot where I was."

Quickly banking a grin, he said, "You've got a lot on your plate, but I have a suggestion. Let's get together when you close the shop."

Her thoughts went spinning. He wanted to get together…just to share a kiss? "But I close at six, and you don't close until—"

"New hire, remember? The restaurant is covered. They'll get by without me tonight."

Emily badly wished she could agree. "I asked Gentry to close for me tonight so I could visit my aunt and uncle during visiting hours."

"What time?"

Wincing, she said, "Five thirty."

"Sounds good to me. I'll get them dinner now that I

know what Sullivan can eat. Should I pick you up here or at your house?"

"I…" Wow, he was moving fast. Her natural urge was to turn him down. What if it was only a friendly gesture on his part and she was misinterpreting things, already envisioning "the kiss," when maybe it wouldn't even happen? What if her absurd flirting had given him the wrong idea? What if, what if?

*Changing it up*, she reminded herself, and tried to look decisive. "Here, to save time."

"Five thirty it is."

Oh. Okay then. A date. Sort of. The smile crept up on her. "I'll be ready."

"Don't forget, dinner's on me." He brushed a knuckle across her cheek and, with obvious reluctance, left the shop. Emily watched him go, even tracked him through the window as he crossed the street, dodging cars, golf carts, and a scooter or two.

An elbow prodded the small of her back, making her jump.

When she turned, Emily found Betty there, now holding a small colorful bouquet and wearing a smile.

Emily smiled back blandly. "Found everything you need?"

"I did." Betty slanted her a look of fascination. "Seems you may have as well."

"What?"

"Don't be coy, my girl," Betty chided. "First you hire that handsome young man, and now you're flirting with Cemetery's most eligible bachelor."

"Saul?" she asked, as if she hadn't heard him called that a hundred times.

"None other. You're certainly getting around."

"I… No. I'm not." How dare Betty suggest such a thing?

As if she didn't hear the edge in Emily's tone, or plain didn't care, Betty said, "I think that boy is good for business."

"Gentry?" Yes, even now he was busy. Never an idle moment for him.

"I meant Saul." Betty leaned closer, her faded eyes direct. "Though your Gentry is a draw as well. You should consider a few posters of him holding flowers. Maybe shirtless." She bobbed her sparse, graying eyebrows.

It surprised Emily so much that she laughed, but with a good deal of uncertainty. Betty used to be so rigid and, well, *mean*. Emily knew how to deal with that Betty: avoidance when possible. Now it seemed Betty was softer, teasing…and into everyone's personal business. "I'll, um, consider it."

"You do that." Satisfied, Betty headed for the door, but not before giving another long, appraising look at Gentry.

GENTRY WHISTLED AS he worked throughout the day, making sure he got as much done for Emily as he could. She looked beat, with stress and worry leaving their mark, her complexion paler, slight shadows under her eyes. He noticed she had to struggle to work up her usual smile.

He had a feeling that she was also thrown by Saul's interest. In so many ways, Emily discounted her own appeal. No way could she be unaware of her looks, but they just didn't seem to matter to her. The woman managed style with casual ease. She didn't need a lot of makeup. Gentry had lost count of the times he'd admired her eyes. They were a unique shade of brown, and she had long, dark lashes. When Emily looked at him, he got the sense that she was completely absorbed.

If he didn't know her so well, he'd occasionally think she was flirting—except that Emily did that with everyone. It was one reason customers liked her so much. She listened intently to everything they said, as if no one else existed, and then she created phenomenal flower arrangements that exactly fit their expectations.

After she wrapped up a transaction with the last customer, Gentry went to get her a water. It had been a busy day for both of them, but at least he'd slept last night. By the looks of it, he doubted Emily had.

When he returned only a few moments later, a frosty bottle of water in hand, he found Emily bent at the waist, her dark blond hair flipped forward as she dragged her fingers through it.

The sight stopped him dead in his tracks. "You okay?"

Turning her head to the side, she smiled at him. "Yes, just rearranging my ponytail. I was getting a headache."

Slender fingers went through her glossy hair again and again, coaxing out any tangles. Propping a hip against the counter, Gentry admitted—only to himself—that it was sexy as hell. He'd bet a week's pay that Emily had no idea how she looked right now, her rump out, the graceful curve of her spine and neck in that position, her thick hair hanging free, exposing her nape…

She gathered her hair together again, slipped a band off her wrist, and secured it. Straightening, she blew out a breath—and caught him staring. "I'm sorry, was I in your way?"

Leave it to Emily to make that assumption. "Nah, I was just admiring the view." He flashed a teasing grin and handed her the water. "I thought you could use this."

Discounting the compliment, she took the bottle. "Thank you. I'm sure it'll help my headache to hydrate. I didn't even think of that."

Gentry glanced at the clock. "Saul will be here soon. Why don't you get your stuff together?" Seeing Emily relax a little would be nice, and besides, Gentry needed her to get going before he said anything else inappropriate.

As soon as he'd gotten the job with her, he'd created a cardinal rule: no flirting with the boss. Actually, no flirting with anyone.

"Vivienne isn't here yet. I can't leave you alone."

Just to tease her again, he asked, "You don't trust me to hold down the fort?"

"Pfft." She gave a light push to his shoulder. "You know it's not that. You've been a godsend, helping out so much. Even today, with me here, I feel like I've been in a fog and you've kept it all going."

Not even close to the truth. "You're better than you realize. You could run this place in a blindfold and never miss a beat. Seriously, give yourself some credit, okay?"

"That's so nice of you, Gentry." She gently rubbed at her temple. "I'm not a good worrier. I take it too far, my aunt always says. When I was younger, she'd make me stop, take a few deep breaths, and then figure it out."

"Did it help?"

Her smile was impish. "Not really, but she thought it did, and that's what mattered. Now she still insists I stop and breathe whenever she thinks I'm getting overwhelmed."

"She loves you," he said, his heart twisting just a little. How nice would it be to have that kind of backup?

"Yeah," Emily said softly. "She really does. I'm so

lucky." Suddenly her probing gaze met his, and she tipped her head. "What about you?"

Trying to put her off, he grabbed a cloth and cleaned a smudge off the glass case. "What about me?"

"Do you have any close family?"

Damn, he hated talking about personal stuff. "Nope." Not anymore. "It's just me." He glanced at her, saw her obvious concern, and asked, "Where's the window cleaner? I think I'm just making it worse."

"I'll get it."

Before he could debate it with her, the door chimed as a new customer came in. Glad for the reprieve, Gentry handed her the rag, then leaned close to her ear. "Hustle up before your date gets here. I'll take care of the customer."

She replied, "He's not a date."

And Saul said, "Yes, I am."

THAT MADE TWICE today that he'd found Emily and Gentry huddled close together. Refusing to accept that he'd missed his chance, Saul smiled, noting Gentry's look of guilt and Emily's expression of surprise. "Am I interrupting…again?"

Coming out from behind the counter, Emily said, "I only need a minute." And then to Gentry, "Are you sure you don't mind? What if Vivienne is a no-show?"

"She'll be here, but even if she's not, I've got it."

"Thank you. You're the best employee ever." After flashing a smile at Saul, she ducked into the back room.

Saul came forward. "She looks tired." Beautiful, as always, but also weary.

"Because she is." Gentry handed Saul an open bottle of water. "I can tell she's worried, plus she has a headache. Get her to hydrate, okay? She's been running around here all day, creating work for herself, maybe as a distraction. I can't get her to slow down, but you might be able to."

None of that sounded like Emily, who, far as he knew, was always composed and in control. Then again, her uncle was hurt and her aunt was afraid. That was likely enough to unsettle anyone, but especially someone with Emily's big heart.

And now he was having second thoughts about his prank, but hearing the growing crowd outside, it was too late to do anything about it. "Seems like you're helping her a lot."

Gentry shrugged. "I enjoy the shop, and I prefer to stay busy, though I admit I prefer to work in the yard."

Saul asked, "The yard?" None of the businesses here had much yard to speak of. They were compact, colorful buildings arranged in neat rows along Main Street and Lakeshore Drive, with easy access to the lake.

For only a second, Gentry seemed surprised. "You know Emily has fields of flowers growing behind her house, right?"

"Yes?" He knew it—but what did that have to do with Gentry?

"It's gotten to be too much work for her, so I do most of the weeding and trimming. In fact, I'm usually there half a day every day, but with her uncle's injury, I'm helping out here a little more. Luckily, there's an automatic watering system. It needed a few repairs, but I got it working again, so the flowers will all be fine."

Stymied, Saul stared at the younger man.

Gentry worked at Emily's house. How had he not known that?

Before he could ask more, Emily came hurrying out of the back room. "Sorry, I didn't mean to make you wait."

"You didn't." He saw that Gentry was right—she was rushing for no reason. "I got here early." *Because I'd wanted time to set up Kathleen.*

Just then, Vivienne darted through the door with a laugh. Pushing it shut behind her, she collapsed back, one hand on her chest, her face lit up with a smile. She was a jovial, plump sixty-year-old hippie who loved the town, the town's name, and especially flowers. In her free time she painted, and often sold her work for added income.

Spotting Emily, she jolted forward, her long graying braids bouncing against her big breasts. "It's genius marketing! Oh my god, I *love* it."

"Genius marketing?" Emily asked.

"Half the town is out there taking pics. They'll be all over the Facebook page in no time. Everyone loves it."

"Loves...what?"

Saul cleared his throat. "Actually, that was my doing."

Grabbing him, Vivienne danced him around in a circle. "You wicked, wicked man. It's so fun it should be illegal, but I'm glad it's not."

"Now I have to see." Gentry strode around the counter, went to the door, and leaned out.

For a few seconds, he said nothing, but the sounds of the onlookers filtered in. Laughter, jokes, a few cheers.

Saul wasn't sure which way Emily would go on it; she'd either enjoy it as much as Vivienne did, or she'd be embarrassed.

Grinning hugely, Gentry came back inside—and

gave Saul a high-five before he paused in front of Emily. "Go take a peek."

"Now I'm not sure I want to." Her wide eyes turned to Saul. "What did you do?"

"A little payback," he said easily, and reached out his hand.

Emily laughed nervously, but she did finally put her hand in his. It felt like a gesture of trust, both friendly and—because it was Emily—intimate. Saul led her to the door, held it open, and waited while she peered around the crowd.

There on the bench outside her door, a bench that Emily kept scrupulously clean and freshly painted each year, was Kathleen.

Long stiff legs stretched out and wearing a tiny bikini made of silk flowers, Kathleen drew attention. Sunglasses shielded her eyes. She had a plastic coconut drink in one hand, and a sign in the other.

Emily covered her mouth, but her eyes crinkled with amusement. "Oh, my."

Relieved by her pleased expression, Saul leaned close. "That's the first time I've decorated a woman's hair."

The grin broke free. "I'm not sure it counts if the woman can't move…and if the hair can be taken off her head."

"Guilty," he said, enjoying the fact that her free hand was still in his. "I put her wig in my lap and painstakingly wove those flowers through. What do you think?"

"I think Kathleen has never looked…" She glanced up at him, her eyes even more beautiful with laughter. "So sexy."

"Great." His attention dropped to her smiling mouth. "Goal achieved."

"What does her sign say?"

Saul tugged her farther out until she could read: The Real Flower Lady Is Inside.

"Oh, no." Emily snickered with glee. "Everyone will think that *I* did this, like an advertisement."

Saul brushed his thumb over her knuckles. "You would have, if you'd thought of it."

"No way," she denied. "Not in a million years. But since you did…" She noticed people taking photos of, or with, Kathleen, and catching the two of them in the background.

Quickly, Emily pulled Saul back into the shop. "Gentry?"

Broom in hand, Gentry exited the back room. "What's up?"

"We're announcing twenty percent off the daisies and chrysanthemums—and you'll need to remove that shirt and go tell everyone."

Gentry stalled comically. "Remove what shirt?"

"Your shirt." She gestured at him as she released Saul and rushed behind the counter to grab a big marker and a cardboard sign. "It was Betty's suggestion." She caught the silence and looked up. "Oh. I mean, unless you don't want to?"

"It's not that I care," Gentry muttered with discomfort. "Not exactly."

Emily blanched. "I'm sorry. I thought… You always work shirtless at my house, so…"

"In the *yard*."

Her face went hot. "You go shirtless to the beach."

"To the *beach*."

Seeing the appalled expression on Gentry's face, Saul

laughed. "Hon, I think you're bordering on sexual harassment."

Vivienne sat there taking it all in. "I'm just imagining both you boys shirtless." She gave a low purring growl.

Emily immediately apologized. "Oh my god, I'm sorry, Gentry. I'm awful. I should never listen to Betty."

"Betty? No, don't tell me." Now Gentry flushed. "It's just…" He glared at Saul. "Stop laughing. Or better yet, *you* do it."

Rolling a shoulder, Saul said, "No problem."

Emily instantly perked up. "Seriously? You wouldn't mind?"

Phone in hand, Vivienne spun on her stool to stare at him with rapt attention.

"You ladies are bent," Saul teased, and then he stripped off his shirt and handed it to Emily. Hell, he ran shirtless on the beach every morning. No biggie to him. "Give me the sign."

Vivienne immediately snapped a few photos, then started typing.

"What are you doing?" Saul asked with suspicion.

"Facebook page. And Twitter." She glanced up. "And Instagram and TikTok… You don't mind, right?"

Saul laughed. "I'm guessing if I did, it's already too late?"

Trying to look abashed and failing, Vivienne said, "Sorry."

"No problem. Just make sure you tag Emily's shop and mention her flower sale." He turned to Emily…who stared ardently at his chest. "Em?"

With his shirt clutched in both hands, she said, "Wait until I tell my aunt about this."

Gentry snorted. "See, this is why I didn't want to do it. It's going to be all over town in under thirty minutes."

"I can handle it." Saul took the finished sign from the counter, and slipped his sunglasses over his eyes—because yeah, he could use a little cover. "I'll be right back, and then we have to get on the road or you'll miss visiting hours."

As he stepped outside, he heard Emily mutter, "Good grief, I forgot all about that."

If nothing else, Saul figured he'd relieved some of her stress.

Once he hit the sidewalk, he held up the sign and gave a loud whistle. "Big sale inside, everyone. Twenty percent off some flowers. You all know you want… some." He added just enough hesitation to make it suggestive.

Catcalls filled the air while Saul held the sign high, strolling through the crowd, answering a few quick questions from vacationers, posing with a few people for photos, laughing with different locals, and all in all, having fun.

Damn, but he loved this town and everyone in it.

It was perfect, like Emily, and if things went his way, his relationships—both of them—would soon be perfect, too.

Several people headed inside, while others gave orders to friends who would do a collective purchase. He straightened Kathleen's hair, adjusted her bikini to "protect her modesty," and then went to collect Emily.

Overall, he'd say their date was off to a good start.

"WE HAVE TO encourage her," Mabel said, sitting beside Sullivan, holding his large, weathered hand in her own.

Thank God he couldn't see her face clearly, because she felt…ravaged. The hospital atmosphere and the awful bruising emphasized the signs of his age, and her heart couldn't handle it.

She'd let him get on that stool, and because of her foolishness, now he was hurt.

"You mean Emily?" he asked, his fingers cradling hers so gently, just as he often did. "We always do, honey. Always."

"I know, but now more than ever, I…" She needed to see Emily settled. Call her old fashioned, she didn't care. She wanted Emily to have what she and Sullivan had. A closeness that surrounded her in support and love and understanding for all the rest of her days. She wanted Emily to have someone to lean on, and someone who would lean on her.

Both things, she knew, were wonderful.

"I love you, baby. You know that."

Mabel sniffled a laugh. How did he always know exactly what she was thinking and feeling? "Oh, Sullivan. You smooth talker, you." She leaned over the bed, her cheek on his chest. "You're my…everything."

"And you're mine." His arm went over her shoulders for a warm hug. "It's just a hip. I'm not ready to kick it yet."

No, he wasn't. But this, seeing him in a sterile bed, tubes coming and going, black-and-blue everywhere, was a harsh reminder that life had its limits. Nothing lasted forever, no matter how badly you wanted it. "Emily feels responsible for us."

"Just as we feel responsible for her. That's all part of it." Amusement laced his words when he added, "That girl is something, isn't she? She came to us a little broken, but you fixed her right up, and now she's just the sweetest thing."

"You helped to fix her up." Mabel felt his strong, steady heartbeat against her cheek. "All that time in the garden, all the fun you two had. She found her calling through you. I think the divorce would have hurt her more if she hadn't been able to throw herself into flowers."

Sullivan chuckled at her wording. "She's always been a pleasure, even when she thought she was acting out." His voice lightened. "A few slammed doors. A belligerent attitude here and there. I think I heard her say 'no' once."

Mabel snorted. "Remember that time she got drunk at a party? I don't think she's touched alcohol since."

"She'd probably only had half a beer," Sullivan scoffed. "The girl never really learned how to misbehave."

"Unlike us, in our own rebel days."

"Aw, Mabel." He smoothed his hand over her hair in that old familiar way, uncaring that it was now gray and not as soft as it used to be. "We've had some fun, haven't we?"

"So damn much fun." Mabel sighed and sat up again, enjoying the ghost of a smile on his mouth. "Now we need Emily to have some fun. That dick ex of hers is why she's still single."

"I agree he was a dick," Sullivan said. "But he hasn't left any permanent damage. Emily's just different from us, that's all. More proper and focused on business."

"I don't think she really knows what she wants, and that worries me."

"You like to worry. Emily got that from you."

"Maybe," she allowed, though few people could

worry with as much verve as their Emily. "Anyway, let's push her a little. Saul seems so nice, and he sure seems ready. If you could see better, you'd know what I mean. How he looks at our girl…he's hungry."

"Hungry-hungry?" Sullivan asked with sharpened interest.

"Like you used to look when I was young."

"What are you talking about? When you were young," he grumped. "Damn, Mabel, you're still the hottest woman I've ever known."

Mabel laughed, in part because she was a short, sturdy, seventy-one-year-old woman with all the signs of a long, happy life on her face and body, but also because Sullivan hadn't been able to see her clearly for years. "You're blind, Sullivan."

His hands caught her shoulders—and then they wandered as he growled, "I can feel just fine, and I know exactly what sexy feels like."

"Ha!" Laughing and squirming, having fun as they often did, Mabel told him, "You're hurt, you silly man. Now behave."

"Never. You wouldn't like me if I behaved."

"Yes I would," she said softly, knowing she'd love him no matter what. She leaned forward for a kiss.

Sullivan put a hand on her hip.

And behind them, Emily said, "Knock, knock. I hope we're not—"

Half sprawled over her husband, Sullivan's hand clasping her rear, Mabel turned her head, and good grief, there was Emily gaping in shock. Next to her, Saul grinned.

Mabel couldn't help it—she laughed. "We're busted, Sullivan. Emily and Saul are here."

He chuckled. "Come on in, kids. You might've just saved Mabel from getting ravished."

Without missing a beat, Saul said, "Guess the hip is feeling better, huh?"

"Son, there ain't no pain ever that would keep me from—"

"Uncle!" Embarrassment tinged Emily's laugh. "For my sake, pretty please censor that thought."

"Can't do that, the thoughts are there, but I'll change the language." Sullivan grinned. "How's that?"

Shaking her head in fond acceptance, Emily went to kiss his forehead. "Thank you. I appreciate it."

Mabel took in the scene of Emily already fussing over Sullivan, and him enjoying the attention, while Saul watched with fascination…like a man falling in love.

How nice it was to witness it all. Saul was a man who, from what she'd learned so far, was worthy of her precious Emily. He was no superficial jerk, like Emily's ex. Tall, handsome, funny and friendly, with a good job and a sense of community—Saul was everything Emily deserved.

All they needed was a little nudge or two, and by God, that was something she could provide.

# CHAPTER FOUR

EMILY WAS A little taken aback when her aunt suddenly embraced her. Fearing they might have gotten bad news, she carefully asked, "Aunt Mabel, is anything wrong?"

"Of course not," Mabel said, hugging her tighter. "I'm just happy to see you." Against her ear, Mabel added, "And with that handsome hunk along."

Ah, of course. Mabel was enthused about Saul. "Tell me how Uncle Sullivan is doing, and then—" she sent Saul a snicker "—I'll tell you what this one did."

"I'm great," Sullivan said. "Walked up and down the halls, ate all my lunch, let them take more blood without bitching too much, so let's hear your news."

"You walked the halls! That's wonderful." She sat next to him on the bed and took his hand. "Did it hurt?"

"Like the devil, but I did it twice today, and I'll do it again tomorrow. I'm told a few more days and they'll spring me." His hand squeezed hers. "I'm ready to go home, Emily."

"I know." Sympathy overwhelmed her. She'd need to talk to him, to both of them, about possibly moving in with her. It would be the only way to ensure they had the help they needed and deserved.

Mabel was busy setting out the food Saul had brought, and that had Sullivan's nose twitching. "I get some this time," he stated. "No restrictions on my diet."

"That's not exactly accurate," Mabel said. "But I already cleared things, so yes, you'll get your share."

Saul leaned against the wall near Sullivan's bed. "Did they tie your gown tight in back so you weren't flashing everyone up and down the hallway?"

Sullivan laughed. "Only after I insisted!"

"He used a walker," Mabel explained. "He'll need one for a few weeks until his hip is well again." With a sigh, she added, "No more chasing bugs."

"As to bugs…" Saul lifted another bag he'd carried along. "I may have a solution."

Perking up real fast, Mabel watched him with interest.

Emily had noticed the other bag, of course, but she'd assumed it was more food or something. Instead, Saul pulled out a box displaying vacuum-type tubing. "This," he said, in the way of a great showman, "is a bug catcher. And it has an extra-long reach." He easily assembled it, then held it out to Mabel with a wink. "A gift for a petite woman."

"Son," Sullivan jokingly growled, "are you flirting with my wife?"

"You more than anyone should know that it's impossible not to." Saul's smile switched to Emily. "But mostly I'm hoping to make it a little easier on everyone, since you don't want Mabel dealing with bugs, but you can't be climbing on things anymore."

"This is genius," Mabel said in awe. "Sullivan, feel it." She handed the contraption over to her husband, who held it close to his face, his hands moving over it, fitting his fingers to the button.

When it whirred to life, Mabel laughed. "It *is* like a vacuum, so all I have to do is point it at the bugs."

"Or I can point it for you." Lower, Sullivan said, "The bugs won't stand a chance."

Stunned by the thoughtfulness, Emily stared at Saul. What an amazing gesture. What considerable kindness. While Mabel and Sullivan tested the vacuum, Emily mouthed *Thank you* to Saul, and he gave her a small, pleased nod.

"Now," Sullivan said. "Let's hear what Saul did that had you so tickled."

Emily told them all about the mannequin in the skimpy flower bikini and how relaxed yet provocative Kathleen had looked sitting all stiff-legged on the bench, her frozen, plastic expression somehow serene.

"That was after Emily sat her against my restaurant like a drunken lush following Yardley's wedding."

Back and forth they went, teasing and exaggerating each story until Emily realized that her aunt was watching her with wonder, as if she'd never seen her be so silly before.

And probably, she hadn't.

Truthfully, she couldn't think of the last time she'd felt this carefree.

They all cracked up as she described how Saul had *strutted* out of the flower shop—a fact he denied—holding the sale sign for her impromptu flower markdown.

For the next half hour, the four of them chatted, having fun and enjoying smoked chicken, potato salad and baked beans with lemonade. Saul fit in with them in a way her ex never had. It wasn't that Mabel and Sullivan had outwardly disliked Rob, or that he'd ever been rude to them. But there hadn't been this level of ease, as if they were all longtime friends.

It sent a weird little fluttery sensation through Emily's stomach to understand the differences in Saul's manner and Rob's. Things with Rob had sometimes felt superficial, especially toward the end of their marriage, after so many disappointments. Yet with Saul, he seemed to enjoy each day, and everyone in it.

"You're not eating," Saul said quietly. "You don't like it?"

"It's delicious." She scooped up a bite.

"Head still hurting?"

"No, I'm fine." It struck her that her tiredness, her tension, and her headache had all seemed to disappear as soon as Saul showed up. Or maybe it was after she started laughing about Kathleen in the bikini.

Actually, it was probably the second he'd casually stripped off his shirt in the middle of her little shop. With the scent of flowers all around them, the colors soft and the blooms velvety, Saul had stood out with stark, raw, hot appeal.

Shoot, she got warm just thinking of it.

Because she knew she was flushed, Emily quickly asked her aunt and uncle, "Isn't the food amazing?"

Mabel stayed beside Sullivan, with his bed raised to a near sitting position and a tray across his lap. She'd tucked a large napkin under his chin and occasionally helped him with the lemonade.

"It's *so* good," Mabel agreed.

"Emily said your restaurant is really something," Sullivan added. "Now I believe her."

Emily and Saul stood together near the window, their drinks on the wide sill, elbows occasionally touching.

Odd, but despite the lack of table and chairs, and even being in a hospital, it was more comfortable than she'd have imagined possible. Saul was right at home with her outspoken aunt and uncle, and he seemed to adapt to any situation. What really surprised Emily was that she so easily adapted too...at least with this, with *him*.

"So," Mabel said, sending Emily an innocent look that instantly put her on guard. "You need to change things up a bit."

"Oh?" She forked up another bite of beans. "What do you suggest?"

"Hot dates, looser or tighter clothes, and a less rigid schedule."

Emily almost choked on her food.

Gently, Saul tapped her back between her shoulder blades. "I can help with the dates, though it's up to Emily how hot they might get."

Everyone, even poor Sullivan with his limited eyesight, stared toward Saul.

"Hey," he said. "I'm not making suggestions on a woman's wardrobe choice, and Emily loves her job, so her schedule is her business."

*That's* what he thought had stunned them?

Slowly, with far too much anticipation, Mabel sat forward. "What kind of dates would you suggest?"

"I was going to ask Em. We could start with a walk on the beach tonight."

Finally collecting her wits, Emily said, "He does enjoy the beach."

Saul slanted her a warm look. "It's quieter in the evenings, and the sunsets are amazing." He turned back to Mabel. "Have you seen them?"

"When Sullivan and I were younger. Back then, the lake wasn't the vacation spot it is now. We'd pack a lunch and head over to Cemetery to find a quiet cove."

She smiled at her husband. "Remember that time we skinny-dipped?"

"One of my favorite memories."

"Oh Lord," Emily muttered with a laugh. "You two." She nudged Saul. "They're always like this."

"In love?" Saul asked, sounding utterly sincere, as if that was exactly what he made of their suggestive comments. "It's nice. My parents are the same. I grew up hearing my dad compliment my mother five times a day. When I was about fifteen, he told me that five was the minimum number of times daily you should say something sweet to the woman you love, just to make sure she didn't forget how much you cared."

What a wonderful memory, Emily thought. "What kind of compliments did he give her?"

"Anything and everything. He'd tell her she was the best cook, or that her hair looked pretty when it was messy. Once she was cleaning the oven and he told her she looked like Cinderella, only with a better ass."

Sullivan chuckled. "I'm an ass man, myself."

Emily rolled her eyes, but laughed.

Smiling, Saul said, "Mom would mention a new wrinkle near her eyes and Dad would tell her that her eyes sparkled. She'd say she burned the cookies and he'd swear he liked them that way." He set his plate aside. "Sometimes they were outrageous, like you two. Mom had picked up weight and according to her, her jeans were a little too tight. Dad said it was just more for him to love."

"I like your parents," Mabel announced.

"I admit, they're pretty terrific. According to Dad, he retired young so he and my mom could travel. He said he wanted to show her the world, but if I wasn't ready to take over the restaurant, he would've hired someone, though he'd always made his preferences clear."

"Did you want to run the business?" Sullivan asked, suddenly seeming serious.

"I'd been working there in one way or another from the time I was twelve. It was like a second home, and I loved it. So yeah, I was happy to do it."

"How old were you when your dad retired?" Mabel asked.

"Twenty-five. Dad had it set up so the switch was seamless. Great employees and staff, an accountant already in place, insurance, all that." He glanced at Emily. "Mimi came to work for me a few years later."

"Yardley's best friend," Emily explained to her aunt. "That's the wedding I just did."

"I remember," Mabel said. "Very sweet girl, adored by the whole town."

And, Emily thought, it was once assumed that Yardley and Saul would get together. Had that ever come about? Had they...dated, and it just hadn't worked out? Emily wasn't sure.

"I didn't need to do much to take over." With pleasant memories in his eyes, Saul smiled. "Dad and Mom took off for a monthlong vacation. He said to call him if I needed him, but he didn't think I would."

"And you didn't need him," Mabel guessed.

Laughing, Saul admitted, "Maybe I did a little, but I muddled through, and pretty soon, I fell into a groove. Now the Pit Stop feels like its own little community. Or maybe a second family."

Family. Emily glanced at her aunt and uncle. They'd never had children of their own, though they'd tried. Did Saul hope to have kids one day?

At one point in her life, Emily had wanted that. A loving husband, a modest little home, two kids and pets. The fairy tale. She'd envisioned herself in a minivan and attending the PTA and soccer games.

But not anymore. At her age, she had little desire to birth a child. Her goals had changed drastically. Now she was too set in her ways, and though her business was already established, she looked forward to ways of making it better. Oh, she'd adjust if she needed to—but she didn't need to. Maybe that was something she should explain to Saul...before they took a walk on the beach.

*Or*, she told herself sternly, *I could stop making absurd mental leaps from a public walk to a life together.*

Stepping away from the window, Saul took his plate and Sullivan's, now empty, and returned them to the bag they'd come in.

Emily hurriedly finished her last few bites and helped out with the cleanup.

Saul surprised her again by producing little individual containers of desserts. "There's a variety," he said. "I hope there's something everyone likes."

Impressed, Mabel peeked into each container. "Good heavens, we'll like all of them."

"There's enough for a few days because my schedule will be grueling the rest of the week. No more visits from me—unless you need me for something. Then I could probably work it out."

"Aren't you just the sweetest," Mabel said.

"He's angling," Sullivan predicted. "And I like it."

"Gotta get on your good side, right?" Saul gestured at the goodies. "Starting with dessert can't hurt."

"It's a damn good start," Sullivan assured him. "You have my blessing to proceed."

Flustered, Emily said, "They like you just fine, and I know they appreciate everything, isn't that right?"

Her aunt and uncle were quick to agree.

"Gentry is ready to cover for me," she promised Saul, "so if anything comes up, don't worry about it. I'll be around, and they can call me anytime." After all, they were *her* aunt and uncle. In no way did Saul need to feel obligated.

"Gentry," Saul murmured, "is so helpful, he should get employee of the month."

There was something in his tone… "I couldn't do that. Vivienne would think I favored him."

To that, Saul quirked a brow. "Don't you?"

Refusing to be drawn in—the very idea of her and Gentry was absurd—she stated, "I have no idea what you mean." There were times when she still felt awkward about relationships, but she tried to cover it with a serene smile. That was her go-to, her way to stay in control whenever she felt lost by nuances. Smile and fake her understanding. Usually it seemed to work.

Mere seconds later, a nurse came in to say visiting hours were over, but she also asked Mabel if she needed anything else—another pillow or blanket, or fresh water in the pitcher.

Emily thanked her profusely for the kindness. It relieved her mind to know everyone at the hospital was treating her aunt and uncle with so much consideration.

After the nurse left so they could say their goodbyes, Emily took her aunt's hands. "*Do* you need anything, Aunt? Something I can bring you from home? Anything at all?"

"Yes. I need you to make that hot date." She grinned at Saul. "You'll see to it?"

"Yes, ma'am. I promise to do my best."

UNFORTUNATELY, ON THE drive home, the sky darkened and rain clouds moved in. Off in the distance, lightning repeatedly brightened the sky. Saul frowned, on one hand disappointed...well, mostly disappointed. On the other hand, it wouldn't hurt for him to get a better handle on things. He could tell that Emily's aunt and uncle understood his intent, but Emily? Hard to say. One minute she'd tease, and then she'd firmly stick him back in the friend zone. "Looks like we might have to put off that walk."

Either Emily didn't seem to share his disappointment, or she hid it well with that patented composed expression of hers. It was one of the many things he admired about her, her ability to always look self-possessed, as if she had everything in hand, even turbulent weather.

She asked, "Will the storm bring in more customers to the Pit Stop, or will it slow things down?"

"It could go either way. People who are already there might linger, rather than run out in the rain. They buy more drinks, but not more food, and that cuts into the servers' tips." As he said it, the first sprinkles started splashing against the windshield, gently at first but then picking up. The headlights and wipers automatically flipped on.

"You're smiling," Emily said with a touch of curiosity. "You like storms?"

"Yeah, I do. You?"

"I don't mind them, but they play havoc with my flowers."

He supposed Gentry would have his work cut out for him, then. "Even as a kid, I always liked storms. Sometimes I'd sit on the back porch and watch the yard fill with puddles. As long as there wasn't lightning, Mom would grab our raincoats and boots and we'd play in the rain."

Wistfully, Emily said, "Your mom really does sound amazing."

Because she was. "She hasn't offered to play in the rain with me lately." They both laughed. A nice, easy laugh. Like being with Emily, it always felt natural. "My house is on the lake. When the weather gets like this, the waves come at the shore like they're ready to brawl, sometimes going over the dock." Glancing at her, he said, "It washes off the droppings from the geese and herons."

Surprised, Emily turned to him. "I didn't know you were on the lake."

"Not many people do. My parents aren't, and that's where I grew up. Everyone around here still thinks of me either at my parents' house or at the restaurant."

She seemed struck by that. "You know, I think I did that. It feels like you're always at the restaurant. I guess I never really thought about where you lived."

He *was* always at the restaurant, but out of necessity, that was one of the changes he'd soon implement. "Dad had bought an acre of lakefront land long before Cemetery got popular. When he retired, he gave it to me."

"You built your own house?"

"Not with my own hands or anything. I know my

way around the restaurant business, not so much in construction. I can do basic stuff, but that's it."

"Repair a leaky faucet, paint a wall."

"Exactly. But building from the ground up? Not my forte." Over the years, his personal time had dwindled even more, but again, he was working on freeing up his schedule for other priorities—one that had dropped on him, and one he'd wanted for far too long. "I looked through designs until I found the house I liked, then I hired a contractor from Allbee with his own crew. I had them leave all the trees surrounding the house, so even though the property on that part of the lake is crowded now, it still feels private. Or at least it does until I reach the dock."

"Then there are the canoes and paddleboards and swimmers."

"All that. I don't mind. The vacationers only wave, but everyone else knows me, so they like to stop by and chat." As if he didn't spend the whole workweek visiting with people. He wouldn't say it, though. It felt ungrateful, as if he didn't appreciate the customers who came by regularly. The Pit Stop was successful because people loved the restaurant and had turned it into its own sort of community. He'd never take them for granted.

"So some people *do* know where you live?"

"I think mostly they assume I'm doing what they're doing—enjoying the lake. Taking time to fish or swim." And he never bothered to explain that he was on his own property. "When I want peace and quiet, I go off to one of the shallow coves and pretend to fish."

Emily tipped her head. "Pretend?"

"Sure. You cast a line, then sit back and soak up the

sun. Other boaters don't come close because they don't want to disturb my fishing spot."

She laughed. "Sneaky." Tucking into the corner of his truck, she half faced him with her long legs crossed, her hands resting together in her lap. "When I want peace and quiet, I just go home."

Alone. He knew the feeling...or maybe he didn't. Carefully, hoping for specific answers, he asked, "Do you ever wish for something different?"

"Sometimes. Lately." She wrinkled her nose. "I've been thinking of getting a dog."

Not at all the same thing as a man, but he didn't point it out. For someone as independent as Emily, a dog probably felt like a safer bet. "Gentry mentioned the field of flowers. He said he works there?"

"They're beautiful. Uncle Sullivan helped me get started, but it's turned into its own full-time job. I don't know what I'd do without Gentry's help."

"You pay him, right?" He hoped that was the arrangement. "He's there as an employee?"

"Yes, but it still feels like a favor because he's so accommodating. He never complains when I need him overtime, or to fill in for me."

It was an odd feeling, this sudden possessive bent for Emily. They'd known each other for a long time, and it felt like he'd been working to get closer to her for a while now. At first, he'd been content to let Emily warm up to the idea. Yet the longer it took to get her interest, the more he wanted it.

The more he wanted her.

Now everything had changed, and getting Emily into his life felt critical, like if it didn't happen soon, it never would.

With certainty, he knew that she was the one.

His every spare thought centered on her. On everything about her. How she looked, yes. Emily was gorgeous and sexy without even trying—which only made her more so. Yet it was beyond that. Like how he felt younger around her, with that same sharp awareness usually unique to twentysomething people. He hadn't felt that in years, and it sparked his system. He smiled just at the sight of her. She impressed him with the way she ran her business, and how comfortably she interacted with everyone. Now, seeing how much she cared about her aunt and uncle…he wanted her to care about him, too. Enough that his changed circumstances wouldn't spook her.

Added to all that, he badly wanted to see her cut loose a little. Not for everyone else—just for him. Intimately. The two sides of Emily…what a tease that was to his senses.

Now that he was trying to navigate all the tricky intricacies of his situation, Gentry kept coming into the picture. "I'd like to see your place sometime."

Instead of picking up on the hint, she did what Emily always did; she smiled. "I love my house, but I'm sure yours, being on the lake, is nicer. You must have amazing views."

"Not bad." He tried to steer the conversation around. "What's your house like?"

"It's comfortable for me. I like that I don't have super-close neighbors or anything. It's a small ranch, but I have five acres."

After that, she went quiet. Too quiet. It bothered Saul. "What are you thinking?"

"A lot of things, actually." Her gaze moved over him

in that concentrated way she had. "First, don't let my aunt and uncle coerce you, okay?"

"I'm thirty-nine, honey. Long past the age of being coerced." Mostly. He had to admit, Sullivan had done a great job of playing the protective parent. Even though Emily was grown and fully independent, Saul respected Sullivan's attitude.

Luckily, he and Sullivan had quickly arrived at a mutual—unspoken—understanding. That part had been easy. Figuring out Emily...not so much.

"So..." Her fingers laced together. "You want to date?"

The uncertain way she asked that both amused him and made him want to pull over and show her all the things he wanted. "That surprises you?"

"It's just that, at least as far as I know, you've never dated much."

"Not around here," he replied carefully. He didn't want to start things out by giving Emily the wrong impression. "Because I knew I didn't have time for a real relationship—" or so he'd thought "—I tended to visit Warsaw, or Kokomo, when I wanted..." Something casual, but that sounded awful. He settled on, "Company."

"You drove over an hour for a date?"

"For one-time dates," he clarified. "Do you understand what I'm saying?"

Her eyes widened, and in a whisper, she asked, "To hook up?"

Lately, he enjoyed everything Emily said, and how she said it. "There's no one to hear us if we talk about sex."

Her eyes went even wider. "So we *are* talking about sex?"

He almost laughed. "You realize I'm not a virgin, right? I'm a grown-ass man."

"Ass man." She snickered, finally recovering from her surprise. "You and my uncle seem to like that part of the anatomy."

Emily's version of flirting totally did it for him. "What about you?"

With false casualness, she added, "I'm a grown woman."

Who had *not* slept around...unless she'd gone to another town, too? He shot her a look, but somehow he couldn't imagine it. Emily was always too contained. Just to tease her, he asked, "So you were chasing tail too, huh?"

She started to speak, and instead ended up choking on a laugh. "No. No chasing tail for me." She continued to chuckle. "You say the funniest things, Saul. I think that's one reason everyone likes you so much."

At the moment, he was more interested in Emily liking him. "The point is, for years the restaurant took up the majority of my time. I've routinely put in sixty-five-hour weeks, often more than that. I'm not complaining, because I love the success of the Pit Stop. I love this town and all the people here, too. When I did have spare time, there were chores for the house or yard, or errands to run. Sometimes Mom would want me to visit, or Dad would want to hear about my plans with the place. There wasn't much time for getting involved."

"I totally get that, since I was the same with my flower shop. There's always something to do. Sometimes just taking a leisurely bath felt like a huge indulgence."

And...yeah. That put a visual in his head real fast.

"Stop it," she said, as if she knew exactly what he was thinking.

Saul grinned. "Sorry, can't."

She broke into chatter, likely to divert his thoughts. "I'm sure you were busier than me. I close earlier each day than you do, but then there's still the paperwork and organizing orders and deliveries, and rearranging the schedule when needed. Taking advantage of sales, or returning calls at a customer's convenience. Paying all the bills." She lifted her shoulders. "Like you, I didn't have room for a relationship."

He wondered how much her divorce might have factored into her disinterest in dating, but now didn't feel like the right time to ask. Instead he said, "Lately, my priorities have shifted." *What an understatement.*

"And now you do have time?"

Time, desire, and the need to settle down. He wanted someone who would be happy with small-town life. With Cemetery, specifically. Someone who shared his values. Someone who would care *enough*…

In so many ways she was the opposite of him, and he wanted her anyway. Or maybe because she was so different.

"You're thinking about that awfully long," she quipped.

"I was thinking about you, actually. You know, I've been laying hints for a while, but you never picked up on them."

With an exaggerated groan, she admitted, "I'm terrible at that. Especially now, at my age."

Was she sensitive about being forty-one? He didn't want to say or do anything that'd feel dismissive of her feelings, but then again, she needed to know the truth.

"You keep saying that like you're old—when you most definitely are not."

"Agreed," she said, notching up her chin. "But neither am I young."

"To Sullivan and Mabel, you are."

That amused her. "I think to them, I'll always be an awkward teenager."

"No way were you ever awkward." She was so serene and competent now, he couldn't imagine her any other way.

"I was the worst."

"I need an example if you expect me to believe it."

He heard the chagrin in her tone when she said, "Fine. Here's one—not long after I came to live with my aunt and uncle, I snuck out to a party. That was bad enough, but then I drank, too, and got so vilely ill… It was awful."

Maybe that explained her aversion to alcohol now. "Consumed a little too much, huh?"

She snorted. "It was like… a beer? Not even a full can. But we'd been eating grilled hot dogs, and I was flirting with this guy, when suddenly I knew I would chuck. Talk about humiliating. I bolted into the house, but for some reason he followed me." She went quiet.

With a bad feeling brewing, Saul prompted, "And?"

Shaking her head, she said, "It was so long ago. I don't know why I'm talking about it."

"Don't leave me in suspense. I'm fascinated." He wanted to know as much about Emily as he could. "You're showing me a whole different side to who you are now."

"It's all dumb. I was a kid then."

"And you're a woman now, but some things stick

with us, right? Memories that never go away. I take it this is one of them?"

She rubbed her forehead. "Only because it got so weird. One minute the guy was telling me not to worry, holding back my hair, and I was mortified like any teenage girl would be. And then somehow his hand...was where it shouldn't be."

Everything in Saul sharpened—his instincts, his attention, his understanding. "He *groped* you?"

"He said it was an accident, but I don't know. It sure felt deliberate. I shoved him back so hard, he almost fell into the tub. Then I puked again, ran out of the house, and kept going...all the way home." Her nose wrinkled. "Except that I stopped a few times to be sick again."

"I bet Sullivan hit the roof."

"No, he and Mabel were both understanding."

No way! "He didn't care that some guy took advantage?"

"I didn't tell him that part." She touched his forearm. "I've never told them, so don't say anything. I just stumbled in the door all sick and disgusting, and they took care of me."

Saul considered that. "Why didn't you tell them what happened, Em?"

"I don't know. I wasn't sure if it was an accident or not, and I'd already embarrassed myself. Plus I felt wretched." She made a face. "When I got to school on Monday, *everyone* had heard about me getting sick. I got razzed a lot, some of it in fun, some of it mean. I steered clear of that guy as much as I could, but he caught me in the halls between classes and apologized. He wanted to see me again, but after that, I just concentrated on getting my act together."

"What does that mean?"

"My mom and dad had died together in a car wreck, and I'd let myself fall apart. I'd always been quiet, had good grades, stuff like that. But then I lost them, and I moved in with my aunt and uncle and did stupid stuff, like sneaking out to a party and getting sick on beer and hot dogs." She went quiet for a minute, before admitting, "That entire school quarter was a waste. I bombed every class so badly, the teachers thought I might fail for the year."

"You were dealing with a lot." Now he knew exactly how difficult that loss could be for a kid, and all the ways it could change things.

Lose both his mother and father like that? Even now, as a mature man, it would devastate him—so it had to be a million times worse for a kid.

There was no way for Emily to know it, but her experience, awful as he was sure it had been, could be a huge help to someone else going through the same thing.

"Aunt Mabel told me I would never fail, but I might slow my pace."

Saul listened closely, devouring every word, hoping to glean a little insight. "Great advice." He nodded as he slowed to turn a corner. "What she said helped?"

"It was more what she did." Emily's tone softened. "She'd lost her only sister, so I know she had to be grieving too, but she was a rock for me, letting me cry when I needed to, then getting me to laugh and keeping me busy baking or shopping. I wouldn't have gotten through it without her."

See, that was gold right there. He committed those words to memory. How to help, what actions might make a difference.

"And Uncle Sullivan…" she continued. "He comes off all gruff, joking one minute and grumpy the next, but he's the most loving guy you'll ever meet. He taught me everything I know about flowers."

Quietly, Saul said, "I'm glad you had them." He only hoped he could prove as insightful.

"Me, too. Without them, I'm not sure I'd have made it through high school, much less two years of college."

Saul started to ask her about her degree, but he knew that at some point during college, she'd married, and then later divorced. Had her goal been an associate's degree, or did the divorce interfere with her education?

She peeked at him. "Only my aunt and uncle know this, but I've never been able to eat another hot dog, and even the thought of beer makes me green."

"Beer and hot dogs are overrated."

"Yeah, right. I'm over forty. You'd think I would—"

"Here's the thing, Em," he interrupted, needing her to see herself as he saw her. "Your age has nothing to do with *you*, so it sure as hell has nothing to do with your preferences. Don't like hot dogs? Don't eat them. I live on a lake and I'm not keen on fresh fish." He rolled a shoulder. "Doesn't matter. Besides, most people would guess you to be at least ten years younger, maybe fifteen." The only signs of age he saw were in her eyes, eyes that had loved and lost, and gained a lot of compassion for others because of it. Was she able to love again?

He sincerely hoped so.

## CHAPTER FIVE

FIGHTING OFF A SMILE, Emily said, "You're exaggerating."

"Cross my heart."

"Well…now I'm flattered. *Really* flattered. I always try to look my best, but a person can't live four decades without it showing."

"Where," he asked, "do you see any signs of age?"

In a very un-Emily way, she fidgeted. "So often, if I look in the mirror, age is all I see. My reflection isn't a disappointment, exactly. Please don't think I'm vain, or only concerned with looks."

"No one who knows you would think that." She was too open, too friendly. Too invested and interested in others.

"It's just… I've given up on a lot, and I don't like that about myself."

The conversation had just gotten serious. "What have you given up, hon?"

"Now I sound all pitiful." She sat back with a self-deprecating sigh. "Let's just say when I was younger, I thought my life would be different. This life is pretty wonderful, though, so I promise I'm not complaining."

He understood. Emily was the type of person who wanted to accomplish everything, regardless of any challenges. Had she once wanted to be a wife and mother? Seemed possible.

It was the opposite for him. He'd once thought of traveling the world, never settling down, definitely never being a husband or dad. Now here he was, firmly grounded in Cemetery with no desire to travel abroad. And yeah, the rest of it…things had happened without his intent, but he was dealing with it, even embracing it.

And damn it, he wanted Emily more than ever.

To keep from mulling over things out of his control, he continued pointing out all the ways that Emily stood out. "On top of looking young," Saul said, "you're nice."

"Everyone in Cemetery is."

He gave her a disbelieving look. "Most, maybe, but not all. Pretty sure you're the nicest."

"I'm starting to blush."

Yeah, she was. And she looked extra pretty with the color in her cheeks. "So that you don't think I'm superficial, I'll point out that you're also reliable, organized, helpful, smart, and—"

"Don't say *perfect*."

His mouth twitched at her warning. "I wasn't going to."

"Oh." There was a long pause while she grappled with embarrassment. "Well…good," she finally said.

Now she'd piqued his interest, though, so he asked, "You have a problem with the word *perfect*?"

"Not a problem, really. I don't think of myself that way at all. It's just that everyone is always saying it to me. Believe me, I know I'm nowhere near perfect, and I wouldn't even want to be."

Maybe not perfect, but she went above and beyond to keep from letting anyone down. "People say you're perfect because you make it all seem easy. You look great, even when everyone else is messed up. Your business is professional, but somehow personal, too. I've heard a lot of people say that within minutes of meeting you, you feel like a friend."

"I'm glad to hear it."

"Customers visit your shop to discuss flower arrangements, then they stop in my place for dinner, and I hear them rave about the *flower lady*."

"I'll admit my flower shop is close to perfect."

"It's you, Emily, who always makes an impression."

She smothered a laugh. "Not much of one since no one can remember my name."

"That's not it. They call you the *flower lady* because your name is synonymous with your product. You *are* the flower lady, and that's a good thing."

"Huh. I'd never thought of it that way."

"People get flowers from you, and from then on, when they think of flowers, you're in their heads."

Just as she was in his. She might not know it yet, but whenever he thought of the future, she factored in. What he needed now was for her to understand that it wasn't his changed circumstances that made him want her.

He'd wanted her all along.

"Hmm," Emily said, with a lilt to her voice. "I need a cool name for my shop, now that it doesn't have to be Cemetery Florals."

Saul snorted. "Thank God Yardley won that battle. At least with your flowers, it didn't sound gross, just morbid. For my restaurant? No one wants to eat at Cemetery Barbecue."

She broke into laughter again.

It was a nice laugh, totally natural and sweet. He hated for the day to end, but they were getting close to her shop now.

"Poor Betty Cemetery," she said. "I understand her pride in the name, since her great-grandfather founded the town. To her, it held a lot of sentiment, and she felt it was honoring him to keep the name on everything."

"See," he said softly. "There you are, being super-nice. Personally, I like it that I've never heard you gossip or say the wrong thing."

With an eye roll, she muttered, "Here we go again."

"Back to being perfect," he teased.

"You know, I do have some bad habits."

Calling her bluff was fun. "Name one."

She thought about it…

After a few seconds passed, he laughed. "See? You can't think of any."

"Naming bad habits is hard."

It was his turn to roll his eyes. "Not if you have any."

"Okay, then, smarty. If it's so easy, let's hear yours."

"No problem." Ticking them off quickly, he said, "I curse too much, am sometimes obtuse, ask a lot from my employees, talk too much with customers, work too much…"

"Hey, I work too much, too!"

He gave her a mock frown. "You don't get to steal my bad habits."

"Darn." Her shoulders drooped. "No, wait. I just thought of one!"

Her enthusiasm had him fighting another grin. "Let's hear it."

"I'm a lousy cook," she announced. Dropping back in her seat, she said in smug satisfaction, "There. I admit it. I'm terrible at it. My aunt is a fantastic cook, but I usually just heat up a TV dinner, or I eat a bowl of cereal, a sandwich, or mac and cheese." She sent him a sidelong glance. "Or I grab something at the Pit Stop."

"That won't be a problem for us, because I'm a great cook."

Her mouth opened, nothing came out, and she closed it. Finally she asked, "It's not a problem…why?"

"I'll do the cooking."

She stared.

*Yeah, take that, Emily. I'm talking about us in a relationship. Deal with it.* One way or another, he'd make it happen. He knew what he wanted, and Emily was it.

It took her a minute, and then she recovered. "Another flaw. I sometimes grumble about people, just not where anyone can hear me. And like everyone else, I have messy days."

His gaze quickly skimmed over her before he returned his attention to the road. Even now, after working all day, then visiting her aunt and uncle, she looked amazing. "Your idea of 'messy' must look great, because I've never seen it."

With a laughing groan, Emily tossed up her hands. "Sounds like I've got you fooled, same as everyone else." Her humor settled into a sweet smile as she stared at him. "It's because of that misconception of me that I'm going to shake things up a little."

He hoped to factor into that. "If we're back to talking about hot dates, count me in." He looked out at the stormy sky. "Can I get a rain check on the beach walk, though?"

Without hesitation, she said, "Sure. When?"

He wondered if she didn't want to invite him over, or if it didn't occur to her. He could probably suggest it—but she'd had a long day, and maybe it'd be better if he didn't rush things too much. He wanted, *needed*, for her to know how much she mattered, not think that she was…what? Convenient? Replaceable?

He shook his head, both to dispel those awful descriptions that could never be applied to Emily, and to convey his frustration. "The rest of this week is crushed." He had things he had to do, but he wasn't ready to talk about that yet. He'd like to actually get the relationship rolling before he dropped anything on her. "How about a Sunday morning walk on the beach?"

"That sounds nice."

"I'll pick you up. Nine or ten?" Not giving her a chance to object, he asked, "And what are your days off next week? I'll tailor my schedule to fit yours."

"Nine works for me." Seeming as enthused as he was, she said, "I haven't done the schedule for next week yet. I can let you know soon, though."

"Sounds good." He pulled up in front of the shop, put the truck in Park, and turned toward her, his arm resting along the console. Emily stared at him, her warm eyes direct and anticipatory. Waiting for his kiss goodbye? He hoped so. God knew, he'd been waiting for too long now.

But not just yet, mostly because he didn't want to let her go. He pulled out his phone. "What's your address?"

She shared it, adding, "It's a white country ranch house. Lots of windows. Super-small. It's basically a starter home, but since there's only me—"

Diverting her from downplaying her house, he said, "Kathleen's gone."

As if the words didn't at first make sense, Emily merely blinked at him. "Kathleen?" Then she quickly twisted to stare out her window at the bench. "I'd forgotten all about her, but I'm glad she wasn't left out in the rain."

"She has synthetic hair and she was wearing a bikini."

"You're laughing at me?" Playfully, she pushed his shoulder. "I loved having Kathleen here. Thank you for bringing her over. It was fun to be included."

*Fun to be included.* That simple statement hit him right in the heart. Everyone in town treated Emily with the utmost respect, because it matched her usual demeanor, yet now he knew she was a lot more fun-loving than he, or anyone else, realized. That would change. Somehow he'd make it so.

With a frown of worry, she added, "I wonder if someone took her inside."

Her concern over the mannequin was sweet. "She'll show up again. She always does." A resounding boom of thunder shook the ground. "I wish I was driving you straight home."

That sentiment earned him a level frown. "The rain doesn't bother me."

No, it wouldn't. Emily was one of the most self-sufficient people he'd ever known. "Since you're not in a rush, I have a question."

She happily sat back again. "No rush, since I'm just going home."

Alone. Damn, he wished she'd invite him along. "In the shop, after I kissed you here—" he brushed one fingertip to the bridge of her nose "—you had a request. One you later canceled."

"Because Betty was right there," she was quick to explain. "I didn't want her to see anything."

Saul allowed the satisfied smile for two heartbeats

before he cleared it away. "Thought you might scandalize the old girl, huh?"

"I have a feeling not much would really scandalize Betty, but I can't wait until she sees the photos Vivienne took! Do you know she called you Cemetery's Most Eligible Bachelor? Like it was a title."

The smile returned. He did love this town, and it loved him back. "I'm honored."

"It's because you've been so elusive. We all see how often vacationers flirt with you. And you—"

She started to say more, but this time Saul touched her cheek, absorbing the warmth and softness of her skin. She turned silent real fast. With the windshield wipers off, the rain on the windows blurred the outside world. No one could see them, and the interior of the truck felt cozy and private.

Keeping his gaze on her mouth to let her know his intent, Saul slowly leaned forward until his mouth met hers. Utilizing iron control, he kept the contact light and gentle.

To his surprise, she made a small sound of hunger and pressed closer—or tried to. The seat belt hindered her. "Damn it." Frantically, she struggled with it, got it open, and landed against him. "Yes," she said, her lips moving against his. "This is where I wanted to be kissed."

*By me*, he clarified in his own mind. *She wanted to be kissed by me.* Emily had gone as relationship-free as he had, but now, together, they'd remedy the situation. Everything else, all the other changes in his life, wouldn't change that.

He hoped.

Savoring the moment, he cupped her face in his

hands. He chose to see this as the start, with his end goals now firmly within reach.

"Mmm," Emily murmured, nestling closer, one of her hands on his chest, the other around the back of his neck. Her fingers weren't still. No, she kept smoothing them over him, exploring him, and he loved it.

It had been a long time since he'd made out in a vehicle, but damn, Emily tempted him. Every time he thought to end the kiss, he deepened it instead. The air inside the truck turned humid and warm, fogging the windows. He tilted his head, taking the kiss deeper, getting a little lost in her taste and warmth—then a blinding flash of lightning split the sky, followed by a rip of thunder, and he knew he had to wrap it up.

Easing back from her, he took in her dazed expression. Her eyes were closed, her lips wet. Damn, she was hot. He'd always known she could be, but she kept herself so collected… Well, she wasn't collected now.

Hating to disturb the moment, but also disliking the idea of her driving in this weather, he said, "The storm is getting worse."

Emily just breathed. Heavily. Until she confessed softly, "I haven't been kissed like that in far too long. Guess I've missed it."

"Em." Unable to stop himself, he took her mouth again. A silky hank of her hair had managed to come loose from her ponytail, and he teased it with his thumb. Reluctantly, he withdrew again. "How long is far too long?"

She wrinkled her nose. "It's embarrassing."

Saul touched his forehead to hers. "I don't ever want you to be embarrassed with me."

Huffing a laugh, she admitted, "I'm embarrassed

with you all the time." And on the heels of that disclosure, she said, "Not since my divorce."

The double whammy threw him, making his brain scramble. Emily was uneasy with him? She'd hidden it well.

And… *Not since her divorce?*

That one really blindsided him. Far as he knew, she'd divorced a few years after college.

Drawing a slow breath, he forced himself to consider the right words. The last thing he wanted to do was embarrass her again. "Okay, first." He could feel her breath on his lips, distracting him. "I want you to be comfortable with me, okay? Always. If I do or say anything that bothers you, just tell me."

"It's not that you bother me. You're always awesome. It's just that… I'm not. I'm just me, you know?"

"Emily…"

"Don't you dare change, though. I think I need to be pushed out of my comfort zone a little."

Since he thought so as well, he agreed with another brush of his mouth to hers. *So damn sweet.* "Second." God, her eyes were compelling, so much so he almost forgot his second point. They were such a unique shade of brown, like warm whisky, framed with lashes several shades darker than her hair.

"Second?" she prompted.

"You're amazing, in so many ways you obviously don't realize. So how is it you haven't been kissed since your divorce?"

She tipped her head back with a groan. "See? It's horrifying." And suddenly the words were tumbling out. "Honestly, until you just planted one on me, I didn't really know I was missing much. My divorce was…

unpleasant, and that's a huge simplification. For the longest time, I wanted nothing to do with dating, and then, like you with the restaurant, I got busy and my life seemed…" As she struggled for the word, her teeth worked her lower lip, and she settled on, "Fine. Full. Satisfying? That's not the best description, but everything was nice enough, my routine was steady and easy, and I'm kind of a control freak—there, another flaw!—but I had what I could control, you know?" She got close again, her lips quickly brushing his jaw, then his throat, and he heard her inhaling against his skin. "I guess it didn't seem worth the effort to try for something more, and maybe not be in control. So… I didn't."

She gave him a lot to think about, especially since his own life was so out of control at the moment. But he was working on that.

And despite the challenges, he wanted her with him.

That remained his top goal for the moment.

The storm and Emily's own unique sweetness scented the air in the truck. When he realized he was still fingering that long hank of her hair, he tucked it behind her ear and smiled. "What do you know? I've managed to muss the always-perfect Emily Lucretia."

"Not always perfect." Easing back, she gave him a heated look. "Seldom perfect, actually. And really thinking imperfect thoughts right now."

"Oh, I dunno." He wanted her, but he also wanted to do this right—meaning not in his truck. "I might consider your thoughts very perfect."

She grinned. "You might." Reaching for the door handle, she said, "I have to go before we both end up mussed, right here in a truck parked in front of my business."

So much for furthering things. "I suppose that'd be a very un-Emily-like thing to do."

Pausing, she playfully warned, "Don't challenge me. I'm not good at being challenged."

"Another flaw? They're adding up." Of course now he'd have to find a dozen ways to challenge her. "Stay put a sec, okay?" Reaching behind the seat, he grabbed a windbreaker and left the truck before she could protest. At the passenger door, he raised the jacket like an umbrella. Rain soaked through his hair, his shirt and his jeans, but he didn't mind. It was worth it, considering everything he'd learned about her today.

Wearing that adorable quirky smile, she held her purse close to her chest, opened the door and slipped beneath the protection he provided. Over the pounding of the rain, she shouted, "What a nice thing to do. Thank you."

Together, with him shielding her as much as he could, they hurried to her car. The little Chevy Spark was also very un-Emily-like… Or was it? He was quickly finding that Emily had layers he'd yet to discover.

That turned him on, too. Clearly, he'd had some preconceived notions, impressions he'd gained from acquaintance without any real intimacy. Now everything he felt for her, all the plans he'd made, were suddenly hotter…and a lot more necessary.

She unlocked her car and slipped behind the wheel, setting her purse on the passenger seat. "I had a great time today."

Despite the rain, he lingered. "Me, too. We're going to do this again real soon, right?"

"I'll work out the schedule and let you know my days off."

Dripping but not caring, he leaned into the car, giving in to one last scorching kiss. "Soon," he repeated, wondering how quickly he could make it happen when he had a load of commitments already lined up. Drenched, and getting her drenched too, he had no choice but to step back and let her close her door.

One little piece of the puzzle had fallen into place.

But the puzzle had also doubled in size.

AFTER SPEAKING WITH her aunt the next morning, Emily opted to skip her early trip to the hospital and instead headed in to work. Aunt Mabel swore they'd both slept well, and along with Uncle Sullivan's breakfast tray, they'd brought one for Mabel. Her aunt said she was now accustomed to using the shower in the room, too, and she'd found all her favorite shows on the TV, so other than the constant noise and disruptions of a hospital, they were comfortably settled.

Angela—Dr. Randall—had already been in and claimed that Sullivan was doing great with his PT. Mabel thought they'd soon release him. Emily knew her uncle would be thrilled, but it'd be one more worry for her.

She really needed to address the situation of them being alone, and soon.

For thirty minutes or so, she went about her routine setup for the shop, getting ready for the day. Gentry showed up a few minutes early, as he usually did, so he, too, could help get things ready.

As always, he looked fresh and energetic, his black hair still damp, a light blue T-shirt fitting snugly over his strong shoulders and chest. It never ceased to amaze her how men could make T-shirts look so appealing.

Emily tended to avoid them, because on her, they merely looked boxy.

"Good morning," he said, catching her looking him over.

"Good morning."

One brow went up. "Everything okay, Emily?"

"So far, so good." She nodded at him. "That shirt looks great on you. You and Saul both excel at the whole casual vibe. You could both be models."

Dumbstruck, Gentry stared at her a moment, then laughed. "Okay. Sounds like you're in a good mood this morning. Does that mean your night went well?"

"My night was wonderful." As soon as she said it, Emily realized how it sounded, and what she'd inadvertently inferred, and tried to backtrack. "I don't mean *that*. We didn't... We visited my aunt and uncle at the hospital, and rode home in the rain..."

Gentry's knowing grin further flustered her.

Trying to sound composed, she said evenly, "Saul and I were going to have a sort-of date, but then it started raining."

His grin slipped. "What exactly is a sort-of date?"

Emily waved one hand, hoping to play it off. "You know, like not an official 'we're dating' date, just a 'friends spending a little time together' kind of thing."

"Like?"

"Just a walk on the beach." To watch the sunset and feel the sand between her toes and be with Saul... Fantasy stuff, all of it. She almost sighed in regret. Stupid annoying weather.

"I think an evening walk on the beach sounds like an official date."

Was it? She wished she was better at this sort of thing.

Folding his arms, Gentry asked, "So why didn't you figure out something else to do?"

"Like what?"

This time, Gentry tried to bank his grin as he walked over to sit behind the computer. "I don't know, Emily. You could have invited him to your house for a drink."

"I don't drink."

Both brows lifted as he scrolled through a page on the PC. "So, a cola? Or coffee?" He kept his gaze on the screen. "Or just to…chat?"

"I heard that pause!"

More serious now, he glanced at her, and whatever he saw in her expression kept him from looking away. "I paused because 'chat' could mean more, right? Something physical?" to give her his full attention, he turned from the PC and rested his arms on the counter. "You're allowed, you know."

In so many ways, Gentry was an amazing young man. Very up-front and plainspoken. She could probably learn a lot from him. "I didn't think of it," she admitted, even though it made her face hot to be so obtuse. "Obviously, I'm hopeless."

Had Saul been waiting for that invite? She felt like a social misfit for not realizing it. And now, damn it, she wondered how differently the night might have gone. Instead of her staying awake late into the night, maybe they would have…

"You're not hopeless," Gentry gently assured her.

Such a loyal friend. Too bad she couldn't believe him. "I'm so far out of the game, I can't remember if I was ever in it." Putting a hand to her forehead, she paced in front of the counter. Then she recalled that she was the serene one, the woman always in control, and she quickly dropped her hand and pasted on a smile. "Thank you for the tips. I'll put them to good use."

After considering her for several long seconds, he frowned. "If you ever want to talk, let me know."

Yes, she'd love to talk. Gentry was young and sexy, and he'd surely forgotten more than she'd ever learn. It'd be great to pick his brain. Unfortunately, that would prove her to be lacking any control, or intuition, and she would appear far from composed. Beyond hopeless. Almost pathetic. Such a depressing thought. "Thank you, but I'm fine."

He did a little more frowning, finally nodded, and started printing out delivery notices.

To herself, Emily muttered, "Today I'll begin shaking things up." She'd start by making a list.

"What's that?"

"Nothing. Just thinking aloud." The day was again gray, with more rain in the forecast. She hoped it wouldn't hamper business too much. In Cemetery, the biggest attraction was the lake. On bad weather days, there was little to no foot traffic, and everything slowed to a crawl. Vacationers stayed in their rooms and played games or watched movies. That is, some places might be busy, like Saul's restaurant, or Sallie's pastry shop. People loved to eat when bored.

However, they did not venture out to buy flowers. Blasted rain.

A sudden thought occurred to her. "Where did Kathleen go yesterday?"

After stacking the delivery papers for her to review, Gentry drew out an apron and tied it on.

He looked good in an apron, she thought objectively, seeing that it somehow enhanced his rugged appeal. Like maybe it offered a stark contrast. Utilitarian apron/ chiseled handsomeness.

"You're staring at me again."

"Hmm? Oh, just noticing how that apron complements you."

Skeptical, he looked down at the two-pocket apron, noted a few stains already on it, and then waited for her to explain.

Emily smiled. "Just an observation. Now, about Kathleen?"

With a long-suffering expression, he let the topic of the apron go. "Just as I was closing up yesterday, I saw a cute girl steal the mannequin."

Ridiculously alarmed, Emily demanded, "Who?"

"I didn't recognize her, but I don't think she was a vacationer. She seemed to know what she was doing."

Oh, thank goodness. Emily assumed she must be a local, then. "What did she look like?"

"Young, probably early twenties. Shapely. Long, wavy hair—some shade of brown. Not as dark as mine is, but it was wet from the rain, so I'm not sure. Brown eyes, too."

Wow.

Never before had Emily heard Gentry make note of anyone like that. Going for subtle prying, she moved closer. "You said she was cute?"

"Very." His grin widened. "From the shop window, I saw her looking around, trying to be stealthy but giggling about it."

"Like she was having fun?"

"Definitely. She ran off with Kathleen over her

shoulder, but she left the coconut drink, so I brought it in. Thought you might want to return it to Saul."

Sitting on the stool that Gentry had vacated, Emily encouraged him. "Tell me more."

Finally catching on to her absorbed interest, Gentry warily dropped his grin. "I told you all of it." He began to set out flowers with industrious haste. "Any sales today?"

Emily was not deterred. "How tall was she?"

"Short."

"How short?"

"I don't know." Without direction from her, he began making arrangements. "I didn't exactly measure her."

*Oh,* Emily thought, *I think you did.* "My height or shorter?"

"Maybe your height." He set out three vases, eyed them, eyed the flowers, and then got out another vase. "Don't forget, you have a consultation today at noon. I printed out the flower deliveries for late morning."

Clearly, Gentry didn't want to talk about the mysterious mannequin kidnapper anymore. Bummer. In many ways, Gentry fascinated her—and there was always a chance she could learn some moves just from observing him. That would sure be easier than admitting her own inept social skills, or coming right out and asking for help. Then again, Gentry didn't date much, or if he did, he certainly was private about it.

Because he was an ideal employee as well as a friend, she decided not to interrogate him further. At least, not right now. Instead, she got to work.

Once they had everything arranged for the shop, Emily started her list. *New hairdo.* Seriously, her ponytail was dated. She'd worn it that way forever, high school, college…mostly because it was easy and tidy. It wouldn't hurt to switch it up a bit.

Next she wrote: *Wardrobe refresh*. She had no idea what she'd buy, because she didn't have a huge budget to splurge, and again, her clothes were *easy* and *tidy*.

And why did those two words suddenly feel like insults? They were almost as bad as *perfect*.

That did it. She'd focus on things that were not so *easy*, not so *tidy*.

Like what? Hard and messy? She puffed out a breath.

What she needed were specific pieces that would change the overall look of an outfit. Her aunt, who favored comfort even more than Emily did, wouldn't be much help with that, but maybe she could ask Angela for some tips. The friendly doctor always looked sharp.

Last, Emily wrote: *Dog*. Then she hesitated. For so long now, she'd had only herself to take care of. An animal would need attention and affection, and there'd be vet bills and other expenses. Dog fur to clean up. Muddy paw prints.

But, her heart insisted, it'd also be a warm companion. Someone to cuddle with in the evening. She thought of sharing the couch with a friendly pooch, watching old movies together and keeping each other company.

God, her life was sadder than she'd realized.

Folding the note, she stuck it in her pocket.

She had time to figure out the specifics of a dog. Right now, getting her aunt and uncle settled was more important.

Minutes later, Vivienne arrived to do the deliveries for the day, which was the duty she most preferred. In the delivery van, Vivienne could listen to music or audiobooks, and she claimed she had to be moving to survive. She was a solid employee, pleasant and easy to deal with, but she wasn't on a par with Gentry.

That gave Emily a thought. She checked out the displays Gentry had just done, all of them more than adequate to highlight their selections while also pushing their newest deliveries. He always seemed to know what to do and when to do it, without her having to direct him. He'd picked up quickly on the business, and on her process of doing things.

Maybe she should make Gentry a manager.

Just like that, the idea took hold. If he agreed, she could hand over more duties, with added pay, of course. That would give her additional free time to devote to her aunt and uncle.

*And Saul*, the voice in her head prompted. *You'll have more time for him, too.* Why hadn't she invited him over? As to that, he could have suggested an alternative to the beach.

So many things he'd said and done had confused her. He'd been blunt about wanting to date, so she wouldn't doubt herself on that. After all, he'd even promised her aunt and uncle that he'd supply the *hot* dates.

Wondering just how hot it might get reminded Emily that she needed to sort out the schedule for the following week. She dug out her dry erase marker and board. "Hold up just a moment, Vivienne. While you're both here, what days off do you each want?"

Gentry shook his head at her whiteboard. "Eventually, you'll learn to do that the easier way."

"Yes, I know. I'm old and set in my ways." Emily added a laugh for good measure, but seriously, it was easier for her to write it on the board, then transfer it into her online calendar once she had it locked down.

"You're not even close to being old," Gentry countered, "so stop using that lame excuse. You're just stubborn and refuse to learn something new—even when it would help you a lot, by the way."

Another reason to make him manager. Emily smiled at him.

Gentry took one look at her and frowned in renewed suspicion. "Why do you keep doing that?"

"What?" she asked with forced innocence.

"Looking at me like you're plotting or something."

Maybe because she was? "I'm considering something, that's all."

His scowl deepened, which had the effect of making her smile widen.

Hands on his hips, he said, "You work too much. You could start shaving off wasted time by updating how you do things."

Vivienne glanced back and forth between them. "Gentry's right, you know. I'm sixty and I know how to set up the schedule online. There's a super-easy software program you could use that—"

"Both of you, hush. I like the way I do it." The idea that Gentry was so keen on a software program, though, was something she could use to tempt him to be a manager. By the second, she was seeing numerous benefits to that arrangement. "Now, days off?"

Vivienne shrugged. "I have a dental appointment Wednesday morning, but you usually don't schedule me then anyway. Other than that, I'm good."

"So, same schedule next week would work for you?"

"Sure," Vivienne said. "You can lock me down for the same every week if you want. If anything comes up, I'll let you know well in advance."

"Excellent." She turned to Gentry. "How about you?"

"Doesn't matter to me. Take whatever time you want and give me something else."

She realized that was always his answer, and suddenly it bothered her. As she considered him, she tapped her marker against the temporary schedule. "There has to be something you want to do."

"Why?" Challenging her, he asked, "What are *you* wanting to do?"

Like there was any comparing the two of them. She snorted. "I don't have anything." Unless it worked out with Saul.

"Same."

"No," she insisted, "it's not the same." Had she been selfishly overworking him?

"Why not?" With the glass fronts now sparkling—which was how Gentry always kept them—he put aside the cleaner and gave her a look of affection. "Why is it okay for you *not* to have plans, but I should?"

"Because I'm the owner and you're…"

"Hot stuff," Vivienne offered, while scrolling through her phone.

"Sexual harassment," Emily reminded her. "We're not supposed to say things like that to him."

Gentry grinned.

"But seriously," she said to Gentry. "I'm sure all the young ladies think you *are* hot stuff. Unless… Oh." Hoping she hadn't been horribly insensitive, she asked, "That's not your preference?"

"That," Vivienne said, "is sexual harassment."

"Yes, of course you're right." Horrified that she'd blundered so badly, Emily rushed to apologize. "I'm so sorry. It's just that we're friends, so I don't mean to overstep as an employer. As a *friend* though, I want you to be happy."

Gentry crossed his heart. "You're not overstepping, I promise. I'm plenty happy. No, I'm not into guys, but at the moment I'm not really into dating at all—so my days off don't matter."

Both women held silent, watching him with keen interest.

Shaking his head, he said, "Stop it, already."

"Okay, but… Am I relying on you too often?" Now that she thought about it, his hours at the shop would make a social life as impossible for him as it was for her.

"Nope. I enjoy the work I do for you."

Determined to be fair, Emily said, "If I'm not giving you enough free time, promise you'll let me know." Somehow she'd figure it out.

"I have more than enough free time," he insisted.

"If you're sure…?"

Grinning again, he tossed up his hands. "Blame it on a recent breakup, okay? Or say I'm nursing a broken heart. Doesn't matter. You can even say that I was wounded and can't—"

"Oh, God." Heart breaking, arms open, Emily rushed from her seat. Gentry had been *wounded*? Why hadn't she realized? She grabbed him close, hugging him tight, tears gathering in her eyes…

Until she finally caught on that he was laughing.

EMILY WAS ONE of a kind.

Gentry had figured that out from day one, when he'd first met her while applying for the job. She seemed to have ten things going on in her head at the same time, and yet she always gave people her complete, undivided attention.

At first that had unnerved him. It had been a long time since anyone listened that closely to anything he had to say. He was pretty sure a woman never had. But it hadn't taken long for him to get used to, and to actually enjoy, her way of centering on a person. And caring.

Emily genuinely cared about everyone, people she knew well, and those she'd just met. Even when she didn't particularly like someone—and yeah, there were times when he could tell that she didn't—she still listened and did her best.

Seeing her now, appearing so heartbroken for him, Gentry laughed harder, which was why he hadn't heard the customer come in.

Not until she said, "I'm free on Thursday, if you want to hang."

Catching Emily's shoulders and holding her back, he looked over—and locked onto big brown eyes and a huge smile.

The girl from yesterday, who'd taken Kathleen.

"It's you," he said, surprised to see her again so soon.

"Me?" she asked, her smile teasing. The way she leaned her elbows on the counter put a nice show of cleavage on display.

*Don't look, don't look…*maybe just a quick look. *Damn.* "I saw you take Kathleen."

"The mannequin? Yup, that was me." Slim eyebrows bobbed. "That's how it's done, right?"

"Sure is," Vivienne said.

"Great." Appearing impish, the girl confided, "I have plans for her."

Emily smiled brightly and offered her hand. "Hello. I'm Emily Lucretia. Welcome to my shop."

"Mila Nash," she said, taking Emily's hand in hers. "I'm a new hire for the Pit Stop. Moved here about two weeks ago, and I don't know many people." Her gaze swung right back to Gentry.

Today, with the fluorescent lighting, she was even cuter than she'd been in the approaching storm. He was right about her hair; dark brown, thick and long, hanging loose to just beneath her shoulder blades.

"This is Vivienne Barker, and *this*," Emily added with an absurd flourish that almost made Gentry roll his eyes, "is Gentry McAdams."

She announced him like the pope, the king, or the president.

"Gentry. What a nice name. I like it."

"Thanks." Gentry thought her smile felt like a dare, and full-on temptation. "It was my great-grandfather's middle name, on my mother's side."

"So... I couldn't help but overhear that you don't have plans."

Damn it. How long had she been standing there? "We were discussing the schedule for next week."

"But he probably doesn't have plans this week, either," Emily offered quickly.

What was she? His pimp? "The schedule is already set this week," he reminded her. He didn't need help getting a date. *If* he wanted a date. But he didn't.

Or at least he hadn't. Now, though...

"So this week is out?" Mila asked.

He hesitated, aware of both Emily and Vivienne suddenly pretending to be busy while no doubt soaking up every word.

His lack of a reply didn't faze Mila. "I figure if you're up to working, you're up to visiting, right?"

Now all three women stared at him. Gentry rubbed the back of his neck. Damn it, he hated being put on the spot.

"What do you say?" Mila leaned forward a little more. "No obligation. I won't tread on your broken heart or ask questions about your supposed breakup, or even your wound."

She was playing with him, and he didn't like that, either. "I'm not wounded." How had he gotten into this situation? "No recent breakup, and I'm definitely not brokenhearted."

Her grin brightened another few watts, putting dimples in her cheeks. "I'm glad to hear you're okay."

"Oh, he's fine," Vivienne said, apparently trying to help, though she kept her gaze on her phone. "Hale and hearty, isn't that right, Gentry?"

Before he had to come up with a reply, Mila said, "Good to know, because I'm off on Thursday, and I could really use some friendly company."

In a silly voice, Emily said, "You're off Thursday, Gentry. Done."

He shot Emily a look. Apparently, he didn't get a say in any of this. "Excuse me a sec." Stepping out around the counter, he indicated the far corner of the room to Mila. After a slight pause, she fixed her smile in place and headed that way.

The shop area wasn't large. There was no real privacy unless he took her to the back room, and he wasn't about to do that. Out here, he'd bet both Emily and Vivienne would be straining to hear anything he had to say.

On the one hand, it was funny. He'd never had any-

one in his life hover as much as Emily did. On the other
hand, he felt his privacy slipping away, when privacy
had been his main reason for relocating.

Mila turned to face him and said in a low whisper,
"I hope you're not leading me over here just to tell me
to get lost."

"I wouldn't." It wasn't in his nature to be that rude—
mostly because he knew what that rudeness felt like.

Not bothering to hide her relief, Mila asked with
exaggerated caution, "So…are you a teensy bit interested?"

How could he not be? "I'm interested." Any guy
would be flattered with the attention she'd given him.
"I need you to know, though…" *What?* What the hell
did he need her to know?

He didn't need anyone in Cemetery to know anything about him. Not really. He needed the chance to
start over. To build a real life and start putting down
roots. Without questions about his past.

Brows up, Mila asked, "What?"

"I don't like being manipulated."

The brows came down hard. "Manipulated? Here I
thought it was playful flirting."

"In front of my boss and coworker."

"Yeah, well…" She gave that quick thought. "I embarrassed you?"

Gentry glanced back at Emily and Vivienne, and
caught them both scrambling to look busy when in fact
they'd been staring. He shook his head and faced Mila
again. "It's a small town. Everyone knows everything,
so it's better not to advertise."

Now she tucked in her chin. "Advertise, as in, you'd
rather no one knew if we went on a single, friendly

date? Gotta say, Gentry, I'm having my own second thoughts now."

He didn't blame her. "That's just it. It's only friendly flirting, right? But I've found that this town likes to take something simple and amplify it a hundred times. Tease like that in front of others, and next thing you know, we'll be on Cemetery's Facebook page as the hottest new couple."

Her lips curled in amusement. "For real? Wow. Okay, so I'll try to be more subtle in the future. Now, about Thursday? Want to visit the beach? I haven't had much chance to go there yet, but it seems to be the hot spot every single night. It's that or the restaurant, and since I work at the restaurant…" She let the words trail off.

"Sure, sounds good." At this point, he couldn't refuse—and being honest with himself, he didn't want to. "Should I pick you up?"

"Nope. We'll make it as commitment-free as we can. I'll meet you there." She stuck out her hand. "One o'clock?"

A casual afternoon thing. So she probably wasn't trying to hook up—and now a part of him was disappointed.

Knowing he still had a lot to work out in his own head, Gentry took her hand in both of his. Touching her sent awareness burning through him. He brushed his thumb over the delicate skin of her wrist, and holding her gaze, he agreed, "One o'clock."

# CHAPTER SIX

MILA GOT SEVERAL yards away, stewing on Gentry's lack of response, before she drew up short. Shoot, she'd forgotten to buy the flowers, which was the very reason she'd gone to the florist shop in the first place. Seeing Gentry was just a bonus—or so she'd thought. Her ego really needed a boost right now, but he'd totally let her down.

Sighing, she looked back, but still hesitated. She was now in front of the sweet shop, but sweets wouldn't do. For one thing, it was another hot, hazy day, and any type of candy was bound to melt. For another, she'd be damned before she let Gentry with his moody gray eyes and ambivalent attitude put her off.

Why were the hottest guys always the most difficult? If only the not-so-hot guys interested her more. Maybe she was just shallow. Maybe she should seek out a mediocre guy somewhere... No. She'd rather skip the whole dating thing than force herself to settle.

She deserved it all, didn't she? A great guy who treated her well and also sparked her sexual interest. Answering her own question, she gave a resounding: *Yes.*

So Gentry wasn't likely to be that guy. He'd still serve as a diversion.

Feeling militant, she stalked back to the florist, but

then instead of entering, she cautiously peeked inside. She didn't see Gentry anywhere. Only Emily was at the counter, luckily, wrapping up a sale with a customer.

Flipping her hair back, Mila walked in as the customer walked out.

Alone with the owner, Mila smiled. "Sorry. I left without remembering why I'd come in."

Emily gave her a blinding smile. "Gentry could do that to anyone, I think."

See? She wasn't the only one who thought he was a hot tamale. "Speaking of him…where is he?"

"He's out back loading up the deliveries for Vivienne. I can get him for you." Emily started off.

"No, wait. I didn't come back for him." Definitely not. Her days of chasing after a guy were long gone.

"Okay," Emily said, then waited patiently, a small smile fixed on her face.

Hoping to wrap up her business before Gentry returned, Mila said, "I need some flowers. Something affordable."

"A bouquet?" Emily asked. "For an occasion, or just because?"

It was easy to see why Emily was known as the flower lady. She was incredibly pretty but understated, and her eyes were…kind.

Odd, but Mila immediately felt like she could trust her. "Actually, I had a plan when I swiped Kathleen from your bench yesterday. I hope you don't mind."

"Of course not," Emily said. "I swiped her from a wedding, then left her with Saul, and he set her up here. It's all in fun."

"Very fun," she agreed. "I wanted to take part, so I figured I'd put her in front of the restaurant again today, with a bunch of flowers in her arms, and a sign that says, "Feel free to take one—from Saul." She grinned. "Won't that be hilarious? Women will be thanking him all day!"

"Yes," Emily breathed, her eyes widened with enthusiasm. "I wish I'd thought of it. It's genius."

Mila grinned just imagining how the women would mob him. "He's a great guy, so this is just a fun way to let him know how much I appreciate him. Despite my lack of references, he hired me, you know, and he's been super-helpful in showing me around."

In a carefully neutral voice, Emily asked, "Showing you around the town?"

Mila laughed. "No, there's been no time for that. We both work too many hours. I meant around the business. He's the boss, but he trained me personally, and even when I mess up, he doesn't get mad."

Emily considered that. "I don't think I've ever seen Saul mad."

"Right?" Mila liked being able to say this all out loud. Being hired by Saul had been the best thing to happen to her, during the worst possible time. She'd been devastated, trying to recupe and pretend everything was fine, and bam. She'd met him, and he'd had her smiling ever since.

Other than Saul, she hadn't made any real friends yet, despite the welcoming work relationship with the other employees. But there was something about Emily that made her feel at ease, as if she'd known her forever. "Usually guys like him are difficult, same as Gentry."

Surprise sent Emily's brows arching high. "What do you mean?"

"Hot guys with great bods—they know it and they're cocky about it."

"You're saying both Saul and Gentry are hot, but only Gentry is cocky?"

"You don't think so?"

A tickled laugh made Emily even prettier. "Saul is often cocky, but in a very fun way. Gentry, though, he's super-nice, too."

"Says you." Liking her more by the second, Mila leaned in as if to share a confidence. "To me, he was just standoffish."

"Your little talk in the corner?" Emily asked with sympathetic interest.

Mila nodded, though she wasn't willing to go into details. No reason to admit that Gentry had more or less brushed her off. Yeah, he'd said he was interested, but he'd also made it clear that nothing much would be happening. Another rejection was not what she needed right now. She had her pride, though, so she'd act like it didn't matter. "I threw out hints, but hey, win some, lose some. I'll just enjoy the couple of hours of companionship, then go about my business."

"Hmm, well, you know, that was probably partly my fault. I did sort of throw him at you without asking him first."

"True, but I threw myself at him first, right?" She smiled as if it didn't matter, when in truth, she was still smarting. "My intention was pretty clear—and then, so was his." Let him make up excuses about broken hearts and wounds, and he could just be happy with his celibacy. Until something more tempting came along, she'd make do with his lackluster attention.

Emily said, "Gentry is..." She hesitated.

"What? Don't want to say?" The hesitancy piqued her interest.

"I might have breached his privacy enough for one day."

Eh, maybe. But now she was really curious about how Emily might describe him. Sensitive? A loner? She could see both, but mostly she thought he just wasn't into her. "Luckily," Mila said, "Saul's not like that. He laughs about everything, and he has amazing patience."

"So...you, er, threw yourself at Saul, too?"

"Ha! No." The way she was going on, she supposed it was easy for Emily to misunderstand. "He's the boss, so that wouldn't be cool. Not that I haven't been tempted."

Showing clear reluctance, Emily admitted, "He is tempting."

"The thing is, I like the job, and I'd just as soon keep it."

"I see," Emily said softly, though to Mila, she looked fairly confused.

Mila asked, "I guess you've known him a while?"

"Saul?" Emily asked.

Wow, she did seem hung up on Saul. "No, I meant Gentry."

That brought back Emily's friendly smile. "I guess when we're talking two gorgeous guys, it's easy to get them confused."

Maybe. Saul was great, but unfortunately, all of Mila's concentration seemed to be on Gentry right now. "They are both very fine." That made her wonder...was Emily involved with Gentry? Was the embrace she'd witnessed possibly something more? Mila eyed her, guessing Emily was older, but certainly pretty enough, and with a very nice shape to her, even if she played it down. Plus she was so darn personable...

Well, too late to worry about it now. She wanted to make her purchase and get out before Gentry returned. "So what flowers do you recommend? Something not too pricey."

As if she were equally grateful for the change of topic, Emily said, "How about carnations? They're hardy, long-stemmed so they'll stay in Kathleen's arms, and the blooms last."

"That'd be great. How many could I get for twenty bucks?"

"Since it's for Kathleen, and ultimately to tease Saul, I'll donate them to the cause."

"Oh, I can't let you do that."

"Of course you can. We're new friends, right? Consider it a first-time shopper bonus." Emily gathered up the flowers, quite a few of them, and wrapped them in pretty purple wax paper before tying them with a length of twine.

"You know," Mila said, eyeing Emily with the purple paper puffed around her. "That's a great color for you."

Emily glanced at the carnations. "White?"

"No, purple. It makes your pretty eyes stand out even more, and it looks fantastic with your blond hair and fair complexion."

A little slack-jawed, Emily stared from the paper, to Mila, and back again. She drew a breath, and a grin blossomed. "Purple? Really?" And then on her next quick breath, "I have pretty eyes?"

"Are you kidding me? They're smokin' hot. Super-pretty. Guys don't tell you that?"

Emily blinked fast. "No?"

"Girl, you're seeing the wrong guys, then." She took in the muted colors of Emily's outfit, and suggested, "You could totally pull off bolder colors. In fact, I bet fuchsia would look great on you, too."

"I have a Nitro Yellow car."

"The one I saw parked next to the building?" At Emily's nod, she said, "Sweet ride. I love it. Bet that hot color really sets off your eyes, too. Seriously, how do you not know how gorgeous they are?" Not waiting for a reply, because she could tell Emily didn't have one, Mila decided that if she couldn't give her own ego a boost today, she sure as hell could boost Emily's. "No lie, okay? You're stunning. The eyes, the hair, and that smile. You should play it all up more."

"With bolder colors?"

"Absolutely."

"Thank you. I think you just gave me some ideas." Grinning, looking even happier, Emily finished prepping the flowers. "Good luck with the jest. I'm sure it's going to be a hit, and I can't wait to hear all about it."

"No, thank *you*." When she heard Gentry in the back room and knew he'd be joining them soon, Mila said, "Promise me you'll come by the restaurant soon for a dessert and coffee on me, so I can repay the favor."

"That sounds terrific."

Rushing now, Mila gathered up the flowers. "Seriously, I'll count on it, okay?"

"I'm already looking forward to it."

"Great." Mila headed to the door with a long stride, and managed to get through it just as Gentry showed up. She heard him speak to Emily, a question in his dark tone, but she didn't wait around to see what either of them had to say.

She hadn't gone to the florist shop to hit on a guy or make a new gal pal, but she'd done both, she thought with a smirk.

One was a hit, the other a miss, but hey, it lightened her heart, knowing she'd left Emily glowing. If only all women were that nice, what a difference they could make for each other—and that, she decided, was far more important than scoring with hot tamale Mr. Gentry McAdams.

EVEN THOUGH SAUL had explained that he'd be busy the rest of the week, as the days went by, Emily missed him. How that was possible, she didn't know. He wasn't really a part of her life, and other than a little playful teasing back and forth with Kathleen, a few visits to the hospital, *and a couple of truly scorching kisses*, they weren't involved.

It was the scorching kisses, she decided, that had him plaguing her brain. She wanted more. She went to bed thinking about it, and woke the same way.

Ridiculous.

It was just… Well, a part of her had thought that he might drop in again, or at least call. But it was now Thursday, and other than when she'd spoken to him on the phone to share her schedule for the next week, she hadn't heard from him.

He'd sounded rushed when he'd told her he'd align his schedule with hers, which meant Wednesday and Sunday off, and that he'd be in touch so they could figure out their plans. Promises, promises…

Then nothing.

"Stop stewing," Gentry suggested.

She looked up, stem cutter in her hand as she'd been

tidying a bouquet. "I'm not." She put the flowers in a fresh vase of water and rearranged them until they looked just right. "I just feel bad that you're in here on your day off. Don't you have a date at the beach with a certain super-cute girl from the restaurant?"

His smile didn't convey a single thing. "In an hour, which means you have time to run over to the restaurant to see Saul for lunch if you want."

No way would she do that. Chasing a man wasn't in her character. "The rush is over now, so instead, why don't you take off? Enjoy the rest of your day." They'd had a massive group of women come in, all of them celebrating a spontaneous engagement for a friend. Apparently, it was a group on vacation together, and a proposal had been made and accepted. Since they all enjoyed the area so much, it was decided that the happy couple would marry here. Emily had spent well over an hour with them, going through the portfolio, helping them to choose flowers, and also showcasing the flowers in her field for photo ops. They'd loved *everything*.

Thank goodness Gentry was free to help out, otherwise she couldn't have accommodated them.

"They plan to visit Yardley?" he asked, rather than taking her up on her suggestion.

She almost wondered if he was dreading the date. He certainly didn't look enthusiastic about it. In fact, when she looked closely, he appeared tense. "I took a play from her book and strongly recommended everyone here. From what I was told, it'll be a true Cemetery wedding." The second the words left her mouth, she made a face. "God, doesn't that sound awful?"

Gentry laughed. "I'm getting used to it."

"Anyway, they'll be in touch with Yardley once her

honeymoon ends. They also love the idea of Saul catering, of Sallie doing their wedding cake—they were going to see her next—and even the Honeymoon Cottage. Isn't that great?"

"It's a nice, but unique, town. Everyone who visits here likes it."

Did *he* like it? She'd never really asked Gentry if he planned to settle here for good. When he had first come to work for her, she'd just assumed… Emily pasted on a smile. "They have more appointments lined up. I've already added them to the books."

"Sounds good."

No time like the present, she decided. "Gentry, do you think you'll stay in Cemetery?"

Seeming surprised by the question, he took a stance, his expression stern. "It's home now. I'm not going anywhere."

Wow. He said that as if he thought someone might try to run him off. "I'm so glad to hear that. Seriously. And since you're now a permanent resident, have you ever thought about other employment?"

His brows slowly drew together. "Firing me, Emily?"

That growled question stole her breath away. "*What*?" she gasped. "No! Not ever. You know how much I rely on you. Too much, actually."

"Not too much," he countered, as the stiffness left his shoulders. "I keep telling you, I like this job. Why would I look for something else?"

Better pay? Benefits? A retirement plan? A lot of reasons came to her mind. Did Gentry have ambitions? Did he someday want a home of his own instead of a rental?

"Emily." He came to stand in front of her, his expression far too serious. "If there's a problem, I'd rather you just say so."

She drew a deep breath, and blurted, "How would you feel about becoming a manager?"

The stark expression lifted, replaced with blank confusion. "Manager?"

"You're staying in Cemetery, this is now your home, so surely you want... I don't know." She tried to find a tactful way to put it without getting too personal again. "A stake in things?"

"Yeah." Slowly, he brought his hand up to rake through his hair. "You're talking about putting down roots."

"Exactly. We never really discussed your plans." Working at a florist shop wasn't generally the type of job a young man would keep long-term. Now that she'd grown used to his help, though, she'd hate to lose him—for any reason. "Since you're staying, and since I wouldn't mind cutting back on my hours a little, what do you think of a manager position? It'd come with a raise." She named the figure she could pay, then, going for enticement, added, "You can use whatever software you want to do a schedule."

He grinned. "So you'd let me drag you into this century, huh?"

"I promise I wouldn't dump more work on you, at least not too much. And I could hire someone else to do the gardening in the fields—"

"I like that part of the job."

"I know, but don't think I'd expect you to put in sixty-hour weeks or anything." She bit her lip, then added, "Gentry, I can't imagine anyone else who'd be as attentive to the business as you. In some ways, I think you love it as much as I do."

"The job, the town…" He searched her face. "You. Your friendship. I love all of it."

Oh wow, pretty sure her heart just turned over. "Wonderful! Oh, that makes me want to dance."

Before she could do anything ridiculous, like twirl, he asked, "Does this sudden decision have anything to do with your aunt and uncle?" He leaned back against the counter. "Or with Saul?"

Right on both counts, but all Emily said was, "I think my aunt and uncle are going to need more help."

"And Saul?"

She hadn't heard from Saul. "I wouldn't mind a little more free time to…date." That sounded so lame coming from a woman her age…but *no*, she would stop thinking about her age. Or the fact that she didn't have a freaking date, hadn't had one in years. "Dating is not a priority, though."

"Dating should be."

She quirked a brow. "That's what I was telling you."

"I meant it should be a priority for *you*." He laughed, then glanced at the clock. "Hold up. This is all sounding serious, and yeah, I'm interested in being a manager, but maybe we should put off talking about the details until later."

"Oh, right." She immediately brightened. "You *do* have a date, don't you? And I'm so excited for you."

Bemused, a smile playing at his mouth, he asked, "Why?"

"I'll live vicariously." She gave him a quick hug. "You'll tell me about it later?"

"Depends."

"On what?"

He lightly chucked her chin. "What Mila and I do, and how it goes."

"Oh." No one had ever done that before, playfully chucked her chin. It was an affectionate gesture and she liked it. Seemed she was having all kinds of new experiences lately.

She watched him turn and saunter for the back room, removing his apron as he went.

Then she said again, "*Oh*," as she finally caught on to his meaning. Right. If things got heated, Gentry definitely wouldn't share details. He was one of the most private people she'd ever met, plus he was a true gentleman.

Emily realized she was grinning.

Maybe Mila was wrong and Gentry was far more interested than the young woman suspected. Emily certainly hoped so. She liked them both, and she'd love to see Gentry get involved.

Especially if that would help keep him in Cemetery for good.

GENTRY GOT TO THE beach a few minutes early. Damn, it was packed, and he had no idea where Mila might be. Squealing kids ran along the shoreline, splashing in and out of the water while parents kept a close watch. Younger couples gathered in groups, laughing under beach umbrellas or walking in the sand. A few romantically inclined couples sat beneath the gazebo, staring at each other and smiling a lot.

He rubbed the back of his neck. This was not his gig, never had been and probably never would be. From an early age, crowds meant gossip, and that meant insults.

He felt as out of place among the vacationers as a don-key would in a flower patch.

"Gentry!"

He turned at hearing his shouted name, and there was Mila on a golf cart at the very entrance to the beach. He'd left his truck parked on Lakeshore Drive and had walked over to the beach, so he headed her way.

Waving to him, she stepped out of the cart—wearing a loose white cover-up. The gauzy material was sheer enough that he could see her black bikini beneath. Could see her body, too. All her curves.

He drew breath so fast, he damn near choked himself.

True, bikini-clad women were always around Cemetery. Some came into the flower shop that way. On a customer, he could ignore it.

On a girl who seemed interested in him? A girl who looked like her? Not so much.

When he got close, he said, "I wondered how I was going to find you."

Her grin was as big and infectious as he remembered, but her eyes were hidden behind sunglasses. "I got this used golf cart for a steal, and it's awesome for tooling around the beach area. Plus I figured we'd ride down the shore a bit to see if we can find a more private spot."

Damn. Now he wished he was wearing sunglasses, too, to hide the sudden flare of heat. "We can do that."

"Great. Get in." She hopped behind the wheel and waited.

He eyed the aged golf cart, glad that she wasn't driving a shiny, recent model. He felt more at home in something dated and in need of new seat covers. Seeing the cooler, tote bag, and towels in the back, he asked, "We'll be swimming?"

"It's a beach, so I came prepared. I also brought food and drinks."

Didn't sound like a quick date—and now he felt like an ass. As he seated himself beside her, he felt compelled to say, "Sorry. I should have thought of that."

"When you didn't want to be here in the first place? No problem. I asked you, so it's my treat."

He hesitated, but what the hell. "Next time will be on me, then."

Appearing pleased, she asked, "Next time, huh? Maybe you'll hate today enough that you won't want a next time."

"Since I already want a next time, I don't see that happening."

Her lips curved the slightest bit in a not-quite smile that looked more curious than amused. "That's a big turnaround."

"Not really."

"I won you over with the golf cart, didn't I?"

She'd won him over when he saw her laughing and stealing Kathleen, but since he'd only just now admitted it to himself, he couldn't see admitting it to her. "I gave you a bad impression at the flower shop. You took me by surprise." When she said nothing, he added, "The golf cart is nice, though."

That got him a small laugh. "Well, I'm determined to have fun, because I deserve it, but I hope you have fun with me."

With no idea what she meant by that, Gentry just nodded. Then he had to hold on as she drove them out of the lot, away from the congested beach area and down the shoreline, over rutted ground, around trees, and past a gaggle of complaining geese.

Not a smooth ride, but the farther they got from the crowd, the easier he breathed.

"I scoped this out earlier," she explained. "It's a lot quieter here because the sand isn't as thick. Mostly it's covered with pebbles and some rocks and shells. Lots of freshwater algae, too, but you don't strike me as a guy who gets squeamish about the water." ·

He wasn't squeamish about anything—except maybe opening up to other people. "It's nice, thanks." The trees here were taller, offering shade, and when she finally stopped the golf cart, he didn't see another person in sight.

"How about I grab the towels and my tote bag, and you get the cooler? Show off those muscles a little."

He couldn't help but grin. "I think I can carry the cooler without showing off."

"Aww, but do it anyway. For me?"

God, she was such a flirt, and he loved it. "I'll carry it. Anything else is up to your imagination."

"Oh, but Gentry, I have an *amazing* imagination, so that works."

The cooler was packed and heavy. He wondered how long she planned for them to hang out. He followed as she picked her way along the uneven ground until they reached a large flat rock very close to the lapping water. Immediately, she kicked off her flip-flops and turned to him.

A willow tree grew to one side, its long, draping branches covering part of the ground and even drifting into the water. On the other side was a mature maple tree, offering protection from the sun.

"How's this look?" she asked.

Cozy. Completely private. And like a place where things could get out of control. "It's nice." A few gulls circled overhead. Somewhere nearby, an insect buzzed. There was no stirring breeze, just the rich scent of the water, the bright blue sky, and the heat of the sun. "Actually, it's a spot I'd have chosen myself, but I thought you wanted to get to know people, and you'd do that better at the busy beach."

"I'm getting to know you, right? And besides, I wasn't up to a lot of confusion right now."

He set the cooler in the shade of the maple. "Busy week at work?"

"It's been nuts, but then, I get the feeling the Pit Stop is always like that." She spread out a blanket-size beach towel and put the second towel, still folded, on top.

So it'd be up to him whether to sit close or open that second towel? Screw it. When she sat, Gentry dropped down beside her and unlaced his sneakers to take them off. After setting them aside, he stared out at the gently rolling surface of the lake. He hadn't worn trunks—so far, he didn't own any—but he did wear board shorts that would do if she decided she wanted a swim.

What she did now, though, was look at him. He felt it, her gaze almost like a touch, so he glanced at her.

Pushing her sunglasses to the top of her head, she asked, "Want a drink? I brought a few colas and bottles of water."

"Whenever you're ready." He half turned to face her, bracing on one straightened arm. The position brought him slightly closer to her. "I heard about your stunt with Kathleen. I guess Saul was busy with women thanking him?"

Her smiling lips drew and held his attention—until he caught himself.

She said, "It was awesome. Everyone wanted to talk to him." Snickering, she added, "I think I totally dicked up his day, but it was worth it."

"Saul seems like a good sport."

"He's the best, but he also threatened to get even." She made a silly face. "Now I have to worry what he might do back, but still, it's all in fun. I've gotten to know him, better than I know anyone else in Cemetery, though I got to know Emily a little, too."

Already knowing the answer, he asked, "You like her?"

"A lot. I bet she's a terrific boss."

"Unbelievably so." A boss who now wanted him to take a more permanent position in the shop. He'd been thinking about it ever since. "Until I met Emily, I didn't know people like her existed." The second the thought was spoken, Gentry wished he could call it back. He rarely shared his personal thoughts aloud. Why would he, when he'd grown up knowing how people would react?

Mila didn't seem to think anything about it, other than agreeing with a nod. "Did she tell you she donated the flowers? Carnations." She lounged back on the towel and stared up at the vast blue sky.

Gentry stared at her body. The thin cover-up didn't even come close to concealing her. She looked good, and obviously knew it.

Confidence was so sexy.

She glanced his way. "I told her I'd buy her coffee and a dessert, so I hope she drops into the restaurant soon."

If Emily wasn't so hung up on Saul, she would probably drop in sooner. Knowing her as he did, he figured if she went there too soon, she'd worry about looking too desperate for Saul—never mind that everyone went to the Pit Stop, often.

Following Mila's lead, he stretched out on his side next to her, propping himself on an elbow. After a laughably brief hesitation, he gave in to his instincts and said, "Nice swimsuit." Even nicer body.

Being coy, she asked, "Do you think so?"

"I think you look sexy as hell, so now I'm wondering if it's to attract me or torment me."

Laughter showed in her big brown eyes, but her tone was moderate when she said, "Initially, I'd have been game for either one, but since you said the attraction was a no-go, I'll settle for the torment."

"About that..." Damn, she was irresistible. "I'd like to explain."

"Hey, I get it. I mean, I found us a private spot so no one will misunderstand. And I am enjoying your company, probably more than I should since you made yourself clear. But being new here—"

The touch of his fingers to her lips quieted her. Her eyes widened a bit...and then he felt her tongue touch one finger.

Gentry withdrew his hand and tried not to react. Wasn't easy, but then, nothing much in his life had been. A little thing like a lick... Yeah, he could handle that. Maybe. "I'm still new to town myself. I've only been here four months."

"Seriously? And you seem like such a local."

That temperate tone was really getting to him and

making him guess about everything. "I can't tell if that's a compliment or not."

Finally, she grinned. "Total compliment. Everyone I've met has been awesome, and you seem right at home with them." She returned her attention to the sky. "So... you being new to town has something to do with why you're not interested?"

"I already told you I'm interested, but yeah, it's why I'm cautious."

"I'm not sure I see the connection, unless you really are brokenhearted?"

"I'm not." Christ, he hated opening up, but he hated the idea of insulting her even more, so he'd explain. "The thing is, I moved here to start over. I get along with everyone—like you said, most of the people here are friendly. But I also wanted to keep my privacy."

"Okay." She looked at him quizzically.

Yeah, nothing he'd said really made sense. "The stuff I left behind..." It always came back to that. He didn't want to be one of those people molded by his past, yet it was always there. Leaving it behind would be like peeling away his own skin. It was a part of him, and he feared it always would be.

Now she came up on her elbow, too, saying softly, "Hey. Whatever it is, it's okay. Seriously, I didn't mean to be nosy."

"You aren't." She'd just been friendly. Flirting, as she'd said. "If you knew me before..." He was making this harder than it had to be, so damn it, he'd just get it said. "I don't want to shout it to the world, but I left a town that pretty much despised me for one reason or another. Either it was my mom that disgusted them, or my grandpa who'd given them hell. Or it was me." He laughed without any real humor. "I was a jerk until I started high school, and by then, everyone had decided I was just like my mother."

Instead of questioning him about his mom, she quietly asked, "Were you?"

"No." Never that. "The thing is, I was guilty by association. No one believed I could be different, even when I was. Once my grandpa passed away, I realized I needed to start over somewhere else."

"Somewhere where no one knew you?"

Glad that she understood, he gave a single nod. "So here I am."

She flushed.

He didn't know how to interpret that until she surprised him by saying, "The reasons I came here are similar, but also different." She avoided his eyes as she admitted, "They're also embarrassing. See, I got spectacularly dumped by my boyfriend in a way that all my friends witnessed. Actually, though, it turned out that they weren't really my friends. Most of them either figured I got what I deserved or they felt sorry for me, like my life was over without him." She made a disgusted face. "There were a few so-called friends who were just glad to have me out of the running."

"But here, no one knows you."

"So no one can judge me." One shoulder hitched up. "Now I'm here, and I feel renewed. Ready to tackle the world."

Gently, because he knew he'd added to her embarrassment, he asked, "And maybe ready to be appreciated?"

"Well, sure. I mean, at first. I saw you and I thought, hey, now there's a hot guy who could boost the old ego."

Her gaze cut his way, but only for a second. "I thought you'd be easy, too. Girl throwing herself at a guy? Usually that's not much of a challenge."

"Believe me, if you'd known my thoughts, you'd have felt pretty good about yourself."

This time her gaze lifted to his and stayed. "Yeah?"

Gentry touched her chin, ensuring she wouldn't look away again. "You didn't know the real me. I'm different now, so I didn't want to take advantage."

"So tell me about the real you."

He shook his head. These days, he wasn't entirely sure who he was anymore. The punk from a few years back, the unwanted kid who made his mother resentful, the burden his grandpa struggled to provide for… the guy who slept around without a thought for the girl, or picked a fight with a jerk just so he could put him in his place? He'd been all of those things, but now he was trying to be a better person.

No, he *was* a better person.

And for that reason, he said, "How about we save that for another time?" From what she'd said, she was vulnerable right now, and he didn't want to add to that, regardless of how much he wanted her. Besides, it'd only be fair if he shared his secrets with Emily first. After all, she'd hired him, and now she wanted to give him more responsibility. He couldn't let her do that without knowing everything.

Mila teased, "I like how you keep referencing seeing me again."

Was he taking too much for granted? "I hope I will." Now that he'd had a small taste of her company, he knew he'd enjoy more. "Unless you want this to be one and done."

"Nope. Now I'm intrigued. I want to hear all about your sordid past." She playfully bobbed her eyebrows. "If you're not so golden, then you can't expect me to be either, right?"

"Sounds fair." For some reason, his heart felt suddenly lighter.

"Plus I selfishly want someone I can talk to. Someone who'll listen to *my* sordid past."

"That's human, not selfish, so count me in anytime." He'd prefer to talk about her over himself any day. Already, she fascinated him.

"You'd have to go first." With a soft-eyed tease, she said, "I'm shy."

She ruined the reserved effect with a laugh that had him grinning, too. "You're something," he agreed. "Not sure 'shy' is the right description, though."

"Sadly true. I'm not sure I have a shy bone in my body, so I'm going to admit I already like you. Now, don't get spooked. I'm not proposing or anything. It'd just be nice to have someone my own age to hang with."

Lightly, he touched her bare shoulder, exposed by the loose neck of her cover-up. Feeling the silk of her sun-warmed skin, he experienced another surge of awareness that went straight to his heart. "And maybe do more?"

"Now you're talking. We'll get there eventually, I think." Then she added with feeling, "I *hope*."

"How about I guarantee it?"

A renewed smile came slowly as she leaned in. "With a kiss."

No, she wasn't shy—and he was glad. The second her mouth touched his, Gentry knew he was in deep. Dangerous, because he felt too many things, only a few of them physical. Things like shared acceptance, understanding, and compatibility. Out of all the wonderful people he'd met in Cemetery, Mila Nash hit him on a whole different level.

She kept the kiss brief, and when she inched away, she appeared pleased with his heated expression. Yes, this was a woman who knew her own power. That reassured him, because maybe she wouldn't scare off easy.

In a voice gone husky, she whispered, "And now it's definitely time for a swim…because I need to cool off."

Not a bad idea at all. Gentry stood and helped her to her feet. "Right behind you."

With both of them grinning, they waded into the chilly lake.

# CHAPTER SEVEN

THE REST OF the day dragged on for Emily. Three times she checked her phone, just to make sure she hadn't missed a call. It made her feel juvenile. And inadequate.

Making excuses for herself, she decided that she only wanted to know what Saul had thought of Mila's joke. Had women mobbed him, going above and beyond in their appreciation of the flowers?

Had he *liked* women mobbing him?

Several had come into her shop and thanked her for the prank, and each time she'd explained that it was actually Mila who'd done it. Most of them asked more about Mila, and they'd seemed interested to know she was new to the area.

Emily had a feeling Mila might have a few new friends now.

How was she faring with Gentry? Odd, but Emily felt protective of them both. She'd almost explained to Mila that Gentry was sensitive and private, and…deep.

Yup, that described him. He was an intense thinker, and she suspected he felt things more keenly than others. Sometimes it seemed that he'd been badly hurt, and she wanted to find a way to make him feel better, to heal him. Not that he'd ever complained. He wouldn't. Plus Gentry smiled often, so she had to believe that he was happy here—in the job, in the town…as her friend.

Still, she saw something behind those smiles, some-thing in his astute gray eyes that was far too serious for a man of his age.

Now Mila, she was a sweet girl, open and teasing, and as Gentry had said, extremely attractive. Yet she'd also seemed vulnerable, almost as if her energetic flirt-ing was a facade to hide a wounded spirit. Emily found herself wondering why Mila had relocated to Cemetery.

And that led her to wondering if Saul was drawn to her. How could he not be? Mila was all the things Emily wasn't… *Nope*. She wouldn't keep doing that. She liked Mila too much to go down the road of comparisons. So the girl was outgoing and beautiful and confident.

At the very least, Emily could claim confidence… most of the time.

Annoyed with herself, she grumbled and got out her note. She'd been carrying the thing in her pocket and so far, all she'd added was a change of hairstyle, a few new clothes, and a dog. Eventually she needed to add more, and then she really needed to start ticking things off the list.

She pondered the note a moment, then quickly, be-fore she could change her mind, she wrote: *Be more assertive*.

There. That's where she'd start—by going to the Pit Stop. If Saul wouldn't come to her, she'd go to him. She'd ask him outright about those hot dates he'd prom-ised. She had expectations, damn it.

Relieved to finally have a plan, she tucked the note away again. A few minutes later, Betty Cemetery came in. Before Emily could even greet her, Betty said, "You missed one of our tea parties," in a way that made it clear she considered that a grave offense.

"I know, and I'm sorry." A few of the local women

had started a tea club to meet the first and third Monday of each month at six o'clock. Normally, Emily enjoyed joining them. There would be anywhere from five to twenty women, based on who was available, but Betty never missed it. Once Yardley had gotten the matriarch to soften up and be a little less strident with everyone, Betty had embraced her newfound gentler persona.

Somewhat.

She still liked to pull the "I'm the descendant of the namesake for this town" card every so often, as she was doing now, with her frown and a tilt of her chin that allowed Betty to look down her nose at Emily.

Emily put on her most tranquil smile. "My uncle had an accident. I'm surprised you didn't know, given how in-tune you are with the town." *Keeping your nose in everybody else's business.* "He's in the hospital, and my aunt is staying with him."

Real concern loosened Betty's rigid jaw, and she put a spotted hand over her heart. "Oh, dear. I hope it's nothing too serious."

"He fell," Emily said, keeping the explanation short. "Given his age, it's scary."

Snorting, Betty said, "He's younger than me," followed by, "Did he break anything?"

"Just badly bruised his hip."

"Well, that's a blessing. Yardley fusses over me all the time, you know, worrying that I'll fall in my yard. People our age can't be too careful."

"So true." And exactly one of her worries. "I know you and Yardley have gotten close."

"Very." Betty rested her folded hands on the counter and softened her expression. "I'm sorry for your difficulty. If there's anything I can do, please let me know."

Wow. Surprised, Emily said, "Thank you, Betty."

"The next time you can't make a meeting, I'd appreciate it if you let someone know. You're one of our regulars, being that you're single, with no one else to take up your time."

Well, that was rude. "Life gets busy regardless."

Betty sniffed, as if she smelled the lie.

Emily's smile felt a little tight. "I enjoy the meetings, and it's true, I usually have no reason to miss them." The truth—but a little galling to admit.

As if she'd read her thoughts, Betty shook her head. "I have a good feeling about you and Saul. It's past time that boy settled down."

Hearing Saul called a "boy" made her smile slip. "He's only a few years younger than me."

"To a woman my age, you're both children. Now. About Gentry."

Emily wanted to groan. "From Saul to Gentry?"

"He's a fine young man. Always polite. I understand he's dating the new girl at the Pit Stop."

"I…" It wasn't a question, but rather a statement. How in the world had Betty found that out so quickly? Cautiously, Emily explained, "They met yesterday, actually, when Mila came in to buy some flowers. I'm not certain about any dating, though." Through a sheer act of will, Emily managed not to look guilty for lying.

Betty studied her closely. "Yes, well. I have my sources."

Emily often suspected that Betty was the keeper of that ridiculous Facebook page. Maybe once Yardley returned from her honeymoon, she could rein the woman in. For now, to change the subject, Emily said, "It's funny that you would stop in, because I had just been thinking about you. I'm going to get a dog, and I know you've been working to get our own shelter set up."

"Wonderful idea!" Betty beamed at her. "Oh, there are so many lovely animals at shelters, and never enough people to adopt. Cemetery's own shelter won't be complete until the spring, so in the meantime I've been learning all that I can."

Briefly, Emily wondered if the shelter would be saddled with the name Cemetery. How horrid would that be? *Cemetery No-Kill Shelter.* She shuddered at the idea, but hopefully the town would have sway in the name now. "I thought you might be able to point me in the right direction."

Betty quickly dug out a card, then used the pen on Emily's counter. "This is a wonderful shelter. They do great work, and they're careful about who they allow to adopt. Don't worry, though. When you go, ask for Berkley. I'll put in a good word for you. She trusts my judgment now."

Whoa. Things were moving along just a little too quickly. "I'm not sure when I can go there…"

"Tomorrow," Betty stated, and her tone made it clear it was already an appointment. "After you get off work. I'll call Berkley now and tell her to expect you." After handing her the card with the address written on it, Betty turned to hurry away.

"But…" Emily trotted after her. "Didn't you want flowers?"

"I only stopped by to check on you. Don't forget your appointment."

"I wasn't—"

"You'll love having a pet," Betty said with a dismissive wave of her hand. She sailed out the door and hurried along the sidewalk, her cell phone already in her hand.

Stopping in the doorway, Emily watched her go, the card held in her hand. Just because she'd said she wanted a pet didn't mean she wanted one right this very minute. Frustrated, she put a hand to her forehead and tried to think what to do.

Yet at the same time, the idea tantalized her. A cuddly pet. One that would love her. Maybe a cute little dog that could sit in her lap. Oh, she could even buy a bigger purse to carry him! She'd seen people do that, mostly celebrities, but still...

*Fine*, she grumbled to herself. *I needed a nudge, and Betty was certainly that.*

Well, nudge accepted. She glanced at the clock, saw she had only another hour to work, and got started on the chores she did every night before closing. The second it was six o'clock, she'd be ready to go. If she hesitated at all, she might change her mind.

Tonight she'd tackle Saul. Tomorrow she'd get a pet. Maybe the day after, she'd even go shopping for something new and different to wear. Something a little more flirty...possibly even sexy.

But likely not.

"Go, Beck!" Saul shouted from the bleachers near the track field. When he glanced at his phone and saw the time, he felt like a jerk.

He had hoped to be done by now so he could give Emily a call, but so far, nothing was going according to plan. It was bad enough that he couldn't see her yet, but he wanted to at least talk with her.

He worried he was losing the ground he'd already

gained in their relationship, but at the same time, *this* relationship was important, too, so there was no way he wouldn't have been here.

His involvement mattered—to him, and to the kid.

A son who, God willing, would soon be his own.

The reality of that made him breathe a little deeper. Emotion got a stranglehold on him every time he thought of it. He *wanted* it. Bad.

He wanted so many things right now, it sometimes felt like he was juggling his life. For far too long he'd been entirely carefree, and now—bam! Was he aiming for too much? He hoped not. His folks swore it'd work out, and he trusted them, but still, the situations with Emily and Beck were unique. It would have been so much better if he could have worked out one before reaching for the other.

Life wasn't that way.

He thought of Emily and smiled. She did that for him, filled him with optimism and hope. Around her, it seemed anything was possible.

And then there was Beck.

A thin, long-limbed and handsome kid of fourteen, at that age where he felt grown but knew he wasn't. Beck wanted to control things, and yet every decision in his life was handled by others.

If Emily represented optimism, then Beck was fear—a fear that Saul would screw it up, that he'd make a wrong move.

Desire warred with responsibility.

With luck, that would change soon. He'd mesh both relationships, both worlds, and—if he could manage it—the outcome would be everything he'd hoped for.

Standing with the crowd of cheering parents, Saul

watched as Beck ran along the course. He'd spent a month watching him compete in the youth running club, and today they were racing in heats. Saul loved it.

Beck wasn't the fastest, but he gave it his all, and as the kid flew past, Saul smiled so big that his face hurt. So did his heart.

Clapping loudly, calling encouragement to all the boys, he headed for the finish line to offer congratulations now that things were wrapping up.

Away from the other kids, Beck paced and breathed deeply, his brown hair matted with sweat and his smooth cheeks flushed bright pink. Saul noticed one of his socks had slipped down around his heel.

When he spotted Saul, Beck gifted him with a rare, sincere smile, and as if Beck's happiness was hardwired to his soul, Saul felt like the luckiest man alive. How was it he'd gone so long not thinking about kids, having no real need or want of them, and now this kid meant the world to him?

Keeping his stride long, he reached Beck and pulled him in for a fierce bear hug.

"I only got fifth," Beck said, laughing and pounding Saul on the back.

"Only fifth? In the final competition?" Saul returned. "Out of what? Four schools and twenty kids?"

"Twenty-two."

"Wow. Very awesome." Setting him back, Saul grinned. "You've got the legs for it." Saul's own T-shirt was now damp with Beck's sweat, and he noticed that Beck smelled a bit like an old gym bag in need of washing, but he didn't mind. He remembered his own youth and how his mom had complained of the smell. She'd often soaked his sports socks, knee pads, and jerseys in a special solution to battle the stink. Testosterone was a bitch. "I'm proud of you."

Averting his eyes while still smiling, Beck said, "Thanks."

Saul knew exactly what he was thinking, that his own mom and dad would have been proud too—if they hadn't died a year ago. Since then, Beck had been living with Warren, his father's distant cousin, who already had four kids of his own, three of them girls, and a son only six years old.

Beck didn't exactly fit there with them. Warren tried. Saul gave him a lot of credit for that. Used to being an only kid, Beck wasn't adjusting well. And the things he wanted to do, like this running club, took up time that Warren and his wife didn't have, not with four kids of their own who had hectic schedules.

Saul wanted Beck. He wanted to show him just how special he was. He had the time—or at least, he soon would. "Your dad was a runner."

Nodding, Beck said, "He told me." Slowly, as if he wasn't quite sure what to do, he headed over to his bag and grabbed a water bottle. It was his last event of the meet. Other than a quick chat with the coach coming up soon, he was done for the day.

Here, now, was not the time for heavy talk, yet when Beck dropped down to sit on the grass, Saul joined him. It took him a second to find the words, and then he said, "The club ends soon." So far, Saul had adjusted his schedule to accommodate Beck, but it wasn't an ideal situation. Beck would like other sports. He'd have other pursuits. Something had to give.

"Yeah." Tipping up the bottle, Beck took another long swig.

"Maybe after that, you'd like to come live with me." When the kid looked away, Saul's gut clenched. He didn't say anything else, waiting instead to see where Beck wanted the conversation to go.

"Dad would've liked that, right?"

"I think so." *If only we'd stayed in touch…* "But right now, I'm more concerned with what you want." It sucked so badly that Saul and Kyle had lost track of each other. Years ago they'd been inseparable friends, but then Saul had taken over running the restaurant, and Kyle had married and had a son. Little by little, they'd seen less of each other. Saul remembered Beck as a baby, and then a toddler. He'd held him on his knee, unsure what to do. Back then, he'd been awkward as hell with kids. Actually, he was awkward still—but working through it. He'd seen Beck take his first steps and laughed at how Kyle and his wife had been so proud.

God, he wished he'd taken videos. Lots of them. But he'd never imagined…

When Kyle had named him as an emergency contact, someone to lend a hand if he or his wife had an issue, or later if Beck got sick at school and couldn't reach his parents, it hadn't been a big deal. Never had Saul imagined this scenario, and why would he? Kyle and his wife had been young and healthy, totally dedicated to their son. Yet Kyle had referenced him, and Saul had agreed, and then…they'd grown apart.

Kyle took a job in Ohio. Saul stayed in Indiana, working sixty-hour weeks. Their visits turned into calls, and then dwindled to little more than Christmas cards each year.

Running a hand over his head, Saul felt the weight of Beck's silence. "I should have stayed in touch."

The kid shrugged. "It's okay."

No, it wasn't. For months now, ever since he'd tracked down Warren, Saul had been trying to get better acquainted with Beck-the-teenager versus Beck-the-little-kid. Wasn't easy, because really, what did he know of either? Sure, he'd been both once, but his life in Cemetery with a doting mom and dad was nothing like the past year of Beck's life. He'd lost his parents in a head-on collision, had been uprooted from everything familiar, and his whole life had changed. As the closest family member, Warren had accepted responsibility for Beck, but the arrangement wasn't ideal.

Until Saul had seen a memorial page on Kyle's sparse social media, he hadn't known that he'd lost a friend, or that Beck's life had been turned upside down. Once he'd reconnected and talked to Beck, he'd also realized that *he* wanted to be the one responsible for Beck.

So damn much.

It wasn't that Warren's situation was bad. Not at all. But Beck was often withdrawn, understandably grieving the loss of his parents, and he had to do so in the chaos of a bustling family. It was one more adjustment for him to have to make.

There were other, financial issues to consider, too. Warren and his wife both worked full-time jobs and barely made ends meet. Adding in another child wasn't fair to them, not when Saul was available, and more than ready to step up.

The silence had gone on so long, Saul asked, "Do you want to tell me what you're thinking?"

Beck hesitated, plucking a blade of grass, then shredding it. Finally he said, "I don't want to move, then have to move back."

An understandable concern. "That won't happen." They'd had this discussion before, but Beck's insecurity remained. "If you don't want to live with me, I swear you can tell me that outright. I won't pressure you, and I'll still be here for you as often as I can. Whatever you need. But if you decide you want to move in, that's it. That's where you'll be. I don't know much about this whole...guardian thing." He wouldn't say *father*, because he knew how much Beck loved his dad, and no way would Saul attempt to replace him. "I'll try, though. We'll work things out together. I'll do my best. You have my word, I'd no more willingly give you up than your dad would have."

Beck dropped his head.

Feeling for him, knowing the kid felt conflicted, Saul clasped his shoulder. "You don't have to decide anything right now."

"I want to."

Saul froze, his hand still on Beck's narrow shoulder, feeling both muscle and bone in the physique of the gangly youth. "You want...to decide?"

He looked up, his blue eyes damp, his voice a little broken. "I want to live with you."

God, he hadn't been prepared for the punch of overwhelming relief and stark gratitude. It took Saul a moment to catch his breath, to ensure his own voice was steady.

Then Beck smiled again, and Saul's reciprocal grin took over, one of pure joy and so much more. He hauled Beck in for another tight hug. "That's great. Really great."

Laughing self-consciously, Beck pressed back, glanced around to ensure no one else had seen them, and then swiped at his eyes. "I want to finish up the track-and-field season, then they're having a party. I wouldn't want to go until after that. Is that okay?"

"Of course." At this point, Saul would do about anything to make this kid happy. Quickly, in his head, he calculated. End of September. Time to get him settled before Halloween...and then Thanksgiving.

And Christmas. Holy shit, he'd have a kid for Christmas. That made everything look different. *Better.*

Possibilities opened up, so many that Saul had to deliberately tamp down his excitement so he wouldn't overwhelm Beck. "Until then, you could visit if you'd like. Help pick out stuff for your room. Check out the area. We could get everything ready for the big day. What do you think?"

"I'll have my own room?"

"Heck yes, you will." Right now, that room was just used for storage, but Saul would get it cleaned out first thing. "You okay with that?"

Beck grinned. "No more little kid jumping on my bed? Yeah, I think I can handle that." His humor dimmed. "He's not a bad kid or anything. I didn't mean that."

"I know." Warren's boy was only six and plenty chatty, which would be tough for Beck. "I was an only child, too, and always had my own room. I liked having *my* stuff where *I* wanted it."

"Not that I wasn't grateful..."

No child should have to be grateful for care. With his throat tight again, Saul nudged him. "Hey, I get it, okay? You don't have to explain to me, I swear."

Now a little embarrassed, Beck nodded. "I'll be switching to a new school?"

"Afraid so." Would that be a big problem for him? Duh. Of course it would. He was fourteen, the age of close friendships. Coming to live with Saul would mean uprooting him and starting over again, but Saul had to believe it'd be worth it to Beck. "I know you'll miss your buddies, but we can't do a two-hour drive each way, every day, right?"

"No, it's okay." Beck surveyed the kids in the running club, most of them hanging with other guys—a few with girls. "It's not like it used to be."

Saul had no idea what he meant by that. "Like it used to be…at your old school?" *With your mom and dad still around.*

"Yeah." Squinting against the sun, he looked up at Saul. "I don't have friends over or anything. Not anymore. I'm not tight with anyone here."

Wow, that hit him hard. Saul wasn't sure what to say—but then Beck cracked a smile.

"It's all right." This time, Beck nudged him. "No big deal, okay?"

"Did I look like a sad sack?"

"Yeah, you did." Still with a small grin, Beck added, "You're funny sometimes."

Only sometimes? Saul supposed that was better than being a clown—or gloomy. Now that he'd been teased with Beck's cooperation and the possibility of making it all official, and seeing Beck act so natural with him, Saul wanted it all even more. "We can hit up the beach a few times before the move if you want. You'll meet some of the local kids there." Not that Saul knew any of them well, but they came into the restaurant with their parents to eat, so he'd met them. "I checked on the sports programs. They've got a lot of options."

"Swimming? I wanted to try that."

"I'm not sure, but since there's a lake, there should

be, right? If not, we'll start a club." That earned him another smile, so Saul continued. "You can hang out at the restaurant, too. Kids your age are always in and out."

Frowning, Beck said, "You work a lot, don't you?"

Beck had probably heard them talking. Warren had worried about Saul's hours, whether or not he'd have enough time to properly supervise a teenager. It'd be an adjustment, especially with his feelings for Emily, but he was determined to make it work. Priorities, he'd decided. Emily and Beck were top priorities.

And he was okay with that.

After so many years of having clear-cut ideas of his future, everything was different now. Emily, Beck, that elusive something his folks had and Mabel and Sullivan shared. The bond that went right to the core of a person.

He wanted *that*. And he knew who he wanted it with.

"You said I could visit." Beck kept his tone cautious. "Maybe for a few days? Then I'd have more time to check it out."

"Want to try it before the move, huh? That makes sense to me."

"It's not that," Beck denied in a rush. "I like the idea of moving, for good I mean, but I was thinking about your restaurant." He hedged, back to picking blades of grass and avoiding Saul's gaze. "I wouldn't mind a job. You know, making some money of my own. I don't know how young you hire, but—"

"I'll give you an allowance," Saul decided out loud. "Plus you could do chores around the house. I think you already cut the grass and stuff?"

"Yeah, and I don't mind doing that still, but I was thinking it'd be cool to work with you, too. Like, even if I just washed dishes, or swept the floor or something. Whatever you needed."

The idea had merit. "I did the same with my father when I was your age." And yeah, he'd also enjoyed having money of his own—wages that he'd earned. It had been a great life lesson for him. Not that he'd overdo it with Beck. Thinking it through, he decided that as his father had done with him, he'd limit the time Beck spent there so he'd still have time for school stuff and friends...

Beck started to stand. "Sorry, I shouldn't have pushed—"

Realizing the kid had misunderstood, Saul caught his shoulder. "It's a great idea."

"Yeah?"

"Definitely. I'd love spending more time with you, and you'd meet more people that way. How about we talk with Warren tonight, see when it'd be a good time for you to come over for a few days, and then go from there. Deal?"

"Sure, thanks." Looking genuinely pleased, Beck pushed to his feet. "The coach is waving me over. Might take a few minutes."

"I'm not going anywhere." Now or ever. "Take your time."

"Thanks."

Watching Beck jog away, Saul checked the time again. Emily was off work now. Once he got Beck back to Warren, would it be too late to call her?

He needed to tell her about Beck, the sooner the better. He'd hoped to cement things with her first, before dropping a teenager into the mix, but it had taken longer than he'd expected to get things going with Emily. Now suddenly Beck's timeline was speeding up.

It wouldn't be the easiest way to start a serious romantic relationship, but it wasn't like Beck was a little kid who needed constant supervision. What he needed most now was unconditional love, total acceptance, and guaranteed stability.

Saul intended to give all of that to him, and then some. Even better, he thought Emily would feel the same. Never had he met a more caring person.

He needed to make her understand, though, that he'd fallen for her long before he even knew about Beck. The last thing he'd want is for Emily to feel used.

WHEN EMILY WALKED into the Pit Stop, the restaurant was hopping. Amazing that Mila was able to have a day off, but the current waitstaff seemed to be keeping up. One young woman balanced an enormous tray full of drinks, while another bustled around clearing empty tables.

Other than on special occasions, the Pit Stop was a "seat yourself" establishment, but the only table available would seat six, so Emily didn't want to take it. Instead, she sat at the bar, something she rarely did, but hey, this was another thing she could check off her list. Not super-daring, but she'd count it anyway.

The young man behind the bar, who she knew was seasonal help for the summer, greeted her with a smile. "Hi. I'm Wheeler, and I'll be helping you tonight. Do you need to see a menu?"

She didn't—she knew that menu by heart—but she did wonder if Saul was busy. Since she didn't see him, she assumed he was. He easily filled every single duty depending on the need. On many occasions, Emily had watched him take orders, bring food, and clear tables. A few times, he'd been the cook and even cleaned the dishes.

"Thanks, Wheeler. I'll take an iced tea with extra lemon wedges, and the chicken salad on a croissant."

"Perfect for a hot day. I'll get that right out to you." He set a glass of water on a small square napkin in front of her, and disappeared through swinging doors to the kitchen.

Emily waited not-so-patiently while still looking around for Saul.

The second Wheeler brought her order, she asked, "I guess Saul is busy?" Before he could reply, she added, "We're friends. I only wanted to speak to him for a second."

"Sorry, but he's off today and tomorrow."

Off? Today *and tomorrow*? Emily stared into Wheeler's dark eyes and wondered if she'd misunderstood. "He's not working?"

"He said something came up. I'm filling in for him. He'll be back on Saturday, though."

Off Thursday and Friday…but clearly not interested in seeing her. Well, now she didn't even want the sandwich, but damned if she'd show it. "Thank you. I'll catch him later, then."

Wheeler's smile warmed. "You're the flower lady, right? Emily…?"

"Lucretia—a hard last name to forget. I own the flower shop, yes."

"Mila said you gave her the flowers for that stunt with the mannequin. We all enjoyed it."

Her return smile came naturally—it always did when she chatted with people. "I'm glad to hear it. You're working here for the summer, right?"

"Until classes start up again, yeah."

"What's your major?" Pretending she wasn't embarrassed by her assumptions about Saul, she bit into her sandwich. As always, it was delicious.

"IT. My dad has a business and I'll become an IT manager, but he doesn't cut us any slack. He asks the same of his sons that he does of his employees, so even though I know the business…" He shrugged.

"You have brothers?"

"Two younger. Mom passed away a few years ago."

The food stuck in her throat. Taking a quick drink of tea and then patting her mouth with the napkin, Emily said, "I'm so sorry."

"Thanks. Maybe it was easier because she and Dad split years ago, and she moved to California. I didn't see her that often growing up."

"That must have been very difficult for your father."

"If it was, he hid it well. Dad's been great." Suddenly, Wheeler looked astounded. He even took a step back. "I have no idea why I'm unloading all that on you. I'm sorry."

To put him at ease, Emily smiled again.

"It's that," he said in amused accusation, pointing at her mouth. "Something about the way you smile. Makes me feel like I've known you forever."

Emily laughed. "I hear that from a lot of people, but then, I love learning about others." She took another drink. "It's much easier to focus on others than on myself."

For another three seconds, Wheeler just stared at her. "You missed your calling, flower lady."

"Oh?"

"Should've been a counselor or a life coach, or something. Maybe even a bartender."

Emily wasn't awkward with him, not the way she often was with Saul. Maybe because Wheeler was so much younger, closer to Gentry's age. Whereas Gentry was dark with gray eyes, Wheeler was blond, with dark brown eyes. He also had very nice shoulders. It struck her that her more intimate interest in Saul might have been what made her nervous.

She smiled at Wheeler again. "Selling flowers is similar, in a way. People often buy them for special occasions, right? Happy times, and not so happy. To celebrate or to mourn. Either way, it's often emotional."

"So you hear a lot of stories?"

"I hear about people's lives." Their loves and their losses. "I enjoy it."

"I can see that you do. Amazing."

"Why is it amazing?"

He laughed. "Most people prefer to talk about themselves."

"I don't." Overall, her life was boring. *But I'm changing that.*

Bracing his forearms on the bar so he faced her at eye level, he said, "Maybe I'll stop in sometime and buy a few flowers."

"We're open nine to six, Monday through Saturday."

After a slight pause, his mouth tipped in a crooked grin. Then he straightened. Though Emily had no idea what had amused him this time, she grinned as well.

Wheeler really was a handsome young man, plus he was friendly and personable, very genuine. She wondered why he hadn't gotten closer to Mila, then decided to fish a little. "I think Mila is close to your age."

"A year younger," he said, then he shook his head while still smiling. "Sorry, let me check on these other customers."

As he went down the bar, tending to two women,

a guy and his kid, and a couple at the end, Emily finished off her sandwich. Since Saul wasn't around, she decided to call her aunt.

Mabel answered on the fourth ring. "Hi, honey."

"You sound breathless." So that she could hear around the noise in the restaurant, Emily held the phone close to her ear and covered the other with her free hand. "Did I catch you at a bad time?"

"Of course not. I'm just trailing Sullivan during his PT." In a hushed but excited whisper, Mabel said, "They have him doing stairs today!"

With the opposite reaction, Emily whispered, "*Stairs*?" But they didn't even have stairs in their house! "That sounds dangerous."

"He's doing great. I explained that our house is a ranch style, but they said he needed to be able to navigate a few stairs, like stepping up to the front porch, or stepping down into the garage. Or even the doctor's office that has two steps at the entry. He'll have a walker for a while—and he *hates* it. Says it makes him look like a feeble old man."

Emily chuckled with her. "Oh, Aunt. I worry about you both."

Going serious now, Mabel said, "Please don't. We really are fine. And guess what? Dr. Randall said we can come home tomorrow."

Panic straightened her spine. So soon? Yes, Emily knew they wanted out of the hospital, and she absolutely understood, but there was a certain security to having them in a place where they were closely watched.

"Emily," Mabel said. "Take a breath."

Dutifully, Emily did just that, and choked a little in the process. She hadn't worked out *anything* yet. Her aunt and uncle should have been her top priority, and instead she'd been selfishly focusing on a change for herself and mooning over Saul.

Somehow she'd figure it out. All of it. "What time are they springing you tomorrow?" She'd be there to get them, of course.

"I won't know until Dr. Randall comes in. Sometimes she's here at ten, and other times not until the afternoon." Oh-so-casually, Mabel said, "I thought I'd call for a taxi."

"A taxi?" She had to be kidding.

Wheeler returned and, with a smile, removed her empty plate. She put a hand over her tea glass to let him know she didn't need a refill.

He slid the bill in front of her and whispered, "If you need anything, anything at all, just let me know."

After mouthing *thank you* to him, Emily said to her aunt, "I'll 100 percent be there to drive you both home, no arguments." It'd give her a chance to discuss the future with them—a future that was still very uncertain. "Maybe as soon as Angela comes in, you could give me a call. I can drive over while they're getting Uncle Sullivan's discharge papers together."

"I know the shop is open on Fridays."

"Yes, but Gentry will be there. He's a dream employee. He can handle anything, believe me."

Mabel laughed. "I'm glad he's working out for you, but I don't think your Saul appreciates how much you admire Gentry."

She scowled. "He's not *my* Saul. Do you know, he asked for my schedule, which I shared with him, but now he's off today and tomorrow and not a word to me."

After a long pause, her aunt said, "Maybe he already had plans."

"He told me he did, remember? He said the rest of his week was packed, and I wrongly assumed that meant he'd be working. But two days off in a row and he couldn't at least call me? Besides, Wheeler said something came up, so that doesn't sound like already set plans to me."

"Wheeler?" her aunt asked, trying to keep up.

"An employee here."

"Here?" Mabel asked. "Where are you?"

"At the restaurant." She lowered her voice. "It was so embarrassing. I asked to see Saul, only to be told he wasn't around."

"Honey, his interest was undeniable, so don't start doubting him or yourself. Just ask him why—"

"That's what I was going to do," she explained. "But I can't when he's not here." She looked up just in time to realize Wheeler was staring at her, looking a little appalled. As soon as their gazes met, he ducked into the kitchen again. Great. He'd probably tell Saul what she said, and it wasn't like she and Saul had anything official going on.

"Crap."

"Now what?" Mabel asked.

She was awful, that's what. The last thing she should be doing was stressing her aunt about her trivial non-relationship issues. Feeling ashamed for pivoting to herself again, Emily shook her head. "Nothing. I think I was overheard, that's all." Firmly planting a smile on her face, she added, "I'll be there tomorrow, Aunt Mabel. I *want* to be there, okay? Just call me once Angela is ready to release him. In the meantime, is there anything you need me to do at your house? Maybe pick up fresh milk, or get anything special that Uncle Sullivan might like? I could run over and dust, since you've been gone a few days. Maybe change out the bedding for you? Catch up on any laundry or—"

"You listen to me, Emily Lucretia. You will *not* waste your time fussing at my house. What you *will* do is call Saul. Tell him your concerns and see what he has to say." After that strict edict, Mabel's voice softened. "Honey, don't screw this up. I know you're uncertain about relationships, and I know you don't need one. You're the most independent, capable woman I know."

*Awww.* The praise felt like a warm hug. "Thank you."

"But Saul is wonderful, and I'm absolutely certain there's just a misunderstanding."

Wishing she was as sure as her aunt, Emily said, "I want to concentrate on you and Uncle Sullivan, so—"

"So," Mabel said, interrupting, "promise me you'll talk to him."

"Aunt…"

"Promise me, Emily. Right now." The stern voice softened. "You deserve him. You deserve everything. Now promise me."

God, she loved this woman. Smiling for real now, Emily said, "I promise."

"Thank you."

Knowing just how lucky she was, Emily said, "I love you, Aunt Mabel."

"I love you, too, honey. See you tomorrow."

# CHAPTER EIGHT

ONCE WHEELER RETURNED, looking a little awkward, at least to Emily's watchful eyes, she thanked him, paid her bill, and left him a nice tip. She started to go, but instead she turned and said, "You overheard me."

For a second, he froze, then admitted sheepishly, "Yeah, I did. Sorry. I didn't realize—that is, I knew Saul was interested in someone, but I didn't know you were her."

None of that made sense, causing Emily's eyebrows to arch in curiosity. "I'm who?"

Even more uncomfortable, Wheeler glanced around, then leaned over the bar to ensure they had privacy. "I heard him talking to Mila about the flowers and the mannequin and stuff. She teased him that maybe he'd get a few new dates because of it—I mean, women were all over him about it—but Saul said he was already caught and other women didn't interest him. They joked back and forth, but I understood that he's already seeing someone."

Ohmigod. "*Who*?" she demanded, overwhelmed with a sense of betrayal whether she had the right or not.

"Um…" Wheeler looked at her askance. "He obviously meant you."

"Me? Oh." But seriously… "Maybe he didn't."

"He said his only holdup was meshing schedules.

You said he asked about your schedule." As if that was all the proof he needed, Wheeler stated, "It's you."

It was her. *So where the heck is he?*

Emily didn't ask Wheeler. It wouldn't be right to grill him, to possibly put him in the middle and make him even more uncomfortable. "Well, we'll see, I guess." Hoping she looked more confident than she felt, she composed her features. "I should get going. I've taken up too much of your time."

"No, it's all good. I enjoyed chatting with you anyway."

Anyway? She didn't understand that, either, but only nodded. "I enjoyed it as well. Take care." With her thoughts buzzing, she headed out to her car. Home again, to…what? Watch television? Sit alone? Mope about Saul? Worry about her aunt and uncle?

No, she wouldn't.

She thought of all the things she hadn't done…like walking on the beach. It was right *there*. A short jaunt from the restaurant. She could even hear the gulls and smell the scent of the lake water.

The night of the wedding, she'd been tempted. The quiet rush of the waves, the reflection of the moon on the water, the remaining warmth of the sand… But there'd been so much to do with packing up her supplies. And then she'd been tempted by Kathleen.

At least that was something new. She *had* taken Kathleen to Saul's restaurant. Bolstered by that, she figured she should continue trying new things.

Determined, she moved her car away from the restaurant so she wasn't taking up a spot for dining customers, and drove the very short distance to the parking area near the lake. It was less than two minutes. Already her heart beat faster.

She parked near the sand, removed her shoes, put her cell phone in one pocket, her key fob in the other, and hid her purse under the front seat. After closing and locking the car doors, she headed for the shore.

Good Lord, the place was still packed.

Everywhere she looked, people were sprawled in the sand, some swimming, others laughing.

Her heart sank a little. This was not the peaceful walk on the beach she'd anticipated.

Well, too bad. She'd do it anyway.

After all, she was already barefoot.

"Emily?"

Glancing up, she saw Gentry just about to get into his truck. It was obvious he'd been swimming. His hair was mussed as if he'd been in and out of the water and then had dried in the sun. There was fresh color on his face, too. He looked healthy and happy, and she wanted to cheer. She'd had a feeling that he and Mila would do well together.

Closing his truck door, he jogged over to her, eyed her bare feet, and smiled. "Whatcha up to, Emily?"

As if he didn't already know. "I wanted to walk along the beach."

He smiled. "Sounds like a plan."

"It's awfully busy, though."

"There are quieter stretches."

"Oh?" She glanced around. "Where's Mila?" Had the two of them found a quieter stretch?

Shoving his hands in his pockets, he said, "She just left. I was about to do the same."

"You enjoyed yourself." It wasn't a question. She

could see that he had, and it filled her with satisfaction. Gentry deserved it, and more.

"Yeah, actually I did."

His tone made her laugh. "That surprises you?"

His own slow grin tipped one side of his mouth. "Guess it does."

Emily touched his arm. "I'm glad," she said softly.

Gentry looked out over the beach. "Do you want to be alone, or is it okay if I walk with you?"

The offer relieved her. "I'd enjoy the company." It'd be a good way to get her mind off things. "I went to the restaurant to see Saul, but Wheeler said he was off— today and tomorrow! Do you believe that?"

"Your uncle was recently hurt. Maybe something like that came up for Saul."

"No, Wheeler said Saul had plans."

Gentry frowned. "Just how long did you chat with Wheeler?"

Long enough to get disappointed. Emily waved off his question. "The point is, I'm here now, and I want to do this whole walking-on-the-beach thing. Having you for company will be a bonus."

Gentry eyed her a second longer, then nodded. "Great. We can talk about your offer."

"My offer to make you manager?" Her steps faltered. "You're not going to say no, are you?" She'd already been counting on his agreement.

"Pretty sure I'm going to say yes—but there are a few things I need to tell you first."

Did that mean he planned to open up? "Interesting. Well then, lead the way." If he led, she could just fol- low, since she wasn't sure yet where they were going. To the beach, yes, but away from everyone else. He led her over thick grasses, beneath a few trees, and past rocks.

"Careful where you step."

He wore shoes. Apparently, she should have as well, at least until they reached their spot.

With another small smile, he explained, "Mila brought a golf cart, and we rode farther down."

"For privacy?" she asked, intrigued.

He nodded. "In the main area, there are too many bodies and too much noise."

"Exactly." It pleased her to know she wasn't the only one who felt that way.

"We won't go as far." He glanced back at her. "You don't mind sitting where there are pebbles and some weeds, do you?"

"Nope." It wouldn't be the same as walking in the sand, but she could see the sun lowering in the sky over the lake, smell the freshness of the air, and feel the slight breeze. And as Gentry had promised, they could escape the crowds.

As they continued on, going farther than she'd expected, she started to sweat a little, and that was disconcerting, until she firmly decided not to care. This was her night for a new experience, and she wouldn't let anything, not even sweat, steal the pleasure of it. She'd have fun, and Saul could just keep his blasted secrets.

A few minutes later, Gentry gestured to a small cove that was more pebbles than sand, with silky green algae floating in the water like a woman's long hair. "Will this spot do?"

Emily blinked twice. Rocks littered the rough shoreline, making her uncertain about what might lurk among them. Snakes? Crawdads? She knew the lake had them, but then, she avoided things like that. By rote alone, her smile appeared, and she declared with forced enthusiasm, "I love it."

He laughed. "Fibber. Don't worry, we won't stay here long, and I didn't think you planned to swim in your clothes."

No, definitely not. "I've never swum in the lake. Isn't that odd?"

"Maybe a little," he said, teasing. Then he patted a large flat rock. "You can sit here."

"Thank you." Carefully, she perched on it, and found it warm to the touch. She opened her palms beside her hips, and despite her reserve, she started to relax. The sky was so blue today and not a cloud in sight. "It's a beautiful day, isn't it?"

"Was, yeah. It's evening now. The sun will set in a few more minutes. Have you ever watched it sink into the water?"

"A few times. Most recently, for Yardley's wedding. The colors just seemed to spread out." A thought occurred to her and she asked, "Will it get dark quickly here? And if so, are there…" She glanced around the ground nervously. "Insects and stuff?"

"I won't let anything get you," Gentry said with a grin. "But I guess that's my cue to get on with it."

"Okay." With a firm nod, Emily prepared herself. If he wanted more money, or better benefits, she'd see what she could do. At this point, she was convinced Gentry was the man for the job. "I'm ready."

"That's my line." He sat on the ground comfortably, forearms draped over his knees, his gaze on the lake. "I'd like the job, but you need to know more about me first, so hear me out."

Oh wow, this sounded serious. Emily forgot all about the heat and snakes and the sweat on the back of her neck. In her heart, she knew whatever Gentry told her, it wouldn't matter. She trusted her judgment, and she believed Gentry was a very good man—regardless of whatever he had to say.

She smiled to encourage him. "Take all the time you need."

That made him scowl, and then he started talking.

DRIVING AWAY FROM Warren's house, Saul was gratified with how things were going. They had a plan. Things were moving along. And best of all, Beck had smiled while seeing him off. Saul could tell he was already anticipating the visit—not as much as Saul, but still, the kid was finally excited about something.

Definite progress.

With everyone's agreement, Saul would return to pick up Beck from school next Friday, and he'd stay until Saturday evening. Beck's first sleepover. Somehow he had to make it special, and yet easy and familiar.

That meant he wouldn't be able to work the weekend at the restaurant as he usually did, but he'd figure it out. He could put in Friday morning and part of the afternoon, and he'd— The ringing of his cell phone interrupted his thoughts.

He saw it was Wheeler and hoped there wasn't a problem. He still had a drive ahead of him before he'd reach Cemetery. Using hands-free calling, he answered with, "Wheeler. What's up?"

"Not much, just something I thought you might want to know. And I'll start by apologizing, but I didn't know, or I wouldn't have said anything or flirted with her."

Watching the traffic and frowning over that non-sense string of words, Saul got his biggest worry out of the way first. "Is something wrong at the restaurant?"

"No. No, it's fine. Sorry."

"Is anyone hurt?"

"No. Man, I'm messing this up." Wheeler blew out a breath. "The flower lady was in here."

"Emily?" Just saying her name aloud felt good. He'd missed her like crazy. And now she'd been at the restaurant when he wasn't there.

"Yeah, her. She's really easy to talk to, and there's something about her smile."

At that, Saul frowned. "What did you do?"

"I was flirting a little—but still working."

Though he already knew, Saul asked, "Flirting with...?"

"Emily. The flower lady. Only I didn't know she was the one you're interested in. She is the one, right?"

"Definitely the one." Saul should have spelled that out to her already. Hell, the whole town needed to know. If only there were more hours in the day.

"Saul? I'm sorry man, really."

It was times like this when Saul felt old. Had he ever stumbled over his words so badly? No doubt. Already knowing Emily hadn't flirted back, Saul said, "It's fine. Just tell me what happened."

"She came in and asked to talk to you, but I thought she was just a customer, so I told her you were off today and tomorrow. She tried to hide it, but I could tell she was irked."

Yeah, he could imagine. "Define *irked*."

"I don't know. Her smile was different. She called

someone and was kind of complaining— Look, I tried to cover. I told her I didn't realize she was the one."

Saul easily envisioned how that went. "Did she even know you were flirting with her?"

"Didn't seem to," Wheeler said, his tone lighter now that he realized Saul wasn't bothered by any of it. "I asked about stopping by her shop to see her, and she gave me her business hours, like she thought I only wanted an appointment to get flowers." He went on with, "Dude, I'm not really used to the brush-off, you know?"

No, he probably wasn't. Wheeler was a big, good-looking kid who stayed fit. "She's out of your league, Wheeler."

"I found that out all on my own," he replied with a laugh. "But hey, I thought you might want to call and explain or something, since she did seem put out that you *hadn't* called. Her words, not mine."

"She said that to you?"

"To the person she spoke with on the phone, but I heard her say it."

Probably her aunt. "Yeah, I'll call her. Thanks for the heads-up."

"No problem."

Before he called Emily, though… "Do you have plans next weekend? I need someone Friday evening and part of the day Saturday. I know, it's a weekend and that sucks, but I'll make it up to you."

"Friday isn't a problem, but I already have plans for Saturday. If it's important, I'll see if I can rearrange things."

"Let me think on it first." Maybe he could get Mila to cover for him. She was picking things up fast. He really needed a permanent manager, someone he trusted so he could be off without concern, but usually those who hired on were seasonal help only. He had a feeling Mila might stay past the summer though, so he was working on her. "Thanks, man. I'll let you go."

After ending the call, Saul wondered if it would be better to wait until he was in Cemetery to call Emily, or get to it right away. He settled on waiting while he sorted his thoughts. He didn't want to blunder, say the wrong thing, or jump the gun and make her leery of getting more involved.

They'd known each other a long time, but their relationship was different now, and he realized that there was a lot about Emily he didn't yet know. She was all the things he already loved—and yet more. He checked the time. It was still early enough that she wouldn't be going to bed anytime soon.

Somehow he had to figure out how to tell her what she meant to him, what he wanted now and in the future.

And then he had to tell her that he came with a kid.

ALWAYS, FROM THE day Gentry had met Emily, she'd been easy to talk to, probably because he never got into anything too heavy. Nothing that would make her like him less or mistrust him. He sat there on the rocky ground, the lowering sun hot on his face, and tried to find the words that would tell her who he really was… and wouldn't cause her to lose her respect for him.

The respect meant a lot to him. It was important. He felt it from her, and cherished it like the greatest gift.

"Gentry." Her small hand settled on his shoulder. "Let me make this easier."

He'd like to see how she'd accomplish that. Right now, he didn't see a way.

"Have you murdered anyone?"

*"What?"* Twisting to frown at her, he said, "No." She nodded as if she'd known the answer—and of course, she had. Emily wouldn't hire anyone she suspected could do such a thing.

"Robbed a bank?"

Damn it, now he knew what she was doing. "No, I haven't killed anyone, or robbed a bank, or stolen a car, or kidnapped a kid. Nothing like that."

Her hand stayed there on him, her gentleness making him yearn for more. Not the same yearning he'd had for Mila. This wasn't sexual, but in many ways it was stronger.

She gave him a squeeze before releasing him. "So you have a few flaws. I consider that a bonus for an employee and friend. We're both now, right?"

He nodded. "We're both."

"I'm glad. There's something that's worrying you, though. Something from your past? Whatever it is, Gentry, you don't have to tell me, but I can also promise that if you do tell me, I won't judge you, and in the end it won't matter."

Oh, it'd matter—if not to her, then at least to him. And who knew how the rest of the town would feel? Tired of trying to sort it out, he stared out at the lake and said, "My mom had me when she was fourteen." He felt more than saw Emily's shock. "Yeah, a kid raising a kid. Though she didn't do much raising, and I can't really blame her. Mostly she left me for my grandpa to deal with."

"Your father...?"

"Never knew him. She wasn't sure, or she wouldn't say, so he wasn't, and never will be, in the picture." Talking about it sucked, so he needed to hurry things along. "My grandma had already passed away, too. I know my grandpa had his hands full. According to him, once my mom hooked up with a boy, that was that. I believe he tried, but there was no keeping her home."

"Even after you were born?"

"Especially after I was born. There were times she'd move back in, but never for long. Where we lived…it was small like Cemetery, but that's where the similarities ended." To him, Cemetery epitomized kindness. Friendliness. Family. "She stayed in the same town. Sometimes I'd see her in the grocery store, or she'd show up at the school plastered." He rubbed his face, images crowding his mind.

Emily's hand returned to his shoulder, and honest to God, it helped. He covered her hand with his own, not because he wanted her pity, but because he appreciated her so much.

"I turned into a jerk. Kids would say something, and instead of arguing or ignoring them, I'd punch."

"I probably shouldn't say this, but yay you. Kids can be so hateful sometimes."

That made Gentry laugh. "Believe me, I was worse. I got used to being in trouble. And I hated her." That was the worst part. Hating his mother for something that had mostly been out of her control. What chance had she had, getting pregnant so young, raised by a widowed dad? "Maybe if Mom had had someone like you—"

"Like me?" she asked in surprise.

"Someone understanding and nice down to the core. It might have made a difference. All she had was

Grandpa, and he had to work when he was raising me—and she had the judgment of the town. They called us trash. Grandpa couldn't or wouldn't hide his shame. Whenever she was around, they shouted at each other nonstop. He'd tell her to get out, or she'd scream that she was leaving." And it was like he hadn't even been there. "More often than not, I just avoided her."

After several heartbeats of silence, Emily quietly asked, "Your grandfather wasn't always like that?"

He knew exactly what Emily needed to know, so he put her mind at ease. "With me, he was different. He lectured me a lot, and more. The man believed in discipline."

"Oh, Gentry."

"Nope, don't do that. He never gave me anything I didn't deserve. What matters is that he was there, you know? I could get into trouble at school or be accused of stealing a candy bar—sometimes because I had, sometimes when I hadn't—and Grandpa was always there for me. He fought with the town, the police, the school and his own daughter to protect me. Finally, when I barely got my sorry butt out of high school, I knew I had to get it together, so I tried to change."

Softly, Emily said, "Good for you."

He glanced at her and saw the slight, proud curve of her mouth. "Thanks. I managed, I really did—only no one believed it. The whole town claimed I was the same as my mother, even though she was arrested every other week, and I'd never been. She vandalized property, stole from people, and everyone assumed I was helping her." In truth, he'd barely seen her. The older she got, the less he saw her.

"Maybe that's why your grandfather didn't want her

around. She was out of his reach, but he still had faith in you."

Faith.

Yeah, his grandpa had always trusted him, and now Emily did, too.

"After several odd jobs, I got employed at the manufacturing plant right out of town. I made enough that I could have lived on my own, but I stayed with Grandpa."

"He wanted you there," Emily accurately guessed.

"Said he did. He was getting older and I didn't want him trying to cut his own grass, or do repairs and stuff. Plus..." Gentry chewed his lower lip while he stewed over admitting it all. "I didn't trust my mom. Everyone knew she was living with a really rough guy. Whenever I'd see them around town, he'd paw her in front of me and laugh about it."

Still in that understanding way of hers, Emily said, "It was smart to stay with your grandfather, then. Smart and loyal."

"And cheap," he joked, though he'd paid his grandfather rent. "In the end..." His throat squeezed and his eyes burned. "In the end, it wasn't my mother who got to him, but his heart."

Leaving her seat on the rock, Emily moved to sit beside him, her arm around his waist, her head against his shoulder.

Gentry let his cheek rest on her crown. Her hair was baby soft and smelled of flowers. That almost made him smile. The flower lady—smelling like flowers. It seemed appropriate. "I went to bed and he was there, and when I woke the next morning, he was gone from a heart attack."

"I'm so sorry."

Gentry nodded. Everyone said they were sorry, but he sensed Emily really was. "He looked so small, when I'd never thought of him that way. We had our routine for mornings. He always got up before I left the house. He'd grouse his way into the kitchen, and I'd pour him a cup of coffee. We'd share a few words, then say good-bye." Memories flooded in, most of them good, sitting with his grandpa, both of them early morning quiet, still sleepy. Comfortable. That's what he missed the most—the comfort of the familiar. Except that he was comfortable now, here, with Emily and the town and his job.

"I like routines, too," Emily said. "There's a type of security in knowing what to expect and what to do."

See, she always got it. She got *him*. "When the morning dragged on and Grandpa hadn't come down yet, I went to check on him. I think part of me knew, but still, I figured out all this stuff I'd say, teasing him about sleeping in…"

Emily scrunched closer, as if she thought her nearness could somehow heal his hurt, and it did help. Likely more than she'd ever realize.

"He left his house to me, Emily. His savings, his truck, everything. I hadn't known. I didn't even realize he had much savings. We lived in such a terrible area, ate mostly home-cooked meals, stuff like that. I thought he was broke, though he wouldn't discuss it much with me, even when I tried to give him extra money. He'd say no, I'd insist, and then he'd leave it on the counter."

"That wasn't what he wanted from you."

No, it wasn't. Gentry swallowed hard. "What he wanted was for me to be different from my mom. He never said that outright, but I know he thought I was heading down that path, and it worried him." It was why he'd changed—for his grandpa. Not for himself, sure as hell not for his mom. "Later, when I was making decent money, I offered to get us a better place, but he told me he was too tired to move."

"If his heart was already bad, he could have suffered from exhaustion."

"Maybe. Mostly, I think he stayed because Mom was there, and it was the only way he could keep an eye on her. They were always at odds. *Always*. But I think if she'd tried to get her life straightened out, he would have helped her."

"I think so, too," Emily said firmly, even though she didn't know his grandfather or his mother. "If you believe it, then I'm sure it's true."

Gentry loved her for saying that. "Mom didn't show at the funeral. It was just me and a few of Grandpa's neighbors. I found her later, after I got his house and most of his stuff sold, and gave her some cash. Enough that she could start over if she wanted." He knew she wouldn't. "Then I left. Got in the truck with a box of memories and drove away."

"To Cemetery," Emily said. "To *me*." She straightened, but only so she could face him, and he saw that her eyes were damp, the tip of her nose red. When she spoke, her voice was scratchy with emotion but still strong. "You're like family to me, Gentry. We haven't known each other that long, but I feel it anyway."

"Yeah," he said softly, because he wasn't sure what else to say. "That'd make me the black sheep of the family."

She surprised him by slugging his shoulder. "Don't you *ever* say anything that dumb, Gentry McAdams. I'm so proud of you. With everything you've gone through, you're still one of the nicest, smartest, hardest-working people I know. Whether you continue to work for me or not, we are friends for life, and I won't let you go."

Relief crept in, crowding out the disbelief, followed by a slow smile. Had he really thought Emily would kick him to the curb? No, but doubts were a terrible thing, and he'd been living with them for most of his life.

He drew Emily in for a hug to his heart, briefly squeezing her tighter than he should have, given how she wheezed. Setting her back, he said, "Thank you."

"Thank *you*. Now." She tugged at the hem of her shirt and straightened her ponytail. "About being my manager."

"I didn't tell anyone where I was going." There was no one to tell—no one who cared. "Doesn't mean my mom won't track me down and show up here someday. With social media and stuff, it's not that hard to find people."

"If she does, we'll greet her together and see how it goes."

Together. It was hard to believe he wasn't alone anymore. After losing his grandpa, he'd felt so isolated, from the world and from his feelings. He'd wanted to keep it that way. How else could he leave his past in the past? But he hadn't counted on Cemetery.

He hadn't counted on Emily.

Or Mila, who—now that he didn't feel the need to keep his distance—sure had his attention.

Gentry cupped Emily's face in his hands. "Promise me, if she ever trips into town, you won't see her without me. She's dangerous, Emily, and the guy she lives with is a hundred times worse."

"I promise."

He studied her, decided she was sincere, and leaned back again. "I want the job."

Squealing in excitement, Emily said, "You don't know what this means to me! I get to keep you, I can update the company, and I can *finally* have some 'me' time."

She made it sound like he was doing her favor. Gentry knew the truth. He'd owe Emily for the rest of his life, and since all she wanted was his friendship, he'd happily pay. She was about to say more when the phone in her pocket buzzed with an incoming call. She jumped several inches.

"Good God, that startled me," she said while retrieving the phone. "I usually have it my purse, not against my backside."

"Emily Lucretia said 'backside.' Will the wonders of this day never end?"

Grinning, she leaned into his shoulder again and then glanced at the screen. "It's Saul."

She hesitated, but Gentry didn't know why. "Answer it."

"I bet Wheeler told on me and now Saul will have some excuse for not contacting me." She wrinkled her nose. "It makes me look desperate."

"Not even. He cares or he wouldn't be calling." Gentry tugged on her ponytail. "Answer it."

"Oh, all right. I suppose I should hear what he has to say, even though I'm already embarrassed." Bracing herself with a big breath, she answered pleasantly, "Saul, hello."

Well, wonder of wonders, Emily sounded completely composed, not a bit of uncertainty coming through.

What a fraud she was, Gentry thought with amused affection. Emily always seemed so serene and in charge, she'd had him fooled—but he was willing to bet Saul had already seen through her facade, and the dude would have a very good reason for why he'd let so many days pass without talking to her.

Emily was too special to ignore.

Saul would have his work cut out for him. Gentry almost felt bad for him.

Thinking she might want privacy for the call, he started to stand, but Emily curled her hand around his arm and held on, a silent bid for him to stay.

And so he did. Pretty sure he'd do anything for her.

Like she'd said, they were now as good as family.

EMILY WAS RELIEVED that Gentry stayed put. For one thing, it was getting dark and she could hear insects, and for another, she felt ridiculously unsure of herself. With their new, more familial understanding, his company bolstered her.

"Are you busy?" Saul asked.

"Just sitting on the beach with Gentry." She kept her tone deliberately neutral so he wouldn't know how his lack of attention had bothered her. She was too proud to start looking needy.

There was a long, low, muffled growl before Saul asked, "You and Gentry?"

"He had a date with Mila." Her chin lifted, and knowing he might question her, she fessed up first. "I went to the restaurant to see you, but you weren't there, so I decided to take a walk on the beach." There. Take that. "But I ran into Gentry. Mila had just left, so he's keeping me company."

Gentry, who could only hear her side of the conversation, silently laughed.

She lifted her brows at him, but he shook his head as if she wouldn't understand. And she didn't.

To Saul, she asked, "Did you need something?"

At that, Gentry started snickering—not so silently.

"Tell him I said to shut up."

"I will not," she snapped. Snapped! Good grief. She never snapped at anyone, so she quickly explained, "He's like a best friend, and he'll soon be my manager." *Because I thought I needed more time off for you.* But no, that wasn't accurate. She was thrilled with her plan either way. She would make the decisions that were good for her, and if Saul wasn't a part of that, well, so what. She'd still stick to her list.

She heard Saul take a breath. "Like a best friend?"

"Exactly." Probably the best friend she'd ever had. "A brother, even."

Gentry smiled at her, and Saul changed tactics.

"Wheeler was flirting with you."

"Wheeler?" Emily scoffed—even though Gentry chuckled again. "There was no flirting. He and I just chatted while I ate."

"Honey, he *told* me he was flirting."

What in the world? Why would Wheeler tell him such a thing? "Well, that's just silly."

This time, Gentry and Saul both laughed. "I won't tell him you said that. It'll hurt his feelings."

"Good grief, Saul. He's Gentry's age."

That did it. Gentry fell onto his back laughing until she poked him in the ribs.

Saul wasn't much better. Around his humor, he said,

"I keep telling you, Em. You're hot. Guys notice. I'm glad Gentry's only a friend—"

"Like a little brother," she insisted.

"—but ask him if he wouldn't have been interested if you weren't his boss. In fact, he probably started out interested anyway."

*"Saul."* Appalled, she glanced at Gentry and was thankful that he hadn't heard. He was amused enough just listening to her. She gave Gentry a brief apologetic smile, and he smiled warmly back at her.

Then he sat up, and said loudly enough for Saul to hear, "She's now my unofficial sister. We just decided. Even if I wasn't her manager, I'd still be around. Hope you're okay with that."

Emily's heart melted. "Did you hear that? I'll have to disagree with one part though. It's official."

Gentry stood, briefly put his hand to her head, then turned to stare out at the lake—and maybe give her a little of that privacy she hadn't wanted moments ago.

Saul said, "I take it you two had a heart-to-heart."

"Most definitely," she replied softly. "He's an amazing man, and a good friend."

"I'm glad to hear it, because Emily, I do need something."

"Oh?" She tried to sound only mildly interested.

"You. What I need, Emily, is you."

Astounded, Emily blinked twice, then cleared her throat. "For...what?"

Saul's rough, low laugh felt like a teasing stroke along her spine. "Pretty much everything. Even more than I'd intended."

What he'd intended?

"For right now," he said, "we need to talk. Is that possible?"

"I…" She looked around and realized the sun was all but gone. "I need to get back to my car. We could talk on my drive home." At this point, he had her curious.

"I'd appreciate that, Em," he said with grave sincerity. "Thank you."

Remembering something Gentry had said days ago, Emily tried to sound casual when she suggested, "Or you could come over." God, she'd sounded lame. "For drinks. I mean like coffee. Or whatever." Slapping a hand over her mouth, she physically silenced herself.

After the briefest of pauses, Saul murmured, "The 'whatever' interests me a lot, but unfortunately, I'm still a good ninety minutes away from Cemetery."

"You're…what? Where? Why?"

"You forgot who, when, and how." With a smile in his tone, he said, "I swear I'll explain everything. Call me when you get to your car?"

"Okay, sure." There was no way she wouldn't now. She had to know what was going on. "Give me fifteen minutes or so."

"Thanks, Em." He disconnected the call.

Staring at Gentry's back, Emily said, "That was the weirdest conversation ever."

Understanding that her call had ended, Gentry turned and offered her his hand. "Hey, men need reassurance, too."

Yes, Gentry surely had. But Saul didn't have Gentry's background. He was carefree and settled, happy in his life. He had it together in a way she couldn't imagine, living by his own rules, his own way.

She envied him that.

Once she and Gentry started back, Emily noticed other people noticing them. In an aside, she whispered, "Are people staring, or is it my imagination?"

"They're staring. Probably thinking I'm hitting on you like Wheeler did."

Surprised that he'd say anything that ridiculous, Emily opened her mouth to speak—

And Gentry said, "Saul is right to be worried. I've met Wheeler. He and every other guy with a heartbeat will be trying to cozy up to you."

"Wheeler's a kid," Emily reminded him.

"He's my age, and I'm not a kid. I see what you don't." His gaze quickly skimmed over her, and he lifted one brow. "I'm sure Wheeler does, too. Definitely, Saul does."

Her head started to swim. "I've lived here for years now, and nothing like that has ever been an issue. No one noticing anything. No one…hitting on me." She felt dumb even saying that. "I don't like how that sounds. It's aggressive. *Women* and *hit* should never be used in the same sentence."

Gentry agreed. "More likely you've always been oblivious to it. Since we're besties now, or whatever, can I give you some advice?"

"I'd love it if you did." For certain, she didn't have a clue what she was doing.

"Don't be oblivious to Saul."

No, she wasn't. "I don't think I've ever been unaware of him."

"Hope not, but you could have mistaken his efforts, right? Thought he was just being friendly when he was flirting?"

Honestly, she didn't know. "It's possible, but it makes me sound really dense."

"Nah. You're always so tuned in to others, seeing the best in them, you miss the subtleties, that's all."

Well, she still felt dense. "So what do I do?"

"Open up to Saul. Tell him what you want."

What an appalling thought. "I don't know."

"Take it from someone who just did a lot of opening up—it feels better than you expect it to." He got her all the way to her car before he spoke again. "From what I can tell, relationships are always a little messy. Sometimes embarrassing. Maybe even annoying. You and Saul are each set in your ways. But I get the feeling he's the one for you."

She had that feeling, too. After years of ignoring men, not even thinking of them, Saul had caught her attention in a monumental way. "It feels risky." After her marriage fell apart, she'd been so leery of involvement. "Feels a little scary, too." She didn't relish the idea of being hurt like that again.

Gentry took her shoulders in his hands. "There are never any guarantees, but I think it'll be worth it. And hey, if things with you two don't work out, it's his loss, right?"

Even though Emily didn't agree, she smiled because she liked his attitude. "You're very good for my ego."

"You're very good for my heart."

Oh, she wanted to hug him again, but too many people were ogling them. "Since we've ironed all that out, can I ask for a favor?"

"Anything."

"My uncle will get out of the hospital tomorrow, but

we're not sure what time yet. I need to be pick them up once we know—"

"Don't give it a thought," Gentry smoothly interrupted. "I'll handle the shop."

How had she gotten so lucky? "I'll come in until I get the call."

"Whatever suits you, okay?"

It suited her to have it all—Saul as a significant other, and Gentry as the closest of friends. If Saul didn't work, she'd still have Gentry, and that mattered a lot. "You're the best."

"Don't say that yet. Tonight I'm going to write up a plan of management. After you see it, you might want to kick me out."

Emily laughed. "Not a chance." Then with a fake frown, "We'll discuss everything."

Amused, he opened her car door, bade her one more goodbye, and meandered off.

It struck her that things were changing big-time. So far, so good, and yet as she'd said, it was a scary, too. Never before could she remember wanting so much for herself. Not like she did now. Before, everything was in her power. For a new business, she'd figured out a plan and stuck to it until she reached her goals.

Now though? Regardless of what Gentry said, she knew Saul had a wonderful, full life with his work, his family and friends. She could be no more than a blip on his radar, and if she fell out of sight, he'd probably carry on, enjoying every day as much as he always did.

She, on the other hand, had such a deep yearning now, one she hadn't even felt with her ex, Rob. Back then, she'd been young and idealistic, and she romanticized many things, including their marriage.

A marriage that had crashed and burned under the first real hardship.

Older now, hopefully wiser, she saw things she hadn't then—like all the ways she could fail. All the ways she could rock her peaceful existence and leave it in turmoil.

If she gave her heart to Saul and things fell apart, would she be able to reclaim the contentment she felt now?

Doubtful.

So with everyone still glancing her way, Emily put on her friendliest smile and waved, which caused a lot of people to quickly look away. Then she pressed in Saul's number, and as it rang, she pulled out of the lot.

Better to get things rolling than to continue to stew in worry.

## CHAPTER NINE

SAUL REPEATEDLY REHEARSED the conversation in his mind while waiting for Emily to call. Earlier, just hearing her voice had reassured him, making him believe once again that he could make it work. He had to.

He already thought of Emily as his.

He thought of Beck the same way.

They were the two people he belonged with, so it had to be possible.

The second his phone buzzed, he answered with, "Are you okay to talk and drive? It's getting dark." And it'd kill him if anything happened to her.

"Hands-free," she said cautiously, as if unsure of his concern. "It's fine."

"Me, too." He wished he was closer so he could sit down with her. In fact… "I'd be happy to come by tonight, if it won't be too late for you."

She paused—a lengthy pause that set his teeth on edge—then, with her typical good humor, she said, "Tonight probably isn't great. Uncle Sullivan is going home tomorrow, so it's going to be a busy day."

"I can go with you." He didn't know the timing yet, or how long it'd take, but he wanted to be there for her anyway. He needed her to understand that despite everything he had going on, she was important to him.

She was…vital.

"That's okay." With the faintest touch of accusation, she said, "Wheeler explained that you had plans."

That was one thing he could easily clarify. "Those plans got rearranged, so now I'm free to go with you." He tried to make it sound like a statement, not a question, but if she told him to get lost...

"What plans, Saul?" Sounding more like her usual caring self, she added, "I know I don't have the right to make demands, but I'm pretty confused at this point."

"You have every right," he assured her. "We have something happening." He held his breath. "Something special?"

"I thought so."

He exhaled and smiled. "You thought right. It's been brewing for a while—" at least for him "—so whatever else happens, I need you to know, I want you. You, not any other woman."

Another hesitant pause. "That sounded...yeah."

"Sexual? Because it is." Most definitely sexual. "Possessive? I would hope so, considering how long I've wanted you."

"Saul," she whispered, sounding both pleased and embarrassed.

It was past time he spelled it out so there'd be no more misunderstandings. "I want us to be a couple, Em. I want a future with you. I want to share everything with you." But "everything" now included a kid. His hands flexed on the steering wheel. "I swear, I won't rush you." *Too much.* "With whatever our schedules allow, I want time with you. As much time as possible."

He heard the smile in her tone when she said, "I'd like all of that, too. Very much. But keep in mind, anything with me is going to include my aunt and uncle.

I'm the only family they have, and I'll always want to help them however I can."

He loved that about her. "I like them. They like me. I don't see a problem." Not with her family. It was his newfound family that he was worried would throw her.

"Know what?" she said. "I made a list."

"A list?"

"Of things I want to do. Things I want to change. To shake up my life, I mean."

To shake up her life? But… One of the things he found most attractive about Emily was her unchanging stability. Her calmness and her gift for staying in control. "Give an example."

"Okay, sure." With excitement and maybe a little triumph, too, she announced, "Tomorrow evening, sometime after I get my aunt and uncle settled, I'm heading to a shelter to adopt a pet."

Huh. Yeah, she'd mentioned it before, so that wasn't too alarming. Maybe, if he worked it right, he could go along with her for that, too. He could turn it into a bonding experience. "That sounds great, Em."

"I also have plans to change my hair."

"Change your hair?" he croaked. He loved her hair!

"I want to freshen up my wardrobe, also. Everything I own is so boring."

"Honey, you are never boring." How could she even think such a thing?

"Thank you, but I want to try new things. Do new things." Her voice dropped. "Being with you counts."

Already Saul's heart was beating too hard and fast. Her tone put his libido into hyperdrive—which meant he was getting ahead of himself. "Glad to hear it, and

I mean that. Hundred percent. But… I need to tell you where I was."

"If it's something that's going to hurt me, or make me mad, this relationship is over before it even started."

Wow. Saul took a second to soak in her blunt words and forceful tone. He'd never before heard it from Emily, so with any luck, it meant she was already invested and just protecting herself—and for that, he'd applaud her. "I hope it won't upset you."

"Good. Because I have to admit, it bothered me a lot to go to your restaurant and find out from Wheeler that you were off."

"I'm sorry." He'd wanted to tell her, but one explanation would have led to another…

"And I've been going over and over it in my head," she continued in a rush. "Torturing myself because I know you're happy and popular in a way that I'm not."

He couldn't really be happy unless he had her. "Emily—"

"But I won't sell myself short," she stated. "I did that with my marriage and it was a colossal failure."

It killed him to hear her say that. "Emily—"

"So if we're going to do this—"

"I hope we are."

"Then no more surprises."

Oh, he had a surprise all right. A big one.

Hurrying to speak before she got started again, he explained, "I rehearsed this while waiting for your call, only now I feel like I should just get it said."

"Yes, do."

His heart thumped heavily three times before he stated, "I have a kid now. He's fourteen."

*"What?"*

"His dad was my friend, but he and his wife died a year ago. Beck needs a home, not a shared bedroom in his distant cousin's house, but a place where he feels he belongs. He needs family who cares. He needs…me." Yeah, that about covered it, except he needed to add, "I'm stepping up, on all counts. *Happily.*"

Silence.

A sense of panic gripped him. "He's a great kid, Em. I swear it. That's where I was today, visiting him because he called. I was going to see him tomorrow, too, except we decided he'd do a sleepover next weekend and I need to find time tomorrow to make a bedroom for him."

More silence.

"Emily? You still there?"

She launched into rapid speech. "Yes, of course. I was just thinking… Helping out with a kid would be another new thing. I mean, I've definitely never done that. I'll add it to my list."

His heart almost stopped, then started to race. *She'll add it to her list*, he silently repeated, almost laughing with the relief he felt.

Saul figured he'd better pull over to the side of the road. He was breathing too fast to drive safely. He checked his rearview mirror, switched lanes, and eased onto the shoulder. Luckily he wasn't on a busy road.

Once again, Emily had knocked him off-kilter. Sweet, compassionate, amazing Emily.

Yes, ultimately he'd hoped she would be accepting. Her incredible empathy was one of the first things he'd noticed about her, along with her calmness, her honest interest in others. But this? To just roll with it?

"Honey, do you understand what I'm saying?"

"Yes."

He swallowed heavily, almost afraid to believe it could be that easy. "I'm not just me anymore, Em... but I still want you. I still want us together." He knew he always would.

"I'm glad he's not a baby," she said. "Diapers, bottles...that'd take a lot of adjusting. Not sure my list is long enough. A fourteen-year-old, though—I remember feeling very grown-up at that age."

Damn if his eyes didn't get glassy with emotion. "His name is Beck." Saul stared out the windshield at nothing in particular and knew if he hadn't already been madly, head-over-heels in love with Emily Lucretia, this would have done it.

It wasn't near enough to convey how he felt, but he whispered, "Thank you."

"Saul," she said gently. "Will you tell me about him?"

"He's great, Emily." There on the side of the road, Saul told her everything he could think of, including Beck's love of sports, his need for space, and his worry about being uprooted again. He explained why it had taken him so long to find out, and now that he knew, he wanted to make things better for Beck.

"Oh, Saul. I'm so glad he has you."

By the way she said that, he knew she felt everything he did, but on a much deeper, more personal level. "It kills me to imagine what he's gone through." *And what you went through as well.*

Confirming that, she said softly, "There are no words to describe the devastation."

His heart ached for the two people he loved. "I thought of Beck when you mentioned your parents. I should have explained everything then, but it had already taken me so long to get your attention, I didn't want to derail things before we really got started." He'd been afraid of losing her...before he ever really had her.

"You've always had my attention. For the longest time, I thought you were interested in Yardley."

Yeah, half the town had thought that, but they'd never really clicked. He'd known it, as had Yardley. "I wasn't."

"There were rumors," she reminded him.

Yeah, he knew that as well. "They weren't true." Now able to breathe a little easier, he got back on the road. For the first time in too long, he truly believed he could have it all, that he hadn't screwed it up and missed his chance with her.

"So..." Emily murmured. "You two didn't have sex in the lake?"

Funny that he could go from tightly strung tension, to laughing, in the space of minutes. Only with Emily— and that, of course, was another reason he loved her. "Have you ever had sex in the lake, Em?"

Offended, she said, "Of course not."

Her scandalized tone amused him. "You brought it up."

"Because I thought *you* had."

And maybe, just maybe, she'd been a tiny bit jealous? A man could hope. "Trust me, I wouldn't recommend it."

With a gasp, she accused, "So you *did*!"

"Not with Yardley, but when I was younger, yeah. Fish nibble, Em. And the water is cold."

She snickered. "Serves you right. That poor girl. It doesn't sound very romantic."

"At that age, romance doesn't factor in, but hey, it was her idea."

"So you were just some poor, innocent lad drawn astray?" She snorted, letting him know what she thought of that idea. "Somehow, that description would never fit you."

No, it wouldn't. "We were all young and innocent once, right?" Though it seemed like Emily hadn't changed much in that regard. Oh, she was a woman with enough confidence and savvy to run a successful business, buy a house, live a full life on her own terms, and give him hell when she thought he needed it.

Yet she didn't have a jaded bone in her delectable body. It didn't take a person long to see that.

She was incredible in a contagious, make-you-want-it way that naturally drew people in.

He certainly hadn't been immune.

Now that he again had control of his senses, Saul got back to the topic uppermost in his mind. "You're okay with the idea of Beck added into the equation?"

"Of course." As if that acceptance wasn't amazing enough, she continued, saying, "Just as my aunt and uncle did for me, you'll make him feel secure in no time. I'd love to help however you want, as much as you want. As long as I'm not intruding."

"Intruding?" Trying not to overwhelm her or scare her off, Saul couldn't help but say, "I'm falling in love with you, Em. I want you with me. How could you ever intrude?" In truth, he was already there. He'd fallen, stood again, and dusted himself off, and now his equilibrium had adjusted to the effect that was pure Emily. He just wasn't sure if he should put all that on her at once. He definitely didn't want her to think that his love went hand in hand with needing help with Beck.

This time the silence grated along his nerve endings until he almost couldn't bear it.

Then she whispered, "Right back at you."

His shoulder muscles relaxed, and relief tugged his mouth into a smile. He didn't want to sound as thankful as he felt when he said, "Then we're in sync." More so than he'd ever been, or ever would be, with anyone else. "I have a feeling you'll be great for Beck. And Em? I want to be great for you. Whatever you need."

"You're going to have your hands full helping him adjust. It won't be easy. Please don't expect him to be fine overnight."

"I won't, but I'll never be too busy for you. Please don't think this is just about Beck." *Or just about me.* "Tomorrow I'll go with you to get Sullivan. We can talk more then." He'd show her every way possible how much she mattered to him.

With the slightest hesitation, she agreed. "If you're sure you have time, then I'd love your company. They've got a lot of stuff stored at the hospital now, and I'm not sure how easy it'll be getting Sullivan inside their house. Plus, I want to make sure they're all set up, so I'll probably run to the grocery, too, only I'd rather not leave them alone right away."

So thoughtful, and so damned sweet. "Hey, Em."

"Hmm?"

"I've changed my mind."

"Nope," she said firmly. "Too late."

That teasing tone broadened his smile, because he knew she felt confident enough in them as a couple to do it. "Not about going with you, but about you being perfect."

"Saul," she laughingly objected.

"You *are* perfect—for me. Thank you for being you."

EMILY FLOATED ON those last few compliments right through the rest of the drive, a quick shower, and a frozen dinner that she nuked just a little too long. She went to bed smiling, and woke smiling.

She had a purpose.

Odd, but until now, she'd felt out of her depth with Saul.

In all the best ways, he was the polar opposite of her, and yet now, he needed her. This was something substantial she could bring to the relationship: an understanding of how Beck must feel. Her heart broke for the boy, knowing the torment he had to feel, and yet she honestly believed she could help.

She *needed* to help.

Her thoughts paused on that as she remembered Wheeler telling her she was a good listener, and Gentry's easy acceptance of her when he was guarded with everyone else. It never occurred to her that maybe she had a gift for putting people at ease. If so, how wonderful would that be when applied to Beck?

Oh, how she hoped she could reach the boy and help him to adjust to the emotional turmoil. Over the years, from listening to others, she'd learned that everyone grieved differently. There were those who kept their emotions contained, and some who seemed overwhelmed by them. People who lashed out at others, and people who took too much on themselves. She did her utmost not to judge, to just listen and be present—because that's what her aunt and uncle had done for her.

Perhaps they were the ones with the gift. Well, if she only emulated them, she was glad. They were the biggest-hearted people she knew.

As she prepared for work, she kept her phone right

beside her in case her aunt called. She felt giddy with Saul's admission—*I'm falling in love with you*—and stressed about her uncle's return home without supervision.

She was already in love with Saul, she knew.

What if her uncle fell again and got hurt even worse? She loved him too dearly for that.

Her mood seemed to fluctuate in a push-pull of excitement, worry, anticipation, and dread.

The minute she got to the shop, she rushed through the prep while waiting for Gentry. He arrived a mere ten minutes later, early as usual, and she immediately unloaded on him, sharing every single thing she felt.

Wearing a thoughtful expression, Gentry finished the prep. "Poor kid. I'm glad he'll have you."

That stopped her in her tracks because, again, it was a wonderful compliment that struck at her heart. "You mean that?" The idea of being seen that way both humbled and thrilled her. She knew she did a phenomenal job with flowers, but people? Children? She'd had no real clue, but for Beck—and Saul—she knew she wanted to try, and she knew she'd do her best.

"I can't imagine anyone better for a boy who's hurting and feeling lost. I mean, Saul is great, but you? You're like an antidote to fear and insecurity."

The heartfelt words made her wonder if Gentry was drawing a parallel to himself, given what he'd faced and their recent conversation. He was a smart, capable man now, not a fourteen-year-old, yet he, too, had been uncertain of his welcome.

In the next second, he disabused her of that notion.

"I had my grandpa. You had your aunt and uncle. It takes someone special, I think, to make things bearable. Someone who understands that it's never going to be the same again, not with what's lost, but it can be something different. Something that's still good."

Oddly enough, her nose tingled, and her eyes burned. "That's beautiful." And so very, very true.

"Beautiful?" As if he only then realized how she was reacting, Gentry stared at her, appalled. "No, it wasn't. Just facts, that's all. Plain old facts."

"Beautifully put." Opening her arms, Emily started for him.

He backed up. "Now, wait a minute!"

"Family is always honest," she instructed, and then she thought to add, "And they hug a lot."

Resigned, he planted his feet and let her wrap her arms around him. He even patted her back awkwardly. "I don't mind a hug," he said, disgruntled like someone who really needed it. "But don't paint me to be some stupid poet. I was just saying, you'll be good for the kid. That's all."

"Saul said the same thing, and I think it's the nicest compliment I've ever gotten." One she was starting to believe.

Gentry held her back enough to see her face. "*That's* the nicest compliment?"

"It has substance." It was a compliment she could sink her teeth into—far preferable to being called perfect.

"If you say so," he answered with a laugh.

Just then, Vivienne burst through the doors, wildly waving her phone toward them. "Have you two seen this?"

Startled by the abrupt arrival, Emily turned to face her. "Good grief, Vivienne, what are you doing here?

You're not due in until— Why are you shoving your phone at me?"

"You're a *hashtag*, Emily!"

The bubbling excitement in Vivienne's eyes made Emily wary. "A what?"

"Look! Right there on the Cemetery Facebook page. It's on the other social media sites, too. Instagram, Twitter—"

"Cemetery has an Instagram profile?" Gentry took the phone from Vivienne, then groaned before reading aloud, *"Emily Lucretia cuts loose."*

Falling back a step, Emily struggled to catch her breath. *"What?"*

"Hashtag The Flower Lady."

Her jaw dropped, then snapped shut. It couldn't be. "Good Lord, what are you talking about?" She snatched the phone from Gentry, and there she was—sort of. The sun setting over the lake made the photo dark enough that the people were more like silhouettes than anything else. Aghast, she lifted her gaze to Gentry.

He appeared equally dumbstruck.

It was a misleading photo of the two of them on the beach, her head on his shoulder, his muscular arm around her. "Gentry…" Swallowing the words, Emily glanced at Vivienne. The older woman was a good friend, but she was also a gossip, and that caused Emily to redirect her thoughts. "Who took this photo?"

"Forget the photo," Vivienne said. "Tell me who he is!"

Whew. Alarm receded, and she caught her breath. Vivienne's question confirmed that Gentry's identity was safe, at least.

Until he gave up with a huff. "It's me, and it's not what they're making it out to be."

Wide-eyed, Vivienne said, "*You?*"

"We were only talking, Emily gave me a hug—something you've seen her do a hundred times, Viv—so this is just someone making assumptions."

Disappointment drooped Vivienne's shoulders. "It's not a hot date?"

Emily almost laughed. "Have you ever seen me on a hot date?"

"No, but I saw über-hot Saul Culver in here schmoozing you big-time, so don't act like it's not possible." Vivienne's phone dinged. She looked at it, and said, "Aha! Wheeler?" Her sly grin stretched with satisfaction. "Emily, you cougar. I'm impressed."

*"What?"* Oh God, she was screeching. In a lower, calmer octave, she demanded, "Give me that." Snatching the phone from her employee's hands, Emily scrolled down through far too many comments. Worse and worse.

"He is a handsome one," Vivienne murmured.

Ignoring that, Emily finally got to the pic that someone had posted of her at the bar chatting with Wheeler. And damn it, he did look attentive, which of course was his job. She scoffed. With great feeling. "This is absurd."

Ding.

Vivienne leaned over one of her shoulders, Gentry over the other, as they all read a comment from Betty, the town matriarch. *Still waters run deep.*

Gentry chuckled. "She's right about that."

Rudely, Emily elbowed him. "It's not funny."

"It's a little funny," he replied.

"I think it's awesome." Vivienne snatched her phone back. "You're a *hashtag*. Now everyone is talking about you being a femme fatale. And I work for you!"

Gentry stepped out of reach and grinned. "Maybe Emily should be marching around outside holding a sign about flower sales. You'd get all the guys in here spending money." When her face went hot, he added, "You can wear your shirt, though."

Which of course reminded her that she'd suggested he remove his—and Saul had strutted around bare-chested. "Shush it." Suddenly she noticed Vivienne texting, and her heart shot into her throat. "What are you doing?" she asked, her tone again pitched too high.

"Replying how awesome you are." Her thumbs flew over the keys. "Some guys are saying they didn't real-ize you were available." Lifting her gaze to Emily, she bobbed her eyebrows. "Now they know, and they're interested."

"Everyone *knows* me!" How could this be happen-ing? "I'm the same person I was last year, last month, *yesterday*—only I'm older."

"You're emphasizing the wrong words," Vivienne said, paying no attention to her panic. "It's that everyone does know you, and likes you, and now you're showing them a new side of yourself."

"There's no new side," Emily insisted...but damn it, hadn't that been her wish? To shake things up a little?

Not like this. Yet still...

This time Gentry gave her a hug, but it was different, one-armed and more teasing than affectionate. "Face it, Em. Saul exposed you."

"Gentry!"

"Your nature, I mean. You did your best to be invisible—"

"I didn't," she grumbled. Being invisible had never been her intent, but neither had she wanted to draw attention to herself.

"—and now that he's more or less said 'look at this smokin' hot babe,' everyone *is* looking. And I bet he's not going to like that, because he wants you all to himself."

"I can't believe that sexist comment came out of your mouth."

Taking no offense, Gentry snickered. "It's what the town is saying."

The possibility that he might be right had her covering her face.

Of course, that didn't stop Vivienne from reading comments out loud. *"Where there's smoke, there's fire."*

"See?" Gentry said. "Smokin'."

*"It's the quiet, thoughtful ones that take you by surprise."*

Offended, she dropped her hands. "Who said that?" She hadn't surprised anyone. In fact, she hadn't changed at all—not yet.

*"I thought she was dating Saul."*

"Has Saul seen it?" Gentry asked. "Anything from him?"

As if summoned, the door opened, and there Saul stood.

Emily soaked up the sight of him, tall, broad-shouldered, and with an intent expression that sent her heart into hyperdrive.

If Gentry thought Saul would have competition, he was completely wrong. She was thoroughly in love with him and had been for a while. As content as she was with her life, he was the one thing she still wanted. The person she craved.

Out of self-preservation, she hadn't dared admit it to herself. Now it didn't look like she'd have a choice.

Striding forward, Emily closed the distance to Saul, her gaze never leaving his. "Vivienne, put that phone on camera."

Eagerly, Vivienne said, "You got it."

In Emily's periphery, she saw Gentry fold his arms over his chest and grin.

Saul just watched her, not quite smiling, not quite frowning.

Stopping directly in front of him, Emily asked, "You've seen the stupid website?"

"Hashtag The Flower Lady."

Fresh determination made her bolder. She glanced back. "Ready, Viv?"

"Oh, hell yeah, I am."

Emily stared up at Saul. "I have something to prove."

His big hands settled at her waist, and his expression warmed with concern. "Not to me."

"No." And she didn't need to prove anything to herself, either. Not really. "To the town."

"Ah, gotcha." Softly, he encouraged her, saying, "Go for it."

So she did. Wrapping her arms around his neck and stretching up on tiptoe, Emily took his mouth the way she'd often dreamed of doing, with a lot of heat, a little tongue, and plenty of enthusiasm.

SAUL COULDN'T STOP GRINNING. Every time he was with Emily, she managed to rock his world. This morning…

yeah. Jealousy had driven him straight to the flower shop—where Emily had made her preferences crystal clear. To *everyone*.

Oh, he'd felt the heat of her blush while she'd kissed him, but the lady had guts galore, more than enough to counter whoever it was starting rumors.

He had to admit, that photo of her on the beach had seemed damning.

Yet Gentry had applauded her, and Vivienne had been beside herself with posting the scoop. She had fun employees, and he'd have liked to stay with them longer, but in the middle of Emily sharing some tongue action, her phone had buzzed with an incoming call. Sure enough, it was her aunt.

Now, as he drove them to the hospital, Saul decided to tease her. "You should sell T-shirts."

Distracted, Emily asked, "What?"

"Shirts, because 'Hashtag The Flower Lady' would be a big seller."

"Ha! Not on your life." She studied him in a warm and intimate way. "Now that I've staked a public claim on you, everyone will move on."

Is that what she thought? In his experience, people never gave up on new fascinations that easily. And Emily was the newest fascination for a town that embraced gossip as an entertainment second only to the lake. "Hate to break it to you, Em, but you've never done public displays before. Vivienne's photo is probably going to fuel the fire."

Given Emily's expression, clearly that hadn't occurred to her.

"Oh, God, I can only deal with one issue at a time." Immediately, he wondered if he'd missed something.

"What other issue is there?" Was she having second thoughts about him? About Beck?

He really needed to find out who ran the town's social media.

Sidestepping his question, Emily murmured, "Now I'm afraid to do anything different. I might have to revise my list."

Oh yeah, her list.

Things were happening fast—in his life, and with Emily—but he couldn't slow them down. When it came to Emily, he didn't even want to try. "I like your list. I've always wondered how you'd look with your hair loose." For as long as he could remember, she'd kept it in a ponytail. Pretty sure he wasn't the only one who fantasized about freeing it from that restrictive band, watching it tumble around her shoulders, feeling the silkiness and weight of it…

Given her reaction to being a hashtag, if he told her any of that, her hair might stay forever contained. Instead, Saul asked, "How else are you planning to shake things up?"

With a side glance at him, she said, "The kiss counts, right?"

"I'd say so." Everything with her counted. A hot kiss? Most definitely. "You said you're going to the shelter tonight. Do you know what kind of dog you want?"

Giving the impression it didn't matter, she lifted one shoulder. "I'll choose from whatever they have. Betty swears that shelter dogs make the best pets."

"Betty has her moments."

"She's softened up some now, but she's still bossy."

Bossy, and determined to keep her iron grip on the town. For whatever reason, Betty always went easy on him, treating him like a favorite nephew. Maybe because he never let her jibes get to him and answered all her nosiness with smiles. "Just consider it part of her charm."

Emily laughed. "I'll give that a try." After a moment, she explained, "I was still thinking about a dog when suddenly Betty had everything arranged. Now I have an appointment on the same day my aunt and uncle are coming home."

And the same day he'd planned to spend working on arranging a room for Beck. "You could reschedule."

"Actually, now that I've been thinking about it, I'm ready."

"What if the shelter doesn't have what you want?"

Another shrug. "I'll be happy with any friendly guy to keep me company when I get home."

This wasn't the time for jokes, so Saul resisted the urge to point out that *he* was friendly.

"Actually, I guess I do have some preferences. I'd like a mature dog, not a puppy, since I spend so much time at the shop. I've heard they'll sleep, right? I could do a doggy-cam or something to keep an eye on him." With sudden inspiration, she added, "And Gentry could let him out when he's working in the yard."

Yeah, Saul didn't want to talk about Gentry, and he didn't want to think about Gentry having a key to her house. Never mind that Emily and Gentry treated each other like family. "Sounds like a plan."

Taking him off guard—again—she said, "Of course, I'll talk to my aunt and uncle about it today, since I want them to move in with me."

"You…" For a second there, Saul fumbled for words, then settled on asking, "When did you decide that?"

"I've been thinking about it ever since Uncle Sullivan got hurt. He is eighty-one now, you know."

"And sharp as a tack."

"Also legally blind and currently injured."

In Saul's opinion, Emily put more worry into Sullivan's blindness than Sullivan or Mabel did. "He's healed enough to go home, or the hospital wouldn't release him."

"Or," she said, eyeing him sharply, "the hospital assumes he'll have the care he needs."

Already knowing the answer, Saul asked, "You?"

Firmly, and with a sort of unselfish satisfaction, she confirmed, "Me."

Damn. Saul recognized a storm brewing when he saw one, and he wasn't talking about Emily's take-control attitude. He and Sullivan had hit it off right away; the man had the same easy familiarity that Emily possessed. From the moment they'd been introduced, Sullivan had treated him like a friend and he'd felt like one.

Like many elders, Sullivan had made it clear that he didn't like being a burden to other people, not even his wife. Especially his wife. He wanted to pamper Mabel, not the other way around. When necessary, he leaned on her, because they had the type of secure marriage that was built on strong love and earned respect.

And Emily wanted to uproot them?

Pretty sure Sullivan wasn't ready for that. Actually, neither was Mabel. From what he'd seen, they adored Emily, and he knew they appreciated her help. Having her as a caretaker, though? Saul already knew how that'd go over.

"You've gone quiet." Chin elevated and expression defiant, Emily stared at him.

Saul knew he had to tread lightly or she might think

he objected to her aunt and uncle, when he absolutely did not. Or worse, she might think he was trying to dictate her life when he never would. He fully respected Emily's capability. She didn't need him or anyone else to tell her what to do.

Still, he hoped they could exchange advice and opinions. One glance at her, and he wasn't so sure. Family was definitely a touchy subject for her.

"Just thinking," he said, giving himself a second to gather his wits. "I know Sullivan's sight issue bothers you, maybe more than it does Sullivan, but it hasn't affected him that much, has it?"

"He fell," Emily pointed out. "Off a stool." She said it as if he didn't already know that.

"Accidents can happen to everyone. They're usually not a huge deal."

"To an octogenarian, they often are."

Her persistence, in Saul's opinion, only showed how much her aunt and uncle meant to her. After she'd lost her parents, her aunt and uncle were all she had left, so naturally she wanted to protect them. "I understand how you feel. My dad fell off the roof a few years back and broke his arm. He was only sixty-one, not in his eighties, and I still felt like shit, like I'd let him down."

By small degrees, Emily eased her rigid posture.

"Dad hadn't told me the roof needed work, and when I suggested that he should have, he wasn't happy." A small grin nudged in as Saul recalled the scene. "He was already in pain, irked that he'd slipped, upset that Mom was upset, and then here I was, 'acting all superior,' to use his words, like I could have done the job better."

"That's different," Emily said, but without a lot of conviction.

"I assumed Mom would side with me, and instead she snapped that I hadn't put my father up there, hadn't told him to be too stubborn to hire a roofer, and if anyone was to blame, it was her, because she shouldn't have allowed him to do it."

"I agree with your mother. Not that she was to blame. I don't mean that. It wasn't your fault, though."

"At the time, Dad agreed with her too, but once we were alone, he gave me hell. I got it, you know? Dad was used to doing things with ease. He told me that if he'd needed my help, he'd have asked for it, and that was that."

With a huff, Emily rolled her eyes. "Great story, but again, totally different circumstances."

"Yet…alike in some ways?" He saw she was softening, so he pushed his advantage. "Just consider it, okay? Sullivan knows he's getting older, and there are things he can't do. That's enough for a guy to deal with, but he also doesn't want Mabel to feel guilty. It's why he's been so grumpy about the hospital. It bothers him to see her sleeping in a chair, refusing to leave his side."

With a hand to her heart, Emily said, "It bothers me, too."

Anyone could see that. "Amplify what you feel a hundred times. Right now, Sullivan is looking forward to being home, *his* home, with his own routine and enough privacy to not only be himself, but to openly love his wife."

Around a small laugh, Emily said, "The way those two carry on."

"They're funny, and still very much in love."

"Yes. Such a wonderful thing."

Exactly what he wanted with Emily.

For a full minute, she kept her thoughts to herself, but finally circled back to say, "I need to find a way to convince him. Both of them."

So she knew Mabel would also resist? Gently, Saul asked, "Because?"

"Because..." After a moment, she admitted, "I'm terrified of losing them."

Those words, said so softly, twisted his heart. Saul reached out his hand, palm up, and then he waited. He could see that Emily was all set to take over for her aunt and uncle, and he got that. He even admired it. But it hadn't taken him long to see things she couldn't.

Love could cloud issues as strongly as any bias.

Finally she laced her fingers with his, and he gave her a gentle squeeze before returning both hands to the steering wheel. "Understand, honey. I have no issue with your family. I like them a lot. If they need to live with you, that won't change my mind about anything." Might alter the plans a little, but family was important to him, too.

"Anything," she repeated, "meaning...what?"

"Us." He had no problem stating it. "Living with you or in their own place, your aunt and uncle are a part of you, and I'm glad. They're terrific people."

Those words relaxed her enough that she smiled. "I bet Beck will like them, and they'll be good for him. They're world-class coddlers who really know how to make someone feel special."

The fact that she was already thinking of Beck sent a flood of emotion through his system. He wasn't used to this, wasn't used to feeling so much, so strongly. Guess he'd have to get accustomed, though, because that was the effect of Emily.

Smiling from the inside out, he said, "I hadn't considered that, but I'm sure you're right." He pulled into the hospital parking lot and found a space to park. "Beck lost his paternal grandparents already. His granddad was gone years ago, and his grandma passed a few years before his parents. I don't think they were ever close with the maternal grandparents."

Putting her hand on his forearm, Emily stated with firm reassurance, "We'll keep him surrounded by love. Kids adapt. I did."

*We.* How amazing was she? "If you say so, I believe it, because I trust you, Em."

That earned him a blinding smile. "I feel the same about you."

Needing her in ways he'd never before considered, Saul turned off the engine, released his seat belt, and caught her face in his hands. "We're going to be good together, I swear it."

Her gaze searched his, but she didn't question him on the finality of that statement. If she had, he could have gone into details, laying out everything he wanted—today, next month, in ten years…for the rest of their lives.

Instead, he left it unsaid, letting her get accustomed to things in her own time and in her own way.

She'd already pronounced to all of Cemetery that they were together. For now, that was more than enough.

# CHAPTER TEN

IT BOTHERED EMILY to admit that Saul was right. When they entered the hospital room, they found her aunt bustling around as she prepared for them to leave, and Sullivan looking happier than he had in days.

Angela was there, giving them both final instructions, but when she spotted Emily, she handed her a folder. "Everything is detailed in here."

"I looked over it," Mabel said as she stuffed her slippers in a tote bag. "Clear as a bell. Exercise, medicine, diet—"

"No diet," Sullivan interrupted.

"That's what I said." Mabel winked at both women. "Your diet is unrestricted."

Angela grinned. "Mr. Thatcher, you really are a healthy man. Just don't overdo it."

"I won't let him," Mabel said. "I promise he'll be on his best behavior."

In a loud stage whisper, Sullivan said to Saul, "She doesn't mean it. She likes me better when I misbehave."

Emily shook her head. They were both so excited to be going home. Her gaze met Saul's, but he didn't in any way look smug.

Obviously, he'd seen things she hadn't. She touched Angela's arm. "Could we talk just a moment?"

That earned a glance from Mabel, so Emily asked, "Do you mind, Aunt?"

"No, of course not. Dr. Randall can go over everything with you, and then if I need any reminders, you'll know." She quickly followed that with, "Not that I will. I promise we'll be fine."

"We will," Sullivan seconded. "Don't you worry, Emily."

Emily managed to smile at them both, then she and Angela stepped out to the hallway. Before Emily could say anything, Angela spoke. "He really is okay. You know that, right?"

"Well, as Saul pointed out to me on the drive here, you wouldn't release him if you thought otherwise."

"I adore a wise man." Angela's teasing eased away, and she asked, "Is he a keeper?"

Until that moment, Emily hadn't realized that she was almost bubbling over with the thrill of her new relationship. She'd had so many things on her mind, and no close female friends in Cemetery, but she felt comfortable opening up to Angela. "Most definitely." Voice low, she confided, "I think things are pretty serious already."

"I am so happy for you!"

"I'm happy for me, too. Honestly, it's been so long since my divorce, I hadn't even thought about men. Now, with Saul, I can't stop thinking about him."

"Your aunt and uncle clearly endorse him," Angela teased. "I guess since we know each other, they treat me as one of your friends more than as Sullivan's doctor, and I like it."

"They're special people." Emily leaned against the wall with a groan. "Don't tell them this, but I was all set to convince them that they needed to live with me."

Right before her eyes, Angela went into doctor mode. "Someday they might, so I'm glad to know that's an option, but for now they're fully capable of living independently. I haven't seen any cognitive decline in Sullivan. In fact, he's sharp-witted enough to compensate for the vision problem and the restrictions of his age. Even though Mabel is small, she's adept at filling in where he needs her." She took Emily's arm and eased her away from the door for more privacy. "Understand, Emily, normally I couldn't discuss any of this with you, but your aunt gave permission."

Uh-oh. "Did Aunt Mabel want you to talk to me about anything specific?"

With a good dose of understanding, Angela patted her arm. "No. I'm sure she wanted you included because she worries about you."

Frustration had Emily groaning again. "I'm worried about *them*—it shouldn't be the other way around."

"Your aunt is clever, Emily, and she loves to tease, but she's serious when she needs to be. You're important to her, so whenever I expressed my concerns, she wanted them shared with you as well. She thought it might put your mind at ease to know all the details."

The door opened and Mabel peeked out, her gaze bouncing from Emily to Angela and back again. "I hate to interrupt, but…"

Emily tugged her into her arms, then squeezed the breath right out of her. "I love you so much, Aunt Mabel." Feeling like a coward, Emily almost hated to let her go.

"Aw, honey." As if she sensed it, Mabel tightened the hug. "You're a blessing to us." She pulled back enough to say, "But right now, Sullivan is impatient to go. Are you ready?"

"There's the wheelchair now," Angela said with excellent timing. She tilted back to glance into the room, swung her gaze back to Emily, and grinned. "Make sure you enjoy every minute of your new romance."

Emily nodded. "That's already on my list."

MABEL WAS SO relieved to get back home, she almost cried. The ride had been rough on Sullivan, but he'd suffered it like a young stud and kept his winces to himself. Mabel didn't fuss, not yet at least, knowing how her husband would feel about it with others there to see.

Saul, bless him, had driven Emily's car, and kept the turns smooth, the bumps to a minimum.

For her part, Emily spent more time peering over the passenger seat to check on them than was necessary. Twice, she'd offered to take them to her house instead.

Both times, she and Sullivan had thanked her but declined.

Sullivan wanted to strip down to his boxers and he couldn't do that in front of Emily. He also wouldn't complain in front of her. Mabel knew he was hurting though, and once they were alone, she'd baby him whether he wanted her to or not.

If it didn't make him feel better, well, at least she'd feel useful.

It was because she needed to do something that she so completely understood Emily right now. Seeing someone you loved hurt... It was awful. If Mabel allowed herself to let go, she'd be bawling like a baby. With fear, with relief, and with exhaustion.

They were the only family Emily had, and the poor girl was afraid of seeing those years slip by.

Nothing marked the passage of time like knowing you were nearing the end. Decades together, that's what she and Sullivan had. Wonderful decades that had somehow flown by.

Would they be fortunate enough to have another? Ten years seemed like a long time, especially when that meant Sullivan would be in his nineties.

Mabel was determined to enjoy every moment with the love of her life, and if one day Sullivan got too old to hold her, to tease and flirt, and do all the things she loved so much, she'd still have her memories.

He'd still be hers.

Just as she knew she'd always be his. Smiling at him, she rested her head on his shoulder and got a kiss to her temple.

Thankfully, the ride didn't take too long.

Once they got to the house, she and Emily made sure Sullivan—using his walker—got inside, and then Mabel helped him to get comfortable, or at least as comfortable as he could be in pants on the living room couch.

Saul carried in everything they'd accumulated at the hospital, and then he ran to the grocery store for them while Emily insisted on helping to tidy up the place.

She knew that Mabel wasn't an immaculate housekeeper, but she didn't allow dust to gather or things to sour in the refrigerator.

"You're both angels," Mabel said, feeling ridiculously weary and emotional now that she had Sullivan where he belonged.

Though he said he didn't need the pain meds, she made sure she put them in a place where Sullivan wouldn't accidentally take one if he meant to get a simple aspirin. Yes, she was a decade younger than him, but at her age, she wasn't sure she'd awaken if he got out of bed and she knew for certain he wouldn't wake her to ask for help.

Finally, seeing the stress on Emily's face, Mabel said to Sullivan, "She thinks we're senile."

"What's that?" Sullivan teased, as if his ears were as faulty as his eyes. "There's an ass grabber around?" He started feeling the air toward her, which made Mabel squeal and Emily laugh. "Come here, Mabel. I'll *protect* you."

"Okay, okay," Emily said with plenty of laughing drama. "I get it. You two want some time alone and a little less oversight from me."

Immediately, Sullivan turned his attention to her. "I love you like my own, Emily. I wouldn't want you any other way. But yeah, honey, we're fine. I'm anxious to kick back—*gently*, Emily," he said, before she could caution him, "and I'm sure Mabel is ready to pamper me in all her special ways."

"Oh, absolutely," Mabel said with a teasing lilt in her voice. "I promise he won't feel any pain."

"Gah." Emily put her hands over her ears. "Cease, please. I'm old, but not old enough to hear this."

They all chuckled, and then, because Emily had done what she could until Saul returned, Mabel insisted that she sit with them in the living room. Once Emily saw that they really were fine and dandy, she'd hopefully worry less.

To distract her, Mabel asked, "So, you and Saul? How's that going?"

For an answer, Emily got out her phone, scrolled a second, and then handed it to Mabel. "That's how it's going."

Putting on her glasses, Mabel peered at the screen,

and cheered! "Sullivan, it's our Emily, and she's making out with Saul."

Dumbfounded, his brows shot up. "She recorded it?"

"No." Emily's rushed explanation started out disjointed but finally turned coherent when she detailed the confusion with Wheeler, and Gentry, and then Saul.

So pleased she could have burst, Mabel leaned against Sullivan's shoulder. "Did you hear that, Sullivan? Emily Lucretia is cutting loose. Hashtag The Flower Lady."

"'Bout damn time," he said.

Emily looked from one beaming face to the other, and scooted to the edge of her seat to share more confidences. "I'm tired of being a Goody Two-shoes, so I'm making other changes, too."

Mabel scowled. "Does our Saul know that miserable ex of yours said such terrible things about you?"

Emily choked. "It wasn't a grave insult, Aunt. I was—am—a Goody Two-shoes. Most of the time."

Mabel nodded at the phone screen. "Not so much now, and we're thrilled. Isn't that right, Sullivan?"

"Saul's a good man. I'm glad you didn't choose one of those other saps. They're boys."

"That's what I said!" Obviously gratified by his backup, Emily nodded. "I'm going to change my hair."

"Excellent idea," Mabel said, bounding out of her chair and striding over to pull off the cloth band so that Emily's hair fell free. "It's so beautiful, but you always torture it into that ponytail."

Smiling, Emily said, "You started that, Aunt. Brushing my hair forever and then tying it back. I just got used to wearing it that way."

"It gave me a reason to take care of you." Gently, she

stroked her hand over the cool weight of Emily's hair. "And you keep so busy, it's easier?"

Emily didn't deny it. "Building a business takes time. Maintaining that business takes even more time." She lifted her shoulders. "Guess the way I wore my hair never seemed significant enough to change it."

"No reason you needed to. It's pretty however you wear it."

"Beautiful," Sullivan agreed. "Always was."

"But now..." Emily glanced at each of them. "I'm thinking of getting it styled differently."

"Hot-pink streaks," Sullivan said. "I hear that's the thing."

Mabel choked.

With a conspiratorial wink at Mabel, Emily said, "I was thinking purple."

Alarmed, Sullivan sat forward, then winced, which had Emily ready to shoot out of her seat while firing off rapid apologies.

"Breathe," Mabel told her, and then to Sullivan, "That's what you get for harassing her."

Carefully, he settled back, sinking into the soft cushions on the couch with a contented sigh. "Damn, that feels good. There's no place like home."

Without a word, Mabel fetched an ice pack and carefully placed it as she'd seen the nurses do. She bent to kiss her husband's forehead, and whispered, "Let me know if it doesn't help."

"Thank you, honey."

When Mabel turned, Emily was eyeing them both as if shoring up new arguments. She cut off those thoughts by asking, "What other changes are you thinking of?"

"Gentry will be taking over as a manager, so I'll have a little more free time."

"Hallelujah. I can't wait to meet him, but if you say he's the one for the job, well, your uncle and I know he'll be as perfect as you are."

"I'm not perfect," Emily said almost absently, as if the denial was made through habit. After nibbling her bottom lip, she added, "I'm also getting a pet. A dog. From the shelter."

Sullivan's bushy eyebrows rose an inch. "Well now, that's an excellent idea. I've always thought you should have a guard dog since you live alone."

Mabel asked, "Wouldn't Saul count?"

To which Sullivan asked, "You livin' with him already, Emily?"

"What? No." She gave an embarrassed laugh. "And I was thinking of a mature, good-natured companion, not a guard dog."

"A dog of any kind would be great," Mabel agreed. "But aren't you and Saul going to—"

"Aunt," she complained with a laugh. "After being called prissy and a stick-in-the-mud for so long—"

"Rob called you that, too?" Mabel asked, appalled. "I wish I had slapped that man just once."

With a tap on the door, Saul pushed it open and stepped in, plastic grocery bags in both hands. Looking as if he'd heard every word, he turned to Emily and said, "Sorry it took so long. I couldn't find the—"

The words stopped. Saul stopped, too.

Mabel watched in satisfaction while he stared at Emily as if seeing her for the first time, and falling hard.

Emily, bless her heart, appeared to have no idea why. "Saul?" She stood and took a step toward him, sending her hair to tumble around her shoulders. "Everything okay?"

His greedy gaze seemed to take in everything at once. "You took it down."

Emily touched her hair, smoothed one side behind her ear, and blushed. "My aunt was just—"

"Agreeing that she should wear it loose," Mabel said. "Isn't it beautiful?"

Still standing there unblinking, Saul said, "Yeah."

Grinning, Sullivan said, "Some of us can't see worth a damn, so if you're happily gawking, son, say so."

Mabel said, "He's happily gawking."

"I am." Finally, Saul finished stepping in and closed the door. To Mabel and Sullivan, he said, "Sorry, but I've imagined how it'd look at least a million times. It's gorgeous."

Because Emily still seemed incapable of speech, Mabel picked up the slack. "It is. No reason to dye it purple, Emily."

Saul went still again, strangling out, "*Purple*?"

And despite everything, Mabel started laughing, which got Sullivan laughing, and before too long, both Saul and Emily joined in.

SAUL WAITED UNTIL they'd been on the road a few minutes before he mentioned her ex. He'd stood there on the front stoop, listening in without meaning to, surprised at how easily their voices had carried through the door until he realized it hadn't closed all the way when he'd left.

He was surprised even more that Emily's ex had apparently misunderstood her in a really big way.

Prissy? No one else thought so. Emily was open-hearted and warm in a way few could claim. Goody-

Two shoes? Okay, so Emily was tactful and reserved. It still amused him to think of how she'd refused a wine cooler based on an experience back in high school. He, however, considered that cute, and he had no problem at all with her choice not to drink. Never, not once, had he seen her judge anyone else for having a casual drink.

And wow, when she let her hair down... Using that to break the silence, he said, "I had no idea what a difference it'd make for a woman to change her hair."

She quickly turned her face away, but not before he saw the twitching of her lips. Probably hoping to affect a casual tone, but still sounding flattered, she replied, "It's not all that."

"Yeah, it is. I hope you wear it that way more often. It's sexy." He waited a beat, then added, "Like you."

She gave a self-conscious laugh—but her cinnamon eyes were bright, and a slight blush colored her cheeks. "Thank you."

"But Em?" He waited until she finally glanced at him, then added, "I've thought you were sexy from the first time I met you."

Laughing again, she said, "No you didn't." It came off sounding like a question.

"It's true. And the night of Yardley's wedding? God, you were gorgeous. You have no idea how much I wanted you then."

Thick lashes lifted, her eyes wide. "I...didn't realize."

"I know." He watched the road as they spoke. "Talk about a hit to the ego. All my flirting and laying hints didn't win you over, though I have to admit there were a few times there when we did the whole eye thing, yeah?"

"The eye thing?"

"The connection? Staring at each other and feeling it?"

Breathless, she admitted, "I did that a lot. You always rattled me. I'd blush for no reason."

Prissy? Not a chance. "You blushed because you were thinking the same things I was."

"Not sure I was thinking at all. No one's ever affected me like that."

Ah, the opening he needed. "Not even your ex?"

Just that quickly, she withdrew. Emotionally, if not physically.

When she said nothing else, he asked, "Will you tell me about him?" And then, because it bothered him that she was bothered, he said, "If you'd rather not, I understand."

"You overheard my aunt and uncle?"

No reason to admit something she already knew. "They didn't like him much, did they?"

"They hid it well for the longest time. It wasn't until I filed for divorce that they finally spoke up." She released a sigh. "I tried, Saul, I really did."

"Hey." He glanced at her, but was pleased to see she looked merely reflective, not sad. "I already know that. Ms. Emily Lucretia gives her all to anything she does, so of course you did everything you could for your marriage. I never had a doubt."

Turning in her seat, she smiled at him. "You honestly believe that?"

"I know you, Em. Clearly better than he ever did."

Her gaze searched over his face, she considered things, then admitted he was right. "Rob had this idea that I should be perfect all the time, but then there were so many things he didn't like about me. He'd say I was too uptight when I didn't automatically like the same things he did."

With awful sexual scenarios playing through his mind, Saul asked suspiciously, "What things?"

"He loved action movies and I loved books. He loved five-star restaurants and I preferred local eateries. He was an evening person and I'm a morning person." Earnestly, she explained, "I'd see those movies with him, and we'd do the restaurants sometimes. I just couldn't always do it, you know?"

He shouldn't have expected that of her. "Compromise is a good thing."

"I like quiet evenings at home. After working all day, I'm tired—and that was true even when I was younger. It was never a good match, really, because he was a football star and I was the studious girl acing my classes with pride. The thing is, I got swept up in the romantic notion of it. Me, backward Emily, chased by a legend."

Saul snorted at that description. Far as he was concerned, Emily was the legend. Anyone who'd ever met her remembered her. What was that if not legendary? "Winning you over is probably the smartest thing he ever did."

That earned him a real grin. "Well, he didn't think so. Not for long, anyway." She went quiet for a bit.

Saul didn't push her. He was pleased that she'd opened up so much already. They had some time yet before they'd reach Cemetery. Their plan was to grab something to eat, then head to the shelter for her dog. She'd already called to check on Gentry, who'd insisted he'd finish out the day and she didn't need to return.

Little by little, Saul realized how important Gentry was to her. Soon, he'd like to get to know him better.

Emily came to a silent decision, and relaxed. "We hadn't been married that long when Rob was in a car wreck. He'd been driving too fast and blew around a curve in the road, taking out a county sign and a guard-rail. Thankfully no one else was involved, but he rolled the car and ended up in a ditch."

Only one thing concerned Saul. "You weren't with him?"

She shook her head. "I was working and he was bored, so he'd met up with friends…" Her breathing deepened, and she whispered, "It was so awful. I'll never forget see-ing him at the hospital. Blood and bruises everywhere. For once, he looked frail when he never had before."

Silently, Saul offered his open palm. Without hesita-tion, Emily put her hand in his. It was something he'd never take for granted, her acceptance of him. Not just of him, but for all the complications in his life right now. In so many ways, he needed her, her trust, her calm, her enthusiasm, and her understanding. This, sharing with her, felt like an incredible gift. "How bad was it?"

"Bad enough to change everything." The breath she re-leased sounded shaky. "He'd broken a leg, his shoulder, a few ribs. His face was a mess, all black-and-blue and swol-len. He could only get one eye open, and it was so blood-shot, it hurt to look at him. Cuts, gouges, bad scrapes."

"That had to be terrifying for you."

"He kept whispering about football, but I think we both knew that was over, not just from the extent of the injuries, but because he'd been drinking, too. We knew… or at least I did, that there'd be legal trouble ahead." Her smile was quick and sad. "For weeks after, I was con-centrating on his recovery, but he was raging about his career. It was like we were in different worlds or something."

Saul gently squeezed her hand. "Raging?"

"Being fined and charged for a DUI, arguing with the college about his scholarship and being in pain, it made him unreasonable about everything, with everyone, and effectively ended his athletic career."

Already guessing the answer, Saul asked, "He took it hard?"

"Very. With his injuries he couldn't drive, but he lost his license for a year anyway. His drinking got a lot worse, and he started misusing his pain pills. When the doctors ended his prescription, he bought them elsewhere." Her mouth tightened. "I was so embarrassed about that."

"He was a grown man."

"He was my husband."

Yes, Emily would take that on herself. Saul knew that about her. "I'm sorry."

As if it didn't matter, she shook her head. "I gave up the rest of my education—"

"Hold up. I thought you said you were working?"

"I did both. My classes were never that difficult, and I had a job at the college bookstore and the café." Seeing his scowl, Emily leaned closer, putting her head on his shoulder for just a moment. "It wasn't bad, Saul, I promise. Not until Rob's accident."

When she released his hand and straightened in her seat, Saul missed her touch.

"Right before my eyes, he seemed to bottom out, and nothing I did was helping. At times, I think I made it worse. Like I was an enabler or something."

"You cared, Em." Apparently, more than her ex had.

"Don't ever feel bad about that." When she still said nothing, Saul couldn't take it. "You had a right to your own happiness, too."

"That's almost exactly what Aunt Mabel said when I told her I'd filed for divorce. It took forever to get everything settled. In many ways, I felt like I was abandoning him, but I wasn't sure what else to do. Staying didn't help him, so I hoped leaving would."

"Did it?"

"He got back on his feet at least." She sent him a crooked smile. "Mostly to meet with a lawyer and try to sue me for everything we had."

Bastard. "How'd that work out for him?"

"Not as he'd hoped, that's for sure. I had to pay to end the lease on our apartment, but I got to keep our car and half of our savings, which wasn't much, really. Overall, it was like starting over, but with a new understanding of myself. My aunt and uncle were with me every step of the way, never once judging me, just being supportive and offering help where they could. I felt like a fool, but my aunt brushed that off and said Rob was the fool for losing me."

"Every minute of every day, I like your aunt even more."

She gave a soft smile. "Yes, she's pretty incredible." Emily smoothed a hand up his arm, over his biceps to his shoulder, then to the back of his neck, where her fingertips played with his hair. "You're pretty incredible, too. Thank you for understanding."

"Yeah?" Her touch was making him a little nuts, so he caught her wrist and brought her palm to his mouth for a kiss. "So, do you think this incredible guy can take you into the Pit Stop for a meal so I can make sure everyone in Cemetery understands the way of things?"

Laughing, she reminded him, "Our kiss is all over social media. People understand."

"So we'll give it a boost. What do you say? There's time yet before you need to get to the shelter."

With a happy huff, she said, "Fine. Let's just don't go overboard, all right? I think I've caused enough of a stir for one day."

"I'll be on my best behavior."

GENTRY HAD JUST finished up with a customer when his phone dinged with a message. Guessing it had to be Emily, he smiled as he pulled it from his pocket...and was pleasantly surprised to see it was from Mila asking if he had time to chat.

Rather than text back a reply, he called her.

She answered on the first ring with, "Hey."

Hearing her voice made him smile even more. "What's up?"

"Please don't think I'm the gossipy sort, but Emily and Saul just came in and wow, they're causing a stir."

Gentry laughed. "Yeah? How come?" Couldn't be just that they were together. No one could be surprised about that.

"Well, for one thing, Saul's acting like he's madly in love, and Emily let her hair loose."

"Her hair loose?" If that was supposed to mean something, Gentry didn't get it.

"Yeah, as in, not in a ponytail." Voice lower, Mila confided, "She looks incredibly fine and everyone is noticing."

Huh. Pretty sure he'd never seen Emily without a

ponytail. Well, there was the one time when she'd had a headache and had rearranged it, but he'd been too taken by surprise at finding her bent forward, rump in the air, to notice her hair.

Sitting on the stool behind the counter, he got comfortable. "I take it you're working."

"Yup. I'm on a break right now, though."

Good, then he wasn't interrupting anything. "The stupid Facebook page has been blowing up all day, and Emily's all over Instagram now." Idly, feeling pleased by it, he said, "I saw your comment."

"Which one?"

More than one? He hadn't realized, but now he'd probably look. "Everyone was talking about Emily and me on the beach." Gentry had already clued in Mila, in case she misunderstood. Fortunately, most didn't seem to know it was him, and Viv apparently hadn't blabbed. He'd remember to thank her for that.

Many people were speculating on quiet, reserved Emily not being so quiet after all, but Mila had simply commented that Emily was one of the nicest people she'd ever met.

Just that, nothing more.

Plenty of people had reacted favorably to her comment, too, meaning Emily was well-liked.

"Hey," Mila said. "As long as the gossip stays complimentary, Emily might actually enjoy it, right?"

He hoped so. Saul had likely taken her to the restaurant to ensure everyone knew she hadn't just kissed him for show, that they were in fact a couple. "If you see anyone saying anything unkind, let me know."

With a grin in her tone, Mila asked, "What will you do?"

He wasn't sure. Shield Emily as best he could. Tell Saul. Hell, he'd go to the town council meeting if necessary, which would completely blow his effort to keep a low profile. "I don't want her hurt."

"Same. We'll both keep an eye out, okay?"

Gentry glanced at the clock. "What time do you get off tonight?"

After a slight but expectant pause, she said, "Unfortunately, we don't close until nine on Friday and Saturday."

"I'm here until six, and then I'm heading to my apartment." He waited only a moment before saying, "You're welcome to come by after work if you're not too tired."

"Definitely not too tired," she said fast, then laughed at herself. "Wow, did I sound desperate much, or what?"

His feelings for her expanded, grew sharper-edged. "Sounded like maybe you want to see me as much as I want to see you."

"Do you?" she asked in another rush. "Because Gentry... Being honest here, okay? I already think about you way too much. Not just because I'm new here but because... I don't know..."

Smiling, his heart beating too fast again—which always seemed to be the case wherever Mila was concerned—he said, "We clicked."

"We did, didn't we? It felt that way for me."

"For me, too."

"Then yes, I'll come over straight from work."

That sealed the deal for him. Gentry knew he'd be watching the clock every minute until then. "I'll text you my address."

"Okay." Softly, sweetly, she whispered, "See you then."

## CHAPTER ELEVEN

RIDICULOUS, BUT MILA felt like a jumble of sizzling nerves by the time she pulled up to the curb at the four-family home. Every part of her wanted every part of Gentry, but she had serious doubts that he was as invested. Interested, yes. She believed that now.

But wanting her like she wanted him? Doubtful.

She was only twenty-three, but she'd known plenty of guys. Heck, since she was sixteen, she'd never been without a date. Her last guy...well, for a while there, she'd thought he could be "the one." Yeah, right. Total nonsense, and she knew it now.

Out of every man she'd ever known, Gentry was quieter, more mature and contained, and he fascinated her on every level. Whenever his gray eyes looked right at her, it was as if he saw things others didn't, good things. Not just looks and a superficial bubbly attitude.

That insight got to her. In a big way.

She stepped out of the golf cart, which, thankfully, no one minded in the small community. She couldn't drive it if she went on any of the busier roads, but luckily, both she and Gentry had settled closer to work, not near the trendy lakefront property.

He'd said his apartment was at the top to the right.

The sun had already set, leaving only a lemon glow along the horizon that faded into the sky to a dusky gray and then blue-black. A few streetlamps lit the area, and somewhere nearby she could hear the quiet drone of kids still playing in a yard. Lightning bugs danced around various bushes, and her heart pounded so hard, it was like it wanted to escape her chest.

Needlessly, she smoothed her hair. She'd brushed it before leaving the restaurant, and she'd even taken the time to tidy up her makeup. There wasn't much more she could do without going home to shower first...

The door to the house opened, and Gentry stood there, backlit by a hall light.

Why did he have to look so good? After getting dumped, she'd sworn off relationships, and seriously, she'd meant it at the time. Heart and soul.

*Have fun*, she'd told herself. *Enjoy guys without risking more hurt.*

Her heart and soul hadn't counted on Gentry McAdams.

Giving her a crooked smile, he stepped out. "Are you waiting for me to come get you?"

Ooooh, would he? That could be exciting, except she was done teasing. So instead she admitted, "Waiting for my pulse to quiet down a little so I can think."

Awareness slowly stole his smile, and damned if his eyes didn't seem to glow.

Wordlessly, he held out a hand.

Nope, there wasn't enough oxygen in all of Cemetery to keep her from going breathless. Shoving the golf cart keys into her pocket, Mila started forward, each step gaining momentum so that by the time she reached him, she was practically running.

Understanding, Gentry braced his feet apart and caught her up against him. His mouth found hers, but not for the consuming kiss she expected—and wanted. Nope, not Gentry. He was way too cool for that.

He brushed his mouth over hers, put his forehead to hers, and whispered, "The things you do to me."

Okay, good. She hoped it was at least half as much as what he did to her.

"Come on. Let's get inside."

Oh, right. She glanced around but thankfully didn't see anyone. Warm with anticipation, she went up the flight of stairs with him, each step sounding like a drumbeat in her head.

Gentry laughed quietly. "So you know, it's an efficiency, a tiny place and as far from fancy as it can get."

"Right now," she replied honestly, "I don't care if it's a shed with tools in the corner." She just wanted to be with him.

He opened the door and stood back for her to enter.

Wow, it really was miniscule. She stepped into one room that held a wide futon, a single chair, and a shelf with a TV on it. Beyond that she saw a galley kitchen with a two-seater table, a narrow fridge and two-burner stove, a single tall pantry, and a few cabinets over the appliances. She assumed the only interior door opened to a bathroom, which meant...

Her gaze came back to the futon, and she noticed the blanket over the back, and bed pillows, arranged as throw pillows, at each end.

Gentry stepped up against her back and loosely draped his arms around her. "You're in my bedroom, Mila."

Her lungs constricted, but she managed to nod. "Seems so."

Smiling against her temple, he said, "I ordered a pizza."

"You…" Wait, *what*? Twisting around to face him, she scowled into his handsome face, opened her mouth to blast him, but he didn't give her the chance.

His mouth settled on hers, and because this was Gentry, it was the most killer kiss she'd ever received. Like melt-your-bones sexy. Whoa.

A second later, a knock sounded on his door.

Stepping back, but with his gaze on her face, he quietly promised, "Soon."

Obviously, she'd hold him to that, but for now, rather than face the pizza delivery person, she stalked away into his kitchen and dropped into one of the two chairs at the small square table, which, she realized, wasn't a table at all but rather a tabletop permanently affixed to the wall in the corner, across from the fridge.

While Gentry spoke quietly with the delivery guy, Mila glanced around again. His apartment was small, true, but modern and exceptionally clean. The dish towel hanging over the sink was folded just so. A magnetic hook on the fridge held two pot holders. Curious, she got up and peeked behind the closed door, and yup, it opened to a toilet, sink, and shower. This room, too, was pristine.

Her hottie was a neat freak. Somehow that made him more endearing.

From behind her, he asked, "Cola, water, or tea?"

"Cola." She pivoted back and went to the fridge. "What about you?"

"I'll take the same."

His refrigerator held more drinks than anything else,

including a quart of milk, bottled water, a quart of iced tea, and two cans each of a variety of colas.

"I wasn't sure what you'd want," he explained.

So thoughtful, but as she took out two cans, she said, "I wanted you, and you know it."

Gentry went still in the act of getting plates from the upper cabinet: arms reaching up, eyes flared, every line of his body taut... Then he drew a slow breath, let it out, and grabbed what he needed. "I'm on board with that, so we're clear right now."

"Great." She sniffed the air, now fragranced with pizza, and realized she was hungry.

They were both silent while getting the food together, her plotting, him maybe...stalling? No, not Gentry. "So." She bit into her pizza, chewed, then asked, "What's on your mind now?"

"I'm staying in Cemetery."

Was that up in the air? "Oh?"

"I spoke with Emily, told her everything..."

The words dwindled off, so she smiled and asked, "Bet she told you not to worry about it—whatever it is. Am I right?"

"Actually...yeah." He sipped his cola. "The thing is, now that she knows, I want you to know, too."

"Oh, good. It's driven me nuts wondering, because you're such a great guy. Just understand, I trust Emily. If she's not worried, neither am I."

Humor, maybe a little relief, too, lifted one side of his mouth. Then he broke her heart telling her about a horrid childhood that he didn't seem to think was so horrid, and a mother who clearly didn't know how to mother, and a grandpa who'd been his whole world before he'd died.

The pizza stuck in her throat, caught there by sympathy and sadness for a boy who'd been trapped by his mother's reputation and lack of caring. She knew people like that existed. Some of her friends had come from less than model homes.

But what Gentry so casually described... His poor mother. Clearly, the woman was lost, and if Gentry couldn't save her, Mila didn't think anyone could. And his grandpa—well, she was glad he'd been in Gentry's life.

She was glad Gentry was here now, too, in Cemetery. And most of all, she was glad she'd gone after him that first day.

"Emily asked me to be her manager, so I'm staying in Cemetery. For good." He watched her closely.

"Awesome."

Gentry didn't blink. "At first all you wanted was a casual hookup, right?"

Before she'd gotten to know him, but she didn't say so, not yet.

"The thing is, I'm not sure I can do that. Not with you."

What did that mean? The way he said it, it sounded like the opposite of an insult.

"Not right now when my life seems to be coming together and my past really is in the past. I only want to move forward—in whatever I do."

She wanted to sing, *Do me*, but again, she waited.

"I'm not saying we have to be serious right off. I won't go all stalker on you or anything like that. But if you're still looking to just play..." He let that trail off.

"You won't play with me?"

The teased words brought his brows together, not in

irritation but in thought. "If you were someone else, I could. But with you? How I feel around you?" He shook his head. "I can't."

She'd never had a guy say so many wonderful, heartfelt things to her. It left her smiling on the inside, but also with her heart cracking just a little bit because she knew both she and Gentry had a few wounds to heal, the kind that came from the soul.

Trying to sound cavalier and likely failing, she said, "If you think all of that will keep me from making demands on your sexy self, you're mistaken. You're staying in Cemetery? Terrific, since I'm here, too."

Slowly, he grinned. "But are you here long-term?"

"I don't know." She held his gaze. "You could try to convince me."

Relaxing into his seat, he said, "Yeah, I can do that."

"It helps that Cemetery is entertaining, I have fun plans for Kathleen the mannequin, I love working for Saul, and Emily is…well, she's a new friend and I really want to get to know her better."

Gentry looked at her plate, which still held a mostly uneaten second slice of pizza. "Will you stay the night with me?"

"Yes."

She said that so quickly that his gaze shot up to hers, and he laughed.

Not at her, she knew, but with her, which made her laugh, too.

"But now you have to work for it, Gentry McAdams. *After* I finish my pizza."

"No problem."

Yet eating didn't hold the same appeal, because they kept making eye contact. By the second, new tension—

of the sexual variety—invaded her every muscle until she felt ready to leap out of her seat.

Gentry finished his plate first. "I have to be at work at nine tomorrow."

"I don't go in until later, but I'll need to be home to shower and get ready and stuff." She didn't want him to think she was moving in on him.

Standing, he found a plastic storage bag in one of the drawers, put the rest of the pizza in it, and stuck it in the refrigerator. "I'm going to run the box out to the trash." He gave her a long, hungry look. "Be right back."

Airily, Mila waved him off, but the second he was out the door, she raced into his bathroom and rinsed her mouth, checked her teeth to ensure there were no bits of pizza stuck between, smoothed her hair and touched up her makeup, all in record time. She stepped back out just as he was stepping in.

Gentry paused, staring at her from inside the front door.

Heart thundering, she stared back.

Reaching behind himself, he locked the door...and that did it.

This time when she reached him, he didn't placate her with a quick, meager kiss. Instead, he kissed her like a man ready to...well, work for it.

And that totally worked for Mila.

UTTERLY EXHAUSTED, Emily stared up at the ceiling and did a mental recap of her current situation.

Everything on Friday had gone so well, she'd thought it was going to be the best week of her life. Her aunt and uncle were home and comfortable, so far doing amazingly well. She'd insisted that if they needed anything at all, they should call her, but she also called them each afternoon and evening. Her aunt was most content when taking care of Sullivan, and he was progressing more each day, so she really had no reason to worry.

Gentry and Mila had obviously become a couple, and they both looked so happy that it made Emily happy to see them. Saturday, Monday, and Tuesday, Gentry took his lunches at the restaurant so he and Mila could visit, but in addition, Mila had stopped by the flower shop on her way to and from work. Each time, she greeted Emily like a close friend.

On one of those visits, Mila had shown Emily an outfit available at a shop right outside Cemetery. She'd taken a screenshot from their website and insisted the clothes would look amazing on her.

Emily waffled, because the white jeans were sexier than she usually wore, made to fit snugly with a row of silver buttons on the fly instead of a zipper. Plus the red top had a draping neckline that went lower than she was used to. Mila was trying to convince her when Gentry had also taken a look and commented that Saul would go "nuts" when he saw her in it, and that decided it for her. She ordered them right then and there, though the garments hadn't arrived yet.

Added to all that fun, Saul was as attentive as a man could be. Just as Mila stopped by, so did Saul. As long as she wasn't with a customer, he greeted her with a kiss. He called on his breaks, and he even called Sullivan a few times, just to check on him.

And…she now had her pet.

She sighed. Things should have been perfect. Unfortunately, they were not.

When the phone rang, Emily jolted, and her heart

shot into her throat. Dread immediately spurred her into action, and she snatched it up from her nightstand. "Hello?"

Her aunt said, "Good morning, Sunshine."

Emily sat up. "Is something wrong?"

"No, everything is fine, and I really wish you'd stop worrying so much."

Groaning, Emily flopped back on the bed. "Sorry. I didn't get enough sleep and I guess I'm extra jumpy."

With glee, Mabel asked, "Did Saul keep you up?"

Oh, she wished. "No. The cat did, though."

"Again?" Tsking with sympathy, Mabel said, "I had hoped it would settle down by now."

Not likely. Instead of a cuddly, sweet puppy, she'd somehow ended up with a very contrary, spiteful cat.

How had the shelter convinced her? Oh yeah, by insisting that instead of a dog, she should take a "very sweet" older cat named Satin, who had the softest gray-and-black fur she'd ever felt. Big green eyes had seemed to stare right through her, as if the cat was lost and alone.

Emily hadn't been easily convinced, but Berkley Carr, a young woman who ran the shelter for the often-missing director, was positive enough for both of them.

Berkley knew all the animals, everything about each one. She'd fascinated Emily with her awesome, modern look: white-blond hair with the ends dyed hot pink and lively, bright blue eyes. She was like a giant splash of color, an animated rainbow of intensity and determination.

While Emily had wanted to look at the cute puppies, Berkley had expertly steered her to a cat enclosure where beautiful kittens and more mature cats all climbed on carpeted towers and ladders and shelves. They played with stuffed mice and yellow balls, squeaky fish and dangling feathers. It was a wonderfully nice area, and all the cats enjoyed playing there with each other.

Except that off in the corner, glaring, was Satin.

That had sent a twinge of anxiety straight to Emily's heart, and she couldn't help but be curious about the standalone cat.

Berkley swore that all Satin needed was a loving home, someone who really cared, and before Emily could say anything, she was told all about Satin's harsh past and the two years the poor cat had been overlooked while living in the shelter, and how *desperately* Satin wanted a forever home.

When Emily had cautiously petted the cat, marveling at the silky, soft fur, she'd gotten a dead-eyed stare in return. No purr, no welcome at all. Just a sort of baleful disdain.

Of course she'd taken the cat anyway. "I still don't know how it happened."

"I do," Mabel said. "You have an enormous heart. Don't worry, honey. Eventually the cat will settle in."

"I hope so." She'd already purchased everything the cat would need, including a carrier. It was quite the investment, and she'd already been reeling when Berkley oh-so-slyly mentioned that Satin and a certain dog were extremely bonded.

At that, Emily had firmly stated that she could only take one animal.

To her surprise, Berkley hadn't pressed the issue. Instead, she'd said that if Emily changed her mind to let her know. She'd gone on and on about how Betty

Cemetery had sung Emily's praises, talking all about her compassion. Berkley claimed that once Emily had time to think it over, she'd know that getting the dog was the right thing to do.

Emily knew that couldn't happen. Her life was so busy right now that an independent cat would be all she could handle.

After yawning, Emily asked, "Did you call for any particular reason? Need me to run to the store or anything?"

"I called only to see how you're doing."

Lying, Emily said, "I'm fine." She rethought that and said, "Better than fine, actually. I love having Gentry for a manager." Which meant on days like today, she didn't have to rush to get to the shop. "And things with Saul are going great."

"I'm so glad you had him to help you get that cat home."

Since Satin had turned into Satan the minute they'd put her in the car, Emily agreed. The brooding cat had transformed into a screeching, angry Tasmanian devil who apparently wanted the entire world to know how much she hated car rides.

"Me, too. Honest to God, Aunt, I've never heard an animal carry on like that." Berkley had stated that the cat was afraid of being abandoned again and that once Emily got her home, she would be fine.

Oh, but Berkley was a terrific liar.

Now, after her fifth sleepless night, Emily glanced toward her bedroom door and wondered what new torment Satan had for her.

So far, the cat hated everything—Emily especially. Every plant had been destroyed. Her curtains sported snags from the cat climbing. No table decoration was safe. The end of her couch was frayed.

"The worst part," Emily said, "is that Satan insists on standing just outside her litter box when doing her business."

Every. Single. Time.

Muffling her humor, Mabel asked, "Have you tried scolding her?"

"Ha. That would only spur her on. You know, she goes, glares at me, and stalks away with her tail in the air, almost as if it's on purpose to spite me."

"Emily," her aunt chided. "That poor cat does not have a vendetta against you. I take it Saul's suggestion didn't help?"

"Not even a little." Saul's advice had been to close the cat in the laundry room at night, so she couldn't destroy things. "Satan literally mourned—*loudly*—for two hours before I gave up and freed her to wreak havoc however she chose."

"Are you sure she just doesn't want to sleep with you?"

"Ha! I tried that, and she screeched like I was killing her. Plus, I leave my bedroom door open, but she never comes in here. My bedroom is the only room not destroyed." Because the cat hated her too much to get that close. It was depressing. "The weird part is that while I'm at work, there's no problem. I have a pet cam set up so I know while I'm gone, Satan is either sleeping or eating."

"Hmm," Mabel said. "Well, it's obviously a contrary cat, because you, Emily, are very lovable."

Emily closed her eyes. So many times, Gentry would

check the camera, and he'd smile, as if he thought Satin was sweet.

Same with Saul. Other than the ride home, he'd noted only a loner kitty, content to go her own way. Emily knew it was hard to align what he saw with what she described.

It made no sense at all, because the second she got home, desperately wanting that sweet cuddle on the couch, the tornado of ruin began. "I tell you, she hates me."

"Well, honey, look at it this way. The cat is adjusting, but in the meantime, you have Gentry to help out, and you have Saul."

Yes she did, but she and Saul hadn't yet had enough alone time to do all the things she so badly wanted to do. Rather than keep complaining to her aunt, though, Emily asked, "Are you sure there isn't anything I can do for you or Uncle Sullivan?"

"You can take care of yourself and be happy. That's all we need."

Somewhere in there, Emily heard something else. She sat up against the headboard. "Aunt? How are you really? Tired, maybe feeling a little worried, too?"

Mabel laughed. "You know me too well." She let out a soft sigh. "I am tired, but in a good way. The type of tired you get when you're doing something you love."

"Taking care of Uncle Sullivan?"

"If only it were that easy. Oh, Emily, he is *so* stubborn. For years and years, he's taken care of me."

"I seem to recall you taking care of each other."

"You know what I mean. Now I want to take care of him, but he grumbles."

"He's doing his PT?"

"He does *extra*, and I can sometimes tell he's uncomfortable, but instead of making it easy and just saying what he wants or needs from me, I have to guess." She blew out a breath. "Last night I lost my temper and told him he was being a damned martyr and I was tired of it."

Uh-oh. Warily, Emily asked, "You two argued?"

Mabel snorted. "The blasted man got all offended and said he wasn't an invalid and that he was bored. He wanted out of the house…so we ended up going to the park."

"You…" Pressing a hand to her forehead, Emily sat forward. "You put him in the car and drove to the park?"

"Emily," her aunt warned. "I'm not an invalid, either. I'm only seventy-one, and I have a perfect driving record."

"I know, but…" Emily let that trail off. True, her aunt was a very safe driver. "I just worry about you getting him in and out of the car." Her aunt was a small woman, and Sullivan was not a small man.

"That part was easy. He's maneuvering much better now, and once he got his way, he was happy to let me help him in and out."

Picturing that lightened Emily's mood. "How'd it go?"

"We had an amazing time. There's a walking path at the park, and we went all the way around it. I was so worried that Sullivan would overdo it, but I swear, he smiled the entire time. He's really good with the walker now. He talked with everyone we met, and afterward we got burgers for dinner and then ice cream."

"Sounds like a full day."

"It was probably a little much for him on his first day

out, but he loved it." Lowering her voice, Mabel whispered, "When we got home, we were both exhausted, so we showered together."

Ruthlessly blocking that image from her mind, Emily gave a noncommittal, "Oh?"

"It was wonderful."

That made Emily smile. "I'm glad."

Still in that very low tone, Mabel confided, "With Sullivan's age and his recent injury, I think… Well, I started feeling our limited time."

"Aunt!"

"No, hush, Emily, and just listen."

Chastised, Emily fell silent.

"We're not getting any younger, and Sullivan is ten years older than me. It scared me." With a slight break in her voice, Mabel whispered, "I love him so much."

"Oh, Aunt," Emily whispered back, wishing she were there to hold her, to offer whatever comfort she could. "I know it, and so does he. What you two have—it's what every couple wants."

"You and Saul included."

Emily couldn't guarantee Saul's feelings, but she nodded. "Yes."

After a deep, bracing breath, Mabel sounded stronger. "From now on, I refuse to be afraid. I'm going to embrace every day. If Sullivan wants to go out, by God, we'll go out. When he wants ice cream, I want to make sure he gets it."

Silent tears fell down Emily's cheeks, and though Mabel couldn't see it, she nodded again. "Yes," she whispered. "We should all make the most of every single day."

"And that's why I called. Make the most of your days,

Emily. If you want Saul, grab him with both hands. Give the social media sites something to talk about."

Now laughter joined her tears. "I'm not sure Cemetery is ready for your plan."

"Doesn't matter. You, Emily Lucretia, are ready. Shake your hair loose, put on something racy, make out with that hot stud of yours, and keep on loving that ornery cat until she starts to love you back."

She wiped her cheeks. "If you feel like going out, you and Uncle Sullivan can visit me, too. Or I'll visit you, whenever you want."

"We'll see. For now, know that we're both following along with the social media shenanigans of *the flower lady*, and we think she's incredibly special, well worth her own hashtag."

Emily's smile went gentle and soft. If she was special, she'd certainly gotten that quality from her aunt and uncle. "While you and Uncle Sullivan are celebrating life with such gusto, keep in mind how much I love you both. Just as you want to take care of him, I want to take care of both of you. So pretty please, if you think of anything I can do, make me even happier by letting me know."

"It's a deal. Oh, and now I hear Sullivan waking. I put some plump cushions on the outdoor furniture, so we'll sit out there to have our coffee. Bye, honey. Enjoy your day as much as we'll enjoy ours."

"I'll do my best." After disconnecting the call, Emily left the bed with new determination. A quick shower helped to revive her. She cleaned her teeth, brushed her hair, threw on some clothes, and crept past her open bedroom door, hoping she wouldn't find a catastrophe waiting for her.

She almost tripped over the cat.

Satan—she refused to call the mean menace Satin—was sitting right there, staring up at her in a way that left her unnerved. "Um… Is your food dish empty?"

Nothing, not even a blink.

"I don't think you're out of water. Maybe you left another mess outside the box?"

The cat simply stared…and then a hopeful thought formed.

Maybe Satan had been waiting for her. Maybe she now wanted to be friends?

With a sort of optimistic desperation, Emily smiled and offered her hand. "Hey, kitty," she whispered softly. "Aren't you getting lonely? I sure am."

The cat's stare almost dared her to come any closer. So far, Satan hadn't deliberately scratched her, but yeah. Emily was leery of those sharp claws.

Moving slowly to keep from spooking the cat, she sat down on the floor. "You really are a pretty kitty," she continued in a coaxing voice. "Wednesdays are my days off, so we could keep each other company. I'd even let you sleep in my bed." *Please, please, please.*

Satan's eyes narrowed. She hissed, then turned and sashayed away, her tail in the air as if to punctuate her disdain.

Emily slumped against the wall. And stayed there. A few seconds later, she heard something crash, but she couldn't work up the energy to care. She was still there, pondering what to do, when a knock sounded at her door.

Saul. *How in the world did I forget about him?* Since today was her day off, Saul had coordinated, and they were supposed to spend the day together.

Done wallowing in her misery, something she'd never in her life done before now, Emily stood, only briefly wondering about her appearance before she headed to the living room and the front door. After ensuring the cat wasn't near enough to dart out, she opened it and said, "Hurry. Come in before the cat abandons me completely."

Grinning, Saul slipped in, closed the door, and hauled her close for a lingering kiss. Emotion, exhaustion, and yeah, excitement, all melded together so that she sank limply against him.

He tangled a hand in her hair and eased up, kissing her cheek, her throat, and then her forehead. "Hey, you okay?" Then he got a good look around and whistled. "Whoa. You didn't exaggerate. The cat has really done a number on you."

"Yes, she has." Heaving a sigh, Emily admitted, "She still hates me."

"She doesn't hate you," he countered automatically. "No one, not even a cat, could hate you."

"Funny, but that's close to what my aunt said."

"She and Sullivan are doing all right?"

Wrinkling her nose, Emily confided, "They showered together."

Saul grinned. "I'd say that's a good sign."

"Yup. Overall, they seem to be doing great. Now if I could just figure out how to please the cat."

"Have you talked to Berkley?"

"A few times." The young woman was always so busy, Emily felt bad bothering her. Each time she could hear the chaos of dogs happily barking in the background. It made her wish even more that she'd stuck with her original plan to get a puppy. Except…that would mean the cat would still be sitting there in the shelter, and she hadn't been any happier there. At least here, Emily could keep trying.

"And?" Saul asked.

"Berkley insists that Satin must miss her dog friend." Of course, that doubled Emily's guilt. She couldn't handle one supposedly independent cat. What in the world would she do with a dog mixed in?

"Ah." In a gesture she now knew meant he was thinking things through, Saul rubbed the back of his neck. Looking around at her house again, he winced. He'd seen it the day she'd gotten the cat, when everything had been undamaged and decorated.

Now it looked as if a herd of buffalo had trampled through.

Decisive, Saul announced, "I'll get the dog. Then they can at least visit, and that would calm down Satin."

"Saul." Resting her palm on his solid chest, right over his steady heartbeat, Emily stared up at him in wonder. The man was trying to cut back at work, readjust his life for a kid and still make time for her, and now, he thought about taking on a dog to keep *her* cat happy. "I don't think a more wonderful human being exists in our galaxy."

"I told you, we're in this together. Plus it'll give me one more reason to hang around." He brushed a gentle kiss over her lips and whispered, "Often."

"You're welcome to do that anyway." He *had* been doing it, with his visits to the flower shop and his frequent calls. Now, on his day off, he was trying to help her when they should be getting things ready at his house for Beck's visit.

Undeterred, Saul said, "Me having the dog would

help with…" he gestured at her house "…this, too, right?"

"This?" she teased. "You mean the disgruntlement and destruction of a cat?"

"I mean life." He cupped her face and kissed her again. "Life, Emily. You're a priority for me. Anything and everything I can do to make it easier for you, to keep you happy, I want to do it."

Now she felt ridiculous for being down about such small things. She had Saul, their relationship grew stronger every day, and even though they hadn't yet sealed the deal, so to speak, her future held a lot of promise.

*Grab him with both hands*, her aunt had said.

Well, maybe she needed to grab her own life first.

Saul added huskily, "Bonus thought—the sooner that cat is appeased, the sooner I can get you alone."

"You know what? That sexy promise has convinced me that *I* should just get the dog. I mean, how much worse can it get? If nothing else, they'll keep each other company in their demolition while I have my wicked way with you."

Satan let out a loud "*Mmrowww*," and when they looked at her, she was standing alert, head lifted, ears forward, and expression expectant.

"Saul," Emily whispered. "Do you think she understood?"

He appeared just as stunned. "Maybe a word or two." Kneeling, he held out his hand and said experimentally, "Dog?" and the cat trotted over to him, head-butted his thigh, and let out another "Mmrowww."

Emily's eyes flared. "Oh my gosh, she *did*."

Carefully, Saul stroked the cat's back. "Honey, I

think that's really it." He looked up at her, amazed. "I think Berkley is right. She misses her pal."

Excited, her heart rapping hard against her ribs—she might have the means to actually make the cat happy—Emily said, "Let me grab my purse," as she ran back to her bedroom.

Saul followed. "We're going to the shelter now?"

"Right now. This instant." She turned, realized he was looking at her bed, and wanted to melt. All kinds of suggestion filled his gaze. "If you're busy—"

"I'm not. I want to spend the day with you."

Excellent, because that's what she wanted, too. "If this works, we could maybe…? I mean, not to rush you, but—"

Putting his arm around her, Saul propelled her back to the door. "I'll drive."

Emily handed him her keys. "Okay, but we need my car so we have someplace to put—" she saw the cat standing in the doorway, her big green eyes widened, so she whispered "—the *d-o-g*." On the way out, she stopped to daringly touch the back of Satin's neck. "We'll be back soon, baby."

The cat curled a lip, turned, and walked away, tail once again in the air.

"I swear," Emily grumbled. "That cat shows me her butt far, far too often."

Snickering, Saul teased, "My imperfect Emily," as he led her out the door. "Maybe she'll stop that once she has her buddy."

After they pulled out of the driveway, Emily called Berkley, who was beyond thrilled and even said she'd give Emily a huge discount for everything. They arrived to find a long-legged hound mix named Snuggles geared up and ready to go. With his entire butt wagging and his tongue lolling out, Snuggles greeted them with undiluted joy.

Emily fell immediately in love with the soft floppy brown ears, the short black, white, and brown fur, and the sheer excitement of the animal. He was too big to be called a lap dog, but he was happy, and she hoped like heck he'd make Satin happy, too.

"A very wise choice," Berkley said, her smile almost as bright as the dog's.

"You," Emily accused with a laugh, "probably knew exactly what I was facing."

"I did, and I'm sorry. I love Satin and Snuggles so much, but no one would adopt them together, so they've been here for two long years. I desperately, *desperately* wanted them to find their forever home together. Betty swore you were the perfect person to make it happen, but she did say you might need a little convincing."

Emily blew out a breath, but she smiled, too. "Oh, when I see Betty again…" She left that half-hearted threat open-ended.

"I added a harness for the cat to everything else. Fair warning, when you take Snuggles out to do his business, Satin will kick up a terrible fit, so just give in and take them together. It's a little more work, but worth it, I promise."

With his arm around Emily's waist, Saul said, "I hope Snuggles is better mannered than the cat."

"Much," Berkley promised. "And you'll see a different side of Satin once you reunite them, but if you have any problems, let me know." She looked at them both as if considering something, then tipped her head slightly to the side. "I hope you don't mind, but I want to give you my card."

Berkley snatched something from a drawer of the reception desk and handed it to her. Surprised, Emily automatically accepted the little rectangle. It reminded her of when Betty had done the same and instantly made her wary. "I already know your number."

"That's for the shelter. This," she said, indicating the card, "has my personal cell phone number. If you ever need to go out of town, please don't leave Satin and Snuggles with a pet hotel, because they'll be separated, and then they'll be miserable again. If you call me, I'll watch them for you free of charge."

Such a kind offer made Emily feel too emotional, but then, she knew she was short on sleep, long on frustration, and she sincerely hoped Berkley was right about reuniting the pets. While storing the card in her wallet for safekeeping, she said, "Thank you. Really. I pray this works, because I'm at my wit's end."

Berkley went one further and stepped close to embrace her. "I promise," she said softly. "You really are perfect for them, and once they get over their snit, they'll be perfect for you."

"Get over their snit?" Oh, she didn't like the sound of that at all. Emily eyed the pooch, who stared back. And now...well, now it almost looked devilish.

"A few days at most, I swear." Berkley's lips trembled with a grin. "Please, please, *please* just give them a chance. I swear you'll only have to be patient a tiny bit longer."

Emily folded her arms. "Describe a tiny bit longer. Days? Weeks? Because Berkley, my house won't survive."

"Two days." She considered, then nodded firmly as if she'd just convinced herself. "Two days," she said again.

Sighing, Emily knew she was stuck. No way would she return that poor, mean, ornery cat to the shelter. It just wasn't in her. And if the dog only amplified the trouble? Somehow, she'd find a way to deal with it. "Just so we're clear, I'm not perfect." Especially right now, when she was so tired she couldn't see straight.

Both Saul and Berkley indulged her with a smile.

"I'm *not*..." Seeing their expressions, Emily gave up. "I'll give the animals however many chances they need." Oddly enough, the moment she said it, she felt better.

Right there in front of Berkley, Saul gave her a quick kiss and a hug. "You ready to reunite these beasts?"

She nodded firmly. "Ready."

Berkley walked with them out to their car, almost like an anxious mother seeing her child off to kindergarten. She said to Snuggles, "You be good now, okay?" Then she hugged him and added, "You'll see Satin soon."

To which the dog woofed happily and got right into the seat, where Emily fastened the special doggy restraint on him.

Even as Emily and Saul got into the car, Berkley lingered. She stayed after Saul started it, and smiled as they began to pull away.

And right before Emily put up her window, Berkley said, "Hashtag The Flower Lady!" and gave Emily a double thumbs-up.

## CHAPTER TWELVE

SAUL VERY, very quietly closed the bedroom door. Then he listened, but he didn't hear a thing.

When he turned to Emily, he found her sitting on the side of the bed, shoulders slumped wearily, and with utter relief. A small, very pleased smile played around her mouth.

*He* wanted to play around her mouth, but for the moment, he leaned back on the door and asked softly, "Happy?"

"Yes." Her lashes lifted, and her beautiful eyes glowed with emotion. "You saw them together. Was that the most amazing sight?"

She was the most amazing sight. "I've never seen anything like it, especially between a cat and dog." Getting out of the car was a trick because Snuggles went bananas, straining at his leash, jumping this way and that, as if he knew Satin waited behind the front door.

And he was right.

When Emily unlocked the door and went to peek inside, Satin shot out past her. Snuggles jerked to get free, and then, like improbable soul mates, the animals met on the sidewalk with remarkable joy.

He and Emily had stood there while Snuggles dropped to his back and Satin crawled all over him, each of them so thrilled that... Yeah. He'd been moved.

Covering her mouth, Emily had silently cried, but he knew it was a happy cry. Bewildered, but happy.

"I should have done this sooner," she'd said. Then she got the leash and urged the dog inside, because that was the easiest way to get the cat inside, too.

Once he'd carried in everything and secured the door, Saul found the dog and cat entwined together. Calmer now, Snuggles groomed Satin's head until the cat's fur was slobbery wet and standing on end. Satin apparently loved it, because she stayed tucked close to the dog's neck.

Emily had torn herself away from the sight to fill the dog's water dish and put out some food, then she'd put the dog bed very near the cat bed…and together, they'd decided to leave the reunited loves alone.

Now he finally had her in a bedroom, and she looked ready to topple over. Not with reciprocal need, but with fatigue. That, more than anything, told him what a trial the last few days had been for her. His organized, always pleasant, *nearly* perfect Emily had never wanted a cat, but she'd taken one in. Not a sweet cat, but one that turned her life upside down and destroyed her possessions.

Emily didn't give up, though; she just wore herself to the bone, because that's the type of person she was.

The type who loved with all her heart.

Who felt the suffering of others, not just people, but pets.

A woman who had so easily stolen his heart, and won over an entire town just by listening. And caring about them.

She didn't seem to realize it yet, but "#theflower-lady" was now the trendiest T-shirt in Cemetery.

Saul sat beside her, causing the mattress to sink a little so that her hip settled against his. After years of her wearing her hair in a tidy ponytail, he'd never get used to seeing it like this, so soft and silky.

He'd never get used to her being his, either.

What he'd like to do—after making love to her—was ask her to marry him so that he knew she'd be his forever. As usual lately, the timing was off for that. Not only was she out of sorts, but Beck would be with him this weekend, and soon after, he'd move in for good. In all fairness, Saul had to give the kid time to adjust before he added anyone new to the equation.

"I can feel you thinking," Emily said, right before she deliberately dropped back on the mattress, her body all but boneless. "It feels like you might be thinking weighty things when I'd rather you think about me."

That sounded like a nice invitation. Stretching out next to her, Saul propped up on one elbow and leisurely took her in. Even now, she looked delectable in pale jeans and a sleeveless V-neck top printed with tiny yellow-and-pink flowers on a white background. "I'm always thinking of you." Lightly, he rested his hand on her stomach. "Always."

"Not when your restaurant is packed."

"Even in the busiest moments," he promised.

Her smile warmed. "Not when we visited with my aunt and uncle."

"Wanna bet? I watched you with them, and I could feel how much you loved them." And he'd wanted that, the closeness and caring, between him and Emily. "Seeing you with them made me think of things I'd missed. For years I went along thinking I was satisfied with my life." He gave her a stern, but teasing, frown. "Then you came along, disrupting my contentment and forcing me to think about things in a new way."

"Hey. I didn't—"

"Purposely do any of that? I know." Very lightly, he moved his hand over the slight curve of her stomach, then to a more prominent hip bone. "You're sneakier. Subtle-like. It was especially torturous since you didn't seem to want me back."

"That's not true. Of course I did."

"You hid it well." Loving that she was so relaxed with him, he leaned forward to brush his mouth over hers.

She drew a breath. "Well, when you're with Beck, surely you don't—"

"I give him all the attention I can." Unable to help himself, Saul kissed her again, and then made sure she understood. "But honey, part of my mind is wondering how Beck will react to you, and you to him."

"Don't worry about me," she quickly assured him. "I love everyone, but a kid going through the same things I did? I promise I won't do or say anything to make him uncomfortable."

"Never, not for a single second, did I worry about that." No, he was concerned with whether or not Emily would willingly disrupt her organized life, not only for him, but now for a boy who, in many ways, had been forced to mature too quickly. Beck would need a lot of patience and understanding. Saul already loved him, but he had to accept that Emily didn't know the kid, and her feelings would be different.

Smoothing out his frown with her fingertips, she whispered, "You're thinking too hard again."

Yeah, he couldn't seem to help himself, not when

so many things were unfinished. He and Emily, he and Beck… He wanted them together, as a family.

Could Emily want that, too?

"Tell me," she murmured, still sounding sleepy but with her gaze as attentive as always.

"From now on, it'll be Beck and me."

"That bothers you?"

She asked it with interest, not censure, and he heard himself say, "No. I want him with me, but I'm always looking ahead to the idea of…" Catching himself, Saul let the words taper off. It was too soon to throw more at her. First, he had to ensure she knew how much he cared. Then he had to get Beck settled so he didn't add chaos to his life.

"What?" Emily slipped her fingertips down to his jaw, then his bottom lip. "Thinking ahead to…?"

"Emily—" he tried to hedge.

"Tell me."

Not what he wanted to discuss right now. He ran the risk of scaring her off, of adding to her burdens when he'd rather help her with her load.

Putting her hands to his shoulders, Emily pushed him to his back and crawled over him, which of course fired his blood even more. "Saul Culver, tell me what you were thinking."

Instead, savoring the feel of her warm weight against him, the press of her breasts and the way her thighs shifted, Saul kissed her again—and wanted to go on kissing her for the rest of his life.

She participated in that wholeheartedly, snuggling closer so that with each breath, he inhaled her intoxicating scent. Unlike him, she didn't lose her head though, and long before he was ready, she lifted her lips away and whispered again, "Tell me."

He gave up. Emily's hair draped down at either side of her face, making her eyes look like heated whiskey, and he wanted her enough that he could barely concentrate, much less filter his words. "Us," he said, his hands coasting up and down her back, each sweep getting nearer to the rise of her backside. "You and me, but now with Beck, too."

"As a family?" She nuzzled her lips to his again, then smiled. "With a cantankerous cat and a slobbery dog?"

God, yes. He tried to draw breath, but she'd just stated it all as if it didn't alarm her, almost as if she liked the idea. It was everything he wanted, the results he'd hoped for, and Emily made it sound possible.

"Yes," he said, pulling her flat to his chest, an arm around the small of her back, one hand at her nape so he could kiss her the way he needed to.

Emily made a small sound of pleasure and moved against him.

Much more of that and he'd be a goner. "Honey." Saul turned her so she was beneath him, then cupped her face. "Tell me you want me."

Giving his words back to him, she said, "I always want you."

That deserved a long, drugging kiss. He was so involved in tasting her, he didn't at first realize that she was working her hands beneath his shirt, not until he felt her hot little palms on his bare back.

Saul drew a chest-expanding breath. "You're not too tired?"

"Don't be silly." She lightly bit his jaw, brushed her nose to his throat, and then nipped his ear. "Hurry it up. Who knows when the animals might decide we're needed. We could hear a crash any moment now."

Around his grin, Saul said, "Reason number twenty-two why I love you. You're always practical." He pushed away from the bed to stand, and then stripped off his shirt.

Emily sat up and did the same, casually, as if baring herself to him was the most natural thing in the world. He went rigid with lust. Her bra was snowy white, edged in lace. Not overly sexy, except that it held her breasts. *Emily's* breasts. And he'd been wanting her for so long, the need had become a part of him, like hunger and thirst.

"Wait," he requested when she started to reach back to unclasp it. "I want the honors." He dug out his wallet, located a condom, and put both on the nightstand.

While gazing at his chest, she asked, "Have you been carrying that long?"

"The condom? I've pretty much kept one handy since I was seventeen." He kicked out of his shoes and unfastened his jeans.

Frowning, Emily also scooted off the bed and stood. In a bra. And body-hugging jeans.

Did she think he was made of iron?

Nodding at the condom, she asked, "When did you… replace the last one?"

Understanding what she didn't quite ask, Saul settled his hands on her proud shoulders. "I put a new one in my wallet two weeks ago, because I realized the one I was carrying was at least seven months old."

She blinked twice, said, "Oh," with satisfaction, but then added on, "Do condoms have an expiration date?"

Leave it to Emily to somehow make everything

unique. "No idea, but I would never take chances with you." As he spoke, Saul slid his hands down her arms to her elbows, brought her a little closer, and then slowly reached around to her back to unhook her bra.

She went very still, watching him as he removed it.

All along, he'd known she was beautiful, but she'd always downplayed her looks and body—not in any obvious way, not with baggy clothes or disregard for her appearance. Maybe it was more that she hadn't shown off her… He hesitated to think *perfection*, since she took exception to the word, but to him, it was the only description that fit. Emily Lucretia, the flower lady, was the perfect combination of curves and character, strength and gentleness.

All her classy, tailored clothes and chic outfits had shown her as stylish, while hiding a lot of raw sex appeal. She had a seriously hot body, even more so than he'd realized. "If you ever wore a bikini, the town would go nuts."

One side of her mouth quirked into a reserved grin. "I'm not the bikini type." She stroked her fingers over his chest. "Maybe we could lose our jeans, too?"

"Good plan." While bending to kiss her throat and explore her warm skin, Saul opened the snap of her jeans and eased down the zipper. He heard the quick inhalation of her breath and felt her stomach tighten in reaction.

Through the years, he'd had to peel many a woman out of her super-tight jeans, but not Emily. The jeans fit her, but not like a second skin, so he did the expedient thing of opening his fingers wide over her hips, slid them down to palm her silky backside, then stroked over and along her thighs, which took her jeans and panties down at the same time.

Just as she stepped out, they both heard a distinct, "Woof," and froze.

It was almost comical, or would have been if he wasn't *this* close to finally fulfilling a fantasy.

When no other noise intruded, he turned back to her. "Should I check on them?"

"Nope." She kicked free of the jeans, turned, and gifted him with an eye-searing shot of her climbing into the bed.

Yeah, that would remain imprinted on his brain for the rest of his life.

"Hustle it up, Saul. If this doesn't happen, I'm blaming you."

Rightfully so. He'd waited so long for her, he'd wanted to make it last, but obviously now wasn't the time. With Emily's fascinated gaze on him, he wasted no time in removing his jeans and boxers, then came down beside her again, this time with them both naked. Skin to skin.

He'd known for at least a year now that Emily was the one for him. At first there hadn't been any urgency. He'd thought to take his time, win her over…yet it hadn't happened. She'd made him change tactics, but now they were together, and here, in bed, they were in perfect sync.

As if they'd been sleeping together routinely for a while now, she countered his every move with one of her own—often with more effect since he was on the ragged edge and trying hard to hold it together.

With a murmur of appreciation, he cupped her firm breasts, drifting his thumbs over her tight nipples and loving the rough sounds of pleasure she made in response. His heart hammered, and he couldn't resist moving against her as he drew one nipple into his mouth to softly suck.

Emily gave a low groan…and then clasped his erection in her small, soft hand.

He was a mature man who'd had his share of sexual experiences, but this, with Emily, was more. She made everything different, sharper-edged and hotter. Being truthful with himself, he hadn't even known it could be like this.

Need escalated, and no matter how or where he touched her, or she touched him, they kept coming back for openmouthed, hungry kisses until he knew he wouldn't last. She was a little bolder than he'd expected, but then, Emily never lacked confidence. He loved it. He loved her.

"I can't wait," he whispered.

Lips damp and her body flushed, she replied, "I don't want you to."

Rolling to his back, Saul snagged the condom and put it on before settling over her again. They both breathed heavily for a moment, waiting, letting the anticipation gather even more.

Staring into his eyes, Emily hiked her slim thighs around his hips.

Another long kiss, a press against her…and he stroked deep. Emily's fingertips dug into his shoulders, spurring him on.

*Yes.* Giving her a moment to adjust, he absorbed the sensations, the taste and scent of her, how she squeezed him, her escalated breathing, and the tightening of her legs…

Absolutely perfect.

She wasn't quite as patient. She lifted her hips against him, a sort of nudge to get him going. Even as Saul smiled, he initiated a rhythm that had her first clutching at him, minutes later panting, and before long, straining toward release.

They moved faster, kissed with more hunger. He went deeper and felt Emily's coiling tension.

In his head, Saul struggled for control, determined to wait for her, determined, *determined*…

As she climaxed, she tucked her face close to his chest so that he felt every heavy pant of her rapid breath, followed by her vibrating groan, and then a long, slow exhalation as her muscles eased.

Closing his eyes, Saul held her close to his heart, and let himself go.

MINUTES LATER, her breathing restored and feeling newly energized, Emily finally opened her eyes and sighed happily. She remembered sex, of course.

She didn't remember anything as profound as that.

Next to her, Saul sprawled on his back, his left hand limp on his firm stomach. She rested close to him, but they were no longer intimately connected.

Emotionally? Yup, she felt very, very attached. Where did they go from here? Realistically, she knew people dated and had sex and sometimes things lasted, sometimes they didn't. Fine and dandy…for others.

Not so much for her. At forty-one, she wasn't looking for casual sex. Her lifestyle, her business, her position in the community—it was all too important to disrupt with a fling.

With commitment, though? Yes, she wanted that.

Saul made her feel things she hadn't before. Not with her husband, definitely not after her divorce.

He was worried about Beck's reaction to her, and she understood that. She also sympathized with his position. She didn't, however, think it would be as big of a problem as Saul assumed. A fourteen-year-old boy wouldn't see things the same way a little kid would. Would he?

She should probably wait and meet the young man before making any decisions on that. Yes, she wanted Saul, but she didn't want him to feel coerced into rushing forward with their relationship.

Wondering about that, she whispered, "Saul?"

"Hmm?" he managed to say.

Humor emerged above the concerns. With feigned umbrage, she asked, "Are you going to sleep?"

The corner of his mouth tilted in a lazy smile. "Sweet, perfect, *hot* Emily. Now, would I do that?" He got one eye open.

Feeling ridiculously happy, she kissed his chest. He was a little salty now, and he smelled wonderful. She wouldn't mind kissing him all over. "I was exhausted clear down to my bones, but now I feel ready to take on the world."

The smile turned into a grin. "You do, huh? Why does that surprise me?"

"I don't know. Why does it?"

"Maybe because most people feel a little lethargic after sex?"

"Maybe they aren't doing it right." She brushed her fingertips through his chest hair, loving that his skin was so warm. "You, Saul Culver, did it exactly right."

"You took part, too, you know." Catching her teasing

fingers, he lifted her hand to his mouth and pressed a kiss to her palm. "Truth is, we're good together."

She thought about her previous sexual experiences and came to the same conclusion. "We are, aren't we?" Before that got out of hand, Emily stretched. "What do you want to bet the animals have finished off the rest of my house? I wonder if I still have furniture. Or drapes. My rugs are likely ruined."

"You don't look too worried about it," he noted.

"A satisfied woman doesn't worry."

That made him laugh, and before she knew it, he'd moved over her. "You can never again claim you're not perfect."

"Is that right?"

"You are most definitely perfect…" he softly kissed her "…in some ways."

"As long you know it's not in all ways."

"Debatable, but I'll let you claim imperfection for now."

This after-sex banter was new for her, and she liked it. "Remember, I have a terror for a cat and now a dog with an obviously very wet tongue."

Saul trailed *his* tongue along her neck in a tantalizing way. "A wet tongue can be useful."

A tidal wave of heat rushed through her, almost stealing her breath. "Hush," she insisted, and then she hugged him. Really, really tight, because she was so happy she felt like she had to hold on or she'd lose it. That was silly, of course. Despite all the unknowns, Saul was a solid guy, as reliable as they came.

But he was going through some big life changes.

*No*, she told herself sternly. *Do not start doubting him.* Wanting to give him the space he needed to sort through everything, she asked, "Do you want to nap while I go check on the critters?"

"And have you think I can't keep up? No way." Another kiss, this one to her ear, before he huskily whispered, "If the pets are doing okay, do you want to come to my place with me? You can keep me company while I paint Beck's room, and then I'll grill dinner for us."

"Sounds like a plan, as long as I can help you with the painting." She sat up at the side of the mattress but couldn't quite draw her gaze off Saul. Man, he looked good like that. Naked.

In her bed.

Another "woof," and this one somehow sounded more urgent. Scurrying from the bed and grabbing up her clothes, Emily headed to the bathroom. On the way, she called out, "Coming, Snuggles! Give me just one minute."

"Do what you need to do," Saul said from right behind her. "I'll check on them."

She turned and found him already wearing his jeans, though they were unsnapped and he hadn't yet bothered with a shirt or shoes. He stepped past her, dropped some tissues in her waste can, then gave her a quick peck on his way out.

Huh. Emily assumed he'd just disposed of the condom, and he'd done it so casually, it felt like they were a long-established couple.

*I'm forty-one*, she told herself. *I can handle the disposal of a condom.* Still, it left her a little flustered—after all, it had been years since she'd dealt with anything like that. Also pleased—because hey, she now had an actual sexual relationship with Cemetery's favorite bachelor.

Humming a little to herself, she cleaned up and was partially dressed when Saul stuck his head in the door. "Hey, um, you have company."

"I...what?" She never, ever got company. Certainly not surprise company. "Who?"

He cleared his throat. "Betty Cemetery?"

"You don't know?" Emily snatched up her shirt, saw it was now wrinkled, and pulled it on anyway to hurry past Saul, who was grabbing his own shirt. "I hope nothing is wrong."

The dog danced around her the second she appeared, so she said apologetically, "Just one second, baby, I promise," and opened the front door a mere crack.

Yup, that was Betty. Standing there in one of her boxy cotton dresses, brows raised and gaze shrewd. "Oh, hi," Emily said. *Had Saul finished dressing?* She heard him behind her, trying to get the cat into her harness.

"Don't be rude, Emily. It doesn't suit you. Besides, I already know Saul is here. I caught him peeking out the window. Silly, since his truck is in your driveway."

"I, um, I wasn't being silly." Fashioning her most practiced smile, Emily said, "I just didn't want the animals to get out."

With pushy insistence, Betty pressed on the door, glanced around Emily, then stepped inside as if she'd been invited. "Berkley said you got both animals. I'm so pleased—oh." Surprise pushed her faded brows into the wrinkles of her forehead for a comical look.

Saul muttered, "Snuggles, wait...damn."

Emily turned to see Saul struggling with the harness for the cat, while the dog hunched up, and pooped. Right there. In front of the town's matriarch.

Appalled, Emily whispered, "Omigod." A nervous snicker escaped her.

Betty just said, "Oh, you poor baby."

She wasn't talking to Emily.

Hurrying in, Betty stroked the now cowering dog's head. "It's okay. They understand, sweetie." Betty shot her a look.

Emily dutifully said, "Of course we understand." She stepped away from the mess and snickered again. She couldn't seem to help herself—especially when she met Saul's bemused gaze. "Everyone needs a little adjustment."

Betty handily took the cat and harness from Saul and seated herself on the couch. Making it look absurdly easy, she snapped the harness on Satin, then attached a leash. "There." She smiled at Emily. "We'll take the animals out while Saul sees to this little accident."

Er...pretty sure there was nothing small about that mess. "It's my house." She eyed the...pile with distaste. "I'll clean it."

"Nonsense," Betty said. "Saul is a man."

And that made him better prepared for dog poo? Emily didn't quite see the logic in that, but Saul gladly handed her the dog's leash.

Leaning near her ear, he whispered, "I got the easy end of the deal. Good luck." Because he always oozed charm, and Betty appeared to adore him, he said, "This way, ladies," and led them through Emily's kitchen to the back door.

Belatedly, Emily caught the way Betty smiled, as if she knew things, which she probably did since both she and Saul were barefoot, and rumpled, and clearly they hadn't let the dog out in time because they'd been otherwise occupied.

The animals were now cooperating, though, Snuggles trotting happily along, with Satin pattering fast to keep up with him.

Betty stepped outside and stalled. She seemed to be looking everywhere at once, taking in the rows of flowers, the fountain, the perfectly arranged seats. "Emily, this is stunning."

"Thank you. My uncle helped me get it started when I first moved here, but it's really filled out."

With that easy and kind exchange, Emily hoped she had herself in hand. Getting to the first order of business, she started her apologies. Not to Betty, who had intruded, but to Snuggles, who now wasn't all that interested in doing his business since he'd already gone.

In her house. Right there, in front of Betty.

What a greeting.

Yeah, Emily felt another unwanted bubble of hilarity coming on.

Quickly, she knelt down and stroked the dog's soft ears. "I'm so, so sorry, Snuggles. That was entirely my fault. You were so very quiet with your demands. Now I know, though, and I promise it won't happen again."

The dog was sweetly forgiving.

Next she turned to Satin, who gave her a "don't even think it" glare, only now it was more comical since the fur on her head was wet and licked to the side in spiky disarray. "You still aren't happy with me?"

Betty said, "She'll forgive you soon. Probably just holding a grudge." She eyed the cat critically. "Why exactly is her head soaked like that?"

"Snuggles enjoys grooming her."

"Ah." Betty patted the dog. "I knew they were bonded. Berkley said she'd been looking forever for the right person to adopt them."

"And so naturally you sabotaged me?"

"Who else, if not you, the town's most perfect person?"

She was not perfect, damn it.

"I wish I could have taken them myself," Betty said.

Emily wondered if that meant Betty considered herself perfect, too.

"Unfortunately," Betty complained, "I'm too old to keep up. I have a feeling that having two pets underfoot would be a tripping hazard for me, and as your uncle discovered, falls for the elderly have consequences."

Wow. That was the first time Emily had ever heard Betty admit to any weakness. She felt sadness at first, because Betty was older than her Uncle Sullivan, and then she felt...well, privileged, because Betty had shared a vulnerability with her.

She looked at Betty's face, seeing the lines of time that webbed around her lips, across her forehead and away from the outer corners of her eyes. "You've had quite the life, haven't you?"

"Indeed." The tiniest sign of humor showed in the gaze Betty flicked her way. "The look on your face when Snuggles had his accident."

"*My* face?" Emily grinned. "I almost lost it at your delicate little 'Oh.' Betty Cemetery, the icon in the community, in my house, watching a dog poo." The chuckles started again, and this time Betty joined her.

"Poor Saul." Betty held the leash lightly so Satin could mosey along a row of lavender, sniffing to her heart's content. "Whenever there's a distasteful chore I don't want to do, I pretend it requires a manly touch, and they, of course, feel honor-bound to handle it." Snuggles chose to sniff Satin, so off they went, like a very short train, taking their retractable leads as far as they'd go.

"Diabolical," Emily said. "I like it."

"You're too independent—and far too young—to use that excuse, though, so don't think to steal it from me."

Emily crossed her heart, then said, "You're good with the animals. Thank you for helping with the harness."

"I love pets." Betty glanced around, saw a decorative iron bench, and luckily the leash was just long enough for her to reach it. She sat primly at the edge of the seat, her ankles together, weathered hands in her lap loosely holding the leashes, and her back as straight as an eighty-six-year-old woman could make it. "I've always loved them, but now that Yardley and I are working on our own shelter, I've learned so much more." Her mouth pinched and her voice softened. "I've heard stories and seen things…things that could rip out the coldest heart." Her nostrils quivered just a bit, and she added, "Animals innocently give so much. None of them should ever suffer."

In that moment, Emily saw Betty in an entirely different way. She wasn't just strident, busybody, pushy Betty. Not just the town matriarch who lorded her position over one and all.

In this single shared moment, intrusive as it had seemed at first, everything had changed. Emily knew she would now forever see Betty as an older, vulnerable, sympathetic, funny and caring person. At her age, she had to have aches and pains. Uncertainties. Fears and needs.

Emily's heart broke a little. As her aunt had said, she

and Sullivan had each other, and they'd always made the most of every day.

Who did Betty have?

She had her beloved town, the history with a hideous name, her pride—and so many people who resented her. Oh, they were all respectful; Betty wouldn't have tolerated anything else. But did they genuinely *like* her?

Yardley did, which was one reason everyone loved Yardley. How in the world had Saul kept from falling madly in love with the woman? How had he instead focused on *her*?

"What?" Betty asked, with a good dose of curiosity. "Why are you looking at me like that?"

"Just thinking about things," Emily said softly. *About how caring you are under the gruff exterior. And brave.* Yes, it definitely took bravery for a woman Betty's age to face each new day with so much grit and determination. Respect blossomed, rich and full, and most definitely deserved.

Betty sniffled. "If you think I'm about to weep, young lady, you're dead wrong."

Emily didn't think she was wrong at all. Betty was near tears. Her second sniffle proved it. If she broke down, Emily would break down with her, because she was suddenly feeling everything Betty felt.

Taking a seat beside her on the bench, Emily whispered, "Neither of us can cry, because animals sense those things."

"Yes, they do. Especially animals as sensitive as these two are."

Eying the cat, Emily said, "You think Satin is sensitive?"

"Very much so. It's why she was so heartbroken to

lose her best friend. That cat went through a lot of neglect, then during her long stay at the shelter she found Snuggles and they grew close. Snuggles was all she had, all she trusted."

Oh God. "I kept them apart."

"And reunited them. Look at them together." Betty dabbed at her eyes. "Thank you for taking them both."

"I'm sorry I didn't do so immediately." Thanks to Betty, she now saw many things in a different way. "I'm glad you stopped in to check on them. I appreciate your concern, and I hope you can visit again." Teasing, she added, "Next time, if I know you're coming, I can be better prepared."

"No dog messes on the floor?"

Laughing, she said, "With these two, I can't make that promise, but I'll try."

Betty idly adjusted the leashes. "I imagine you'll be busy going forward, what with two pets and Saul panting after you."

"Betty!" The wording made her laugh.

"I would enjoy having you back at the tea club. We miss your beautiful flowers, and we miss *you*. Everything is calmer and easier when you're around. Everyone smiles more."

That had to be the nicest thing Betty had ever said to her. "We're fortunate that most people in Cemetery are wonderful." Emily let her shoulder rest against Betty's. "There's you, and Yardley."

Smiling, Betty said, "And you and Saul."

Wow, Betty was quickly growing on her. "Gentry and Mila."

"Cemetery is expanding. I like it." She shooed away a bee that buzzed too close, then heaved a soft sigh. "I'm hoping the shelter will be successful here, because there are always animals in need."

A sad truth. "You know…" Since Emily tried not to say unkind things, she wasn't quite sure how to put her thoughts, then she shrugged and just stated the truth. "Some people shouldn't be parents to kids or animals."

"I agree. You, though? I knew you would be amazing with them. You have the calm patience and attentiveness required." She slid a teasing look Emily's way. "At least I'm sure you do when hunky bachelors aren't hanging around distracting you."

Something shifted in Emily, some subtle emotion that usually warned her to be on guard with Betty, but now brought her closer to confide, "I think I distracted him, actually."

Snorting a laugh, Betty cheered, "Good for you!"

They chuckled together in the nicest camaraderie, until Betty caught herself.

Primly, she smoothed her skirt as she gathered her decorum around her. "I've always thought you would be a wonderful mother as well."

The prodding didn't offend Emily. Instead, with her new insight into Betty, she felt complimented. "I think I would have been, too. I hope so, anyway." Odd, but she found it easy to confide in Betty. "When I was younger, I wanted children. Several. I had visions of reading books to them at night, and playing ball in the yard and big dinners around a well-worn table." In so many ways, those dreams seemed a lifetime ago. "Then I got divorced and put all my attention on my business."

"And you're happy." How nice that Betty stated it as fact and not a probing question.

Yes, she was happy. Lifting her shoulders, no longer

invested in that dream, Emily said, "At forty-one and being where I am in my life, I'm content to enjoy other people's children." Funny, but she thought of Beck as she said it. At his age, he certainly didn't need anyone to read to him, but there were other things to be done as a family. The idea of the closeness, of dinners together, holidays as a family, the day in and day out sharing— that appealed to her in a very big way.

"Exactly how I feel," Betty said, agreeing with a firm nod. "Now, what about Gentry?"

Drawn from her thoughts, Emily asked, "What about him?"

"He's also a very handsome bachelor."

That again? Emily shook her finger at Betty, which was something she wouldn't have dared to do just the day before. "I told you, he's an employee." That didn't come close to covering it, so she added, "And now a very good friend. I consider him part of my family."

"He's a charmer."

"Yes, he is." Emily almost said that Gentry was interested in Mila, but she caught herself in time. "He's also very private, and only twenty-five."

Saul stuck his head out the back door. "Mess is up, but you have a call."

Alarm brought Emily to her feet. "My aunt?" If she was calling again, something must have happened.

"No, it's Gentry."

"Speak of the devil," Betty murmured deadpan. She glanced around theatrically. "I don't suppose Wheeler is here somewhere?"

Suspicion brought Saul's brows together. "Wheeler?"

"Never mind. A private joke between Betty and me."

Emily started forward, ran out of leash, and asked Saul, "Would you…?"

"I've got it," Betty said, taking the handle from her. Since the animals were sprawled out, resting in the sun, it wouldn't be a problem.

Saul asked, "Can I get you anything to drink, Betty?"

"Such a nice host," she noted. "Tea?"

Saul turned to Emily in question, and she nodded. "There's some in the fridge." As a warning, she said to Betty, "I'll be right back."

## CHAPTER THIRTEEN

A MINUTE LATER, Saul handed Betty her drink and joined her on the bench. He even stretched out one arm along the back and slouched comfortably. Betty slyly watched him as if he should be uncomfortable, but now that the initial surprise of her visit had passed, he wouldn't let her get the best of him.

Silently, wearing a small smile, he waited for Betty to speak. He knew she wouldn't be able to stay quiet long—and he was right.

"So." She sipped her tea. "You and Emily?"

"Betty," he said, sounding absurdly sympathetic. "You having trouble with your eyesight?"

She sniffed. "You know my eyes work just fine."

"And your deductive reasoning is still sharp?"

"As a tack."

"Then why ask me silly questions?" To follow that up, he smiled even more. "I thought Emily would keel over when the dog dumped on her floor. Thanks for taking that in stride."

Betty softened. "He's a beautiful dog. He'll need time and attention to get used to the new environment."

Like Beck, he supposed, not to compare a teenage boy to an animal, though remembering his own youth, there were similarities. Saul was determined to give Beck everything he needed, and more.

At that moment, dog and cat were curled together, snoring in the sunshine. "Emily will see to it." He, too, sipped his tea. "The cat hasn't been easy. First time I saw her house, it was picture-perfect."

"Like Emily."

Very much like Emily. "The cat's taken her temper out on the furniture and drapes. Do you know, Emily hasn't lost her patience at all? I mean, she's a little sad that the cat isn't warming up to her, but she continues to try." Even when she called the cat Satan, her tone had been calm, gentle and mild.

"I never doubted that Emily was perfect for the animals."

Quieter, with awe, Saul admitted, "I'm amazed by her."

"So when's the wedding?"

Did Betty think to throw out a stunner of a question and take him off guard? Probably. The old gal did like to plow through people. Saul understood her, always had. Betty was easier to charm than to fight, so that was the tactic he most often used.

Now, when it concerned Emily, he'd just be honest. "If I could make it work tomorrow, and she'd agree, I'd marry her then."

Betty's brows shot up, turning her forehead into an accordion. "Did you ask her?"

"Not yet." His mouth twisted. "She hasn't been easy to win over. I had to give it my all, several times, in fact."

"Your all is quite impressive, I'm sure."

That deserved a full-fledged grin. "Thank you, Betty. I try."

"Bah. I'm sure if you ask—"

"Not to get into the nitty-gritty, but Emily and I only just worked out a few things. I think if it hadn't been for her uncle getting hurt, she might still be putting me in the friend zone." He'd caught her at a vulnerable time, and while he hated that she worried for her family, he knew she'd needed a little backup. Saul was glad to be that, and more. Whatever she needed, whenever she needed it.

"From what I saw, you're out of the friend zone now."

How odd to be discussing this with Betty. "Yeah." He smiled with genuine pleasure. "I love her. I've told her so. The thing is…" He glanced at the back door. How much longer would Emily be? Gentry had said there wasn't anything wrong, just an appointment he needed to set with a customer.

Saul turned to Betty…and spilled his guts in a quick, concise way. He told her about Beck, and about his plans. "I'm a package deal now, so there are a lot of things to consider."

"Hmm, yes," Betty said thoughtfully. "Taking on a fourteen-year-old certainly factors in."

"I'm happy to have him with me." Saul never wanted any doubts on that. "But to move him in, then add a wedding… I don't know if that'd be fair to him."

"If you'll forgive an old woman's interference—"

Saul nearly choked. "Since when have you ever hesitated?"

"Yardley is softening me up." Showing great satisfaction, Betty said, "She's like a granddaughter to me, you know."

"Yeah, Yardley is great."

That earned him a shrewd look.

"No, stop right there. Yardley and I were never involved."

"There were rumors," Betty said.

"Yardley and I both heard them." For a while there, things had been awkward. He and Yardley were friends, but they'd never had the chemistry that he had with Emily. "Yardley's awesome—"

"But she's not Emily?"

Since he loved Emily to distraction, he said, "Exactly."

"So." Betty stood, which prompted both animals to look at her. "Begin as you plan to continue. You and this young man are now a family unit. Emily understands that."

She did.

"Well, you and Emily should be as well."

"Absolutely." Saul stared at Betty, hoping to glean some solid advice. "It's asking a lot, but I want them both."

Her expression softened. "Dear Saul, you deserve it all. Don't you know that?" Before he could react, she turned brisk again. "Honesty is the most important thing in a relationship."

"With you so far."

"So be honest with Beck, the same as you were with Emily. Tell him nothing will change how you feel about him, just as nothing will change how you feel about Emily." Betty lifted her shoulders. "I would think he'd prefer you to be up-front, rather than treat him like a child."

"He's only fourteen."

With a mysterious smile, Betty looked off in the distance. "Oh, at fourteen, I was so sure I was grown."

Thinking back, Saul knew he'd felt the same.

"As long as you make him feel secure, he won't be threatened by another person in the picture. Look at it this way. No young person can have too many people to love him. Right now, you're all he has. Wouldn't it be wonderful if he had Emily, too?"

Saul soaked up the words of wisdom, then stood and impulsively gave Betty a hug. "You're right."

She blinked fast, flustered. Clearly, she hadn't expected that. "I've been around a few years, seen a few relationships, and witnessed a lot of people interacting. Emily is as bighearted as they come, and kids are remarkably adaptable. I predict they'll get along amazingly well, but don't dillydally."

"Dillydally?"

She waved that away, further rousing the animals. "You understand my meaning. Emily is now a hot commodity."

Though he fought a grin, Saul felt compelled to say, "I'm not sure I like how you put that."

"Doesn't matter. Everyone is currently interested in her."

A sudden hunch hit Saul like a tsunami. As he took the leashes from Betty, he asked, "You're not, by chance, the one running the social media and hashtagging Emily, are you?"

Flattening a hand to her heart in dramatic display, Betty breathed, "Me?" with over-the-top incredulity.

Oh, he was on to her now. But then Betty lifted a finger to her lips and whispered, "Shh…" and with a wink, she moseyed away.

Incredulous, Saul stared after her. Was that an admission?

He would never, ever, underestimate Betty.

Prompting the animals, he asked, "Well? What do you say we go inside and find out what's keeping Emily?"

The cat and dog glanced at each other, and instead of standing, they flopped back down and closed their eyes. Huh. He sure hoped their attitudes changed before Emily got her feelings hurt. Then he shrugged. Didn't matter.

One way or another, he planned to keep Emily a very happy woman.

BY THE END of that week, the hashtag sensation had grown. Somehow, for some reason, Emily found herself being discussed on every social media site affiliated with Cemetery. People who didn't even live in Cemetery were getting drawn in. It made her head swim.

As Gentry pointed out, it also brought in new business.

Business was good, of course, but while smiling and being extra friendly, people continually watched her. When she parked at the florist shop in the morning. When she left in the evening. When she and Saul had dinner out… Emily didn't know what to think. She'd never been the center of attention before.

It was the most bizarre thing, but online, everyone seemed to have a comment—not about the floral shop, but about her hair and her clothes. Fortunately, most of what she read was kind.

On Friday, in between the steady flow of customers, she went down the rabbit hole of a long thread that started when some anonymous person claimed the flower lady was getting a makeover.

Emily had no idea who'd posted it since it only said "page moderator" and so far, no one seemed to know who that might be.

She eyed both Gentry and Vivienne. "You two swear you aren't the ones posting this stuff?"

"I comment," Vivienne said, "but I haven't initiated anything."

"Same," Gentry promised.

"The suggestions are pretty outrageous." Did no one from Cemetery really know her? "As if I would ever."

Gentry took in her frown and decided to read over her shoulder. After a second, he scoffed, "Piercings? People actually think you'd do that?"

No, she wouldn't, but was she so predictable? "I have pierced ears," she pointed out, then she thought of Berkley and grinned. "The woman who runs the shelter where I got Satan and Snuggles has several piercings in her ears, and she looks incredible. Very sharp."

Folding his arms, Gentry leaned a hip against the counter. "Somehow, I can't see you going for that."

"I'm not Berkley," she agreed. "I couldn't pull it off."

"I think they're talking about piercings in other places, anyway." Vivienne gave her a pointed look. "You hiding anything interesting, Emily?"

Scrunching her nose, Emily said, "Absolutely not. I don't want anything that hurts."

Vivienne said, "Guess that rules out a gnarly tat then, huh?"

"I saw where you commented that!" She laughed at Vivienne and pointed to the comment so Gentry would see it. "Tattoos were never under consideration."

"Darn."

Feeling impish, Emily said, "Although… Can you

imagine if I got a small, colorful flower someplace nice, like my wrist or shoulder?"

Bemused, Gentry asked, "Are you really considering that?"

Leaning closer as if in confidence, she let her gaze go from Gentry to Vivienne and back again, holding them in keen suspense, then she whispered, "I could do a temporary tat, just to give them something to talk about."

"Ha!" Laughing, Vivienne chanted, "Do it, do it!"

Gentry shook his head. "It'd stir up the town, that's for sure."

Funny that anything she did would stir up anyone. Little by little, Emily was getting used to it though. Not that she had much choice, given how her week had gone. "Did you guys see Kathleen?" She still couldn't believe how the mannequin had been pulled into service. "One day she was in front of Sallie's with a sign that said, 'Recommended by Hashtag The Flower Lady.'"

Amused, Gentry said, "Mila wanted to put her out front of the Pit Stop with a sign, too." He held up his hands, as if to frame the words, "*Hashtag the flower lady eats here*. Saul wouldn't let her, though."

Saul, at least, understood how it all flustered her. He still enjoyed it and teased her about being famous, but he promised not to add to the chaos.

"Did you see Kathleen outside the place selling souvenir T-shirts?" Gentry grinned. "She's been there a few times now, always sporting a new *hashtag the flower lady* shirt. I hear they're the hottest thing."

Lifting a brow, Emily eyed his chest. Those very words were displayed in white on his black T-shirt. "Ahem."

"I wear it with love," he said, bending to kiss the top of her head.

Because she wasn't yet used to Gentry being so demonstrative, Emily caught him in a tight hug before he could straighten away.

Even better, he hugged her back. Ever since their talk, Gentry had been a different man. Or maybe it was his relationship with Mila that had instigated the change. Whatever the reason, she loved that he wasn't as guarded anymore.

Releasing him, she said, "On you two, I don't mind the shirts. They're almost like uniforms for the shop."

Every day, Vivienne wore a different slogan shirt to work. "I get mine free."

Well, no wonder she had a whole wardrobe of them. "You're kidding? How come?"

"Lawson Salder," Vivienne sang in a dreamy voice.

Unlike Emily, Vivienne often dated. This name was unfamiliar, though. "I don't think I know him."

"He's new," Gentry explained. "Opened shop right before you got hashtagged." He grinned. "You've been a little too busy with Saul to keep up."

"He wants to meet you because you gave his new business a boost." Vivienne followed that with a throaty growl. "The dude is smokin'. Wavy blond hair, light brown eyes, and scrumptious shoulders. So far, he's always dressed in board shorts and T-shirts. Don't marry Saul until you've given this new guy a look-see."

"Hey." Gentry shot an indignant frown at Viv. "Our loyalty is to Saul." He turned to Emily. "Forget she said that."

Emily felt herself blushing. For heaven's sake, Saul hadn't asked her to marry him, and even if he seemed to want the whole forever thing, she knew it wouldn't be anytime soon. Hoping she didn't look as uncomfortable as she felt, Emily snorted. "Like anyone could steal Saul's thunder? Not likely. Believe me, he has no competition."

That seemed to appease Gentry, but he still shot Vivienne another look of warning.

To distract them both, Emily said, "We had an amazing day on Wednesday."

"Yeah?" Sitting at the other end of the counter, Vivienne propped her chin on her hands and bobbed her eyebrows. Her long braids, interwoven with the occasional purple bead, trailed down her chest. "Tell me *every* lurid detail."

For a middle-aged hippie, Vivienne was mightily entertaining. Playing along, Emily leaned closer. "We painted a room in his house."

Viv scowled. "You *painted*? A room?"

Still in a hushed voice, Emily said, "Then we shopped for some things to go in that room."

Viv rolled her eyes.

"And then…" She leaned closer still, until Viv seemed to hold her breath. "We grilled our dinner."

Slumping, Vivienne complained, "Sounds—*yawn*—exciting."

It had been absolutely amazing, and Emily just knew Beck was going to love his new room when he visited today. She wished she could be there to see it all, but of course she understood that it needed to be a private moment between him and Saul.

"You also walked Snuggles and Satin," Gentry pointed out.

"How do you know that?"

He took her phone, scrolled farther down on the Facebook page, and then pointed at the post.

"Good grief!" Emily stared. "Is nothing sacred?" Yes, they'd walked the animals together on the sidewalk a few days ago. Emily didn't think anyone had seen them, though she had to admit, it was a novel thing to walk a cat. Didn't matter to Satin. Wherever Snuggles went, she went, too.

The animals were truly inseparable…which had worked in her favor afterward, when the dog chose to nap across the cat bed, and the cat had curled up with him, which left Emily and Saul with a private hour that they'd spent in her bedroom.

Definitely, Saul was it for her.

Watching Emily, Gentry grinned. "See that look in her eyes?" he said to Viv. "When you're with someone you care about, everything is awesome—even walking a cat."

Vivienne patted his shoulder. "Speaks the lad who is all ate up with a certain beautiful young lady."

Not in the least bothered by Viv's teasing, Gentry agreed. "Mila *is* beautiful."

An easy answer, but Emily knew it wasn't just Mila's looks that drew Gentry. So far, they'd connected in important ways. She really thought they might have fallen instantly in love.

Vivienne lowered her head to the counter with a thud. "All this love talk is nauseating. Didn't you two ever hear of wild flings without commitment? Having a good time?" She peeked over her arms. "One-night stands?"

Emily and Gentry shared a glance, and both grinned.

"Blah. I think I'll take off on those late deliveries."

Vivienne pushed up from her seat. "C'mon, stud. You can help me load up."

Off they went, two of the best employees Emily could have asked for.

With the added business, Vivienne had happily taken on more deliveries. And all the changes Gentry had made! Yes, an updated, online scheduling program had been his first order of business, and she had to admit, it really was easy. He'd also changed out her dry erase boards for a trendier chalk board permanently affixed to the wall.

The coolest thing, in her opinion, was the vendor-type machine he'd put in with a few rows of colorful flowers that people could get for a set price. They sold out every day because customers could come in, gawk a little, sneak a photo of her or the shop, and then pay for a flower without having to wait in line.

All in all, Gentry was a genius.

It was also nice that business often spilled over next door to Sallie, who sold pastries, and M.J., who sold candy.

Wheeler had even come in a few times, and yes, it did seem as though he flirted, but in a fun way that wasn't serious. Everyone took photos, and she figured that was why Wheeler did it. He'd later confirmed that, whispering to her in an aside that she was good for his social life.

Emily had cracked up, but Gentry wasn't at all amused. She was finding that her new "brother" was calmly, quietly protective.

A new group of customers came in, and that kept Emily busy through most of the afternoon. She wondered if Saul was with Beck now. If he'd yet seen the house.

When she'd find out what he thought.

Later, right before closing, Mila rushed in. Emily and Gentry greeted her with a smile.

"I have thirty minutes," Mila said, "before my last break of the day is over, but I wanted to—"

Gentry said, "See me?" Then he leaned over the counter and kissed Mila.

Right there in front of her. Emily couldn't stop grinning. It wasn't a sexual kiss, but a warm greeting that implied a deep relationship.

She knew people, understood their motives and emotions, and she knew in her heart that they were meant to be.

"What?" Gentry asked when he saw her expression.

"You two are just so cute together."

The compliment had him snorting, but Mila gave her a wide smile. "Thank you. Did Gentry tell you I'm staying here in town?"

"You are?" Actually, Emily hadn't thought about her leaving now that she and Gentry were involved. "I'm glad to hear it."

"Originally my plan was just a summer job, a little time away. Maybe a summer romance." She wrinkled her nose. "I had a bruised ego. Guys can be such jerks."

Dutifully, Emily said, "Not Gentry."

"No, not him." Mila gave him another fond smile, followed by another quick kiss.

Gentry didn't seem to mind at all. He looked pretty content, actually.

"Now I don't want to be anywhere else. I love Cemetery, Gentry is too special to let go, and you." Her gaze softened on Emily. "You made me feel so welcomed, like we were old friends."

Gentry said, "Even when I was a jerk."

"You were never a jerk," Mila protested. "I just came

on too strong." She leaned into him. "I wanted to share some awesome news with both of you." Now beaming, Mila said, "Saul asked if I'd manage the restaurant." She sent Emily a knowing smile. "And… I said yes. Isn't that awesome?"

"Wow." With obvious pride, Gentry gave her another kiss and a squeeze. "When does that start?"

"In a week or so. There are a few more things he wants to show me. Then I'll get a raise."

Emily assumed that Saul was freeing up time for Beck, which made sense. "Congratulations. I know he's glad to have you."

Mila's smile gentled. "Just so you know, Saul told me about the kid, and he said it was fine if I told Gentry." In short order, Mila explained the situation with Beck while Emily stood there in mute surprise.

She'd thought everything to do with Beck was private, but Saul didn't mind sharing?

"Fourteen." Gentry whistled. "When I think of myself at that age…" He turned to Emily. "Let's just say, I'm glad Beck will have you and Saul."

Since Emily didn't yet know what role she'd play in things, she merely smiled.

"If he turns out half as wonderful as you, he'll be awesome," Mila said. "With you and Emily so close, Saul figured you'd be meeting Beck, and he didn't want to catch you off guard."

Now Emily's mouth almost fell open. Beck would be meeting Gentry? That was news to her—so how involved did Saul want her to be?

Her aunt was correct; she should have come right out and asked him.

Mila added, "With everything going on, Saul really

needs someone permanent to learn the ins and outs of the restaurant so he doesn't have to keep working fifty- to sixty-hour weeks." Cheerful, she held out her arms. "He said he trusts me, that I'm a natural. I'm excited to get started."

"I'm excited for you, too." Emily's thoughts danced in different directions. She and Saul were both cutting back to spend more time with each other. He'd told her that she was a priority and that he wanted to share his life with her. A good thing, since he was a priority for her, too. "With your outgoing personality and smarts, you'll be perfect for the job."

Mouth twitching, Mila asked, "How do you know I'm smart?"

"You chose Gentry, right? Went after him nearly the moment you saw him. I'd say you're smart and have great instincts."

"High-five to me!" Mila lifted her hand.

Laughing, feeling a little silly but glad to be included, Emily smacked her palm. She really did adore them both, and thinking that, she considered all the times Gentry had filled in for her recently. That made up her mind. "You two have plenty to talk about before Mila has to get back to it, so how about I finish closing up so you can visit?" She glanced at the clock and the dwindling time. "At the very least, Gentry can walk you back to the Pit Stop." That'd give them a few minutes alone.

Looking around, and probably deciding there really wasn't much more to do, Gentry agreed. After grabbing a few things, he reminded Emily that he'd added a few consultations for her to look over. Then he made sure the back door was locked. "If anything comes up, I'll be at the restaurant."

"There's only a half hour left before closing. I'm fine, so go on." Even if a big group suddenly converged on her, she was more than capable of handling it. "Have fun."

"Thanks." Gentry took Mila's hand and off they went, already talking low together.

In Cemetery, very little went unnoticed, so Emily knew Mila had stayed the last few days with Gentry. It seemed obvious that they'd be together again tonight. The new intimacy between them was apparent even to her.

Just because she'd been single for so very long didn't mean she'd forgotten those early days of her relationship with Rob, when sex had been a top priority. Funny, but by the time things had ended, she'd all but forgotten about sex.

Now she was back to prioritizing again—with Saul.

Not seeing him this weekend would be tough, but she loved that he was focusing on Beck, and she wouldn't want to detract from that.

Her time with Saul would come. Until then, she could be patient. After all, she'd spent more time being single than she had as a couple. Maybe she could use the weekend to win over her new pets… But yeah, knowing the cat's attitude and the influence she apparently had on the dog, Emily wouldn't hold her breath.

SAUL WATCHED AS Beck looked around the house, his eyes a little wide with awe.

After the drive to pick him up after school, then the drive back to Cemetery, they'd stopped to eat and then Saul had shown him around the town, with a little time spent at the beach.

Finally, they'd gone on to his house and Saul was on pins and needles waiting to see Beck's reaction.

Each silent second that passed ramped up his tension until he forced a smile. "Well, what do you think?"

"It's awesome." Beck went still, his head slightly cocked. "I hear something."

Saul listened, too. "Frogs on the lake. They're just getting started now, but they're even noisier at night and in the early morning."

"Frogs," Beck repeated with a wondering half smile. He went to the patio doors and looked out at the dock and trees and the gently lapping water. "We took a vacation a few years before…"

Before he'd lost his parents. Saul shifted uncomfortably. "To a lake?"

"Yeah. Bigger than this lake, and there were houses all around us. I remember waking up early and seeing people skiing. Barefoot." He grinned. "Guess they wanted to get out there before the water got choppy."

"Probably. We're back in the cove, so no skiers here, but you'll see them on the main body of the lake. Jet Skis, too. The sandy stretch of beach is protected by a no-wake order so boats can't get too close." Abruptly ending the sales pitch, Saul said, "Let's check out your room."

With excitement in his eyes, Beck followed as Saul led him down a short hall. "Bathroom," he said, indicating a room on the right, "and overall, it'll be yours to use. I have another off my bedroom, which is here." He indicated a large room on the left that faced the lake. "Your bedroom is here." On the right, and it struck Saul that it would have been better for Beck to get his room, so he could use the deck with the great view of the cove and—

"Wow." Eyes wide, Beck eased inside and slowly looked around.

The room was smallish with a twin-sized bed, night-stand, and bookcase, but a mid-size walk-in closet gave him plenty of room for storage. Saul and Emily had painted the walls a light bluish-gray—Emily's choice—and a colorful quilt, simple but tidy, was folded back on the bed. A large oval rag rug covered much of the hard-wood floor. Above the bookshelf, Saul had hung a televi-sion, and on the bookcase was the newest game system.

Beck breathed a little deeper.

Unsure what he was feeling, Saul rested his hands on Beck's shoulders. "I want you to be happy here, okay? If something should be different, just let me know."

"Are you kidding? This is awesome." When he turned to face Saul, his eyes looked glassy. "Really awesome. I..." He shook his head and swallowed. "You painted it? I mean, I can still smell the paint."

Damn. "We'll open the windows and let in fresh air."

"But you painted it? I mean, for me?"

Did he have to sound so surprised, as if he'd expected Saul to stuff him into a broom closet? "Hey, we talked about this, right? I like my comfort. You have a right to your comfort, too."

"It's great." Locking his hands behind his neck, Beck looked around yet again. "You didn't have to do all this. I mean, I love it. I just don't want you to think I expect stuff."

There was no way Beck could understand how those words slayed Saul. Hell, everyone had expectations. Things they wanted. Things they'd work for and things they took for granted.

He didn't want Beck to be any different. Sure, he hoped he had a fair appreciation of things, but he didn't want him to be surprised by every scrap of consideration.

Taking a seat on the edge of the bed, Saul mulled over what to say. "You know, when I first found out about your parents, about you, I went through all these emotions. Like fear, worry, relief that you were okay, grief because I loved your dad." Not the way Beck loved him, no, but it was important for the kid to understand that all the things he felt were normal. It was important for him to know that Saul got it, because he'd felt it, too. "I had this driving need to get to you, to let you know we'd face things together." Saul suffered it all again, because Beck was here now, quiet and alert, and it was incredibly hard to read his expression. Maybe even impossible. "I was...afraid."

Beck stared at him. Silent.

"Mostly afraid that I'd mess it up. That I'd say or do something to make it harder for you. From the minute I knew what had happened, I wanted you with me, and I wanted you to know it was by choice, that I didn't feel forced into anything. Your dad knew that about me. He knew how I'd react, but how could you know that?" It would forever shame Saul to admit the truth. "You didn't know me—but you should have. If I'd been around, you wouldn't have had to worry about what would happen or where you'd go."

Chewing his lip for a moment, Beck seemed to make a decision. He looked a little awkward, but not really unsure. "I was scared, too. Like, I wanted my mom and dad back, you know?" Shoulders tightening, he looked everywhere other than at Saul. "I didn't really have anyone to talk to about it. It's like no one would mention their names, so I didn't, either." Briefly, his gaze collided with Saul's. "You were the only one who talked about them with me."

Molars working together in frustration, Saul took

that like a hit. It hurt. "I'm sorry it took me so long to find out."

Shaking his head hard, Beck said, "No, I wasn't saying that. I mean... I'm glad you're here now. I'm glad *I'm* here now. With you and stuff." He ran a hand over his face. "Guess I'm trying to say thank you. You know, for everything." He gestured at the room. "For this, but also for just...remembering them. With me."

Words escaped Saul. The room was so quiet he could hear Beck breathing and felt his own heartbeat in his ears. Maybe some of Beck's awkwardness in explaining was because Saul, too, felt awkward. Betty was probably right. If he was straight with Beck, it might make it easier for Beck to always be straight with him.

Smiling at that thought, Saul looked around the room again. "So you like it?"

"You kidding? I love it." He flung out his arms. "Privacy!" His shaky laugh broke just a little, but still, it was natural and fun.

Which allowed Saul to laugh with him. "Emily helped me to choose everything. Helped me paint, too." He watched Beck closely. "She's a woman I'm seeing. When you're ready, I'd like you to meet her."

Beck's grin went lopsided. "Hey, I'm ready whenever you want. I'll thank her, too."

Huh. *Thank you, Betty.* "From the moment I knew about you, I wanted you with me, so I figured... Eventually you two will get to know each other."

"Yeah?" Beck leaned his back against the wall, looking older than his fourteen years. "That's cool with me."

"I wasn't sure how you'd feel about it. I swear you'll like her. Everyone likes Emily."

This time Beck laughed. "Hey, you don't have to sell me on her. I've been reading up about her online."

In an instant, Saul went blank as his brain tried to scramble to remember everything that had been posted about Emily. He'd seen only nice stuff or he'd have already demanded that Betty take it down. But that kiss? Had Beck seen it, too?

Immediately, he knew how embarrassed Emily would be. He could tell that, although she hadn't yet met Beck, she already cared. He couldn't imagine a more empathetic person than Emily. It probably hadn't occurred to her, either, that Beck would know things about her before they were even introduced.

"Hey," Beck said. "It's no big deal."

"No, it's just that I hadn't even considered it." Of course at his age, Beck was on social media.

Man, he had a lot to learn about teenagers today.

Seeing Saul's expression amused Beck even more. "All the flower lady stuff is funny, isn't it? Did you two really walk a cat?"

If Saul hadn't already been sitting, he would have fumbled for a seat. "Yeah," he said cautiously, "we did. See, Emily recently adopted this really contrary cat." For the next few minutes, they talked about the animals and all the issues Satin had caused. He also explained about Emily's sudden fame online, and how it had happened.

"Will I get to meet Kathleen, too?"

"You know Kathleen is a mannequin, right?"

"A mannequin who gets around." Beck shook his head. "Some of that stuff is hilarious."

That statement led Saul to tell a few more stories, which got Beck asking questions. They talked while going through the house, and they talked while sharing colas out on the back deck. Pretty soon they were on the dock, feet in the water, watching the sunset and laughing like old pals.

It was nice in a way Saul hadn't anticipated. Easy. Really enjoyable.

After a while, Beck pulled off his shirt and squinted out over the water. "This place is amazing."

Luckily, with the sun hanging so low, Saul didn't have to stress about sunscreen. "I like living on the water."

"Yeah, that too, but I meant all of Cemetery. Such a weird name but a cool town."

Yup, that pretty much summed up Cemetery. "The people are nice. Like a big extended…" He stalled.

Beck didn't. "Family? I get that."

In many ways, Saul was more cautious than Beck. Apparently, he needed to get over that. "They can sometimes be a little overwhelming, but in a nice way."

"That's everywhere, right?" Beck scooted closer to the edge of the dock.

It was a new sensation, to be responsible for someone else, to worry. "The water is shallow here, but still, I want to know if you're coming down to the dock, okay?" Beck shot him a look that Saul couldn't interpret. "I don't mean to be overprotective or anything, but it could be dangerous." Fumbling a little, Saul added, "You could trip or something, hit your head."

Beck rubbed away a smile. "I'm glad I'm here."

Whew. "Me, too. This is nice, right?"

Shoulders hunching just a little, Beck stared down at his feet in the water. "I was worried about messing up your life."

"You're not," Saul assured him. "You never could." Then, emphatically, he stated again, "I *want* you here."

"I'm not so worried now."

The urge to embrace the kid kicked his heart into overtime, but Saul resisted. "Good. If you do get any worries, let me know, okay?"

"Sure." Beck watched with interest as a heron, silhouetted against the red horizon, soared over the lake. "So, when will I meet Emily?"

Saul was surprised all over again. "Whenever you want."

"You going to marry her?"

Since they were doing the whole heart-to-heart, Saul decided it was time to be straight with the kid. "I love her, so yeah, that's my plan. I haven't asked her yet, though. Like I said, I wanted you two to meet."

"You're sure I won't get in your way with that?"

That did it. Saul slung an arm around his shoulders and gave him a gruff squeeze. "Not to make you uncomfortable, but I already love you, too. Any problems you have, any concerns, I hope you'll come to me. I'm not perfect and I know it, but I swear I'll do my best. No matter how it rolls out, when I mess up, or when you think you've messed up, we're in this for the long haul. Problems will happen—there's no way around them—but you will never be in my way. I swear."

Beck inhaled an audible breath, then slowly blew it out. He skipped past most of what Saul had said, which made sense for his age, and instead stated, "So let's go see her."

Searching his face, Saul asked, "Now?" It was getting late. He assumed Beck would want to chill, maybe jump on the laptop or play a few video games.

Beck grinned. "Or tomorrow? Is she working? Whenever is good."

"She got off at six today. Same for Saturday." His thoughts rushed in three different directions. Sunday she was off, but he'd agreed to bring Beck back Saturday evening.

"I wouldn't mind visiting her shop tomorrow." Looking happier than Saul could have ever hoped for, Beck grinned. "I'm curious about this web sensation."

"The flower shop is great. Emily is great."

"Figured she had to be if you're hung up on her."

*Hung up on her.* What a simple way to describe everything he felt for Emily, things he'd never felt before—things he hadn't even known existed. New determination energized him. "How about I call her? If you're serious, we could probably swing by her place tonight." She was likely alone, and he hated that. Nothing would give him more pleasure than getting her and Beck together. As enticement, he added, "You can meet the animals, too."

Already pushing to his feet, Beck said, "Let's do it."

Again, Beck seemed older than his years. Grief might have done that to him, but Saul preferred to think it was the love of his mom and dad, something Beck would never forget, that had given him that confidence—a confidence Saul could now detect in his easy smile.

Withdrawing his phone while following Beck back to the house, Saul hoped that, in some small way, happiness also played a role. Happiness for a new future, new hopes and plans. Beck now had something to look forward to—and so did Saul.

Maybe everything would be just a little easier than either of them had expected.

## CHAPTER FOURTEEN

AFTER THE PHONE call with Saul, Emily raced excitedly around her house trying to tidy it. A futile endeavor since Satan had destroyed so much.

Not lately, though. Since getting Snuggles, Satan wasn't as angry all the time.

The cat still didn't like her, but at least she didn't seem miserable.

Snuggles always greeted Emily when she got home, and she was now proficient at leashing both animals and getting them out the back door before accidents occurred.

The last thing she did was quickly scoop the cat box, because—ta-da!—it had been used, which was much better than Satan going outside the box.

She patted Snuggles on the head and said, "Good dog," assuming he was the one responsible for that positive change.

Wagging his tail, Snuggles turned his face up to Emily, until the cat intervened by gliding between them, leading Snuggles away.

Jealous little cat.

Huffing a breath, Emily hurried down the hall to the bathroom, where she washed her hands and quickly brushed her hair. She was considering changing from the clothes she'd worn all day—but then the knock sounded on the door.

Absurdly eager to meet Beck, Emily took a moment to compose herself. Then, over the noise of Snuggles barking and Satan meowing, she called out, "Coming." Blocking the dog from the door was a little trickier than blocking the cat, so after she ensured it was Saul—oh, and look, Beck was such a cute young man!—she unlocked it, grabbed the dog's collar, and said, "Come on in."

Carefully, Saul peeked in, saw that she had control of the animals, and hurried Beck inside.

Snuggles went nuts with glee, as if a teenage boy was his most favorite thing in the entire world. Shooting right past Saul, he started dancing, his tail swinging wildly, and jumped against Beck, who laughed and tried to pet him while dodging a wet doggy tongue.

"Oh, my goodness," Emily said. "I think Snuggles considers you a treat."

The cat quickly got into it, too, twining around Beck's legs until the kid gave up and sat on the floor, right inside the door.

Grinning, Saul leaned in to greet Emily with a quick kiss. "Hope you don't mind us visiting so late."

"No way." When Saul slipped his arm around her, she assumed he'd explained her to Beck. "I'm thrilled for the company, just not quite as thrilled as the animals, obviously."

Laughing, Beck somehow got Snuggles to sit beside him, and allowed Satan to climb into his lap.

"Beck, meet Emily."

From his spot on the floor, he smiled up at her. "Hey."

Oh, this one was a charmer for sure, she thought, smiling back.

Then, in an attempt to warn her, Saul casually re-marked, "Beck has seen you on Facebook."

Emily froze.

"It's cool," Beck said. "You're like an internet sen-sation."

After missing a beat or two, her heart started trip-ping. "I didn't exactly plan it. I mean, it just sort of... happened?"

"He knows." Saul gave her a squeeze. "I explained."

"You should enjoy it while it lasts." Casting a sly glance at Saul, Beck added, "I'm surprised the local papers haven't interviewed her."

Immediately, Emily shook her head. When that didn't suffice, she gave a silly laugh that sounded a little too high. "Really, no one wants to interview me. I'm just...me." That came off so weak. Desperate, she turned to Saul. "Don't you dare give anyone ideas."

Beck thought that was even funnier. Now that the animals had sort of settled down, mostly *on* him, he idly stroked them both.

"Fickle animals," Emily said. "I wish they liked me a tenth as much as they apparently like you."

"I love animals."

"I can tell."

"I've never had any pets of my own because my mom was allergic to animal fur."

"Oh?" Forgetting everything else, Emily stepped away from Saul and joined Beck on the floor. Not too close—she didn't crowd him—but she showed her in-terest as she tentatively stroked Snuggles. "Are you sure you didn't inherit the allergy?"

"Nah. My friends had pets and it never bothered me." He smiled at a memory. "Sometimes I had to put my clothes straight in the wash, though, because if she handled them, she'd get watery eyes and start sneezing."

"That must have been miserable for her. I bet she loved animals anyway, didn't she?"

Beck's gaze flicked to hers and held. "Yeah, how did you know that?"

"By the way you greeted them. Not everyone would let someone else's pets accost them." She gave him a friendly nudge. "They're from a shelter and still adjusting, so I haven't even attempted to teach them manners yet." Emily released a soft breath. Teaching them anything would be hard to do when the cat despised her.

"Mom always collected stuff for the local shelter, and she and Dad donated to SPCA. She felt bad because we couldn't have pets."

"She wanted you to love animals, too, and you obviously do."

He nodded. "Dad did, too. Sometimes when Mom had a hair appointment or something, we'd visit a local farm. The guy there was my dad's friend, so we could feed the chickens and ducks, and talk to the cows."

Picturing that, Emily laughed. "Horses? Donkeys? I bet they had goats. I love goats. They're hilarious."

"They had all that. We'd take photos for Mom, since she couldn't be there." Lifting a hip, Beck pulled out an aged phone and quickly scrolled through his photos. "Here's their goat, Max."

"What a cutie." While admiring the goat, Emily also noted what a handsome man Beck's father was. Melancholy clutched her heart when she saw the happiness in Beck's face, how he leaned against his dad, and how carefree he looked.

A lot had changed for him in a year, much of it unbearable.

"Here's another." This time, Beck turned the phone so Saul could see, too.

Profound emotion brought Saul closer, until he knelt beside them. "Frame-worthy," he said. "Maybe we could hang it on the wall in your room."

"Yeah." Quieter now, Beck tucked the phone away.

Saul shared a lost look with Emily.

"Maybe you could grab us some drinks?" Emily gently stroked Snuggles's ear, giving Beck a moment. "We have bottled water, lemonade, or cola."

"Sure." Saul stood. "What would you like, Beck?"

"Water is fine." More solemn now, he kept his attention on the pets. "Mom hated for me to drink too much cola."

"It's not great for kids," Emily concurred.

While Saul slipped away, she and Beck remained there on the floor. Emily wasn't uncomfortable with the situation, and she hoped Beck wasn't, either. She wanted to say that she understood, and that he should take all the time he needed, but sometimes saying nothing was better.

"Saul told me all about these two." Leaning down, Beck put his cheek to the dog's head. "Oh, and thanks for helping with my room. I like it."

"I'm so glad." Scooting away a little bit, Emily rested her back against the wall, stretched out her legs and crossed her ankles. "I was a little older than you when I moved in with my aunt and uncle, and I remember that they made this big deal about my room."

Lifting his head, Beck asked, "Why did you live with them?"

"I lost my parents, too." For an extended moment in time, they each held silent, until Emily whispered, "It was the hardest thing I've ever gone through."

Rather than withdraw, Beck nodded. "I think about them all the time."

Emily noticed when Saul paused in the kitchen, his body tense as he listened in. Because she'd been in Beck's shoes, she felt compassion, but she didn't shy away from the topic, either. "My aunt used to tell me that when we think of people in heaven, they feel it like a warm hug."

Pain deepened Beck's breathing. "Do you think she was right?"

"I do." She fought the urge to reach out to Beck and instead kept talking. "It was like I had permission to think about them as often as I wanted."

Worry pinched his brows. "I sometimes try not to."

"That's understandable. You can't stay in a place of grief nonstop or you wouldn't be able to function. You have school and sports and friends. I'm sure your mom and dad wouldn't want you to miss any of that. More than anything, I bet they want you to be happy."

"Yeah." He busied himself petting the animals. "I still love them."

"I know. Even after all this time, I think of my parents often." Emily looked toward the kitchen, smiling at Saul. "When Saul asked me out that first time, I wanted to tell my mom about it."

"How come?"

"I've been single a long time. It was a big deal for me, and I used to share everything with Mom."

A quick grin appeared on Beck's face before he subdued it. "Saul probably felt the same."

As if. "I might be the flower lady, but he's Cemetery's hottest bachelor, you know."

That brought his grin right back. "Sounds like a match."

Oh, how she adored this kid!

Uncertain, he hesitated a moment, then blurted, "Only now Saul will have me, too."

"A bonus," she said. "Like Snuggles and Satin." Emily brushed the back of one finger over Satin's head—and got a look of warning. Frustration caused an audible huff of breath. "Did you see that?"

"What?" Beck asked.

"How that cat just mean-mugged me?"

Humor had his mouth twitching. "Did she?" For him, the cat purred. "If I could tell my mom that, she'd crack up. She used to say animals knew she was allergic and so they laughed at her."

She grinned with him. "Your mom sounds amazing."

"She was."

"You know, you'll always miss talking to her, like I miss talking to my mother, but the memories won't stay as painful. Time doesn't steal them away, but it does blunt things a little."

"I know. It's been great talking to Saul and stuff, too."

"Saul is so easy, right?" She hoped Saul knew the impact he'd had on Beck already. If not, she'd be sure to tell him at the first opportunity. "Having my aunt helps me, too. She never tried to replace my mom—" *just as Saul won't try to replace Beck's dad* "—but I know how much she loves me, and she's always there when I need her."

Without saying a word, Beck looked toward the kitchen, and his gaze met Saul's. The understanding was there in his face: Saul was here for him and Beck knew it.

Unable to help herself, Emily felt tenderness well up—for both guys.

As if beckoned, Saul reentered. "I'm sure you'll meet Emily's family soon, and I bet they'll make you laugh." Taking a seat on the floor again, Saul handed them each a drink. "They're pretty funny."

"So, you're staying with Saul tonight, right? What do you two have planned tomorrow?"

Saul said, "That's up to Beck. He might want to check out the town a little more."

"We could swim, too."

"The beach is loads of fun," Emily said, as if she had a clue. Never, not once, had she gone swimming there.

"Once you're ready to move in," Saul said, "we can pick up some games, too. I have no idea what's popular right now."

Using the excuse of petting the cat, Beck dipped his head, avoiding eye contact. "You don't have to buy me things."

Emily's brows went up. "Wow, I swear, I said almost the exact same thing to my uncle once. Know what he did?"

Diverted, both guys turned to her.

"He got me working."

Blank stares.

"It was a great strategy. It not only gave me something to do, but I earned my own money."

"Saul said I could work part-time at the restaurant."

"What a perfect solution."

Beck shifted the animals so he could better face her. "Did your uncle help you pick your job?"

Getting into the story, Emily sat forward. "Even better, he took me shopping for flowers." What a life-changing moment that had been. "At first, I didn't really care. I just went along while he looked at so, *so* many plants. He kept drawing me in, too, asking which ones I liked."

Saul smiled. "Got your interest, didn't he?"

"It was diabolical. I didn't have a clue about flowers, so I'd just pick one that seemed pretty. Uncle Sullivan would tell me if it was easy or difficult to grow, if it needed sun or shade, if it needed a lot of water or if it needed to be dry." To make sure she kept Beck's interest, she asked, "Did you know there are some plants that don't like wet toes?"

Beck and Saul shared a look.

"Right? Toes on a plant? That's how my uncle put it." The memory drifted around her like a warm blanket. She ended up petting Satin without even realizing it at first, and wonder of wonders, Satin didn't complain. "Some plants only like surface water and if their roots get too wet, they wilt. Opposite is true, too. Some like squishy toes."

Both guys grinned.

Opening her arms wide and turning up her face, Emily said, "Some flowers embrace the sun." She peeked at Saul. "Picture Uncle Sullivan doing this, okay?" She closed her arms over her head. "And some flowers are shy and duck away from too much sun."

They both laughed.

"You'd have to know my uncle, Beck. He's a tall guy, and it cracked me up to see him doing all this stuff in the middle of a garden shop. People were staring, but he didn't care."

"Your uncle sounds fun."

"He is. He taught me about planting flowers so some will shade others, and what will bloom when, so I always have color in the yard."

Saul nudged Beck. "Want to see her garden out back?

The sun's almost gone, but it's well lit and I think she's hinting to show you."

"I was not," Emily lied theatrically with enough humor to make Beck laugh again. "But of course I'll happily show you."

The dog immediately bounded up at the word "out," which meant the cat came alert, too, and soon they were all strolling outside, up and down the rows of flowers. Suitably impressed, Beck asked about different flowers, and even smelled a few.

Emily asked if she could get some photos, which became silly fun as Beck and Saul indulged ridiculous poses with different blooms, pretending to smell some, framing their faces in others, all in all clowning around and having fun.

When Beck requested a photo with her, she was so flattered she couldn't stop smiling. She, too, incorporated the flowers. Then Saul got them all clustered together, including Snuggles and Satin, and stretched out his long arm to get a group selfie.

Soon all three of their phones were full of photos. Emily knew she would cherish hers, but it wasn't until Saul whispered to Beck, and Beck gave an enthusiastic nod, that she realized their group selfie was being posted on the Cemetery social sites.

Immediately, people started responding, which impressed Beck.

Seeing his happiness, Emily didn't mind the social fame at all.

GENTRY RESTED AGAINST the headboard with Mila nestled into his side, still catching his breath. He'd known lust, of course. Quick attractions, just as quickly forgotten. He'd been distracted and he'd been tempted.

None of that came close to this.

Idly, he coasted his fingertips up and down Mila's slender arm, enjoying touching her, allowing himself to sink further under her effect. Her skin was warm and smelled indescribably good. Turning his head so that his nose brushed her hair, he breathed her in.

Everything about her offered him a peace he'd never dared to expect. No, he didn't assume that she was the solution to his every worry. Naivety was not a quality he possessed, not any longer, not since his early teens. Yet with Mila, the worries weren't as powerful.

It defied reason, but he already knew he loved her.

At least, he believed this all-consuming, turbulent, and tender mash of emotions must be love. Nothing else made sense. With her, he felt more like the man he knew he could be.

The man he wanted to be.

Better than his past, and actually, even better than the future he'd figured on.

Yes, he'd dated other girls, and probably slept with too many back when he considered sex the easiest comfort to get.

None of them had ever done to him what Mila had, and she'd done it so easily, just by being herself.

Maybe it was the circumstances he was in now: more secure, settled, with a clear direction in mind. Or it could be Mila's outlook on life: tackling problems head-on, going after what she wanted—namely him. All he knew was that he'd met the right woman at the right time, and he wanted her forever. Here, in Cemetery, with all the quirks of the town. This place came with laughs, open-armed acceptance, and people who were now so important to him.

Emily. He had to smile. She thought herself a big sister, but he knew it was even more than that. She, too, owned a piece of his heart.

"I came here straight from work," Mila murmured sleepily.

"To me." There were no words to tell her what that meant to him.

"Mmm." Stirring, she looked up at him. "I was fine all day. Doing my job, staying focused, but the second I clocked out…" Her voice dropped. "I wanted you."

Not because he was the best lover in town. Not because he was the only available guy, either. Whatever twist of fate had brought them together, they had "it." Strong chemistry, an unbreakable connection. A bond that he knew would grow—and last through the years.

Did she know that, too?

Kissing her forehead, Gentry thought about all the things he wanted to say, and how he wanted to say them, but the words weren't coming together. Early on, he'd learned to keep his mouth shut, and when necessary, to say as little as possible. Emily had cracked those defenses already, and now Mila had lovingly battered her way through the rest.

But vocalizing things? Pretty sure he'd suck at it.

"Gentry?" She angled her face up to see him. "I didn't go by my apartment to get a change of clothes, and I need to be at work earlier tomorrow so Saul can spend the day with Beck."

His arms closed around her, wishing he could hold her close enough to change the facts. "You don't want to stay the night?"

As if she saw things in his expression that he hadn't yet identified, she dropped her head to his chest and laughed. In the next second she sat up and faced him. The sheet slipped to her waist and yeah, her bare body caused a massive disruption to his concentration.

To get his attention back where she wanted it, she cupped his face. "That could have gone either way, yet you took a total wrong turn." To punctuate that, she gave him a hard, fast kiss.

Another hot distraction.

Settling his hand on her hip, he let his thumb play over her skin. He absolutely loved her body, but that wasn't why he loved her. "You're going to have to explain that to me, because I—"

"I want to live with you."

Several sensations hit him at once. Soaring elation. Searing heat. Instant concern, because his place was so small...

"Say something," she insisted.

Honesty was his only option. "I love you." Surprise widened her eyes but he didn't retreat. "I want you with me when I sleep at night and when I wake in the morning, and I want every minute we can find together around work."

Nodding, her breath quickening, Mila began peppering him with kisses, to his throat, his shoulder, his chest. "I want that, too."

Gentry caught her shoulders and held her back. "This place is so small."

*"I don't care."* More kisses, followed by a damp love bite in the spot where his neck met his shoulder. It sent his blood surging. "My apartment is a tiny bit bigger. We can stay wherever you want."

Tunneling his fingers under her hair to clasp her nape, he kissed her, then turned her beneath him. "I thought I might spook you, talking about love."

"Why?" She hugged him with all her might. "I feel exactly the same, Gentry McAdams. I have wanted you from the moment I saw you."

No way could he hold back his smile, but he tried to keep his tone serious. "We haven't really known each other that long."

"So?" Her small shove to his shoulder didn't budge him at all—pretty sure it wasn't meant to anyway. "Emily and Saul have known each other for years, and they're just now figuring it out. Love happens when it happens."

For him, it had happened so fast, he'd been left floundering, trying to catch his bearings. Good thing Emily had already steadied him with her trust, her affection, and her support. Otherwise, he might have taken off, and then he'd have missed out on this, on Mila. On love.

Again, she kissed him. "We will be so amazing together. I promise."

She sounded so sure that he started to believe, too. "We have a lot ahead of us. I want to share it all with you, but if you need time to think about it, I'd understand."

Getting emotional on him, Mila touched his mouth. "Silly Gentry. I don't need more time. There's always been something about you that set you apart. It was like my heart kept screaming *he's the one*, and my usually argumentative brain just happily agreed. If *you* need more time, I'm okay with that. I instinctively trust you more than I've ever trusted anyone. I can be patient, or we can go at Mach speed. *I love you*, and I swear that's not going to change."

Breathing became a challenge, and speaking was impossible. So instead Gentry kissed her, and kept on kissing her. He didn't have to sort out next month, or even next week. He had Mila now and tomorrow, and together they'd work out the future.

BY THE TIME Saul and Beck left, Emily had smiled so much her face hurt. She loved it. She loved both of them. She'd had the absolute best time.

Snuggles and Satin were sociable during the visit, loving Beck as if they'd known him forever. While he'd played with them in Emily's living room, she and Saul had made milkshakes—and Saul had stolen a few kisses and bestowed some awesome compliments.

He thought she was a natural, and he'd been awed by how easily she'd conversed on touchy subjects.

Emily didn't think she could take credit for that. It was Beck who'd opened that conversation by sharing about his mother's allergies. He'd been upfront, almost anxious to talk about his parents, which made sense. She'd felt the same after losing her own.

Yet she'd only felt that way with certain people, and remembering that brought back the ache of long ago, along with a huge dose of gratitude for her aunt and uncle.

On an impulse, while she tidied up the house, she sent her aunt a text to see if she was still up, while also assuring her that nothing was wrong. A second later her phone rang.

Smiling, Emily answered with, "You're sure I'm not disturbing you?"

"We just finished watching a movie."

"Well then, I want to tell you what a wonderful time I had with Saul and Beck." Having previously told her aunt about Beck, Emily didn't have to go through the whole history again. Instead, she told her aunt about the parallels she'd noticed. "I learned so many things from you and Uncle Sullivan. You know how much I appreciate you, but I have the growing urge to tell you again. You not only helped me more than I can ever say, but you helped me to help Beck, too."

After a few beats of silence, Aunt Mabel spoke softly, with a lot of emotion. "We learned a lot from you as well. There were so many times Sullivan and I wanted kids, but it just didn't happen. For years, I felt like less of a woman because of it."

"Oh, Aunt Mabel." Emily had never heard that sentiment before and tamped down her current enthusiasm.

"Sullivan had all this love to give, love he wanted to share. I had so much room in my heart for more family."

Dumbstruck, Emily sank blindly to the couch. "I knew you'd tried for children, but I didn't know it meant so much to you. I thought that, like me, you'd ended up with a similar choice and…chose not to." Had it been a true choice for Emily, though? No, in the beginning she'd wanted babies of her own, but she'd decided to go a different route after the failure of her marriage.

Occasionally she had a few mild regrets, but she had too many other blessings to get bogged down by it. In so many ways, her life not only satisfied her, it fulfilled her.

Aunt Mabel said, "When it didn't happen for us, I'd already planned to devote all my love to you. I was going to be the most doting aunt a niece had ever seen."

Overwhelmed with love, Emily said softly, "You were that, and more."

"When the unthinkable happened…"

Closing her eyes, Emily finished that thought. *When my parents died.*

"I was so afraid I'd screw it up."

"You didn't," Emily promised. "From the day you moved me in, I knew I wasn't alone. I've always known you loved me. You call me perfect, but I know the truth. You're the perfect one. You and Uncle Sullivan both."

"Oh, now, see," Mabel sniffled, giving in to a breathy laugh. "You're getting me weepy, and this is a happy call about your fun day."

"It's just turned into a call about my happy life." Wiping the tears from her eyes, Emily smiled. "Beck wants to visit the shop tomorrow, and he's anxious to meet you soon, too."

"We could come by." With new enthusiasm, Aunt Mabel said, "Sullivan gets bored, you know. He would enjoy the trip. We could go by the park again after. What do you think?"

Used to be, Emily would have worried about her aunt driving and trying to assist Sullivan to and from the car on her own. Now she realized how her worry and love had been overprotective. Instead of trying to inhibit her aunt and uncle, she should have been encouraging them. Realizing it now only made her stellar day even better. "I think it sounds wonderful, thank you. Even if you get to the shop before them, you can still meet Gentry, and I can show you the changes he's made. I'm sure Uncle Sullivan will have some opinions on that, too."

There was a moment of surprise before Mabel excitedly said, "Sullivan will love that."

Emily heard him in the background. Then of course Mabel explained to him, and soon they were both enthusiastic about the visit. Why, oh why hadn't she realized all this sooner? Going forward, she would encourage them both in any way she could.

And thinking of that... "Until then, check out the Cemetery Facebook page. We posted some photos of us together. Tell Uncle Sullivan that Beck loved the flower rows he helped me get started."

"Soon you'll have him planting with you," Mabel said. "You know Sullivan would love to sit out there and give advice on that, too."

Awesome idea! "I'll get him a comfortable padded lounge chair for the yard."

Another beat of silence, then Mable asked, "You mean that?"

Didn't her aunt know she'd do anything for either of them? "I'll take care of it on my next day off."

Proving she was touched by the offer, Mabel's voice brightened. "That would be wonderful, honey, thank you. I can't wait to tell Sullivan. Now I have to go. I don't know how to look up social media while I'm on the phone, and I'm ate up with curiosity about Beck and the photos."

Emily laughed. "Give Uncle Sullivan my love." After she finished the call, she took the animals out one more time, and since they were no longer interested in more petting, she grabbed a quick shower.

It was getting late, and she had a full day tomorrow, so she went up the hall to say good-night to the animals.

Snuggles started to give her a tail wag, until he caught the cat's look of disdain, then he ignored her as thoroughly as Satan did.

"Contrary animals." Emily stared down at them. "So you love Saul, and you love Beck, but you're still annoyed at me?" For some reason, the way they ignored her actually hurt her feelings. She dropped onto the sofa, stared at her feet and… So many feelings flooded her, she slumped back and closed her eyes.

Defeat because her animals hated her.

Love because Saul had brought Beck to meet her.

Joy because she and Beck had hit it off.

Sympathy, knowing what he'd been through, and yet pride because he was a pretty amazing young man.

When the sofa jostled, she went still…until she felt a small furry weight settle at her side.

*Satan*.

Cautiously, Emily opened one eye—and found the cat gazing at her. Not with hatred, or at least it didn't seem so. Tentatively, oh-so-slowly, she reached out, and Satan butted her head into her hand.

And OMG. Was that *purring*? It was! Satan—no, Satin— was purring. Her heart completely melted. Quietly, filled with emotion and afraid to move enough to look, she whispered, "Where's Snuggles?"

Then she heard the whine and saw the dog standing at the side of the couch. Oh no, now Satin would abandon her…but no. When she patted the cushion beside her, the dog agilely leaped up and with a loud doggy yawn, plopped down beside her.

Holy cow, what a day.

She had won over her pets! Next, she'd win Saul.

Not to be greedy, but now she wanted Beck, too. As she'd told him, he was a bonus.

And she, imperfect Emily Lucretia, Hashtag The Flower Lady, now wanted it all.

HIGH ON CONTENTMENT and driven by determination, Emily pulled into her parking spot beside the little flower shop early Saturday morning. Today she had an agenda, and she couldn't wait to get started.

Rather than the sunny skies that had been predicted, hazy clouds blanketed the area, making the morning dim and gray. Undeterred, she continued to smile...but she worried about the animals. They'd finally decided to like her, and she didn't want to leave them home alone if storms were rolling in. She had no idea if they got nervous over thunder and lightning.

Today, she arrived ahead of Gentry, but then, she'd be willing to bet Gentry's mornings were a little more exciting these days. Thinking of him and Mila sharing coffee and talking before they started work only added to her newfound happiness.

Actually, she wanted to talk to Gentry about possibly adjusting the hours of the shop, so that instead of opening at nine o'clock, they'd open at ten instead. She, too, hoped her own mornings would soon be spent in better ways than rushing in to work.

October would be a good time to implement that change. It was a slower month, and then in November and December, their usual foot traffic would all but disappear.

Dressed in cropped white jeans with a tan tank top and sandals, her hair once again hanging loose, she felt breezy and comfortable more than fashionable. Didn't matter. Nothing could dent her spirit... That is, until she went to the front door and found Kathleen there.

Expertly posed with arms up, the mannequin held a bold sign: Who Will Marry #theflowerlady?

Good grief. Appalled, Emily stared at Kathleen's blank yet somehow provoking expression, and then at that awful question. It made it sound like she was desperate to marry but didn't have any prospects.

She had Saul, damn it!

Emily gave quick thought to dragging Kathleen inside, but a subtle glance around assured her that too many people were already aware and watching for her reaction. Had the mannequin been there all night? Emily didn't think so. This close to the beach, the humidity would have already curled the sign.

With any luck, Kathleen would get rained on.

Forcing a calm smile and waving to the onlookers, Emily turned, unlocked her door, and gratefully disappeared inside. She moved away from the big front window so no one could see her and, after a few calmly drawn breaths, decided she didn't care.

This was *her* day, by God, and she wouldn't allow some prankster to ruin it for her.

Determined to stay upbeat, she went about prepping the shop. With Kathleen out there, no doubt they'd have a busy day, despite the gloomy weather.

Minutes later, Gentry came in. He approached her warily. "You saw Kathleen?"

"Yup." She shot him a look. "I assume you and Mila were too busy to set her up?"

Sympathy brought him forward. "You know I wouldn't, and Mila was with me until just a few minutes ago."

"That's what I figured." She accepted his brief hug, returning it with affectionate gusto. "You two are getting serious."

"I love her."

Wow. He dropped that little bombshell like it was nothing. Pressing him back to search his expression, and seeing nothing but contentment there, Emily grinned. "I gather she feels the same?"

Attempts to keep a straight face failed, and he cracked a smile. "Why do you think so?"

Oh, how she loved him. She cupped his face in her hands. "Because you, Gentry, are one heck of a catch."

He started to laugh, then suddenly frowned and turned his head so quickly that her hands fell away. "Well, hell."

Following his gaze, Emily saw several people on the walkway peering in at them. Of course, they quickly darted away.

Snorting, Gentry said, "So nosy," without any real heat.

"Of all the…" Knowing what they'd think, Emily started toward the door.

Pulling her up short, Gentry said, "Forget about it. I'm happy. You're happy. Who cares what tales they tell?"

Great attitude. She opened her mouth to agree when her phone started dinging with notifications, and she could just imagine why. Snapping her mouth shut, she glared at her purse with dread.

"Ignore it." Using his hold on her arm, Gentry guided her around the counter and to the stool. "I can tell you're excited this morning. Tell me why."

Leave it to Gentry to see something Emily hadn't yet expressed. "You first. Have you told Mila how you feel?"

"Yeah, and it wasn't real smooth." He ran a hand over the back of his neck. "I just sort of blurted it out there. I thought I might've botched it, but then she said she feels the same."

"Of course she does." Emily hadn't had a doubt, but

she was still relieved to have it confirmed. "Have you guys made any plans?"

"Only that we'll live together. My place is barely big enough for me to turn around in, and her apartment isn't much better, but…"

"You'll be together, and that's what counts."

"Yeah. That's how we see it." He propped a hip against the counter. "It's a huge move for both of us, and for now it's enough."

Hmm. Thoughts crowded in, bringing with them possible solutions. If she and Saul—no, *when* she and Saul—finalized things they'd have one house too many. She wondered if Saul had considered that…and she wondered how Gentry would feel about taking on added responsibilities. If anyone could handle them, she knew he could. With the flower fields that Gentry already helped maintain, there'd be an added benefit to her and the shop. For that reason, she could justify to him why he got a really good deal.

"Emily."

With her thoughts interrupted, she glanced at him. "Yes?"

Sincere gray eyes studied her as Gentry took her hand. "I don't think you realize your role in things, but you've helped me so much."

"I feel the same about you."

Bemused, he shook his head. "You don't understand. It's because of you that I feel like this town is my home. A real home. More than anything else, more than the friendly people or the great job…" Struggling, he glanced down; his hand cradled her own, his thumb brushing over her knuckles. "I thought I had plenty of confidence and that I was ready to tackle anything, but

I wasn't, because the idea of letting anyone in..." His voice dropped. "It scared me enough that I avoided it."

Squeezing his hand, Emily stepped closer. "How do you not know what an amazing person you are?"

Self-conscious over the compliment, he gave a gruff laugh. "No one ever told me that before you. I knew my granddad cared, but that was more about being blood-related. It was responsibility and the fact that neither of us had anyone else." Unease had him shifting his shoulders. "When I lost him, I didn't want to get close to anyone else. I'd been an outcast in my own home-town, and I didn't want that to happen here. I was all set to stay apart from everyone, but you wouldn't let me."

Wincing playfully, she asked, "Did I push my way in?"

"Yeah, and I'm glad. If you hadn't, I probably wouldn't have given Mila a chance." Those words didn't sit well, and he shook his head. "That is, she gave me a chance, and because of you, I took it. Now I can't imag-ine losing either of you."

"Well, you couldn't lose me if you tried. For the lon-gest time, it's just been my aunt, uncle and me. Now there's you, and you're bringing along Mila."

"And you have Saul," he said as a verbal nudge.

*And Saul.* "Maybe Beck, too." She'd always taken pride in her perfect little flower shop, and she'd been at peace with her life, but the contentment she felt now was richer, fuller. With utmost sincerity, she said, "I love seeing my family grow."

"About that?" With a final gentle squeeze, he re-leased her hand. "It's your turn—so what's happening? You seem extra happy today."

"I am." Refocusing, Emily told him first about her visit with Beck, and then how Snuggles and Satin had finally cozied up to her. "It was the most wonderful day ever already, because Beck is incredible, but then for Satin to come around, too? I couldn't believe it. She and Snuggles even slept with me, at least for most of the night. At some point, Satin went back to her bed and Snuggles followed, but they greeted me again this morning."

Grinning with her, Gentry said, "I'm not surprised."

"I am. I was trying to be patient, but man, it was tough to see them like everyone but me."

"The cat couldn't hold out forever. You're irresistible."

"And you're good for my ego." She was about to say more when another string of notifications sounded on her phone. She gave a heartfelt groan.

"We can silence those, you know."

"Yes...except that last night I told my aunt about the photos I'd posted with Saul and Beck, and now I'd like to share them with you, too." She made a face. "I've never been addicted to social media before."

"I imagine being the main topic changes things. Want me to look first?"

As if to mock her, more notifications dinged. Exasperated, she shook her head. "No. Everyone else is going to see it, so I may as well prepare myself." Practically lunging at her purse, she yanked out her phone, clicked on a notification...and then she wished she hadn't.

## CHAPTER FIFTEEN

INCREDULOUS AT WHAT she saw, Emily turned to Gentry. "Oh, no."

He strode over to her. "What's wrong?"

Turning the phone for him to see, she thrust out her arm and waited for his equal umbrage.

To her surprise, he laughed. "This town never gives up."

Unable to credit that reaction, she asked, "Did you *read* it?"

"Yeah, so? It's just more nonsense."

"They're making bets!" Squeezing her eyes shut, she shared the worst part. "On who I'll marry."

He nudged up her chin. "Wonder what Wheeler thinks about being included."

Imagining that, Emily dropped her head back in mortification and groaned. It was bad enough that the poster acted like she was interested in both Saul and Gentry, but to include Wheeler? And Wheeler had actually reacted to the post with a laughing emoji!

Done wallowing in her embarrassment, Emily squared her shoulders and decided to take charge. "I have to clear this up."

In the middle of sending a text, Gentry said, "Don't worry about it. Eventually you and Saul will do your thing, and the gossip will die down."

"Who are you texting?"

"Mila. She saw it, too."

Dread gripped her. "And?"

"She also thinks it's funny."

Well, of course she did. "It's ludicrous for anyone to think I'd get romantically involved with an employee—especially one so much younger than me."

"The town disagrees." Gentry's gaze briefly met hers. "Mila and I both think you should use this for promo."

Disbelief widened her eyes. *"Promo?"* The nonsense had her heart pounding through her chest, and Gentry thought nothing of it? "You can't be serious."

"Why not? Play along. Have some fun." Unconcerned, he nodded at her phone. "Turn the tables. Don't let anyone get the better of you. It can only bother you if you let it."

As the words sank in, her reaction ebbed and gradually settled. Of course he was right. "How did you get so wise?"

"Living the hard life?" His grin teased her. "Post a reply and say something like, *Hints come with flower purchases.* Then add a wink and flower emojis."

Emily could only stare at the incredible way his mind worked. "Ingenious," she had to admit. "I'm so glad you work for me and not against me."

"Just so you know, I'll always have your back."

That promise helped her shake off the last of her agitation. "Ditto."

Just then, Betty Cemetery entered the shop at a brisk pace. "Good morning, all." Low heels tapped on the tile floor at her no-nonsense approach.

Emily could always identify her by the rapid rhythm of her walk.

To Gentry, Betty said, "Young man, I'd like a dozen colorful flowers to counter this dreadful, dank weather."

"Yes ma'am. Anything in particular?"

"Something moderately priced. No roses." She eyed Gentry. "I'll leave the choice up to you."

Since that wasn't an uncommon request from Betty, Gentry nodded. "I'll make sure you get the freshest we have."

"Naturally." Next, Betty aimed her shrewd gaze at Emily. "I saw the photos you posted."

Why Emily had expected something else, she couldn't say. It might have been the assessing way Betty looked her over. "You mean of Beck? We enjoyed a very nice visit."

"He approves of you and Saul?"

Her jaw loosened, but words didn't form. Finally, Emily said, "Why in the world wouldn't he?"

Flapping away the question with an impatient hand, Betty glanced around. "You misunderstand my meaning. You're a lovely girl, so of course he liked you. I knew he would."

"You knew…" Feeling as contrary as her cat, Emily lost her smile as she straightened. "What exactly do you know about Beck?" How much had Saul told her?

After taking her measure, Betty changed tactics. "I meant that anyone who met you would, of course, appreciate the kindness that overlays your steel."

With every word, Betty confused her more. *Kindness that overlays my steel?*

"Saul, Gentry, Wheeler." Betty smiled. "Do you have a preference?"

Oh, that did it. Frustration shot through her, stiffening her neck and making her shoulders go tight. It seemed circumstances today were determined to sour her mood no matter how many times she countered it. She was supposed to be the unflappable flower lady, damn it.

It took an effort, but with a few quiet breaths, Emily regained her composure and even found a tight smile. "Now Betty, you know perfectly well I'm not involved in *that* way with Gentry, and Wheeler and I barely know each other."

Brows lifted in inquiry, Betty said, "Oh? You haven't seen the social media sites blowing up?"

Stealing Gentry's attitude and claiming it for her own, she negligently lifted one shoulder. "I saw, I just don't care. In fact, Gentry has a brilliant idea for promo."

Perfectly timed, Gentry reentered from the back room with a stunning bouquet of flowers. "What do you say, Ms. Cemetery? Colorful enough?"

She looked over the flowers with a critical eye. "You have wonderful taste, young man. Thank you. Those will do." Tempering her smile, she said, "About this promotion idea of yours?"

Ignoring her dig for information, Gentry carefully wrapped the flowers. "Emily and I will discuss it." He rang her up.

Far from deterred, Betty paid him while speaking to Emily. "Now, about Beck. Does he accept that you and Saul are together?"

The gall of Betty, to try to put her on the spot. Well, she'd just steal from Gentry again. Lifting her nose, she said, "Saul and I will discuss it."

After a stretch of heavy silence, Betty's eyes squinted, and her mouth pursed.

Oh no. That was a new look for Betty, one she'd never seen before, and it obliterated some of her attitude. "Um... Thank you for the interest, though."

Chin wobbling, Betty choked out a sound.

*Is she about to cry?* Regret brought Emily darting out around the counter. "Betty—"

The first chortle escaped, followed by a snort and a weird squeaking sound that might have been... Yes, that *could* be considered a laugh.

Emily wasn't positive, because they were sounds she'd never heard from Betty Cemetery.

She turned to Gentry, but he stood there grinning, not in the least alarmed, so she looked back to Betty.

Rounded shoulders shaking beneath her sensible cotton dress, Betty slumped against the counter. She lasted three seconds more before losing her battle to hold it in.

The most unruly, outrageous sounds rattled around the little shop.

What in the world? Wanting verification, Emily leaned down to try to see her face. "Are you laughing?"

The question only ramped up the odd sounds. Braced on the counter like she needed the support, Betty roared.

Definitely hilarity.

Emily's mouth started twitching, too.

In the middle of all that, Saul and Beck arrived.

The second Saul spotted Betty, he bore down on her with a purpose. "What in the world?"

Flapping a hand again, this time to let Saul know she didn't need help, Betty continued to wheeze and snuffle.

Nonplussed, Saul cocked a brow at Emily. "She's hysterical?"

Giving up all pretense of decorum, Betty simply put her head back and laughed some more.

Gentry wore an enormous grin. "I'll get her a water." He moseyed off without a care.

"Betty?" Starting to get alarmed, Emily patted her shoulder. "Really, it's not all that."

"You," Betty gasped. She lifted a fist, her eyes watering and her face flushed. "With *gumption*."

Seeking an explanation, Saul and Beck looked at Emily.

She had no idea what to tell them. "I didn't want her to bully me."

Saul took Betty's shoulders. "Take a breath before you make yourself pass out."

Nodding, tears still swimming in her eyes, she patted his chest. "Yes." The slow breath turned into another laugh, which she indulged while hanging on to Saul, but the next breath went a little better, and on the third, her hilarity died down to occasional chuckles.

"Better?" Saul asked. He took the water Gentry offered, opened it, and pressed it into Betty's hand.

She sipped, chuckled again, and blew out a loud breath. "Whew. I've been storing that up forever."

"Feels good to cut loose, doesn't it?" Gentry asked.

"Oh, indeed."

"What brought it on?" Saul wanted to know.

At that, Betty grinned at Emily, but patted Saul again. "Oh, you've picked a good one, my boy, yes you have."

"I agree." Rocking back on his heels, Saul looked at each of them before zeroing in on Betty. "So why did you post that nonsense about Emily choosing between me, Gentry, and Wheeler?"

*"What?"* Emily couldn't believe what she heard.

That got Betty laughing again.

With a roll of his eyes, Gentry turned to Beck and held out his fist. "While Ms. Cemetery has her meltdown, I'll do the introduction. I'm Gentry, and I assume you're Beck."

"Emily said you work on the garden." Beck bumped his fist to Gentry's. "It's nice."

"I work here, too." Leaning forward, Gentry whispered, "Flowers can be pretty cool."

To that, Betty strangled out in a high voice, "Like Emily," and off she went again.

Fed up, Emily huffed. "That's enough out of you." To Saul, she explained, "Betty came in here trying to strong-arm me, but I didn't let her."

"No," Betty said, wiping her eyes and still looking very pleased. "You didn't." After two deep breaths, she smiled at Beck. "Hello, young man. It's very nice to meet you."

Uncertain, Beck chewed the inside of his cheek. "Saul said it was probably you who posted that dumb question?"

"*Motivating* question," she kindly corrected, then with a not-quite-apologetic glance at Emily, she said, "Yes, it was me. It's always me, you know. I'm the namesake of this town, and I won't ever let any of them forget it."

"As if anyone could," Gentry teased.

Emily couldn't believe Betty had just dropped that bombshell like it was nothing. "It was you all along? You started all this with that photo of Gentry and me talking on the beach?"

Betty nodded impishly.

Suspicions grew. "You started the hashtag, too?"

"Oh Emily, you're so perfect, you deserve a hashtag."

*"I am not perfect."* Hearing herself, she muttered, "Perfect women do not screech."

To that, Saul grinned. "A woman who is perfect for me can screech whenever necessary."

Betty approved that comment with a nod. "Nicely put, Saul."

Looking around at each of them, Emily saw that she was the only one bothered by what Betty had done. "You'll have everyone wondering, when in fact Gentry is with Mila, and I'm..."

Saul took a step forward. "With me."

Her heart swelled.

Delighted with his show of possessiveness, Betty elbowed her. "Well?"

"Yes." Emily nodded fast. "I'm with you."

"Wonderful. I'm glad that's settled."

"It was never up for question," Emily reminded her.

"Ah, but questions make things more interesting." Primping, Betty touched her hair and smoothed the skirt of her dress before giving Emily a covert glance. "Perhaps you should fight fire with fire." She took another sip of her water. "Just a thought."

Yes, she really should. After all, Betty was a master manipulator, and Emily figured she could learn a few things from her. Accepting the challenge, she made a sudden decision. "Are you heading straight home, Betty?"

"I don't have to, dear. What did you have in mind?"

"Gentry, do we have any appointments scheduled for today?"

Wearing a rascal's grin, he shook his head. "Nope."

To Saul, she asked, "Where were you two headed?"

Intrigued, Saul took her hand. "Nowhere important. We were going to visit with you, then grab lunch at the restaurant."

"Wheeler is working with Mila?"

"Just for a few more hours."

Bolstering herself with a deep breath, Emily took a step forward.

When she just stood there, working up her nerve, Betty whispered sotto voce, "You've got this."

Yes, she really did. Staring up into Saul's beautiful green eyes sent a certain kind of peace settling around her. "I love you."

"I love you, too."

Beside them, Beck grinned.

"I also want to marry you."

Satisfaction warmed his expression. "Is that right?" He reached for her.

"It is." Shifting away before Saul could touch her, she placed her hands on Beck's shoulders. This was important, because Beck was important. "It doesn't have to be right now."

Startled, Beck's eyes widened. "But he wants to marry you, too."

Despite the sudden tripping of her pulse, she forged on. "I know you need to get settled in and—"

"I don't! I mean, I am." He turned to Saul. "We agreed I'd be moving in soon, right? No reason for her to wait."

"No reason at all," Saul softly agreed.

"There, see?" Beck smiled at her in encouragement. "We can make it any time you want."

*We* can, he'd said, and oh how happy that made her.

To be sure, she asked, "You'll take part in the wedding?" Since she and Saul hadn't talked it through yet, she quickly added, "Whatever and whenever the wedding will be?"

"Heck, yeah. Count me in."

More joy bubbled up, and she just naturally drew him in for a big celebratory hug.

"Get used to it," Gentry advised from beside her. "She's a hugger."

Awkwardly, Beck patted her back, but his good mood didn't dim. "I don't mind." Then he actually returned the embrace.

Suddenly Saul's arms were around both of them.

Blindly reaching out, Emily snagged Gentry's hand and pulled him closer, too. So much joy just might make her laugh as wildly as Betty had.

No sooner did she have that thought than she heard a soft, melancholy sound that drew her gaze. Betty was nearby, but apart, watching them all, her hands clasped together and her eyes wistful.

Emily couldn't bear it. "Betty." She beckoned to her, but Betty shook her head.

Saul leveled a look on Betty, too. "You started this group hug." He wiggled his fingers at her. "Come on, my girl. Get in here."

Flustered, Betty said, "Oh, but I…"

And Gentry, probably understanding Betty's distance more than most, carefully slid an arm around her shoulders and gently urged her in. She was so much shorter than everyone else that they just naturally circled her. When Betty spoke, her voice came from somewhere in the middle. Sounding amused and very touched by the caring, she said, "I need a photo of this, otherwise, no one will ever believe it."

IT SEEMED APPROPRIATE to Saul that they'd go to his restaurant to make the fun announcement.

Emily had put up a Temporarily Closed sign at the flower shop. Gentry had laughingly dragged Kathleen along. Mila, who'd been forewarned, had cleared a spot for them.

Even better, her aunt and uncle had arrived for their visit just as they were all stepping out of the flower shop. He could tell that Emily was reassured by how competently Mabel assisted Sullivan in exiting the car.

It was a short walk, and Sullivan, full of good spirits, swore he was up for it, especially with his walker. Saul had even reached his parents with a video call, so even though their vacation had taken them to Niagara Falls, they were able to take part.

Beck was all smiles, loving every second of it, and that made Saul so damn happy it was all he could do not to crush the boy close. He knew he and Beck had passed some hurdles, and Emily had helped to seal the deal.

But Cemetery, with its odd name and quirky habits—like a mannequin that got into mischief—had really won Beck over. It was a wonderful place to live, and an even better place to raise a family.

*His* family. Saul loved them all.

Off to the side, Gentry and Mila shared some close talk and a few tender touches. Anyone could see that they were very much in love.

Emily asked Wheeler, "So you're on board?"

"Absolutely. I've struck out with a few women because they thought I was in love with you." When Emily rolled her eyes, Wheeler clarified, "Not that I don't think you're awesome."

Saul stared him down.

"Awesome for Saul," Wheeler emphasized with a grin. "But I'm enjoying it here, and I'm thinking about staying on, so it'll be good for everyone to know the facts."

Saul agreed.

Anticipating his moment of fame, Wheeler hammed it up, especially after a few vacationing women made their interest known.

Reigning supreme in the middle of it all was Betty. She organized the patrons who gladly took part, with Kathleen set up atop a table, one arm raised high, a lot of tape affixing an empty drink in her hand as a toast, while the other hand held a sign saying, *It's official. The flower lady has chosen.*

Mabel, with the help of Sullivan, stepped up onto a chair. She had Emily's phone to take the photos. "Gentry?" Mabel called out. "You and Mila need to get in the shot now. Beck, you stand in front of Wheeler. Oh, Wheeler, that's a nice pose." To Sullivan, she explained, "He's flexing his muscles."

"Show-off." Sullivan laughed, then did a little flexing of his own.

"Emily?" Saul tipped up her chin. With her cinnamon eyes full of excitement, he had to give her a soft kiss. "I love you."

Beaming, Emily whispered, "I love you, too."

He'd spent so much time wondering how to juggle it all, how to align his priorities in a way so that no one misunderstood how much he cared, and now, thanks to a very perfect flower lady—who would vigorously deny perfection—he had it all. "I need to get you a ring."

Waving that off, she said, "I have an idea about us each having a house."

Loving that she'd already put some thought into it, he asked, "Do you want a long engagement?"

"I want to be with you." This time she went on tip-toe to initiate the kiss. "In your house. Is that okay?"

Her lack of interest in a ring couldn't have been more obvious, and it made him laugh. Nothing with Emily would ever be predictable. "Beck is partial to being on the lake."

"Then the lake it is." Emily smiled fondly at Beck. "Do you think we could be married quickly?"

"Depends on what type of wedding you want." Before she could ask, he said, "It's completely up to you." He already had everything he wanted.

"I'd prefer we just gather our families together and get it done." She screwed her mouth to the side. "That doesn't sound very romantic, does it?"

"Having you as my wife that much sooner? Sounds perfect to me." Meaning it, he said, "We can marry today, if that's what you want."

Her laughter sounded throughout the restaurant. "Well, I think I can wait a few days so that our favorite people can be there."

From his phone, his mother said, "Give us three days at least! We have to drive home."

Impatient, Betty asked, "Is everyone ready now?"

Hooking her arm through Beck's, Emily announced, "We're ready."

Together, Emily, Saul, and Beck stood as a family. Beside them, Gentry and Mila embraced while still mugging for the camera. Holding his arms up as if empty-handed, Wheeler grinned behind them.

Mabel took a zillion photos, a few with Saul on one knee before Emily, and another with Beck and Saul both hugging Emily.

Betty took a few photos as well so that Mabel and Sullivan could be included—until Emily insisted that she join them also. With no reticence at all, Betty handed over her phone to a customer, squeezed in next to Beck, and flashed double peace signs with a big goofy grin and eyebrows arched high in delight. While she posed like that, the rest of them cracked up.

All in all, it was a wonderful announcement to the town.

At the speed of light, photos were posted, but it was Betty, who ran the Facebook page—and apparently all the social media for Cemetery—who added text to the image so that above Saul, Emily, and Beck, it stated, *Together*, and above Gentry and Mila, it stated, *Together*.

Atop Wheeler, it said, *Still up for grabs!*

While those in the restaurant cheered, Saul promised his parents that they'd meet Emily as soon as they returned from their vacation.

After he ended the video call, Emily nudged Saul. "Watch Betty work. She's a professional."

"She texts faster than me," Beck added.

That gave Saul an idea. With Emily, Beck, Gentry, and Mila all huddled around him, he added text to a photo, too.

The second Betty's post went live, he put his image in the comments. It was one of the group shots that included Betty, and above her he'd written, *Cupid*.

With a lot of snickering, they watched Betty for her reaction.

Aghast at first, she sternly searched the crowd for the culprit. When she caught them clustered together watching her, Betty accused, "You're ruining my rep."

Mabel and Sullivan suddenly flanked her. "If Emily is your friend, your rep is guaranteed to be favorable."

"Exactly what I don't want," Betty grumbled.

Without missing a beat, Sullivan asked, "How can you help us plan Emily's wedding if you're going to act like a badger?"

Taken completely off guard, Betty gaped at them.

"You can't," Mabel answered for her. "Now, come join our table. Saul? You'll bring us some drinks, won't you?"

"I'm on it," Mila said. After a farewell kiss to Gentry, she got back to work.

Customers settled down at their tables, but the majority still had out their phones.

Beck surveyed it all. "I think the flower lady just went viral again."

Sighing, Emily leaned into Saul. "At least it's only in Cemetery."

"For now." Ready to get back to work, Gentry gave Emily a hug, shook hands with Saul, and shared another fist bump with Beck.

Into the chaos, a new guy entered, late twenties or early thirties, tall, relaxed, dressed comfortably. Spotting Saul, he approached with his hand extended. "Hey, you're the owner here, right?"

"Yes. Saul Culver."

"Lawson Salder. I run the new T-shirt shop." He held up his phone. "I saw that congratulations were in order."

"They are." Saul pulled Emily close and introduced her.

Lawson took her hand with an enormous smile. "Now I can thank you personally for the boost to my profits."

Emily donned her usual friendly, composed smile before saying, "I'm glad something good came from it." Then she laughed. "I mean, I'm getting married to Saul, and that's the best, but a little hashtag fun is fine, too."

In his free hand, Lawson held some papers and a shirt, making Saul curious. "What do you have there?"

"A gift." He held up a pink shirt that read, *I AM the Flower Lady*, which he handed to Emily. "No obligation to wear it, just another way for me to thank you. It's the only one I printed, by the way, and not for sale."

"I'll wear it to the shop," Emily promised.

Holding up the papers, Lawson asked, "Since you have a crowd, mind if I hand these out? They're discount coupons for the next purchase of a shirt."

Unsure how Emily would feel about it, Saul deferred to her.

"Okay by me." In a magnanimous gesture that proved she didn't mind her newfound fame, she added, "Stop by the flower shop, if you want. Gentry can give them to our customers."

"Hey, that'd be great." Looking around, Lawson noted, "This place is always busy, but that flower shop is really a happening place."

"It's a perfect little flower shop," Emily agreed.

And Saul knew it had the perfect flower lady.

COMPARED TO YARDLEY'S wedding on the beach, their ceremony in the flower field a mere two weeks later was intimate, serene, and best of all, fast.

She and Saul were now married.

In addition to the beautiful colors everywhere, a few accommodating birds sang, numerous butterflies fluttered around, and every face wore a smile.

Saul's parents had welcomed her to the family with open arms, and they were thrilled to meet Beck. Anytime they glanced at their only son, their pride was obvious to see. They'd already stated that their travels would be on hold for a while so they could get better acquainted.

Throughout the brief ceremony, Aunt Mabel had done this hilarious combo of grinning and weeping at the same time, which amused Uncle Sullivan and prompted him to be even more outrageous than usual.

Betty, who they all now realized had a wicked sense of humor, took great delight in egging him on, in between posting online. The woman clearly relished her social media presence.

Gentry and Mila were almost speechless over Emily's plan to rent her house to them for the same amount Gentry had already been spending on rent. Despite her explanation that she needed him there anyway, and the fact that she considered it part of his benefit package as her manager, he tried to insist on paying more.

Emily had talked him around by explaining the importance of her field of flowers. It was a token of the love Sullivan and Mabel had given to her after she'd lost her parents. She could never have handed it over to strangers.

As understanding as always, Gentry had accepted and promised to take very good care of everything. Then he'd gone one further and asked Sullivan for advice on planting new spring bulbs. Her uncle had been thrilled to be included, which of course thrilled Aunt Mabel, too. They treated Gentry as if he really was her brother. They were just plain wonderful that way.

Satin and Snuggles didn't exactly take part in the short ceremony, but they'd remained nearby, in attendance throughout, with Beck holding their leashes. Emily couldn't be sure, but the cat appeared happy for her, and Snuggles continually wagged his tail.

Vivienne took as many photos as the photographer did.

And there, standing among the many blooms, flowers in her hair, was Kathleen. Even though the mannequin's expression couldn't be altered, Emily thought she still somehow managed to look excited. Or maybe that was Emily's happiness making everything look different.

Saul's arms looped around her from behind and he pressed a kiss to her temple. "Mom and Aunt Mabel are getting the food together. Hope everyone is hungry."

Composure was her stock and trade, the very reason so many people wrongly labeled her *perfect*, but after gaining Gentry as a brother, making Betty a friend, marrying Cemetery's most popular bachelor, rounding out her family with Beck, *and* surviving her time as a hashtag, Emily was too euphoric to be composed.

The flowing fabric of her long white sundress flared out as she spun around to grab Saul for a laughing hug.

Smiling with her, Saul smoothed back her hair. "Did you know I have the most amazing wife in all of Cemetery?"

Emily glanced around at their family. "I don't know about amazing, but right now, I'm certainly the happiest."

THOUGH MABEL KNEW Sullivan couldn't see well, he still picked up on the festivities happening around him. He was comfortably seated on the cushioned chair that

Emily had gotten specifically for him. Saul had put another chair just like it on the deck at his house with the invitation for them to visit often.

Bringing Sullivan a plate of food, she remarked, "They're absolutely perfect for each other."

Sullivan surprised her by setting the food aside, taking her hand, and tugging her carefully into his lap.

"Sullivan! Your hip…"

"You won't hurt me."

Glancing around, she laughed and blustered, and yes, sniffled a little. "You're causing a scene."

"Let 'em look." He kissed her knuckles and hugged her close. "You're still the love of my life, and I don't care who knows it."

Tucking her face against his neck, Mabel smiled. "I love you, Sullivan."

That earned her another kiss. "I always wanted the same for Emily."

"Me, too." She looked up in time to catch Saul kissing Emily—yet again. "Now, at last, she has it."

\* \* \* \* \*

*Here's a sneak peek at* New York Times
*bestselling author Lori Foster's*
*next all-new summer read,*
The Love Shack.

CARRYING A COLORFUL bouquet of flowers and a pastry box, Berkley Carr strolled down the sidewalk with her dog, Hero, while taking in the sights and sounds of the eclectic little town where she'd recently relocated. A bright afternoon sun heated her shoulders as she breathed in the unique freshness that she'd never experienced anywhere else.

She'd made the right decision when she'd accepted the new job and, basically, a new life. The notoriety that so often haunted her couldn't possibly bother her here, not in this quaint rural setting bustling with activity and filled with kindness.

As she waved to the owner of a sweets shop, and then, on the opposite side of the street, the proprietor of a seasonal ice cream parlor, she decided that the full-time residents were...almost too good to be true.

Not perfect, no. How boring would that be? They varied in age and ambition, with vocations that spanned the imagination. Most of the businesses were clustered here on the main street, but others were farther out.

None, however, were near her new home and The Love Shack, the amazing animal shelter she now ran. Privacy, that's what she had. Peaceful, wonderful privacy.

As if he'd read her thoughts, Hero gazed up at her,

his tongue lolling out one side of his mouth and his muscular body moving in time with her long strides. The brindle pit bull boxer mix loved these walks as much as she did.

Berkley smiled down at him. "It's nice being a stranger, isn't it?"

Hero licked his chops and then sniffed the air, possibly smelling a squirrel in one of the mature trees that provided blessed shade everywhere, or perhaps he'd picked up the scent of barbecue that permeated the air from a not-too-distant restaurant.

A vacationer walked by with two kids in tow, no doubt headed for the large recreation lake. As the girl, who looked to be around six, reached out for Hero, the woman asked with caution, "Is he friendly?"

Berkley stopped. "The friendliest." With his tail wagging, Hero snuffled against the kid and made her laugh. The girl's shier brother came forward and gave Hero a hug, then the mom knelt and gave him a few pets, too. As always, the dog loved the attention.

After the woman wished her a good day and corralled her kids along, Berkley resumed her walk.

The vacationers were the easiest for her to deal with because they had only a passing interest in her.

The residents, though, they had reason to want to know more about her. Most of them were caring, involved, determined—with a few quirks thrown in. A few were nosy, others liked to gossip and of course there were often assumptions.

So far, their assumptions about her hadn't come anywhere near the truth. No one here knew her history, her infamy.

If she could help it, no one ever would.

She no sooner had that thought than she saw Hero go on the alert. Berkley followed the direction of the dog's stare and encountered a very fine male behind.

Maybe if the guy hadn't been leaning into the well, things would have gone differently. But there he was, legs braced with a muscular tush on display in board shorts, his head and part of his shoulders hidden inside the well. She and Hero weren't the only ones to notice, either. Berkley saw several women taking in the view.

It was her distraction with the other women, as well as the packages she carried, that made her lose hold of the leash when Hero launched forward, already on a mission. She shouted, "Hero, no!" But of course, it was too late.

Hearing her, the man straightened too quickly and smacked his head on the roof frame of the well. Before he could complain, Hero had him by the seat of his shorts, determinedly tugging him to "safety," which made the guy lose his footing on the gravel lot. He fell forward with a barely subdued curse.

Filled with dread, Berkley sprinted forward, dropped her flowers and pastry, and grabbed for Hero's leash. "He's fine, bud. I swear. Hero, *drop him*."

Obediently, the dog released his grip on the shorts, then wagged his tail, very proud of himself. And damn, she was pretty proud of him, too. He'd gotten much better at following commands. "Good boy."

Grumbling, the guy pushed to his feet, dusted off his knees and stared down at her.

Holy crap. *She knew him.*

Lawson Salder, in the flesh. She hadn't seen him in

nearly a decade, and honestly, that wasn't long enough to suit her. She would have been happy to never again see anyone from her old neighborhood, her old life, anyone who knew of the god-awful scandal that had overtaken her existence.

*Why had no one told her he lived in Cemetery, Indiana?*